Chloe and Olivia

BELL GALE CHEVIGNY

Chloe and Olivia

GROVE WEIDENFELD   NEW YORK

Published by Grove Weidenfeld
A division of Wheatland Corporation
841 Broadway
New York, NY 10003-4793

Published in Canada
by General Publishing Company, Ltd.

Library of Congress Cataloging-in-Publication Data

Chevigny, Bell Gale.
    Chloe and Olivia / Bell Gale Chevigny. — 1st ed.
        p.   cm.
    I. Title.
PS3553.H438C4   1990
813'.54—dc20   89-29606
                                                        CIP

ISBN 0-8021-1182-3

Manufactured in the United States of America

Printed on acid-free paper

Designed by Brush Horse Books

First Edition 1990

10 9 8 7 6 5 4 3 2 1

For Katy and Blue

ACKNOWLEDGMENTS

I wish to thank Karl Bissinger, Rachel Field, Rachel Fruchter, Leslie Haines, Denise Kahn, Bobbye Ortiz, and Joan Snyder for background information. And for indispensable encouragement, Paul Chevigny, many good and wise friends, especially Carol Ascher and Antonia Meltzoff, and my wonderful editor, Joy Johannessen.

"*Chloe liked Olivia,*" *I read. And then it struck me how immense a change was there. Chloe liked Olivia perhaps for the first time in literature.*

—Virginia Woolf
A ROOM OF ONE'S OWN

Chloe and Olivia

Except for a few months in Italy at the beginning, Chloe and Olivia never lived in the same place. Yet whenever they got together, in whatever part of the world, their friendship colored the place and their talk confounded time. Often, they admitted to each other, this made them wonder if their friendship was quite real. But sometimes the other reality paled and they looked in amazement at what they had made.

Spring 1961

Chloe liked Olivia the moment she saw her. A tall dark girl grinning at a heap of skulls. Lips drawn back over long straight teeth, she fronted their toothless gape, intimate and unafraid. So sharply did the sight etch itself in Chloe's mind that for years it was to rise with the thought of Olivia.

Surliness alone had driven Chloe into the dim underground chapel of Santa Maria della Concezione on a sunny Tuesday afternoon of early spring. Her strategy when her work soured was to flee the books and walk around Rome, sometimes with Sandro, but increasingly, by preference, without his provocative guidance. In the abrupt brightness of that day she felt oppressed by the specific gravity of her body and sought the dark. The bones of four thousand Capuchin monks had gone into the lacy patterns on wall and ceiling—odd, morbid, perfect. Dropping her coin in the bag the glowering friar shook at her, she stepped in.

The time was gone when the place inspired awe. Cobwebs dripped from chandeliers of wired bones, graffiti on the skeletons abused the rival soccer teams of Lazio and Roma. The long room smelled like sweaty socks. No one was there but the guard and one couple, and Chloe had not noticed the man, so struck was she by the canny, uncompromising grin of the girl. When she realized she was staring, she turned to study a skeleton hanging from an arch fashioned of crania. The man came up behind her silently.

"Who's your friend?" he drawled, thrusting his chin at the skeleton. Chloe started and her yelp bounced off the stone walls, but the friar in the doorway practiced deafness. The man muffling his laugh was the celebrated Karl. Never had they spoken, let alone laughed together, but at the university back home they had known each other by sight. He was on a fellowship too, it turned out, painting in Perugia. And now in Rome to visit the girl, one Olivia, at work on Italian literature. Fumbling for Chloe's name, he introduced them. Vivid grin gone, Olivia seemed different, at once waifish and austere. She stood slightly behind Karl, her dusky wedge of a face hanging beyond his shoulder, watching Chloe with startling large eyes, a broad severe mouth.

"Frank folk, the Capuchins," Karl deadpanned, walking back down the room between the women, "no skeletons in *their* closets." He pointed out the more bizarre creations, the crosses made of knucklebones, a large cranium topping a pyramid of skulls stacked like so many melons. "*Ti amo Claudia*" was carved above the eye sockets. "Wear their hearts on their foreheads."

Chloe was surprised. At Michigan, Karl had been so aloof she had not imagined he could joke at all. His rocketing reputation in the painting department made him seem to lean away from ordinary mortals. With his dramatic good looks—tall, hair so blond it was almost white, cat's eyes, strong nose— Chloe took it for granted that he was crippled by vanity. But so friendly now! Was it just that she spoke English and he was having a rough time with Italian? Or had this Olivia changed him? Maybe dead things made him lively. He said he was taking Olivia on his "*memento mori* tour of Rome."

"Who could meditate on the last things in the middle of all

these Valentines and doilies?" Chloe grumbled. "It's kitsch death."

Olivia's smile, breaking out of that stark beauty like something fetched up from the depths, was splendid. "Want the real thing, do you?"

"Let's leave the Capuchins in their cellar," Karl suggested, "and get a cappuccino."

Was the man propelled by puns? He might not be so bad after all, Chloe thought, but Olivia was a find.

At the cafe, Karl's mask crept back over his face. He seemed to fade, his bright blondness canceled by the sunlight of the Via Veneto. But Olivia held her own. It was hard to believe that she had just graduated from Swarthmore and was only twenty-one. She sat with her back to the crowd streaming down the sidewalk and stalled in the Roman manner—"*Boh*"—before ordering Campari with a flawless accent.

"Never mind her," Karl told Chloe, "she's really a Roman," and he ordered his cappuccino in English.

Chloe asked for Campari, imitating Olivia's lilt. "*Per cortesia,*" she added.

"Not quite," Olivia corrected Karl. Her mother was Italian, and she'd been born in Italy just before the war, she said, and lived here again for a few years right after it. Now she was studying the writers who burst into print in the postwar period. Looking for a way to place herself as well?

"What writers are you working on?" Chloe asked. Lame grad school code for "Who might you be?"

"At first I thought Moravia, but no. All that alienation—in the end it's just glib, a reflex." Who, then? She loved Carlo Levi, but right now she was reading nothing but Pavese.

Karl stirred at the name. "Pour me a little of me, Olivia," he said, yawning.

She laughed. "Pavese said that what we ask of others we

have inside ourselves—though it's pleasant to have a pitcher to pour yourself into and drink yourself from."

They didn't touch or even look at each other. Lovers of long standing, Chloe surmised.

"The only heroic rule is to be alone, alone, alone," Karl quoted slyly, glancing at Olivia for the first time.

Olivia grimaced. No explanation this time. Sipping her drink, she leaned back and surveyed the people at other tables. "Funny," she said at last. "Those bones are playing tricks on my eyes. I look at these people and see the skeleton under the flesh." In Olivia's own cheeks there were faint shadows. But she turned to Chloe warm and intent when she mentioned that she lived alone.

"Really! How did you happen to come to Rome anyhow?"

Chloe found to her surprise that she wanted to amuse them. She told how it had happened on the spur of the moment, when a half-year study grant fell her way. She heard her voice ring. "It was a small grant, but it's so much cheaper here, I knew I'd be rich. I've never been to Europe, and I've got a job lined up for next year. It was go right away or forget it. So I cooked up a Roman topic in American Studies. And who needs to *study* Italian? thought I. Don't I know all the arias in *Don Giovanni?*" Karl grinned, but it was Olivia's low chortle that made Chloe, right out there on the Via Veneto, sing, *"La ci darem la mano,"* extending her own hand to them.

When they asked about her work, the heady mood held. "Innocents abroad. Hawthorne and especially James. No one had solved his riddle, I argued to my sponsor, one had to return to the scene of the crime. I was improvising madly, and of course it's nonsense. It's a different Europe entirely, this side of the war—but *ecco!* I'm here."

While Olivia was taking down the phone number of Chloe's

landlady, Karl mentioned that they were about to go to Spain. When? Day after tomorrow, for two weeks. Chloe's elation collapsed so fast that she feared it showed. She looked into her empty glass while the bright afternoon wheeled away from her. Fool, she berated herself, how desperate you are. As soon as possible, she said goodbye.

By the next day Chloe had forgotten Olivia and turned to her thesis as if it were a life sentence.

"Of course you have a block," Sandro said on the phone. "An American in Italy writing on American writers in Italy! It's the serpent biting his tail! Impossible. Unless you have distance. And here I am—on the far side of the Tiber."

Chloe was immune at last to Sandro's cleverness. Two months earlier it had melted her, she mistook it for kindness. Then, when she knew it was not, it caught at her pride, as if it were a point of honor not to flee from a man who was quicker with words. She imagined him lounging on his sofa, legs crossed, one foot stroking the air, with the patience of the Mediterranean ages and a malicious gleam in his eye.

"I've tried that, thanks," she said. "Now I'm going to sit at my desk until I break through." She didn't mind sounding clumsy and bullish. Maybe he'd give it up. "I'll call you when I can," she lied. It was never clearer to her that Sandro fed the confusion that drove her words away.

"*Attenzione*," he murmured. "Don't become the block."

It was easier to end the talk when he was cool and superior. Easy too, when she went back to her desk, to put him out of her mind. Not so his incredulous words the night she broke suddenly away from the kissing she had started: "But you don't know how to live!" No matter that they were melodramatic, opportunistic, the words settled deep in her inner ear. She thought them at Hawthorne and James, she wrote savagely about their American characters' blithe ineptness in the Old World. The elusive mystery of Europe that drew and alarmed them—what did it amount to but sex? She filled pages all afternoon, and the next morning threw out what she had written. The malaise of her authors—Hawthorne's unrelenting ambivalence and James' mystified evasion—became accusations she leveled at herself. I will have to give it up, she decided, I will have to go home. But the thought of her father deterred her. Without having to say a thing, he would repeat Sandro's charge: *You don't know how to live.*

Her father began to peer up at her from the page of writing. The hawk stare, inescapable, even when he was saying good-bye. He stood at the door, her mother just behind him, smoothing her skirt with splayed fingers, always in the background, the field to his figure. He leaned toward her, he leaned out of the frame, looming into her life. Chloe amused herself trying to write over him, to press him back under the paper with her pencil. But her tangled sentences gave way to a different script, in which she was telling her father the truth. "You were right, I was bluffing," she began. "I fooled them in Michigan, I fooled myself, my own words fooled me, but they fail me here, and I see you were right. It was never me." No—she tore the page—I can't give him that. "You were right," she said, "but you'll never know it."

When Olivia called, Chloe was studying a schedule of transatlantic flights. She didn't know the voice at first—Olivia! the girl grinning at the skulls—and then she wondered at the husky music of it, a voice so full in a body so thin.

"We just got back from Spain, Karl's gone back to Perugia, and I have something for you. Are you free for dinner?"

The timing was perfect. Dinner that very night would be great, Chloe said, especially if Olivia, who really knew Rome, would name the place.

"My favorite has no name, but I'll tell you how to get there."

It was raining, and the sallow old waiter was perplexed that Chloe wouldn't wait at a table. "I'm not sure I'm here," she said in Italian, then felt the flush. Trying to undo her mistakes usually made things worse. And she didn't want to sit all lit up and alone in the empty trattoria anyhow. So she waited under the awning outside.

Chloe liked standing there watching the street. She liked its stink, more acrid in the rain, the deeper ochre of the wet walls, the gleaming cobblestones. Her thin sandals were soaked, even her legs were splashed, but the air was warm. Across the street a boy in a long blue apron fished upward with a pole and brought a shutter crashing down over the face of a shop. Then he prodded a box stuck in the flowing gutter till it sailed freely away. Chloe must have smiled. "*Ecco, signorina! Un bel sorriso per me!*" said a dark face an inch from her own. Smile at *me*! Chloe hadn't seen him coming, and now he was gone without breaking stride, the taunting grin flashing over his shoulder. She felt her face stiffly retracting its smile, the familiar dip in her belly that she hugged away with her own arms. The color drained from the building opposite, and her father loomed again from his doorway. You were right, she told the wraith, I can't make it, but not for the reason you think. The street was darkening. She counted the lights coming on in the buildings opposite. When there were six, Olivia would arrive, or else— Chloe was thirsty. Where was Olivia, anyway?

Olivia heard the clock strike at the corner, but she was held by the mirror. Tying a scarf around her neck, she stared at the oval mole under her chin that Karl had brooded over, stroking, frowning. She couldn't make out if he liked it or not and was damned if she'd ask. Exasperating to spend even a moment wondering about it, and she had spent several. The mirror made a disgusted face. Then, at the street door, the rain sent her clattering upstairs to find an umbrella and change out of the new Spanish shoes. Halfway down, she spun back for Chloe's present. Finally, in the street, the cheap umbrella gave way, and she had to hold its broken wing out with her other hand, her bag swinging wildly from her elbow as she hurried over the cobblestones. Two men in a doorway hissed insinuations, and one held out a mock helping hand. From the corner of her eye, Olivia shot him her drop-dead look, and he backed off.

It was a relief to be back in a country where she understood the whole insult. She took comfort even from the raucous darkness of these narrow streets. Madrid was dark in another way, grim with constraint. Yet she and Karl had never been closer than in the Prado, when he showed her how Goya found menace in the sunniest scenes. "Goya knew all about malice," he said. "He drew everything from it." But she had thought it was grief, as if Goya looked backward from death. That way he could make no mistakes. When she told Karl, he turned his naked look on her, the one that made all the difference every time. Karl bright against that darkness, drinking it with eyes wide. Was that desire or fear? "An artist has to be in danger, or it's nothing at all," he said once. And then chortled, delighted with himself, kissed her palm, and pulled her into bed. But what about the other times, when he was petulant, or deaf to her? Should she heed the signals, call it off now? When she tried to ask him, what did he say? "More than you think depends on you." His typical move, passing it back to her. Two women scuttled out of a shop, clutching their shawls and cackling at the rain. One shook her fist at the thick sky. What a pleasure, the noise of those black pear-shaped Roman ladies. Hell, the rain wasn't bad at all. She folded the fractured umbrella under her arm. Glad to be back and alone.

A church bell started counting. Damn, she was late. Would Chloe mind? She lives all alone. None of the other Americans even try that, look what a botch I make. Went by herself to those Capuchin chapels, lucky thing Olivia had gone along after all. Karl forever on the trail of the ultimate in art, for how little artists could use, how much they could bear. But the Capuchins hedged their bets, fudged it. Kitsch, yes, as Chloe said. Still, Olivia found the bones beautiful, the hollows like petals, the satin finish of their tapering spans, the yellow other-worldly light of them even under the dust. Vulnerable, but enduring. A passing Fiat splashed her. She glared, flung up her hand, and yelled, *"Porco!"* The driver skidded to a halt, leaned out the window with an evil smirk, sent her a noisy kiss, and dug out again fast. Imbecile.

Chloe. Volatile woman, dancing on the balls of her feet as she talked, as if to refuse and transcend her shortness. Every-thing about her keyed up, red cape, high blazing cheeks, wiry yellow hair standing out all over her head. The uninhibited way she sang *Don Giovanni* at them, sotto voce and a bit flat, holding out her small hand. Skittish, showy, Karl called her. Likes his women quiet. Imitating Valentino: "Lie still, you little fool." But Chloe grinned up at him, entertained by the golden boy in a skeptical sort of way. Refreshing response, intriguing. And beneath the flamboyance, something driving, intellectual but *personal*. Bet she wants to live out James for herself, reenact the quest of his heroines.

Karl hadn't known Chloe at all well at graduate school. Not his type, clearly. She worked at a secondhand clothes place he passed often. Never saw her not talking, he said, always sur-rounded by people. Sometimes they stood around among the old coats reading aloud to each other. He thought she held little weekly parties, bring-your-own salons, someone called them—Chloe never had any money. No, Karl had never gone, of course not.

A woman coming to live all alone in Rome, just like that, on impulse—it took chutzpah. Twenty-four and already writing her dissertation. She had it all figured out. And so *interesting* the way she laughed at Karl.

And here she was, in the classic pose of a woman waiting, arms folded, leaning on the wall, curvier than Olivia had remembered, half in the yellow light of the trattoria, half— God!—in the rain. She was looking for Olivia in the wrong direction. "Chloe!" she called, and Chloe whipped around, shot up her arms in welcome, and stepped forward altogether into the rain.

"You're always late," Chloe grumbled a year and a half later in New York. "Like our first dinner at the trattoria. I have to tell you, I almost gave you up that night. I was about to go home—"

"Were you?" Olivia returned. "That would have ended it for me. You'd already run off the day we met, remember? When you left me and Karl sitting on the Via Veneto, flying away in your red cape, I was afraid we'd bored you silly—"

"Bored me! I was crazy with disappointment—"

"You seemed too good for us. A free spirit, a woman who knew her mind—"

"When in fact—I don't believe this. I'd been so desolate before I met you—all that spring sunshine wasted on me. Rome seemed as false as a stage set, and then there you were— like a torch in that cavern. And then at the cafe, I thought you were—I don't know—the soul of Europe. But when I found out you were blithely taking off for Spain—"

"Taking off! Blithely! God. Sedated was what I felt, and under tow. I was full of dread whenever Karl and I were going somewhere, like I was out of control—"

"You hid it well enough," Chloe replied.
"Well, of course!"

"It's a miracle we took to each other at all," Chloe went on another four years later in Oregon.
"It always is. The whole thing's a long shot," Olivia agreed. *"Each time I'm a little nervous in advance, afraid we'll have changed too much."*
"I am too. But what I meant—it's a miracle because we were reading each other so badly."
"Oh? I'm not so sure. And do you think we each could read our self any better? Or can now? Anyhow, the miracle was all my work. It was awfully good of me to remember you in Spain when you were busy forgetting me in Rome!"
"What are you talking about?"
"You forgot me. Just turned your back, tucked into your thesis, and forgot all about me. Why are you staring? You told me so yourself later on. Have you forgotten that?"
"I don't believe it. I don't remember. I must have been exaggerating."

"I can admit it now," Olivia said still a year later in Washington. *"You intimidated me in Rome, me drifting along blindly and you on the verge of becoming a high-powered literary scholar—"*
"Oh, yes! On the verge of a veritable hotshot, look at me—"
"It took nerve to call you, really, and then I was afraid you'd hate my corny present—"
"That present got us going."

They had the restaurant to themselves. A waiter she didn't know showed them to the table she liked by the window. Olivia shook the water out of her hair, and Chloe did the same. They both wore their hair long and treated it with voluptuous neglect. Olivia didn't want to talk about Spain, but Chloe pressed her.

"I didn't realize what bothered me about Spain until just now, coming through these streets, with everybody throwing their hands around. People in Spain were so wrapped up, so mute. Resigned. Romans are forever indignant!"

Chloe agreed emphatically, and Olivia gave her the package. A Spanish wineskin, the authentic article, hide still prickling with hair. Obscene, Karl said, and wouldn't try it, but Chloe was delighted. When the waiter brought the bread and the carafe of house wine, she said, "Let's try it out, what do you say?"

Olivia tried to pour the wine into the thin-necked skin. Wine puddled with rainwater on the floor, and then, when she tried to demonstrate, the red arc shot past her ear. "*Ufa!*"

"Oh, let me try," Chloe said. She was game, but she didn't understand how to grasp and fold the thing. Olivia took her hand and wrapped it around the rough bladder. "Okay," said Chloe staunchly, clutching the bag at arm's length. "No fair holding it close, right?" She stretched her mouth wide and shot a red line into her thick hair. They burst out laughing, and the waiter did too. Gasping, Chloe extended the bag to him.

"This is what I mean," Olivia said. "This would never happen in Spain!" Of course, everyone in Spain would know how to do it. In the end it was the waiter who triumphed first. He held the wineskin high above his head and arched his back like a matador in a poster as he shot the jet. Olivia praised him.

When the waiter went off for the pasta, Chloe asked, "You use the *tu* with him?"

So she had slipped back into the familiar form—it hadn't happened for a while now. Must be going out of the country and coming back, or the coziness of the evening. "It comes from learning the language as a child and leaving before you grow up." Chloe pursed her lips, Olivia could see she wanted to ask more. But to answer would mean, sooner or later, telling about Esther. Olivia looked away—not ready yet—and Chloe dropped it.

"Must be nice, seeing Italy in the familiar voice," she murmured in a moment. Incredibly flattering, that intelligent gray-green gaze. "Make you feel safe." Olivia did feel safe, now that Chloe mentioned it. Strange as that was, in her mother's country. Was it because Esther wasn't here anymore?

Chloe was asking how she'd met Karl. Olivia saw his face when she spoke to him, mistrustful, beseeching. "All us fellowship people came over together," she said. "The first afternoon on the ship, everyone was out on deck getting acquainted. Except Karl. He stood apart, leaning on the rail, squinting at the horizon. I heard two girls carrying on about him. 'Have you ever seen anyone so gorgeous?' 'So melancholy!' "

"Ha," said Chloe. Olivia felt a minute perfidious thrill.

"I thought I saw something different. I went up to him and asked if he was feeling seasick. 'Oh, I don't know,' he said. 'Well, maybe just a little.' So I sat him down at a table and told him to pick out something and look at it very hard."

"I've never heard of that!" said Chloe.

"Neither had I. It just came to me. But he did it. He sat there staring at the salt and pepper shakers. 'What am I looking for?' he asked me. 'Their secret,' I said. He looked at them for the longest time, completely serious, then he said, 'They're so angry at each other they won't speak!' And his nausea had passed!" Chloe had a laugh that began with a little shout. Karl's laugh was pantomime.

After fueling up with a great forklift of pasta, Chloe said,

"Let me tell you what happened to me yesterday." She described a hill of wild flowers she'd found above a path in the Borghese Gardens, overlooking a grove of ballooning pine trees, the massive Pinciana gate, and the city spreading to the horizon beyond. Chloe had a way of watching her listener, searching first one eye, then the other. But her talk was a headlong rush. Olivia knew no one who plunged like that.

"I was lying there in the grass, reading, when this troop of schoolboys came walking and joking down the path below the hill. What a picture—white shirts and dark jackets, all dappled by the sun coming through the trees. One of them spotted me and called out. I ducked into my book, but it was too late. He glided up the hill while the others watched. When he was directly above me, he said, '*Bel-la!*' "—Chloe's voice sang in imitation—"and he swooped down and plucked a daisy right out from under my hip!"

"What nerve!" Olivia cried. "Only in Rome!"

"Then he swung back down the hill to his friends, who were all hooting with laughter. I was dumbstruck."

"But you—lying in the grass!"

"It was irresistible. These things never happen to you?"

"I don't lie in the grass. No Roman girl would dream of it! But"—Olivia could just see Chloe curled up on the daisies—"I think it's great that you did!"

"What I mean is," said Chloe, "how do you manage to move around in this town?"

Could she be serious? She looked it. Olivia roused herself; she could help with *this*. "The trick is, you can't let them throw you off balance. Sometimes you can stop them with a look. Or say something before they get a chance. Then they're startled, and that gives you time to get away."

"Nervy is best," Chloe said thoughtfully. "But you have to be in the mood."

Olivia giggled. "It's got to be tougher for you, being blond. There's always rudeness, don't forget. You can say something nasty." Chloe looked doubtful—maybe nastiness was beyond her Italian—but ready to learn.

On the street, Olivia thought of the cold stone floor of her room and invited Chloe to come back with her. She resurrected the umbrella as best she could and held it over them as they ran back through the rain. A barrel-chested sailor jumped out of a doorway, planted his legs wide in front of them, and wouldn't be ignored. His eye jumped from one woman to the other as he ran down the usual list.

"*Francesi? Parlez-vous français? Danesi? Tedesche? Inglesi?* You spiks inglis, babee? Eh? *Americane?*"

Cutting her eye at Chloe, Olivia said coldly, "*Siamo Italiane. Romane di Roma. Vai via.*"

The sailor shifted his weight. He grunted, and his leer slackened. "Eh? Eh?" But he didn't budge.

Chloe pressed forward, hands on hips. She went toe to toe with the man and mimicked his whine. "*Ma lei che è? È danese? È svedese? O polacco?*" He glowered, and with a glance at Olivia, Chloe stepped closer. "*No? Allora, è inglese? O irlandese?*" The man yanked at his cap and brushed past them. Chloe turned to Olivia, jubilant.

Olivia squeezed her arm. "It worked! I don't believe it! We did it!"

"O Rome!" Chloe apostrophized the street. "Bring on your worst. We're ready!"

Strings of rain-soaked laundry framed the view of the Roman ghetto. Chloe hung out of Olivia's window taking in the jumbled rooftops, the squared gray dome of the synagogue gleaming faintly. The stroke of a clock somewhere came heavy and round through the wet.

How could she have dreamed of leaving Rome?

Olivia seemed amused. "You make me think better of the place." When Chloe admired the painted wooden carvings on the wall, she said, "I picked them up at Porta Portese. You don't know the flea market? I'll take you there." On a stand was a slender clay vase. Swelling below the narrowest of necks, it was like the idea of an elegant woman. "It's a lachrymatory. The ancient Romans used them to preserve tears shed for the dead—imagine! I'm told it was found on a dig in Sicily. It's probably fake, but I don't care."

Olivia knew how to live.

Chloe eyed the stack of Cesare Pavese on the bookshelf. She knew very little about him, a dark figure brooding on destruction—Olivia in front of the skulls. Chloe said right out that all she knew about Pavese was that he'd plotted out his suicide in his diary.

"It makes me furious," Olivia said. "Everyone, from extreme right to far left, seized on that diary to prove their point about Pavese's politics. Not one of them gave a damn about the last thing the man wrote in his suicide note! You know it? It's great. 'I forgive everyone and ask forgiveness of everyone. Okay? Not too much gossip, please.'"

"What is any criticism, when you look at it drastically," Chloe wondered, "but gossip? It must make it hard for you to write about him yourself."

Olivia laughed. "That must be why I'm so unproductive." But when Chloe asked her to tell more, she said, "Pavese had such an intense response to small things. Let me read you a passage I love." Chloe perched on the windowsill so she could listen facing the view. "The swiftest, surest way for us to waken the sense of wonder," Olivia translated, "is to stare fearlessly at a single object. Suddenly, miraculously, it will look like something we have never seen before."

What patience, Chloe thought. Well, we know it cures sea-sickness. Pavese would have no use for a big view like this, though. He'd stop at that fraying towel. Turning from the window, she said, "It's great." Then she asked, "How did he get through the war?" It was her first question of all Italians. Sandro and his friends had gone into exile. "He never left Italy, did he?"

"He was banished from Turin at one point, but no, he didn't leave Italy. The hard thing was keeping his mind alive, Fascist culture was so stultifying. Pavese holed up and read Melville and Whitman. He loved their exuberant, barbaric language. He translated them, he wrote about them, and for the Fascists, that made him an intellectual traitor. But he stuck by his Americans and learned from them how to forge his own literary dialect."

"How wonderful! And how clever and devious," Chloe exclaimed. "Using the Americans to say what he meant, it's like being a smuggler, isn't it?"

Olivia laughed. "Yes!"

"And then, how perfect for you, with your two languages, two countries. The most interesting thinkers have no fixed homes, do they? None of us do, of course, but most people never find it out."

"Exactly," Olivia said, and she smiled. The spectacular gift of that smile, Chloe thought, owed everything to the melancholy severity of her face in repose. Olivia brought out a bottle of wine and two glasses, invited her to settle at the other end of the old sofa, and drew her out about James, whom she liked too. It struck Chloe that James was like Pavese turned inside out.

"Pavese got closer to his Italy by translating the Americans, and James went to Italy to find his America. Except he never really could find it. His best Americans have no home, no place to go."

Olivia liked that. "No real home except in consciousness," she suggested.

"Or in finding one or two people who might understand," Chloe said.

"Oh, yes," said Olivia.

They talked about Yeats, Bach, and Camus. About college and high school and how it felt to be pushed through a year or two younger than their classmates. Chloe thought it made you incurably young, but Olivia said it forced you to be strong.

Cross-legged at her end of the sofa, Olivia set her wine aside, drew a long breath, and began to wonder aloud about love. She had had a bad time with Karl in Spain, she said, and was thinking she should break up with him.

"The way Karl is—he smothers me, I don't know why, but he does. And then, other times, he makes me feel so alone!" Olivia confided with a kind of deference. She seemed to assume that Chloe, being three years older, knew proportionally more. Chloe wanted to protest that she was six inches shorter, that she was in a crisis of inexperience, that each motorbike that burned past her with a girl welded to the driver's body parched her throat with fearful longing. She had a bad moment when, after a long appraising look, Olivia asked, "Do you know what I mean? Have you ever felt intensely lonely right after making love?"

Chloe weighed the four months she had spent alone, fending off Sandro, feeling raw and exposed in the sensual glare of Rome, against this evening with Olivia spinning a cocoon in the rainy world with her *tu*. She refilled their glasses and, knocking Olivia's lightly, silently promised her a truthful future.

"Not even once," she said. "But I think I know what you mean." Olivia's serious gaze made even that come true—for suddenly Chloe could see what she felt. "Are you sure you didn't feel lonely just before as well?"

It was a lucky guess.

"Not a total guess, though," Olivia said six years later in Washington, "because you had known Karl at graduate school. Only slightly, true, but you were clever enough to guess that the closer one got to Karl, the lonelier one became."

"Not clever enough," Chloe replied with chagrin, "to warn you not to marry him."

"You warned me, you warned me. You forget. You warned me in your own way. But it made no difference."

Still four years later, in Ontario, Olivia amended, "It might have made a difference, if we'd had more time together. You believed so intensely that I could think for myself, it might have begun to happen."

It's as I thought, Olivia told herself. She's twenty-four, she knows things, she goes after what she wants. She doesn't let herself moon about men and sex every minute. Olivia decided to trust her.

"Loneliness isn't the problem," she began. "I mean, I want it, I want to be alone. *You* know what I mean, don't you?" But Chloe looked unsure. "What I *want* is solitude!"

"Ah!" said Chloe. "Like Pavese."

"Pavese, no. Solitude was his vocation, he's too extreme." If Pavese were still alive, she had often thought, she'd contrive somehow to divert him from his terrible anguish. She explained that she had wanted to make her year in Italy a test in self-reliance. Before Karl came to go with her to Spain, she'd been running an experiment on her character. "I was trying to see how many days I could go without speaking to anyone, simply to see how I liked my own company."

"You need to be in a strange place," Chloe laughed, "to take your own measure."

"Is that why you're here?"

Chloe grinned at her frankness. "In a sense, yes. I was doing better in graduate school than I'd ever done. It scared me. One day I saw my reflection in the library window and I didn't recognize myself. Everything was too familiar there. I was too accepted. Damn good thing this grant came through. I had to get away. And I can't help feeling that Americans who come in couples and live together in Rome are missing the point. They're cushioning the impact, they're muting their own experience."

"Absolutely!" said Olivia, amazed that another American girl put so much stock in strangeness and solitude. So avid and so nervy, coming without the language. Chloe's accent needed work, but she had picked up a lot. However had she done it?

Chloe said she was learning Italian and politics at once from her anarcho-syndicalist butcher, Bruno, a beetle-browed veteran of the Sacco-Vanzetti wars. He had met his wife Pia in the struggle, and they had married in jail to avoid the pain of separate prisons. "And now he serves me up news of the States with my daily slice of veal," she said. "Just yesterday, he put down his cleaver to hold forth on racial discrimination in the American South. I like to see the States through his wrathful eyes. It's so terrible, but it's romantic too. He talks about the Negroes picketing Woolworth's—'Vulvart,' he said, I could hardly recognize the word in his mouth—and now they're sitting at segregated lunch counters until the police carry them away. Have you heard about it?" Olivia had not, but she said yes not to slow Chloe down. Chloe showed her how Bruno saluted the demonstrators who braved arrest, kissing his bunched fingers and thrusting them in the air.

"But wait—" Chloe backed up. "Your experiment—Italy's not a strange place to *you*, is it? Do your parents ever come back? Tell me about them."

"My father . . . is dead. It's all right," she reassured Chloe. "It was a long time ago. He was a fine person, I think. I know he was a wonderful journalist. He worked in Europe before the war and wrote important pieces on the anti-Fascist movement. I've seen some of them. He was making a real contribution, but—"

There was no getting around the melodrama of her story, and Olivia knew it could draw or distance her listener. She had picked up the scent of Chloe's intensity and was gambling on catching her.

"He couldn't bear to stay out of the war. He always regretted that he hadn't gone to Spain to fight with the Republicans. After Pearl Harbor, he went back to the States to enlist. But his vision was so bad the army wouldn't take him, so he memorized the eye chart and finally got in. He was killed before he'd been in the Pacific a month."

Chloe asked if she remembered him.

"I was three when he died. I don't remember much. He rocked me. He sang to me, I think." She closed her eyes, and at that moment she thought she remembered a low hum, a warm swaying, a musk of wet wool and tobacco. She put it away.

Chloe was silent, all her vivacity banked down and concentrated in attending to her. Olivia liked her sympathizing scowl, the way she caught her lower lip in her teeth.

"You were born in Italy," she said at last. "How did he meet your mother?"

Olivia sighed. To tell about her mother, she needed to dig in her bag for cigarettes. Chloe took one too.

"He met her when he was working in Milan and she was in
the chorus at La Scala. It was when Mussolini was handing
down one anti-Semitic decree after another. The other Italians
sheltered the Jews as well as they could, it drove the Nazis
crazy."

Chloe nodded, she'd heard about it.

"Esther is Jewish, and maybe my father hoped he could
shield her with a Gentile name. They got married and I was
born right away, then Andy. When he left to join the army, she
was working with the anti-Fascist partisans. She kept her job as
a cover, but essentially she gave up her career. She did everything, printed pamphlets, organized strikes in the factories, and
after the German occupation, she was a *staffetta* for the armed
resistance. That's a courier—she rode around on her bike to
deliver messages. They couldn't be written down, she had to
memorize them, and they were usually in code. Esther said later
that it was easy after memorizing all that music. Sometimes she
put a tune to them."

Chloe was entranced. Pride rose in Olivia like heat, but the
taste of metal was in her mouth. It had been easy too for Esther
to siphon off the attention of her daughter's college friends.
And she recalled the man she had met here in Italy a month
before, pale eyes wet with pleasure, who told her that he owed
his life to Esther. Enough, she would keep that to herself.

"To me, Esther was treacherous, through and through."

Chloe gasped.

"She helped the Resistance, but she plunked down me and
Andy, *ffft!*"—Olivia shook her fingers at the floor as if casting
off something noxious—"with my father's third cousins on a
farm in Massachusetts until the end of the war. When the war
was over, she wrote to them—Andy and I found this out years
later—asking if they wouldn't like to keep us indefinitely. They

couldn't, they had three children of their own, the wife's father was sick. They weren't mean, just worn out. They said no. So Esther dispatched her new lover to bring us to her in Italy."

Olivia remembered that big shambling man better than anyone in Massachusetts, the way he huddled over her and Andy to teach them Italian nursery rhymes. "He was very good to us," she said. "But by the time we all arrived in Italy, Esther had taken another lover and wasn't ready for any of us. Oh, she was at the dock all right. She met us with crushing hugs, made us feel all we had missed. She brought us big bouquets of flowers, heaped baskets of fruit, as if we were about to take a voyage instead of just finishing one. Which was the case, in fact. After two days we were shipped off to a beach town with a nanny."

Chloe moaned, and Olivia relaxed a little. "What happened to the guy who brought you?"

"Vanished," she answered. "We never saw him again. Esther's like that—seductive, hungry, always awake to her next move." Olivia's rancor hit its stride, and she told of Esther's two other marriages, the move back to the States, the fat years and the lean. "No marriage lasted long. But she never once admitted failure. Living on the edge, she calls it, that's what she likes. It makes her feel alive."

Pride stirred again, but Olivia didn't mind it, Chloe looked so aghast. "She's always on stage. That's why we can't trust anything she says. And her own life fascinates her to distraction, so she remembers her children only in spasms, though she loves to display us from time to time." She even told Chloe about the worst years, when Esther gave voice lessons at home, and Olivia and Andy had to keep quiet and out of sight while she spoiled and pampered her adoring students. "We grew up, Andy and I, tiptoeing around the back rooms of God knows how many apartments. We raised each other."

"My God!" said Chloe, sagging back on the sofa. "That's awful. I've never heard anything like it." And after a while, "You've been *alone* enough, as far as your mother was concerned."

"You would think so. But Esther is always present somehow, even—and I know this sounds odd—*especially* when she completely forgets my existence."

"It doesn't sound odd," said Chloe. "It sounds like she's so self-centered—and magnetic, too—that you have to go far away if you're going to invent your own life and live it."

Invent your own life. A woman like Chloe might know how it was done.

Her new friend's exotic pain made Chloe's face hot with sorrow and inadequacy. To love a father that way! To be virtually abandoned—and by a mother like that! Puzzling that Olivia had fled to the very ground of her mother's troubling heroism, but Chloe did not say so.

"Enough." Olivia's sigh was a whistle. "What's your family like?"

Chloe felt green. She'd lived all her life before college in the same house in Syracuse, New York. Olivia's past made her own feud with her father, which she liked to call "asphyxiating," seem a meager thing. She had two parents, but she did not call them Simon and Jean; she was sure they were monogamous, and they had been conventional enough to raise their three children themselves. Sometimes, it was true, she felt like an only child, because her sisters were so much older—nine and eleven years—so close to each other, and now so married and so far from Syracuse. But there was nothing remarkable in that. Yet Olivia had told so much, and if Chloe didn't respond in kind, friendship would be impossible. It was like a law: you had to take your turn.

Chloe got up to open the window a crack, let out some of the smoke. She perched on the sofa arm and began. "My mother. There's nothing to say about her . . ." Then she laughed self-consciously. That could never be true, could it? She sprang up and said, "I mean, there's really nothing to say. She's a good mother." Good! How empty it sounded. But it was true. She and her mother had never quarreled about anything, though her mother's tongue had been sharp enough once for raging behind her husband's back. The dark of Olivia's eyes went so deep. Chloe wasn't going to tell a woman with those eyes that her mother had become a sincere and cheerful Christian. "The point is, my mother is so devoted to my father, to his every smallest need, that"—she tugged at her hair with both hands— "that it makes me impatient!"

"What do you mean?" Olivia asked. "I don't know the first thing about good mothers, good wives." She looked as though she didn't much credit their existence either.

"Oh, murder! It's that, I don't know, I just can't see what she gets out of it, gets for all her service. I mean, my father"— and, more easy as soon as she shifted to him, Chloe settled on the sofa—"my father cares only about what he's lost."

Her father was a failed playwright, "bitterly failed," she said with satisfaction. "So he throws his histrionics into the advertising business. When I was little, I thought an ad man was someone who had to shout on the telephone."

Olivia beamed, and Chloe took off. "The trouble is, he made my sisters and my mother do penance for his failure. There were horrible scenes when he didn't get his own way. So everyone just played to him. When I came along, he got a different idea. He looked to me to make it up to him. He taught me to read at three. He gave me a typewriter at five! To this day, my handwriting is illegible."

Olivia's laugh was gusty.

"He's so wrapped up in the idea of me as the writer, in my so-called gift"—Chloe made a face—"that if it ever existed, it's disappeared, gone into hiding. Permanent hiding."

"I guess it's hard to be the chosen one," Olivia mused, "especially if your father is unhappy."

Chloe liked this view of herself, and when Olivia asked the painful question, why she had gone to graduate school, she wanted to be honest. "It was my own idea, not his. It seems second best, but it's the only way I know to live near the quick of art—" But she couldn't tell Olivia how queasy she felt sometimes, nor of her secret plan to live her life as if it were a novel.

"We both have made narrow escapes," Olivia said, "we're both refugees." It was the kind of overstatement that from someone else at another time might have embarrassed Chloe but flattered and impressed her now.

"We have to find our own country," she heard herself assert. Olivia rewarded her with that high-voltage smile.

"I did think you thought for yourself," Chloe insisted in Ontario ten years later. "You'd been through the most devastating suffering, Europe, war, you'd been worse than orphaned, and you were struggling with this artist—"

"None of it did me any good, though. And that first night we talked? I played it all up for you. I thought you were brilliant, so I showed off as if my life depended on it. I was so pretentious."

"We were both as literary as hell. And thank God! It's how we got each other's attention. I was awfully shaky, remember. I was ready to give up when I met you. But you stunned me. I thought you'd cut right through the surface of Italy, and I had to work so hard to match you."

"Work? I thought you were pouring out your soul!"
"I was courting you, Livia! It was hard labor."

Neither of them could remember later what they talked about the rest of that night. But they talked until the wine was gone and they were hungry again. Olivia found some artichokes that they boiled and ate, and then they talked until they were out of cigarettes. When the sky began to bleach behind the shutters, they made up the couch for Chloe. Exhausted, manic, they couldn't believe their good luck.

"What time is it anyhow?" Chloe asked. "My watch has stopped."

Olivia shrugged. She didn't wear a watch. "I don't know. What year is it?"

"Where are we?"

Summer Solstice
1961

After that first night, Chloe and Olivia got together three days out of four, though sometimes, in deference to the project of solitude, they shunned each other for days. Olivia tried to read with Chloe in the Borghese but found it hopelessly distracting. Chloe liked to turn up late in the afternoon at the dusty palace library where Olivia read. Then they would wander around until it was time to find a restaurant. They learned to make a modest meal luxurious by lingering for hours.

If, toward midnight, they found themselves nearer Chloe's place, they would take one of her two thin mattresses and thump it onto the floor for Olivia. The narrow space was more like a corridor than a room, a bit of thick red carpet Chloe's only luxury. Bed, wardrobe, desk, towers of books, and a hotplate were ranged down one side, and the wall opposite was papered with index cards of provocative quotations for her thesis. In the course of that spring Olivia read and discussed all four drafts of Chloe's introductory chapter, and Chloe read Pavese. They compared their authors with each other and with themselves. Suicide, self-sufficiency, the consolations of art, and the impossibility of "home"—these were their themes. They debated the merits of realism and romanticism, they wondered whether love could be free of illusion, and, as the

Roman air held daily more heat, what besides love a person might find in the larger world.

Olivia taught Chloe the best Italian curses. Their favorite was redundantly malicious: *"Ma va a mori mazzato!"* Drop dead murdered! Chloe persuaded Olivia to take the bus with her to the beach at Ostia where she would have ample opportunity to practice it. At the flea market at Porta Portese, Olivia bought Chloe a Sicilian puppet on impulse. It was the only way she liked to buy things. Chloe admired that, but she could never succeed in forgetting her tight budget. Near the end of each month it was she who lent Olivia money to tide her over until her scholarship check arrived. One week they made a little money working as extras for a movie. Reasoning that they now were women of means, they resolved to reward themselves with a trip before going home. Olivia talked of Corsica and Greece, but Chloe had heard of Lipari, an island near Sicily where the boat stopped only once a week. When the agent said it was dangerous—*"molto pericoloso"*—that decided it.

As the spring ripened, they sometimes referred to the longer future. Olivia thought she might be able to hook up with an archeological crew at Erculano or Gela, the Sicilian town where the lachrymatory had been found. Or she thought about graduate work in comparative literature or linguistics. Of course she would write eventually, and teach or translate to survive. All that was certain was that she could not live in New York with Esther there. In any case Olivia would come to New York for a couple of weeks to show Chloe around. Chloe had a teaching job waiting for her there, but she had never spent more than a weekend in the city. She looked forward to it, but abstractly. The future, life after their season in Italy, seemed unreal, and they never tried for long to imagine it. They made it a point of honor to live in the present.

* * *

Chloe asked Olivia to go with her one afternoon to see Sophia Loren in *La Ciociara*. Olivia had not read the Moravia novel on which it was based, but they knew it was about a Roman woman taking refuge from bombardment in the hills during the war. At first the apparently unconscious sexuality of Sophia Loren as Cesira made Chloe anxious, and Cesira's aggressive self-assertion only seemed to expose her to more danger. Then Chloe was melted by the tormented idealism of the pacifist Michele and the community of refugees in the hills, but she worried for Olivia. Olivia read her mind. "I never saw anything like this," she whispered, "and I don't think Esther did either." When Cesira and her daughter Rosetta, still only twelve years old, were raped by Moroccan soldiers in the church, Chloe shrank down in her hard seat, clutched her belly, and covered her eyes. It got worse. The stony-faced child refused to speak afterwards, and when the soldier who was giving them a ride bullied her into singing tunelessly along with him, Chloe couldn't bear it, she thought she would have to leave the theater. Only when Rosetta learned of Michele's death and wept in her mother's arms did the hot tears of relief pour down Chloe's face.

The lights came on. Olivia's cheeks were wet too. They left the theater with heads bowed and walked along the Tiber without a word. The sun was low, and little birds swooped above the dry-eyed river. A girl leaning on the wall slapped the man she was with, then laughed at him and pulled him toward her. Italy was all right, it had recovered from that terrible time. Chloe's chest lifted with the sense of possession. But Olivia continued to stare at the pavement. I know so little really, Chloe thought, chastened, and Italy seemed strange again, alien passions under its dark clothes. Now it was Olivia's silence that Chloe couldn't bear. She touched her arm.

"Livia," she began, "it was too close, wasn't it—"

"Not at all!" Olivia jerked her arm away and wheeled toward Chloe, glaring. "There's nothing in common! That woman took her daughter with her! She wanted to protect her herself, but Esther—" She stopped short, her face flaring.

"Oh, God," said Chloe miserably. "It's awful, if only I—" There was no way to embrace this tall suffering girl.

"Shhh," said Olivia, touching her elbow and turning. "Let's just walk."

In late April Olivia got a call from Chloe. "Olivia, have you heard? I was just at the butcher's, and Bruno told me the most horrible news!" It took a minute for her to get it out. Kennedy had tried to invade Cuba. "I remember thinking last fall it was safe to leave the country once Nixon was defeated. But now this! They say Kennedy counted on the Cubans to rise up against Castro. Does he really believe everyone thinks just like him? Or doesn't he care?"

Olivia was disgusted but not as surprised as Chloe. She didn't expect as much as most Americans seemed to from their presidents.

"I can't just go back to my work. I can't concentrate at all," Chloe complained.

"What the hell," Olivia laughed, "that's as good an excuse as any. Let's take the day off. We'll go sightseeing."

At the bus stop, Olivia saw Karl's back bending over a fruit stand. Flame ran up the length of her like a zipper, laying her so open that the man, turning and seeing her face, fumbled his orange. As he bent to retrieve it, staring boldly, an ordinary man, any man, no one, Olivia mounted the bus and fled. She knew now why she had not refused to talk to Karl when he called last week. Now she would have to figure out what to do. Chloe was waiting for her in front of San Giovanni in Laterano. She would have to talk it over with her.

Poking around the huge church, Chloe seemed to forget her upset. But outside again in the sun, she fretted. "I can't explain it," she said, "there's nothing I could do back there—but the whole thing makes me miserably homesick!"

Always preferring to work things out in a cool place, Olivia steered Chloe toward a round church with an inviting bench in its porch. She leaned back and languidly stretched her legs out, while Chloe tucked up and hunched over hers.

"I don't know why it eats at me so, but Americans are so ignorant, and they're too arrogant to know it!" Facing a low stone wall, they watched an American couple fuss over their cameras, the woman scolding her mate. "How ridiculous they are!" Chloe sputtered. "They can't look at anything except through that little box, can't go anywhere without that harness of apparatus, can't do anything alone!" Olivia lolled her head sideways.

"What's up, Chlo?"

"Couples everywhere you look!" Chloe growled. "Creeping out from under their rocks when the sun shines! Two and two, lovers everywhere! I can't stand it! And it's not just lovers"— her voice was rising, cracking—"it's these absurd tourists, even, ha! the nuns, the soldiers!" Her attempt to laugh died, strangled. "Ow-oooh! I'm the one who's ridiculous!"

"Chloe—" Olivia tried to catch her eye, but she ducked her head like a runner.

"You can't understand. I promised myself I'd tell you—I didn't mean for you to think—because, I'm still—I've never— oh, what a fool I—" Tears sprang from her eyes. "I'm afraid I'll never—*never* go to bed!"

Reflexively, Olivia took Chloe's damp hand. How small it

was! Poor Chloe—what an awful feeling! With her other hand she hugged Chloe's head to her shoulder, stroking her tangled hair, so familiar and suddenly so strange. Astonishment vied with sympathy. How could she have been so far off? She had thought Chloe—full-breasted, big-hipped—so sexy! Abruptly she realized what she had only half registered. Chloe did not use her body but wore it almost unconsciously. She had none of that brooding inward look of women monitoring their flesh. She never talked about sex. Olivia had thought, She's right, sex is overrated. Fixed on other things, Chloe could take for granted her place in the larger world. She would sail into it deftly, without ballast, and Olivia might have followed her course. Where were they now?

Chloe pressed her hand. "I meant to tell you sooner." She drew back and peered up through gluey lashes. "Do you forgive me?"

"For what? You weren't obliged to—" Olivia felt a belated sting of betrayal, but it gave way to relief. Chloe knew no more about it than she! Less.

"Yes, but I let you assume—and that made it harder. And then I was too embarrassed—I hated your thinking—"

"Forget it." Olivia thought of Karl's call, folded it up like a letter, and stuffed it away. "I couldn't help assuming." She felt expansive. "The way you look—you could catch anyone you want. And you seem so game, so aware, there's no way I could have guessed—"

"That's what Sandro says."

Olivia dropped her hand. "What? Who?"

Then Chloe brought her confession to its point in the present. There was an Italian film critic she saw from time to time, a much older man, and she simply didn't know what to do with his three-month standing invitation.

It couldn't be, but it was. The same Sandro Olivia had looked up when she first arrived in Rome. One of Esther's old cronies from the Resistance, who had also gone the route of disillusion to a mannered, hedonistic cynicism. What was his line? That he would take her with him everywhere, like his umbrella over his arm. That was supposed to be such a treat! What was Chloe doing with that old fraud? Everything was coming loose! Could Olivia herself have read him wrong? Maybe he was different with Chloe. When Chloe pressed her now, she only mumbled, "I don't know him well. I didn't like him much. I thought he patronized me, because he knew my mother."

"Livia! It's uncanny! Sometimes I don't like him either. I certainly don't love him. He can be awfully condescending. But he's been nice to me, and he's funny." Her thesis on American writers in Rome was apparently a fount of entertainment for Sandro. One evening, Chloe said, he showed her the sites where the virgins of American literature had languished—the Colosseum where James' Daisy Miller had caught her fatal fever, the tower where Hawthorne's pale Hilda had fed her doves. Maybe, Olivia thought again, she was wrong about Sandro. But he didn't matter. What mattered was that Chloe, so clear about everything else, was so wretched. "Nothing is happening," she was saying, "and I'm leaving Rome in a few weeks!"

"You don't have to be at the mercy of the calendar, you know. You can anticipate time." Chloe looked grateful but still confused, so Olivia elaborated. She felt powerful and gentle, fluent with invention. "Why should the passage of a few weeks dictate how things turn out? Don't you have any say?"

"You mean it's up to me?" Chloe stared at the stone wall in concentration. "I suppose it is. But which should I do? End it, or pull him into bed?"

"Either one," said Olivia, happy with the sweet taste of her bounty. "Your first initiative would be to answer that."

Hugging her knees, Chloe rocked and nodded, still focusing on the wall. "Look!" she cried. There among the rough stones of the porch wall was a piece of marble with a trumpeting angel carved on it. It had been turned on its side like a brick to fill in the wall. They crouched in front of it.

"Sandro—you really despised him, didn't you?" Chloe asked ten years later in Ontario.

"Ugh. I couldn't understand why you saw him at all. He was so vain! Those routines! He offered both of us his black Russian cigarettes with the gold tips at just the right moment late in the evening, remember? Pathetic. And it puffed out his feathers to show up at his screenings with a new foreign girl. Thirty years younger if possible. If she can't speak Italian and has to depend on him for everything, so much the better."

"Jesus, he wasn't that bad! And you were nicer about it in Rome, thank God. I was having an awful time. I couldn't figure out the first thing to do with him, and you helped. Maybe you couldn't think for yourself, but you thought for me."

"I did? Good for me!"

"Maybe I should have asked the angel its opinion that afternoon," said Chloe a few weeks later on the deck of the boat from Naples to Lipari. People were sleeping all around them, in dark mounds or familial heaps, so Chloe kept her voice down. She had booked deck passage since their funds were slim. Besides, there were two good reasons to sit up all night—not to miss the volcano when they passed Stromboli (though the eruption at dawn would prove a matter of barest courtesy, like a tugboat salute) and to catch up. They hadn't seen each other for a week.

"But I did it on my own. I took the initiative. Actually I took both of them, one after the other. I offered myself to Sandro three nights ago, and he turned me down. So then I ended it."

"He turned you down!" Olivia caught her arm in a bony clutch.

How good it is, Chloe thought, unwrapping the truth with a friend. "He just looked at me and said, 'But you're leaving now.' Then he asked how I could have thought that all he was interested in was a one-night stand."

"Do you think he thought it was more than he could handle?"

"Maybe." Chloe had wondered the same thing. "Maybe the role of seducer, the pose of it, I mean, was all he really wanted. But still I felt shabby. He seemed so, well, sad. He told me he had had a suit made because of me."

"My God! Chloe! He was in love with you!"

"You look stricken," Chloe laughed.

"It never crossed my mind. He was in love with you."

"Cut it out! I'm not so sure he was. He'll live, anyhow, and after all, he rejected me."

Olivia's guilty sympathy for Sandro seemed to evaporate, and her fervor was all for Chloe. "God, yes! Were you all right?"

They both laughed, and a sleeping man raised his head to beg the signorinas for mercy.

"I was a mess while it was happening. But by the next day," Chloe whispered, "I was fine. Cleaned out. It's mad, I suppose, but I feel as calm as if I'd done it, put it behind me. I don't think I'll be afraid next time."

"There's not so *very* much to it," Olivia said kindly.

"Don't condescend! Your advice was good, no matter what happened. To take initiative may just be"—and Chloe began to giggle—"as good as being initiated."

"Better!" said Olivia, choking back her laugh. "If you're rejected! It's purer."

"*Hssst! Zitto!*" A dark form rose from the deck and threw something at them.

"It was a shoe, I tell you," said Olivia five years later in Oregon. "I should know. It was my hip that caught it." And she rubbed that long shank now. "But you know, I never remember that. I never think of that night, or that week we had on Lipari, except as extraordinarily peaceful."

"It was lovely. But peaceful?"

"An interregnum. Free time. A time for us, and a respite between hard bouts with men. Yours with Sandro before, mine with Karl after."

"But Livia! How can you forget the men of Lipari? The local crooner—Ciccio! Who was so hot for you? With his shirt split to the waist, remember?"

"With holy medals caught in the hair! I remember, of course!"

"Okay, then. Peaceful! Do you remember the day he and his friend took us out in his boat and when we got back to Lipari—don't you remember? Peaceful!"

"What?"

"The boys waiting at the dock? To tell us Ciccio's wife was looking for you, and if she found you she was going to drag you through the streets by the hair?"

"We were crazy to believe that, Chloe, don't you think? Who knew if Ciccio even had a wife? We never saw her, and—"

"I don't know. Anything seemed possible. The agent said 'pericoloso.' There were no other Americans. And we were stuck. The boat to Sicily wouldn't come for a week. We were in trouble!"

"*And so you kept us on the lam! That very night we had to go out fishing with those kids. Sit in that boat with them till dawn waiting for their nets to fill. You said—oh, Chloe, you said so solemnly: 'It is safer on the open sea.'*"

"*What's so funny. It is! It was! Besides, that was the only night the boys could get the boat, wasn't it?*"

"*Sure, Chloe! And it would have been criminally wasteful— immoral!—to pass up a chance to go fishing all night for squid. And that wonderful lamp they hung over the prow—so pictur- esque! And when we got back, we looked at each other, and our faces—*"

"*Were black with soot—*"

"*And soot in our hair—our scalps stained black as the ink of the calamari. But that wasn't enough. You made us get out of bed after almost no sleep and clamber over the rocks to try to find a secluded beach.*"

"*Was that the next day? That wasn't so clever. We only drew attention to ourselves. Remember the army of little boys?*"

"*The further we went, the faster they came. No women ever out on the beach, let alone in bathing suits. And they wouldn't leave us alone—*"

"*Until you turned on them, Livia, and let rip with your whole repertoire—*"

"*And slipped on the moss, and cracked my elbow.*"

"*You were a hero, saving the wine bottle.*"

"*And you came running to help me, and you slipped and gashed your knee on the shells.*"

"*Yes! And the people on the cliff began yelling to us to pour the wine into the wound.*"

"*And then, after all our trouble, you had to let them prac- tically carry you back to the dock. And that guy was just poised there with the motorcycle to spirit you off to the hospital.*"

"By then the whole town was there."

"And you went off behind him practically naked, nothing but your blond hair streaming behind you—"

"And blood streaming down my leg, not knowing where the hell I was going. And all I could do was worry whether Ciccio's wife would find you. Peaceful, yes."

"But you know, Chloe, it was. Even that. Compared—"

"You're right. It seems idyllic now."

"Yes. And sometimes, especially now when things seem unendurable, I get this wild longing for our last day there. The summer solstice, remember? Longest day of the year. When we had the world on our own terms. Just held our lives back a little, you know? For the last time, really."

"You mean—oh! The day we ran away?"

"Over the mountain. Yes."

"Yes! You mean the cave."

"The cave. And that woman."

"Oh! What she said."

"Yes."

They left the town early in the morning when a haze lay over the harbor. This time they remembered their hats, and they carried some figs and bread in a net bag. They followed the road to the top of the first hill and looked back on the olives and fruit trees, the scattered houses, the rocky horseshoe harbor and the ribbon of black graphite that made a beach. Another hill swelled ahead of them. There were only a few huts, gnarled stumps and scrubby bushes. The sun ducked in and out of the clouds. Olivia talked a little about the sad beach town where her mother had dropped her and her brother for their first summer in Italy so she could concentrate on her new lover.

"This place is simple, but that place was poor! There was so little to eat, and Andy was bitten by a rat. My mother had told us we needed the sea air, so God help us, we made the most of it! We dutifully stood hand in hand by the seawall each morning and filled our lungs."

Without thinking, both Chloe and Olivia stopped and drank the pungent air. They laughed sheepishly.

"You were tough, kiddo," Chloe said shyly, stroking Olivia's silky hair.

Olivia pressed Chloe's hand to her head before pushing it away. "Blind stubborn is all! Hanging on to whatever she gave us, ignoring all the signs."

Olivia tried again to teach Chloe her half of the women's duet from Bach's cantata. Chloe had explained that it meant they were hurrying with feeble but eager footsteps to Jesus for help. It didn't fit them exactly, but it had become their song. Soon they could no longer see the harbor, and the bushes gave way to pale plants and brambles, scarcely darker than the gray rocks they grew on. There was a single apricot tree with bright fruit tumbled promiscuously about its roots. They sat and ate until a man on a scooter paused to warn them they would get sick. Walking on, they put together fragments of Ciccio's song. Then they fell silent except to remark how the hill kept rounding over itself, how each summit concealed another. There were no more trees, no more huts, no more people.

It was past noon and they seemed improbably high when the greener ocean appeared on the far side of the island. At the foot of a series of cliffs was a tiny crescent of sand. The sun showed it to them for only an instant before a cloud erased it. The road followed the cliff's edge for a while without conviction, then surrendered entirely to what might be only a creek bed. Without a word, Chloe began to pick her way down, and Olivia followed her. In the smooth stretches Chloe leaped ahead, but in the hard places she handed Olivia around the big boulders. They were on a ledge more than halfway down when the sun disappeared for good. No bottom could be seen, but they hesitated only for a moment before plunging down the rest of the hill.

Reaching the scarf of gray sand, they looked back at the cliffs tilting toward them and discovered a shallow cave at the base just as the first rain splashed their backs. Olivia made a large scorpion vacate the cave for them, and they sat on dry ground. Hollowed behind their backs and curved over their heads, the cave had the form of a seated woman. The rain was huge, but it did not reach them there. They chewed their bread and sucked on their figs while they watched a river carry little stones, then large ones, down what had been their path. Neither one had brought anything to drink, their thirst grew immense, and there was nothing even to catch the rain in. Their useless hats wilted in their hands. But they grinned at each other and agreed that extraordinary as it was, they felt only safe, even joyous.

The rain stopped abruptly, and they watched a black wall in the sky slide across the horizon until it escaped their sight. They stripped to their suits and swam far out in the sea. From there they could see halfway up the mountain a broad plateau with a hut at its edge. When they dressed in the cave, it seemed as familiar as an old house. Olivia methodically brushed the sea out of her long hair while Chloe shook her tangled yellow mane and danced around looking for the scorpion.

They climbed up slowly then, Chloe in the lead. Olivia fixed her eye on Chloe's calf muscles, which jutted like her cheekbones. Sometimes they slid up to their knees in the muddy sand, and the late afternoon sun drove on their backs. When they reached the thatched hut, a woman and a girl were standing just inside the door. The woman was dressed in black, and black cloth bound her head. She studied Chloe and Olivia without surprise while the girl's green eyes flew from one to the other.

In a torn rag of a voice, the woman sent the girl to the well. After bringing a bucket of water and a cup, the girl retreated a few feet and watched them drink. Chloe and Olivia could see a few sheep grazing at the far end of the narrow scrubby field. As they drank and drank again, the woman slowly told them how her first son had died in the war and how the second had been tending the sheep near the cliff's edge when a huge boulder rolled down the mountain and carried him into the sea. While the slender girl hovered behind the well, the woman pointed out the rock's trajectory. Now only she and her daughter were left. She said she climbed over the mountain to go to market at the harbor once a week, but she was uneasy there and hurried home. Chloe said, "I can understand that," and Olivia said, "It's so beautiful here." The woman's face relaxed in assent. When she understood that Chloe and Olivia had come not only from the harbor town of Lipari, and not only from Italy, but from further places, other countries, she twisted her mouth and squinted long into their faces.

Then she asked in a whisper so the girl wouldn't hear, "The rest of the world, is it better?"

"We both said no at once, remember?" Chloe asked in Oregon five years later.

"I meant it," said Olivia. "It was all she had. And it was so beautiful. I still mean it."

"But the rest of the world! What about this Oregon coast!" marveled Chloe. "And what was better? That woman's meadow and cliff and seascape? Her tragic tale? Or our day's adventure, our cave?"

"It's a riddle, isn't it? We said it, and we have the rest of our lives to figure out what we meant! But we both felt so full—"

"Yes! We thought we understood everything. We were sure we understood each other, anyhow. It was like being drunk. You know, Livy, I think we thought we were the same."

"We were wrong about that. But listen. When we both said no, Chloe—it was a kind of pact."

"For what? To find something better?"

"No. To live out our lives with what we'd found that day."

"It was beautiful, even the giving and taking of life," said Chloe still one year later in Washington. "That woman had lost so much. And taken in the loss, made it a part of her."

"That's your idea, Chloe. We don't really know anything about her. I'm sure we romanticized her."

"How could we not have? We were so young—"

"Precocious but callow! Still, whatever she really was, we made her and her question a standard for our lives."

"And for us too, Livy, for our friendship."

"Jesus! No wonder it's been hard."

"My God, how we romanticized that old woman in Lipari," Chloe moaned four more years later in Ontario. "She was desperately poor. It embarrasses me to think of it."

"Well, it doesn't embarrass me," said Olivia. "That's how we were then. Why can't you accept it? And besides, it wasn't really her, it was us, our world, that moved us—as we'd made it that day. Nothing seemed better than that. Of course it was unreal. Conditions were all skewed in our favor. We'd put all those men behind us, and the island was so small we could hike across it. So we thought we could do anything."

"An illusion bequeathed us by our class—"

"And our heady experience. The bottom line was, we believed in each other. A deal we struck without realizing—"

"The interesting thing is, each of us held the other to it!"

"I relied on you to hold me to it, Chloe."

"It weighted down the friendship at times. But it was the only thing—look how far apart we went!—that held us together."

"Listen, Chloe, we had to be far apart for it to work at all!"

Summer 1961

When Karl stepped off the mail packet onto the dock at Lipari, the eyes of the men and boys around Chloe and Olivia turned inward. The brightness of his hair in the hot light seemed to stun them. When he kissed Olivia, they melted away without farewell. In the next few days in Sicily, Chloe learned to invoke Karl's aid. On the way back from the temple at Segesta, the man leading Chloe's donkey had dawdled until the others were far ahead. Then he sprang up behind her and, insisting hotly on the Greek authenticity of a coin he offered with one hand, chafed her thigh with the other. Chloe managed to shove him off, and even laughed with her friends over her "hush money," but the next day she shrieked, "Karl!" when someone goosed her in the streets of Agrigento. In one fluid motion, Karl dropped the luggage he was carrying and pivoted toward the offender with palms turned forward. The man vanished. Chloe called it Karl's "Olympian gesture" and kept it in mind.

Willy-nilly, despite her prejudices and his distance, Chloe began to know Karl. Often he seemed preoccupied, burdened by his beauty as if by a public charge. But when he spoke of his parents, his childhood, his work, a bountiful intelligence lit up his features, he warmed to his subject, and his kindness spilled over onto Chloe. Karl's love for himself is contagious, she warned herself, and she wondered for her friend.

Agrigento gave them their best day. They strolled all morning among the temples on a bluff now high above the ocean,
but at one time so close that seashells had washed against the
columns and nestled between their ribs. Olivia took Karl's hand
and made him feel the mysterious scallop, its perfect architec-
ture vying with that of the Greeks. Chloe found a stone giant,
fallen or asleep, in the grass. Karl stretched himself out on it,
and Olivia pronounced that he came short.

"My dreams dwarf giants," Karl said orphically. The color of
the air made him miss his work, he said. "You know something,
Chloe?"—he gave her an odd look—"I'm a better painter than
I am a person." Chloe felt his power then, but she could not
define it.

After lunch, they hitched a ride to the little town below the
ridge. Karl reminisced about learning to sail off the Maine coast
at five, and Chloe found herself boasting about her own infan-
tile boating in Canada. She had been only three when her father
took her into the shivering bottom of the canoe and placed her
hands next to his on the double paddle, making her feel what
she long believed was the rhythm of pure flight.

Olivia spotted a tiny boat for rent. She had rowed only a
short way when Chloe noticed they were going in circles.

"Your move, Chloe," drawled Karl. "Show her how it's
done."

Chloe was game, but something was wrong. After one
clumsy stroke, she figured it out.

"The right oar is shorter, look!" She levered them up. "But I
have an idea." She took two short strokes with the right for
each one with the left. The boat wobbled but held its course.

"You're a genius!" Olivia cried.

Karl was attending to her rhythm. "Long, short-short, long,
short-short," he conducted, triangulating the salt air. "You see

that, Olivia? Chloe rows in waltz time." He groaned the *Blue Danube* in time with her stroke.

Olivia cracked up. "It's the death march," she gasped.

Karl leapt up, heedless of boat balance. "Slide over, pip-squeak, and let me have the short one." Chloe slid, but not past the touch, the good acrid smell of him. He made her laugh too, giant with a tiny oar, lunging forward and back to lengthen the stroke. Olivia laughed so hard she began to hiccup. Karl dropped his oar and made her stand up with him in the pitching shell. When Chloe began to shout and curse in real alarm, Karl explained simply, "Fear is the only cure I know for hiccups." It worked, Olivia hugged him, and Chloe looked away, so famished all at once that she was frightened.

Later Chloe strode the beach beside them. In the waning light, the sky curdled over the sea. Olivia lowered her voice to ask Karl something. He didn't answer. Instinctively, Chloe dropped behind. Now, replete with the long day, she felt generous. She watched the shifting design of her friends' silhouettes. Head down, hugging herself, Olivia was concentrating her force. As her outline clenched and shrank, Karl's expanded jauntily. He scooped up a shell to skip at a fishing gull. He gazed, arms akimbo, at the mottled sky. Olivia's thin fingers, darting at his shoulder, stopped short. Then, her profile craning, she asked again. A violent roar shattered the sky. They all wheeled to see a yellow seaplane trying to lift itself from the water. As the noise tore the air, Karl turned to Olivia, and his large mouth began to work silently. Screaming, the plane seemed stuck in midair, and Chloe and Olivia pressed their ears. But Karl's lips pleaded and swore as he clutched his heart, slapped his brow, bunched his shoulders, and clasped his hands before Olivia, dancing all the loverly attitudes of anguish, chagrin, and renewed ardor. The need, naked in her eyes, darkened to rage just before she shut them. At last the plane moved off. Then Olivia was laughing helplessly.

"And that's the way it is," Karl pronounced in basso. "That's how, deep down, I feel. It wasn't easy for me to say it, Olivia, but now at least you know. Don't ever ask me again."

The next day Olivia thought the heat had made them crazy. After she nearly passed out in the amphitheater of Catania, they had jumped on a train that bore them south to steamy Siracusa. The sight of the white *Star of Malta,* shivering and swimming in the heat waves of the harbor, made Karl babble of cool night breezes. He was about to book them passage they couldn't afford when they reminded him that Malta was even farther south.

But when they were in the train escaping to temperate Taormina, Olivia realized it was Karl's own climate, the electromagnetic field he projected around him, that was at work on them. His peremptory stance, his conviction that everything began with him, had been the first thing she noticed when they met on the boat. His summons that first night, his cutting her away from the others to inhabit the space he defined, even his insistence that they stand side by side at the mirror in the ship's lounge, had seemed to her lucid, irrefutable. Following his speculative gaze, she took in their paired legs and flat hips, her small breasts next to his slightly narrow chest, and his shoulders jutting over hers. The top of her head, she remembered, was level with his eyebrows, but her eyes, black with alarm—oh, God!—were incomparably wider than his judicious hazels. Only then, smiling as if he had won a bet with himself, did he lead her silently to the bed in his cabin. Karl's clarity still stopped her breath, and his chariness with words deepened his authority. He transcended explanations. To be with Karl, she figured, she would have to become a paragon of independence. It was too hard. After Spain, she had thought she was through with him. Not talking about him with Chloe, she pretended she had forgotten him. But she so watched for him with her peripheral vision that she sometimes thought he lived in the corners of her eyes. When he announced that he would join them to go to Sicily, she had not hesitated. Transportation to Gela and the archeological dig was difficult, so she gave it up. It didn't matter where they went.

When Karl took her on one arm and Chloe on the other, Olivia pretended to feel festive. He conferred safety on them, but it was not the safety she and Chloe had imagined in the cave. And Karl was not the same. She realized late that she had hoped to display him to Chloe, but the intelligence that had drawn her seemed sunk into cleverness, his ambitious curiosity into probing and teasing. Was he different because of Chloe, or was she herself seeing him through Chloe's eyes? Sometimes Karl argued with Chloe, and she fell in with it. Olivia felt that she had lost them both, and sometimes she hardly cared.

At a flyspecked juice stand where the train paused half an hour, Karl asked Chloe how she got her name. Chloe knew what was coming. She stalled, talking about her father and the Greeks, his insurmountable envy of Euripides. By the time it came she was ready.

"Daphnis and Chloe—aren't they the ones who couldn't figure out how to do it? What did your father have in mind?"

Chloe didn't blush, though she had to sacrifice her father to keep her poise. "My father did all he could to slow me down."

Back on the train Karl pretended he thought her thesis was about American virgins in Rome. When Chloe stared at her friend, Olivia stammered that she had told him about Sandro's

tour of the haunts of literary virgins. Chloe wasn't convinced
that was all.

Crossing Sicily with these tall friends, Chloe had become
sensitive about her height, and Karl wouldn't let up about it.
When the train pulled into Taormina that evening, the porter
told them the town was very crowded. Karl said not to worry,
he'd ask at the hotel for a room with a crib. In the end they
found two tiny adjoining rooms, the last in the hotel. At dinner
Karl started in on Chloe's frizzy hair.

"No accounting for tastes," said Chloe coolly. "I was told
just the other day that my hair makes me look like a Fra
Angelico."

"Oh," said Karl. "You mean the picture of the Virgin getting the news?" He grinned, benign with triumph, then cocked
his head to appraise her hair. "Yeah, there's something in it. If
the Fra had his finger in a socket."

Was he competing with Chloe? Olivia wondered. And if so,
was it to win Olivia or to feed a whim? Couldn't Chloe see he
was mocking her? Or was he flirting? Why did she rise to his
bait? When Chloe caught his tone, Olivia didn't recognize her.
Once Chloe startled her—and she looked startled herself—by
drumming her fists on the table. Karl only smiled. They stuck at
dinner as if fated. Then Karl leaped up to take a walk, and
Olivia went up to take a shower. She stood long in the soft
stream, washing and washing her hair.

Yesterday he had ignored Olivia's hints that he and she do
something alone, and now he goes off by himself. Chloe was
sorry Karl had come, then sorry she had. She hung out the
window over the darkened valley until she heard Olivia brush-
ing her teeth. Then she went into the bathroom between their
rooms and said she'd ask in the morning about another hotel.

Olivia spat into the sink. "Forget it. From what they said in the station, we're lucky we found anything."

"Well, we're here for a few days. Maybe I'll take a little side trip by myself."

Olivia swilled water from a glass, spat again, and glared at her friend in a mirror now weeping steam. "Do what you please, but don't do it for my sake. The way we are, it's what he likes."

Could he *prefer* the threesome? Why? "But—"

"Chloe. Take my word—"

Chloe watched her image redden with indignation. "But he's so mean to you!"

"You assume a lot," said Olivia with a severity new to Chloe. "You're sure I want to be alone with him. But I've had it, it's finished."

"Then why are you angry at me?"

"I'm not!" Olivia smiled without conviction and ran water into the glass.

Chloe was grieved by her bleakness. "You said it was over after Spain."

"This time it's different."

Chloe was doubtful, but she could not mistake the tone of warning. She turned away before Olivia spat again.

When Karl threw his arm over his face to block the sun, Olivia woke. She sat up in bed and looked at him. He didn't move. Above the elbow on his soft inner arm, a pulse jumped. Her cheek laid there lightly caught the tremor, then she slid down beside him, fitting herself in his hollows. He didn't stir. After a while, she edged away, breaking contact the length of their bodies. Driftwood left by the tide. It was then—oh, of course—that he rolled to her. She tried in vain to call back the desire that had thudded through her moments before. She fought bitterness, and failing to defeat it, managed to hide it, till he lay back again smiling. How mean he is, as Chloe said. Olivia went and stood by the window. In all that color nothing would register. What was she doing here?

Karl hummed a little, and she stayed at the window while he called down for coffee, rolls, fruit. She went into the bathroom and pulled on the clothes she had left there. When she came out, for the first time on this trip, Karl had taken out his tiny set of oils and was working.

"Ha! That was close. It was almost perfect. But not." He chuckled. "That scares me, Olivia, do you know that?" He didn't look up. "It doesn't happen often. But sometimes, with the very first strokes, it looks as if an angel just passed through. Then it's hopeless. There's nothing I can do." He concentrated on dabbing and poking, humming a single note. He didn't need her to say anything. "I have to sneak up on myself. If I think I'm painting, I'm dead. I need it to be like something left behind by mistake and then I just mess with it." This was how he wooed her, by not wooing, by letting her watch him, figure out what he wanted. "Someday, when I get good," he went on, "when I get really good, it will be like some terrible freak accident, some awful trouble, and I'll just be the someone who has happened down the road that day. Otherwise I'd never have the nerve." He might have had her pinioned, she was just where he wanted her, exactly at the point between near and far. She took a few experimental steps toward the door, like a person paralyzed all her life trying to walk. His voice was barely audible. "Olivia, don't go." He didn't ask where she was going or why.

"Why not?"

"I want you here with me." He still didn't look up, though his hands were motionless now. She couldn't speak, couldn't leave, couldn't stay. In that silence, his pride touched her and she burned for him. When he said softly, "This is the way it's possible, Olivia," she had strength only to sink into the nearest chair.

As soon as she woke, Chloe decided to take off by herself. Shutting the door, she tried to fasten some latch in her head as well. Immediately she felt less alone. She realized she had been constipated for days, and she drank espresso until she was cured. It was the end of her long vacation, and she decided to look for the house D. H. Lawrence had lived in. Her inquiry for *"la casa di Day Acka Lorenchay, il scrittore"* puzzled the towns-people. Is he blond? Does he walk with a red dog? No, no, said Chloe, he's been dead for many years. They exchanged looks of alarm as they sent her down the road. She heard one explain to the others that the signorina was looking for a dead man. At the road's end a rosy house stood alone, surrounded by cypresses and chickens pecking in the yard. From an open window came the eerie but unmistakable music of a typewriter. A middle-aged man spotted Chloe through the window and stepped out on his terrace, sweeping a robe on over his shorts. He was from Great Britain and had rented Lawrence's place hoping it would help him finish his novel.

"From sheer osmosis," she told her friends back at the hotel.

Olivia laughed, but Karl looked distracted. He'd been paint-ing all day, Olivia explained, and she showed Chloe a row of tiny abstract seascapes. Chloe pretended to look, but she was weary of artists. She was ready to go home, to start her life.

Before putting Chloe on her plane, Karl insisted that they stop at the cathedral in Palermo to check out the catacombs there. "Chloe wants to," he improvised. "For old times' sake. To round out the circle." The skeletons were supposed to be fabulously costumed as kings, queens, and judges. Chloe didn't care one way or another. She was going home to be maid of honor at a friend's wedding. Karl and Olivia had decided at the last minute to go back to Italy together by boat, see the ruins near Naples, then go their separate ways, he to France, she to Milan. Olivia still did not know where she would end up next winter, but she promised Chloe that her first move would be to touch base in New York.

At the entrance to the catacombs, Olivia turned sharply. "I can't, Karl, I'm sorry. I don't want to go down. I'll wait outside."

Karl gazed at her coolly, without reproach or apology. Olivia's look matched his. They seemed to Chloe like deer in the forest, full of beauty and their own cold understanding. She watched Karl turn one way to descend, and Olivia the other to make her way out to the sun. These two would not press each other, but the strange intimacy that bound them had never been more palpable to her. After a minute she went out and saw Olivia sitting on the steps, staring into the piazza. At her approach, Olivia glanced up from under her straw bonnet. She smiled faintly and extended a cigarette. How deeply she sits inside her mysterious life, Chloe thought. She sat beside her, and the two smoked in silence.

Olivia felt the sun on her legs and arms and shoulders begin to draw out a chill deeper than that in Karl's dank catacombs. Good to have Chloe near and silent. She didn't want to explain how Karl had seemed like a current drawing her down into his own dark. This was only a momentary reprieve anyhow, a brief resistance to the drift she was giving herself to. She was in the sun, but she was after all waiting for him. The sun brought out the sweat on her shoulders whose sweet scent had soothed her since girlhood. Turning toward Chloe, she saw a man with a

camera in front of them just as triumphant laughter burst from
behind. A pair of young Italians sprang to their feet. They had
been crouching behind her and Chloe for an Italian classic—a
shot of two men with their foreign women at the portal of a
cathedral. Now they bowed deeply and, throwing kisses, ran
off with the photographer.

"Who are the boyfriends?" asked Karl, materializing suddenly beside them. He was in a good humor all the way to the
airport—"Imagine what they'll say about you when they show
the picture around in Reggio di Calabria, or will it be Brin-
disi?"

Olivia let him talk and fell into a little dream. The two
Italians were actually the promised spouses of herself and
Chloe. They would live out their lives, all four together and
without Karl, in a little town by the sea.

At the airport, Karl clowned his goodbye to Chloe. She
clasped Olivia, and Olivia suddenly clung.

*"That hug threw me," Chloe mused ten years later in On-
tario. "I'd been thinking for days that you wanted to be rid of
me to be alone with Karl."*

*"Goodbyes sometimes terrify me. I hate them! And I was
miserably confused. I was determined to break with Karl, but I
was suddenly afraid that with you gone, I wouldn't be able to
manage it."*

It was two months later, at the end of summer, that Chloe
heard Olivia's voice again, and it was so tinny with panic she
had trouble recognizing it.

"Where have you been, Chloe? I've been calling for hours.
How do you like the Village? How's your apartment? Yes, I
just got in last night. Yes, *here* to New York. Brooklyn. My

mother's apartment. But we're not going to stay. You've got to come immediately. We're getting married this afternoon. What? Yes! Yes, of course, Karl!"

When Chloe simply asked for directions, Olivia moaned with relief. It doesn't matter that Chloe and Karl don't like each other, she thought, just as long as Chloe's here and sees it. But hanging up the phone, she realized she couldn't summon Chloe's look. Feature by feature she could find her, but she couldn't assemble the splinters.

When Chloe buzzed, she flew down the stairs, crying, "How pretty you look!" Chloe was wearing a white Mexican peasant dress and had wrested her hair into a French twist. It was Chloe's way of cocking her head to search her face that Olivia had oddly forgotten. Chloe's hand went to her throat, and her face drained of color. Olivia ached with fear. She hugged Chloe, swaying, till it passed. "I'm so glad you came," she said brightly, and thought suddenly, I need you here, you more than anyone. Then she said it aloud, thrilling them both. "I need you here, you more than anyone." Olivia felt she had never spoken more truly, that her words had become transparent as glass.

Chloe was glad too, but she couldn't speak, she didn't know why. Olivia's dark eyes pleaded, flying up the staircase and back to her. They had only a few minutes to whisper in the hall. Chloe stammered, "Are you all right? What's going on?"

Olivia sucked her cheeks. "Here's the story," she said. Her voice regained its low music. It was Olivia all right, though Chloe would never have dreamed her into this draped dove-gray silk, this hairdo, this elusive fragrance of lilac. Olivia took Chloe's hand from her throat and held it. She talked rapidly, glancing at the door at the top of the stairs.

"Yes, I had called it off! It's no wonder you're surprised. I told Karl right after your plane took off that it was over for me. He didn't believe me, and I didn't push it. After all, we had booked passage together back from Sicily. In Rome I said it more clearly. He went off without a word. Then, yes, I went to Milan—remember Patrick, that nice guy with the motorbike? The historian, also on fellowship? He was great, terrifically nice really. We traveled around northern Italy together till our money was gone. Then we went back to his place in Milan—it wasn't serious, but I liked him, it was a relief just to be easy. And we were there one morning, Patrick was still asleep, and the doorbell rang. It was strange—no one had ever come to visit—but I went down without waking Patrick. I knew somehow. And then there was no one at the door. He was standing just outside, facing the street, with his arm up on the wall, leaning."

"You mean, with his back to you?"

"Yes! Yes! With his back to me!" Olivia's eyes glittered. "God knows how much trouble he'd gone to to track me down, but he didn't even turn when the door opened."

"Why? What—"

"He was leaving it to fate. Or to me. He was giving me a chance to see him and go away. Well, I didn't go away." If I can just make Chloe see it, then it will be all right. "I didn't go away. How could I? I knew what he was up to. But I stepped around in front of him. And he looked terrible. He was stary-eyed, like—well, like he'd been starving." Chloe flinched and Olivia felt encouraged. "Neither of us said anything for a while. Then he said, 'I can't stand this. You've got to marry me.'" She sighed. "I can't tell you how he looked, Chloe." But Olivia saw and felt that look again, as if Karl were showing the face behind the bland, nearly expressionless face he gave the world, showing it only to her and for that time only.

"I said I needed time to think, but I really didn't." Chloe
could believe it. Olivia's drama made her not want to think
either. "We went to a bar. I didn't even wait for the coffee."
Mockery tugged at the corner of her mouth. "But it's different
now, it's altogether different." To prove it, Olivia smiled what
Chloe thought of now as her heroic smile—unequivocal, like
the one that dazzled her at first sight in Rome, but protracted in
a willful way—and turned to lead her up the stairs.

"Chloe, Chloe, say something! No, don't! Just give me your
blessing."

Chloe was flustered. "Of course," she said.

Just inside the door, Olivia's mother and brother turned
identical crooked smiles on Chloe. She blinked and made herself recall that one had nearly destroyed Olivia while the other
had been her partner in survival. Andy's shyness called up
Chloe's own. Soft and unformed, he seemed more than just a
year younger than his sister. But then Olivia was still twenty-
one. Andy had a year to go at Brooklyn College, Chloe remembered, and Olivia was praying he'd get far away from their
mother after that. They had just begun to talk when Esther—
Chloe was to call her that—pulled her away, clasping Chloe's
hand to her own ribs almost roughly.

The flesh of Esther's face had gone soft over the fine bones,
but she was erect and deep-chested and had the imperious
charm of a woman who had once been irresistible. Her heaped
hair was dark red. Most of her accent was polished away, and
the trace that remained seemed oddly deliberate, put on like
perfume. Tilting her head, she treated Chloe like an old aunt of
these adorable children and her own intellectual peer. Olivia
had once said that her mother always tried to seduce her
friends, and Chloe was carefully polite. The way Esther talked,
the wedding might have been her own invention. Karl would

take Olivia to see his parents in Vancouver at Christmas, she explained. Pointless for them to come so far for such a brief time. She gleamed as if she herself were family enough for all.

Esther released Chloe's hand to clasp the slender nape of the young man at the piano, the accompanist at her students' recitals. "This year's treasure," she murmured. Then she passed Chloe on to Olivia's two oldest friends, women who had grown up in New York and made Chloe feel as though she had never left Syracuse. One was a dancer, with hair to her waist and mascara to her temples. The other, a singer who had already cut some records, smiled as if everything had a second meaning. But they were far away. Olivia had said that astonishing thing: You more than anyone, I need you.

Standing before the judge, Esther's old buddy, Olivia was bemused by the mole in the cleft of his thumb. Andy, playing father, hooked her right hand in his arm. But twice today she had caught him watching after her in bewilderment. After so many partings, why should this be difficult? She squeezed his arm, and he pressed her hand with his. Knowing Esther was on his other side, she didn't dare look up. She had no use for her mother's public joy. When she had asked Esther to stand up with her, she meant it to underscore some point about her leaving, but now she couldn't recall what it was. Her mother's creamy hands lay one on the other as if she were about to sing a solo.

The pain of the morning—when Esther and Karl had carried on like long-lost cousins—swept over her again. Esther had set herself at Karl—that was the only way to put it—and Karl had been enthralled by her energetic style and classy gossip. Esther in turn caught fire from him. And there was more, something avaricious in her response to his golden beauty.

But now she felt Karl's shoulder touch hers and she drank

the wool smell of his jacket. He leaned there deliberately for just a moment. This had to be. He held out his hand, and its beauty smote her. His fingers were perfect, brown still, longer than hers, the knuckles strong and elegant, the nails square. But when he turned it to take hers, the palm was like a yearning face, as expressive as its handsome back was silent. Lying in his palm, her own thin fingers looked like jointed bamboo. Olivia marveled: his hand was trembling slightly. This was hard for him. The tips of his fingers just curled over hers but did not clasp. She could trust them not to. She was safe.

From where she stood, Chloe could see only Andy and his grieving smile. When it was over, she hung back. Olivia's friends buzzed about her, but around Karl they made a kind of hush. Catching Chloe's eye, he stretched his mouth, mugging terror. She moved forward to kiss his dry cheek, and he shot her the cunning glance of the cheerful winner. He rehearsed what she already knew, that they were leaving that night for Arizona, where the master's program was about to begin. "The train is the honeymoon," he said, affecting a world-weary drawl. "We've had it with beaches and olives and temples." Then she knew, from the scent of lilac, that Olivia was behind her.

"Oh, Chloe." Olivia had no words. Looking into that dear face, full of the surrender of her, Olivia poured all that she could not say. "We'll write!" She could see that Chloe didn't believe her. But she nodded and smiled, her blue eyes brimming bright.

"Like the law of gravity," Olivia went on in Ontario, "I knew it was inevitable. Not that I thought it was right. I knew it was a terrible mistake. But it had to be. I was mid-dive! Karl— it was my destiny. I knew he'd be bad for me, but I didn't think

I had a choice. And I knew in another way, obscurely, that I was also saving a part of myself."

"Come on, Livy. You couldn't have thought all that."

"I did, though. I thought it was a mad fatality. Until you arrived. When you came, I was scared, because with you there—you knew me, you knew how I'd felt—I couldn't pretend it was fate, it was a choice. I was sure you'd know it was wrong, but I counted on you to understand it somehow, interpret in some way I couldn't for myself. Then it just might be all right."

"What did you want from me? Complicity? You could have had it. Cheap."

"Something like that. But I saw in your face what I really needed: you were for me, whatever I was up to. Still, you must have noticed I didn't give you a chance to say anything. I was afraid of your disapproval."

"Disapproval! What an idea of me you had! I was worried, I was desolate. But disapproval! I was too much in awe."

December 1962

"Chloe, I'm here—with the baby! We got in early this morning. I'm dead, but I can't wait to see you! I don't know how I can budge from here till tomorrow night, my mother has all these people coming anyhow. Karl, no. He's mired in a big painting. Can't stop, you know, for fear of losing it. He already took time off for Thanksgiving, we went to Vancouver to show Hannah to his parents. She's wonderful! It's not hard, just scary. You have to see her. When can I see you? Christ, it's almost a year and a half! How have you been? What are you doing?"

"I—well, I have a snake."

Chloe was clearly nervous about the baby. It didn't help that Olivia had been late and Hannah entered screaming, having to be changed first thing. Chloe scarcely looked at her and then dampened the washcloth with water so hot Olivia had to cool it at the sink. While she found the pacifier, wiped, powdered, and pinned, Chloe stood with her hands clasped behind her. But she had made a nest of pillows in a Japanese wicker swing hanging from the ceiling and was keen for Olivia to use it as a cradle. No sooner had Olivia rinsed, wrapped, and packed the diaper than Hannah was asleep, thank God, her fist in her eye as usual.

Olivia strode the length of Chloe's one big room to get the feel of her life. Leaded windows, working fireplace, a real Village apartment, the kind she might have found if she'd stayed in New York.

"How wonderful all this stained pine is—what a difference from your little cell in Rome! Your Sicilian puppet looks great here." But the plant on the windowsill was forlorn. "Is that Washington Square over the rooftops? What a relief to be out of Brooklyn."

"Was it bad? How is Esther?" Chloe asked. "How is she as a grandmother?"

"Perfect," Olivia growled. "Perfectly ghastly! If only she could be honest! But then she wouldn't be Esther." Funny things in this apartment, a jar of peacock feathers collecting dust. "When I was so sick, for instance, in my seventh month, she didn't even answer my letter. And then, when Hannah was born, she wouldn't even consider coming to Arizona. And yet she made a fuss you wouldn't believe about sending on the ancestral silver cup and spoon!" Chloe made a vague sympathizing sound. Of course, it would be all Greek to her. She should wind it up. "Hell, it's par for the course. I'd been a fool to expect more. But now!" The hurt was so fresh she couldn't stop. "Esther's cooing so over the baby in front of all her friends—it's unendurable. She's such a fraud! I thank God it's only a short visit."

Basta. Hannah might just be tucking into her first solid sleep in New York. And she was with Chloe at last. "Why don't I pour us both some wine?" In a butcher's apron that came to her shins, Chloe was arranging anchovies in stripes over oiled bread crumbs, capers, olives, and charred red peppers in a casserole. A spatula marked her place in a fancy Italian cookbook. A far cry from the plain boiled artichokes they devoured in the middle of the night in Rome. But that Rome was so far away Olivia sometimes wondered if she had dreamed it all up. "Here's to you, Chloe," she said, "and life in the Village!"

Chloe returned the toast. "Here's to Hannah and her ma!"

Chloe seemed different, more easy in her body somehow, but also remote. Olivia felt awkward. "Getting anywhere with the thesis?" she asked.

"Please," Chloe muttered, diving into the cookbook. "Don't talk trivia. I'm trying to do some serious work here."

Still stalled, apparently. Unless she thinks it's all over my head now. Olivia asked quickly about the teaching, which she knew Chloe enjoyed.

Chloe snapped the book shut and smiled. "It's okay. I teach them grammar, they teach me the city." She thrust the casserole into the oven. "And that's not all." Shiny with some secret, she pressed Olivia down into a wicker chair. "Just sit, Livia. I have something to show you." She disappeared into the bathroom and reemerged like a diva in triumph, arms raised wide, with something like oiled rubber around her shoulders and extending from hand to hand.

"Oh, Jesus Christ."

"It's my snake, I call her Fascination." Chloe posed, grinning. Her hair was wriggling out of its bun, and the creature wrapped and sliding around her made her look like that snake goddess in Crete. Chloe advanced toward her slowly, and Olivia could see the forked tongue darting like black lightning. She glanced apprehensively toward the swing, but Chloe gave it a wide berth and stopped mercifully a few yards from where Olivia sat cringing.

"She's utterly harmless, Livy. I'm holding her firmly at the back of the head." Chloe unwrapped the snake as if taking off a scarf and turned its head toward her own, smiling indulgently

at that tongue. "Isn't she gorgeous?" Olivia said nothing, but
Chloe was oblivious. "You think she's jet black all over, and
then you see this long blue mark on her belly. That's why she's
called an indigo, but look! Look at that rosy, rosy throat! Isn't
nature too much?"

Olivia looked. It was rosy, it was strange, but stranger still
was Chloe's little rapture. She willed Chloe not to make her
touch the thing.

Chloe stepped back and held the snake at arm's length. Its
flailing tail swept the floor. "She's exactly five foot four, like
me," she said. "That was the point of the gift."

Olivia said nothing.

"It was a present for my twenty-sixth birthday," Chloe said
ingratiatingly, tossing the snake back over her shoulders.

Olivia was seized with fury. Why was Chloe doing this?

"There's this girl, a student of mine," she went on. "Gifted,
funny. Also slightly crazy. She wouldn't stop giving me things.
Little things at first, like tiny cacti, those peacock feathers. And
last month, for my birthday, nothing would do but an indigo
snake, exactly as long as I am tall. She's from the Everglades, so
I put a box in the bathroom with a lightbulb to simulate the
tropics, confuse her into surviving." She gestured an invitation
for Olivia to go look.

Olivia only grunted. Is it possible, she wondered, that Chloe
doesn't notice? No.

"Oh, don't look like that, Livy. She's fun. Besides," she
beamed, "a snake is just a snake. What people think is not its
fault. A snake doesn't know itself for a phallic symbol." She
giggled. "If you asked the snake, it would say a penis is a poor
metaphor for a serpent! This snake is extremely snaky."

Chloe notices, all right, but she doesn't care. So why the hell
am I here?

Her silence finally got to Chloe. Her sparkle subsided, her shoulders drooped. "This student's obsessed with challenging me. Actually, Livia," she said thoughtfully, "she worries me. She lives by herself, she's very alone. But instead of asking for something, she just keeps giving me stuff."

"Are you sure she's not asking?"

"No. But I can't quite catch the question. So I decided if I took it militantly at face value, simply as an unusual gift, it might defuse things a little. What else could I do?"

"Are you seriously asking—"

"All right, okay, maybe I'm wrong. But that's how I saw it." Distracted, Chloe wrapped her wrist in the snake's tail. "The girl graduates in January, she's going abroad, so I may give up the snake then. Or sooner, if—"

"January!"

Chloe turned away then to deliver Fascination to her false tropics. Sooner, if— She decided not to tell Olivia about the snake's refusal to eat the mice she bought, the humiliation of returning the mice to the pet shop, the phone consultations with the zoo's snake man, their fear that Fascination was yielding to fatal despair. And it would probably not help to tell about when the snake shed her skin, how Chloe had to work it down like a tight stocking. Not all her friends were keen on the snake, but Olivia was taking it badly. Why had Chloe felt impelled to show her to Olivia anyhow? She had missed Olivia sorely, especially that first winter in New York. Was she punishing her for going so far away for so long? As she closed the snake in its box, Chloe felt ashamed.

Washing her hands at the sink, she knew it was the baby. She had been able to bear the marriage, but when Olivia wrote that she was pregnant, Chloe felt she had lost her irretrievably. Storming through the streets of the Village to work off the news, she had said to herself, "Never once, never once in all that time did we talk about babies!" Then it was over, and she had sent Hannah that splendid picture book—premature, she knew, but the only thing she could think of, and babies grew fast, didn't they?

Now she bent over the swing to peer at the stranger. Those narrow chips of mica were real fingernails, and that round cheek was covered with finest down. The flesh of the face looked as though it would dent if she touched it, and the reddish fuzz could not protect the scalp. She watched the little stomach rise and fall, and the moist breath laved her hand. A thrill of panic came and went. Olivia, she thought, this is your life now. Without a word, she went to Olivia and hugged her, and after an instant, Olivia hugged her back. A baby. It was hard. Others of her friends had had babies, but they had not sat up till dawn talking with Chloe.

"I don't know how—is it like—does Hannah, I mean, do you—does she always sleep like this?"

Olivia still had that transfiguring smile. She reached up from her chair, clasped Chloe's head in both hands, and pulled her thick hair. How Chloe had missed this Olivia! Now it would be all right. She carried the wine and their glasses across the room to what she called the garden, and they sat on cushions under the potted rubber tree. They toasted each other again, but this time they looked each other over. Olivia was positively plump. Always small-bosomed, she held her arms awkwardly beside her swollen breasts, but she looked slyly pleased.

"I smell like a dairy, I know."

"I don't know the first thing about it, Livia," Chloe confessed heartily. "What the hell is it like?" Olivia laughed. This was how she should have begun. Plainly Olivia wanted her to understand everything, and Chloe longed to meet her. Olivia talked about colic and sleeping patterns and rashes and a problem with nursing. Chloe set down her glass, concentrating on every word as if learning a foreign tongue, and heard almost nothing. She prayed it didn't show. Little as she loved him, it was easier for Chloe to imagine Karl. She asked about him.

"I think he's happy now. He gets up sometimes at night just to watch me fix her. He won't change her himself, but he watches. Her tininess, he can't get used to it. He has these wild protective schemes. Even in the hospital, he said we would have to build a wall around the house so no man would ever get at her."

"That's nice. But 'happy *now*'?"

Olivia hesitated. "For a long time, his work didn't get off the ground. He carried on, you know, in his comical despairing way. He said painting was all used up, it was obvious there could be no more paintings. What I think, he was having a hard time with Arizona. We both were."

Chloe recalled an enigmatic postcard. "What was that all about last summer, Karl's having to see the Hopis?"

The corners of Olivia's broad mouth dipped down—a new look. "I can't explain it, Chloe. He can't work at all in a new place till he finds it. Finds something, he never knows what it will be, that belongs to him. So he was between courses, and we'd heard this story about how the Navajo kept crowding the Hopi, and the Hopi were as pacifist as the Navajo were aggressive. Well, there are three Hopi mesas, they stick out on the desert like long fingers." She showed Chloe three of her own. "So finally the Hopi just gathered on the three mesas and pulled up the ladders behind them. You know how that would get to Karl."

"Pulled up the ladders!" Chloe marveled at Karl and the Hopi. Perverse of me, she thought, to like him best when he makes himself most separate. "But you explain it very well, Livia. Why do you say you can't?"

Olivia punished her cigarette stub and glared. "Chloe!"

Chloe flinched, but still she examined her friend, searching one eye at a time in that earnest way that had first drawn Olivia. And didn't it still? Olivia looked at Hannah. Exhausted by the commotion in Brooklyn, poor kid, and the way I was feeling didn't help. Her head was thrown back, she was in her most abandoned sleep. Olivia relaxed too.

"The Hopi had nothing to do with it. He just couldn't stand me so big. Said it made his own body feel funny. I didn't want to hear about that. So by the time he went away, I was glad."

"But also sore."

"Damn straight!"

"I'm sorry, Livy! Was there anyone around?"

"No one. Oh, there were people. No one that mattered. I didn't mind, though. I wanted to be by myself to think about what was happening to me. And so I was. It wasn't great. It was okay. Anyhow, it's—"

"Like what? Think about what?"

"About me becoming this incubator, and—my God!—a mother!" she cried impatiently. "I mean, it happened so fast! I was just about to get a course to teach and then—we never sat down and planned it. Last year I was just me, but now, now—"

Last night at Esther's she had waked to black silence. She had held her breath till she heard the baby's in the crib, and then she matched its rhythm with her own. Lying there then, she fancied herself a vast province whose boundaries had fogged over.

"Who in the world else could you be?" Chloe sounded edgy.

"You're so literal, Chlo! I feel like all of me stretched out for the baby—not just my belly—and I'm still out there, flapping in the breeze."

"That could be interesting. As an experience. As long as you get your old shape back soon."

Olivia stiffened. Chloe understood nothing but adventures, and they had better be efficient ones at that. Olivia had never known a woman less maternal. At least Chloe had the grace to be embarrassed.

"Don't mind me. I don't know what I'm saying, Livia. I mean it, I don't understand the first thing. Does Karl, uh—feel the same as you?"

"Christ, no! Not that I'd tell him. He'd be too jealous!"

"You have to spread yourself pretty thin and go about it awfully carefully, don't you, Livy?"

She understood something, then. "Well, now it's different. Karl's getting to be a great father."

"Really? And what about his trip? Did he immerse himself? Did his painting get started?"

Olivia wasn't sure that Karl had even gone to the Hopi mesas, but she couldn't tell Chloe how she felt. There were no words for it, or there weren't the kind of words that she and Chloe used. She thought differently when she was with Karl—if it could be called thinking. "I don't know," she said. "He didn't paint anything while he was away. But then, he never paints except at home." She warmed to this. If she could make Chloe know some of her life, she wouldn't feel so divided. "August and September were awful. But then he made a breakthrough. He said he felt like a seal who had just found a hole in the ice!"

Chloe whistled. She took to Karl's words more readily than anything else about him. "Wonderful!" she said. "But must be scary, no? I mean, what if he doesn't find it?"

Exactly. Chloe asked about the new work. "Quirky" was all she could say. "More like Karl himself when he cuts loose." The quickening feeling in her gut came again as she spoke. How strange it was, in the same months, to feel Hannah kicking and Karl straining to some new life in himself. And because of her!—he had almost said it once.

"You look like you take it personally," Chloe said gently. "You must feel very close to this work."

The old Chloe! "I do. Sometimes he even needs me to be in the house. It's strange."

Chloe watched her. "Does that make you feel good?"

"It should, shouldn't it?" She was abruptly grateful that Chloe insisted on Olivia's slim old self, the one no one else discerned. Karl's wanting her made her feel good, but lopsided. Olivia felt constrained again, as if a wire were drawn across her middle. "At least I'm good for something."

"Livia, for heaven's sake, you're—"

"Yes, yes, I know, I'm wonderful." Enough of this. "How are *you* managing? Do you ever see the Old Movie Man?"

"Why are you changing the subject? That was over nearly a year ago! I must have written you—"

"You made it sound so allegorical. How did it go? He invited you to *Modern Times*?"

"Right. And the next week I took him to *À Nous la Liberté*."

"And thence to bed?" What fun suddenly to be in New York, quizzing Chloe about sex at last! No more grief over the mockery of Roman schoolboys! For a moment Olivia regretted the passing of that dewy Chloe. But then, she hadn't changed so much. Chloe's new urbane casualness didn't take her in.

"A week later," Chloe said. "After Carl Dreyer's *Day of Wrath*. A very sexy movie, actually."

Olivia laughed aloud, and now Chloe half hoped she would wake the baby, but Hannah didn't stir. Chloe got up to check the casserole. Barely warm at the center.

Olivia beckoned her back. "And then?"

"It was all right, but when I made a date with another man at a party, he was hurt." Chloe didn't say she had sat up all night wondering whether she was in fact cold.

"And the man at the party was which? The Conceptual Artist? The Reichian Analyst? The Bomb Shelter Man?"

"The Bomb Shelter Man. He's *against* bomb shelters, you understand. He was trying to get people to picket *Time* magazine because it had run a cover story in favor of bomb shelters. Four of us went. We made posters: 'Don't Put the Unthinkable in Your Cellar.' But people were rude. I was surprised. They wouldn't even take our fliers."

"And so you gave up and went to bed with him? What happened to him anyhow, the Bomb Shelter Man? And don't any of them have names?"

"He was overprotective." That made Olivia laugh. "I'm not being funny, he was. You're going to wake the baby. No, none of them have names."

"No, but seriously, Chloe. Talk to me. Isn't there someone? The Reichian." She was relentless. "You had another name for the Reichian—you wrote me—"

"Livy, don't be feeling sorry for me, please. It's just the dead of winter, you know?"

Startled, Olivia softened at once. "Oh, was it rough? Would you like more wine? Do you really not want to tell me—"

Chloe was powerless before that low music. "Creature Comfort, I called him. Creature for short." She couldn't stop the heavy heat in her cheeks.

"That's it. How come? When you wrote that, I didn't understand why you were being so ironic. Against yourself, I mean. What was wrong with him?"

"Everything! Chiefly, I was in love with him." Chloe surprised them both.

With that look, Olivia didn't have to say anything.

"Livia!" Chloe pleaded. "It was all *done* by the summer. You don't live here, you know! It's not so easy to stop and start like this!" She was bewildered by her rush of anger. It wasn't Olivia's fault! Had she hurt her? "Now, don't *you* be sad. I'll talk! I'll talk! You know, it's actually got its funny side. Give me a cigarette." Even so girded, she checked Hannah in the swing. No help there. She was merest sentience. "That's a kind of sleep we know nothing about."

Olivia was silent, her eyes waiting on Chloe's.

"He had eyes too." Chloe groaned, set down her cigarette, and did three perfect deep knee-bends.

Olivia was touched by the display of physical control. Chloe sank down on her cushion in the yoga position.

"Not like yours," she went on. "Gray. And they always had this puzzled look except when—Livy, we made no sense. When we'd met, years ago, before college, everything was easy. So when he turned up again, I asked him here. He brought—I didn't write you this—he brought Bach. Not your Bach. I already had a record of your cantata. But he brought another. 'Wachet auf.' Do you know it?"

Olivia was stirred—my Bach, she says, my cantata.

"There's a love duet between God and Zion, and it's something else! You know the part?"

Olivia said yes, it was extraordinary.

"So full of yearning!" Chloe cried. "Well, it was wonderful at first, and so natural. He talked about marriage even the first night. I laughed, but he kept at it. Livy, we didn't understand each other at all."

"Didn't understand what?"

"Didn't understand anything but putting on that record and getting in the sack. I mean, that was a lot, but we practically

wore out the second band. Being in love is the pits. Well, it's a
nice thing to have behind you, if you know what I mean."

How could she have felt so much and put it aside? "But *what*
didn't you understand?"

"Olivia! Simply *everything* else! He wanted to get married
right away, find us a *house,* just shut the door and make babies.
Oh! what am I say—" Chloe smacked her head and shot a wild
look of apology at the swing. "I mean—Livy, babies weren't
the problem. It was us, him. That Reichian stuff just seems silly
to me."

Chloe looked miserable. Why had she run from this? "Why
is being in love the pits?"

"Because, if it's not going to work—I mean, those moments
in bed when you think you could just die—"

Olivia couldn't let her stop now. "It's overwhelming?"

"Yes. No. I mean, I had no idea before, despite Old Movies
and Bomb Shelter. No idea what it could be like. There's no top
and bottom, do you know? You can't tell who's getting, who's
giving. And when you think you can't take any more, it starts all
over again. How could I have imagined all that? Even you
never told me."

It's just that our timing is off, Olivia thought. How many
times had she told herself that, as if it were only bad luck,
something beyond them, like the weather? Nothing wrong
with Karl and me, we both feel a lot, we're just not in sync this
time, or the time before, or the next time. Her voice felt
clogged.

"Maybe it's not that way for me."

The hateful question rose again: Was Olivia really all right?
But Olivia was asking pertly, "If it was like that, how could you
want it behind you?"

"Because it *is* too much if it goes with nothing else. We had no feeling for each other's work. Finally it was even clear to him. Don't laugh at this, but—what am I saying? Go ahead, laugh, I *want* you to laugh." In fact, she did. "There was this organization of scientists who were talking to groups of people in living rooms about just what nuclear testing does. He laughed, my Creature Comfort. He couldn't believe I wanted to do it—have a gathering like that. And when he realized I was serious, it really upset him. So it ended. But I still can get a chill"—and she did at that moment—"when I think of that door closing on his dream house."

"You do have a cool head, Chloe," Olivia said, wagging her own. "But I'm glad there was someone you felt that way about. It must have been hard, believing it was right to let him go."

"Oh, it was. At first I thought the hardest part was giving up the creature comfort—" When Olivia started to protest, she held up her hand. "I know! You hate my putting it that way! But feeling right about it *was* harder. He believed *so strenuously* in that house of ours. And those eyes!"

"His house. You realize what it is, don't you?"

"What?"

"Another bomb shelter!"

"Livy, you're a genius! And me, look how consistent I am!"

"You were afraid for me, weren't you, when I gave up Creature Comfort," Chloe asked nine years later in Ontario.

"Yes. You made it sound so good, I didn't know if you were just afraid of all that feeling."

"Maybe I was."

"Maybe. But now I think you were taking care of yourself with some uncanny instinct."

"This is your myth of my powerful omniscient self-control."

"Don't be silly. Who knows your weaknesses better than I?

*But the Bach duet would have done me in, I'd have let that
door slam in my face."*

*"This is your myth of you as natural prisoner. Still, if I had
to live in a house, the Creature's wouldn't have been the worst
in the world."*

"You would have died in it, Chloe, that's all."

"Please note the wine," said Chloe. It was from Segesta, and
the label pictured the temple they had visited on muleback. She
believes you can hang on to it all, Olivia thought. She served it
with the pepperonata casserole and artichokes fried in deep oil,
carciofi alla giudecca.

"Chloe, this is so elaborate."

"It's feast or famine here." She laughed. "Sometimes, when
I'm alone, I get to thinking cooking is too utterly contrived.
Table setting. Sometimes I can't see any reason for a place mat,
even a plate seems absurd. Once I just drew my chair up to the
refrigerator! But this—this is a salute to our past. Do you
remember the night we splurged in the Roman ghetto?"

Olivia remembered well. The restaurant was in what had
been Beatrice Cenci's house. "Yes, and you told me the story of
Beatrice doing in her father."

"And then you, sly fox, made me talk about *my* father."

Olivia nodded. She might forget the Cencis' tragedy, but
never Chloe's account of her father getting drunk and falling
down the stairs the night after her mother took a job, so she
would have to stay home to care for his broken bones.

"I think they must have used more tender artichokes,"
Chloe was saying. "Well, it was an experiment."

"How is your father?"

Chloe sniffed. "Well, I haven't poisoned him yet. Just his
life." Her father's blood rushed to her neck. A few weeks earlier,

Chloe explained, they had fought bitterly over the missile crisis. "I couldn't believe Kennedy would level that ultimatum. Some of us stayed up all night so as not to sleep through the end of the world. My father thought because the Russians had backed down it proved Kennedy had done the right thing."

"Where was your mother?" Olivia could never fully imagine that retiring female.

"She was there, is that what you mean? She tried to make us quit. I think she agreed with me, but she hates quarreling. She got up and went into the kitchen. What's the use of that? Then my father told me the story again about the bully on the block. I can never get the point of that little homily. If the Soviets are bullies, what good does it do us to bully first? My father and I, we have no common ground."

Olivia watched Chloe beat a little tattoo on her knees. "Are you sure you have no common ground? Not even temperamentally?"

"*O-liv-ya!* What does temperament matter?"

Hannah answered with a loud bleat.

Out of that long stillness, so much violent sound! Chloe was alarmed. But Olivia was already making the buttons of her blouse fly open, chattering to Hannah the while. "I'm coming, I'm coming, Hannah, I'm right here. Your lovely nap in Aunt Chloe's magic swing has made your lungs so strong! Look, here I am!" She opened a flap in her brassiere and picked up the baby. So modest in Italy, she now tugged her breast out matter-of-factly and thrust it in Hannah's mouth, quenching her wail. Olivia laughed. "Quick, Chlo, look at these eyes, before she's off again." Dark violet eyes unseeing, heavy with the sating of desire.

Chloe rearranged the pillows in the wicker swing, and Olivia sat in it to nurse. Chloe started to clear the table, glancing regretfully at Olivia's unfinished plate. Too much clatter. So she laid a fire in the big marble fireplace, the pride of the apartment. Then she sat on the hearth between the swing and the fire, smoking. The baby sucked noisily and Olivia chuckled. How much of her does she drink anyhow? Chloe wondered. Won't there be a deficit? The way she had handled that breast, it was like a thing that belonged to the baby. Olivia tucked one leg under her in the swing and slowly stroked the child's thin hair. She might as well be back in Arizona, all the ladders pulled up behind her.

The weight of Hannah, her surprising heat—these things gave Olivia rest deeper than sleep. Hannah made every inch of herself sink against her belly, like heavy water, seeking closeness to her first home—how long, she wondered, would this part last? The tiny leg she clasped had a rubbery firmness. Hot frog.

The only sounds were of bark crackling and baby sucking. Chloe sat on the floor brooding. Olivia remembered herself young, sitting up late with her mother, getting Esther talking so she would only half notice the child leaning against her legs, pressing against her side, seeking the bones under her flesh. When Hannah took a rest between breasts, Olivia tried to tell Chloe how amazing it felt, like nothing else. Sometimes, she said, it was hard to tell who was the baby, who the mother. The thought of Esther came and went. The way Chloe looked she might have been thinking about Esther too.

"This is what I should have given you last time," said Chloe as she served Olivia Yankee pot roast two winters later. "I felt so mortified after you left, feeding you all those oily things, those brown artichokes, the capers and anchovies. And you so milky, Nursing Mother."

"I managed. It was a little difficult at first. But not because of the food."

"*You were pissed about the snake!*"

"*I was not! But the way you came back at me on the phone—'I have a new baby,' 'I have a new snake'—it was too much!*"

"*It was true! You had a new baby, I had a new snake. I didn't mean anything more than that. I knew it sounded ridiculous. I thought it was funny. I didn't mean to piss you off.*"

"*You didn't piss me off. You were going through a lot.*"

"*A lot of nothing. Nothing but weirdness. I think I lived on oil and garlic. And the snake was just there. I think you were pissed, Livy.*"

"*Chloe. I was not pissed. I was afraid you wouldn't accept me with the baby.*"

"*Accept you!*"

"*You know what I mean.*"

"*I didn't know how to act around the baby. I was scared of her, if you can believe that. After you left, I had a dream that all my plants died! But when you nursed, I saw how much she meant to you. I felt awful afterwards. I thought I'd failed you.*"

"*You've never been willing to talk about that business with the snake,*" Olivia said five years later in Washington. "*When I got in and called you to say—*"

"*Oh, let's do the snake again! Never been willing!*"

"*Are you annoyed? We can skip it.*"

"*Let's not! Let's have it! The snake! The snake!*"

"*Chloe, I used to think you were hostile. But now I believe it was your moment of greatest loneliness.*"

"*You goof! I was strange, I was experimenting, but I had people everywhere. All those men! And I didn't want to have a child.*"

"*You didn't hold her. You didn't want to touch—*"

"*You didn't hold my snake. You didn't want to touch—*"

"Ah!"
"Christ, Olivia! It's a joke!"

"Olivia? Remember the snake?" Chloe asked nine years later in Ontario. "What it was—I'd been afraid of men too long. And thought, simplemindedly, because by then I'd slept with a few, that the fear was gone. Having the snake proved I didn't need them. And the nicknames for the guys? Pure machismo."
"You might put it that way."

December 1964

The night Chloe fed Olivia Yankee pot roast was colder than usual for mid-December. Olivia and Karl had come to town to show his work to some galleries before deciding whether he should take a job with an Oregon museum art school. Cozy in navy surplus, Chloe went to meet them at five on a midtown corner. They were already there, a still island in the turbulence of the New York rush. Olivia was grim around the nostrils, as though holding her breath. Her even tan gave no protection. More handsome than ever, Karl looked somehow vacated. His big coat might have been swinging from a hanger.

Olivia hugged Chloe warmly—she was wearing a spicy scent—but she seemed distracted. Karl's offered cheek was a slab of slate. In a booth at a Madison Avenue bar, he hunkered over his double scotch like a man warming himself at a flame. Things had gone badly, but there was no other subject.

"How do you like our dealers," Chloe asked.

"Darling," said Karl, "every last one. Of course, we have our favorites. Olivia's mad for the Pop Wop, but give me the Op Fop every time."

That was when Chloe learned that Olivia's heroic smile could be as fixed as glass. She laughed uneasily. "Op and Pop— they haven't taken over the whole city, have they?"

Karl made a show of looking at his watch. "I got here

twenty-five minutes too late." He sucked his teeth. When Chloe opened her mouth again, Olivia said, "Later." She leaned back into the leather booth and snapped her lighter. Karl fiddled with a swizzle stick and pretended to survey the place. But he looked evicted again. They sat there waiting for the next thing.

Chloe broached his shows in Arizona—two of them!—but he wouldn't bite. Olivia's eyes flashed a warning, and she suggested he show Chloe his slides. Even through the tiny hand viewer, Chloe felt the pull and pressure of the paintings. She thought of de Kooning but managed not to say so. Besides, this was different, the recklessness was tamed. Precipitous planes burst from dark cores of brooding, but they caught their balance. Karl shook his head at her praise.

"It's not Now," he said mildly. "It ain't Happening. My work's Already Been. I call it To Hell and Gone." Then he announced he had to go to Westchester, an old friend was inviting a dealer to meet him. He was on his feet, throwing on his coat and turning, when he did a double take and kissed Olivia an energetic goodbye.

Chloe wanted nothing more than to get her out of there, but Olivia snagged the waiter and asked for another round. The waiter twinkled at Olivia, who looked good, tired or no. When she ignored him, Chloe recalled her easy intimacy with waiters in Rome and realized how unhappy she was. But struck with shyness, all she could do was babble about how elegant Olivia had become. "Is that real suede? Remember what ruffians we were in Rome?"

Olivia looked pointedly at Chloe's thick braid, loose blouse, and heaped beads. "Those days are gone. The suede," she said, smoothing it, "is an item in the New York campaign. I got it to meet the dealers. But it's not doing the trick. The dress is from Saks, but Karl's painting is provincial."

"But!" Chloe sputtered. "What do you mean? Isn't it action painting?"

"Chloe, Chloe! Where have you been? Who would guess you live in the metropolis? They look at Karl's work and all they see is abstract expressionism. And that is *finished*, haven't you heard?"

Chloe had not seen Olivia's irony before, and it worried her more than the suede. But it didn't last. Olivia burst out, "So please—don't give me a hard time about this dress! We'd heard about the brutality of the New York art scene, but we hadn't seen it for ourselves. You wouldn't believe the snideness. Karl's shows in Arizona, for instance, you think they help? They make it worse. A guy this afternoon just smiled when Karl mentioned them and didn't say another word."

"That's disgusting! But also, Livy—you don't need me to say it—it's ridiculous. I mean, who needs them? Why make a fetish of New York galleries? Wait, I mean it. Those pictures are strong. Karl's started selling in Arizona, they understand what he's doing. Wasn't this trip supposed to be a long shot anyhow? You're not going to knock the shows Karl had just because some Madison Avenue provincial—"

"Jesus, here come the drinks. I don't really want one, do you? I hate this kind of place, this part of town. Let's just go."

Olivia lingered in the Italian bakery, drinking in the hot restorative fragrance. "Sure you don't need anything else?"

"You want to walk around a little? There's time—dinner just needs warming up. You're not cold?"

"Not seriously. I still like the Village, even though it's changed so." She slung the long loaf in one arm and took Chloe's with the other. "Show me the places you like."

Chloe led her along Washington Square, to which she said

more and more Negroes came every day from uptown, all of them bent on starting up a conversation.

At least Chloe hadn't changed! "You still try to read in parks!"

"Well, not in the winter, Livy, but otherwise, why not?" Olivia squeezed her arm, and Chloe showed her a Middle Eastern jewelry store on the corner of MacDougal. Then, with apologies for Eighth Street's becoming so touristy, some blue and green Mexican glass in a window.

"One more place, okay? Just a block further. How's Hannah, by the way?"

Olivia was instantly on guard. Had Chloe written her off intellectually?

"I have trouble imagining her. Tell me what she's like? What does she do now, for instance?"

I'm unfair, she's trying, Olivia thought. "Dress up every minute she can," she said. "All the time. In anything. Her idea of putting on the dog is to sling on one of Karl's neckties. Then she sticks out her chest and preens! It tickles him." Astonishing how much she missed Hannah all of a sudden. "She's so extravagant! The other day she hugged me and said, 'I want two mamas, I want ten mamas.' I couldn't tell if she was complaining or cheering me on."

"Maybe both," said Chloe, clearly approving Hannah's appetite. She led Olivia into a tiny knickknack shop. "Hi, Eva," she said to a shriveled woman on a stool. "I want to show my friend the Russian doll." It was a pear-shaped peasant in a babushka, made of thin wood. Chloe opened it at the middle to reveal another doll inside. In that doll nested another.

"How much do you think it is, Chloe? Hannah loves to fit things—"

"It's already done," Chloe said nonchalantly, and put the

doll back on the shelf. "Thanks, Eva." When Olivia stared, a grin cracked Chloe's face. "I've got one for her at home, bought it here last week. I just wanted to check." But she couldn't help confessing, "I asked a colleague who teaches child development. I was such an ass last time. So long, Eva."

Then Chloe took Olivia home, gave her a drink, and sat her down to call Hannah, and while the dinner was reheating, she built her a fire.

"A blaze like this almost justifies the savage weather," Olivia said. Zipping off her boots, she shed the day. She rotated slowly before the fire, swinging and bending, watching her hair redden in the light until Chloe called her to the table.

"You'll have to face the cold again if we're going with Gabe to that bar in Harlem," Chloe warned. She pressed more pot roast on Olivia for several reasons, all having to do with insulation. "It'll pad you against the cold and line your stomach against the booze to come—you don't know what booze is until you've been to Harlem!"

She wants to cushion me retroactively too, Olivia thought, against the shocks of midtown. She gave Chloe's roast her entire attention, and felt restored.

"We can change our minds and stay here, you know, if you like," Chloe said.

Olivia didn't like. "I said I want to see how you live, and I meant it."

"Well, this is how, right here. I don't exactly live in the Purple Manor. I've only been there once."

Olivia considered Chloe's big room, her Japanese swing, her things glinting coppery in the firelight, already a happy part of her past. But she had missed the city. "How much time do we have before Gabe picks us up?"

"Hours. We're invited by the woman who works the bar.

We'll go a little before midnight. She gets off then, I think her husband is coming, and we'll have a drink together."

Olivia said, "That makes it easy. We'll do it all," a formula for which she knew Chloe would hug her. She threw a big cushion in front of the fire. Deep comfort first and then a prowl in Chloe's New York—ideal!

Chloe ensconced herself in the swing and waited for Olivia to get settled. "If nothing comes through here, will Karl take the job in Oregon?"

Olivia was as dry as the desert. "We can't stay in Arizona forever."

"Ah!" Now it could begin. "Tell me, Livia. What's wrong?"

"It's suffocating."

Chloe threw her cues. "The people? Your life? Your house?" Olivia wrote so little, none of it was real to her.

Olivia couldn't explain. The school housing was terrible—no space to turn around in, paper-thin walls—but they couldn't afford better. "And last year Hannah was really cranky—teething's a bitch. Karl flung himself around saying he couldn't work in such a madhouse. Then I felt resentful—of him, of everything. Even Hannah. And that was miserably depressing. Because I'd promised myself when she was born never to resent her. But now that's over, thank God. She's got her teeth, and Karl's enjoying her again."

"So what's suffocating?"

"Not Hannah, not at the moment. Yeah, it's the people. It's the damn women. The artists' wives. The way they carry on about babies—they swaddle themselves in their babies' diapers! Babies in general, I realize, bore me silly."

Chloe shrugged. She couldn't quarrel with that.

"Sometimes I wonder if they like babies at all or just use them to hide behind, they're so timorous. And at parties,"

Olivia went on, "the women literally stay on one side of the room as if they're under some sort of curse. There's an invisible line, and when I cross it to hear what the men are talking about, the tension is so thick it spoils my fun." But parties weren't the issue anyhow, it was more the general zeal of wives for houses and their show of rancor toward every foray outside them. Olivia had a tight new smile, a nod to the unfunny. "Even my little two-bit teaching job, a single course—remedial English, no less—is taken as an affront."

Olivia conceded that Karl backed her up, but her mouth wrenched down at the corner. "It's easier for him to simply let me do what I want. . . . The other woman who teaches is all right, but she's kind of a professional academic. It's like a class difference. She doesn't even know how condescending she is. . . . The teaching itself does grab me, more than I could have predicted, but damn it!—it's all deadly, I can't explain it."

Olivia's words strayed like sheep on a prairie. Chloe was a harried sheepdog, running, circling, and yelping. "But didn't you say—? . . . But is it really that? . . . Then why can't you—?" Olivia wouldn't be herded, and Chloe regretted her little protests, which hung ringing in the silence that fell between them.

It came over Chloe then that her dismay was bone-familiar. Olivia's irony and paralysis—they were like her mother's. Running from one grievance to the next, getting nowhere, the way her mother used to fume and rant behind her father's back in the old days, before she got religion. Now everything that had once fueled her wrath seemed heaven-sent to nourish a new forbearance, even equanimity. Yet the sharpness of her tongue when Chloe was young matched only her weakness of resource. Chloe had not seen it so clearly before. But this was Olivia—*she was not meant to be like that!*

In front of the fire, looking up at her blond inquisitor, now

in baffled meditation—a little cross-legged Buddha in a swaying basket—Olivia felt her edges smoothed, her slackness
firmed. Her life was like runny dough that Chloe was trying to
pat into shape, knead into consistency. It couldn't be done that
way, but Chloe's effort made Olivia tender. If she wanted so to
draw off Olivia's tension, well, she could have it all. Olivia lay
back on the rug and stretched her arms over her head.

Then Chloe asked flat-out, "It's Karl, isn't it? Karl and
you."

Olivia sat up at once, as if Chloe had dropped the cake. "Karl
and me? This gallery ordeal has brought us pretty damn close.
There are always the times he goes off by himself. That was
rough on me at first, but I understand it now. I can live with it."

Chloe looked grave. Olivia roused herself—this was true,
wasn't it? "The point is, things are better. Karl is working in the
house again, like in the beginning. He calls me to show me
things, sometimes even when I'm asleep. He can be pretty
ardent when he wants my response." Once, when Karl had
woken her, she clung to the watery depths of sleep and the
dream on its sea floor—something precious, sad, and wonderfully early, her mother a young woman and she herself scarcely
older than Hannah. When she rose to the present, to Karl's
urgent whisper, to their dark bedroom, all that remained of the
dream was a sequence of colors: silvery bliss, orange excitement, purple danger. But that much held, and she moved
blurrily to his studio, almost without transition, and saw his
painting as if through thick layers of water. "Sometimes it's like
going from dream to dream," she told Chloe.

"Livia, how wonderful."

Chloe looked smitten and humbled, as she had been in Italy,
in the presence of feelings mysterious to her. Then it seemed
that Chloe could imagine Olivia's passions better than her own.
But she had since let men come close. What explained it now?

"How lucky Karl is," Chloe was saying, "that you respond that way."

Olivia smiled. That night Karl had been as ardent taking her back to bed as he had pulling her out.

"He must know how rare you are."

The memory recoiled. What was rare was a moment like that. She studied Chloe, so tenderhearted on her behalf, so suggestible. It was too hard to tell her all of her burdensome love, but essential to let her feel the pain. "Look. Last year there was someone. A pretty little undergraduate."

Chloe jerked as if she'd been slapped. "Jesus, Livy!"

"Yeah." Olivia sat up now and held the sides of the swing. "She worshiped him."

"Livy! You never told me!"

"Well, I'm telling you now. She adored him. He liked that."

"Oh, damn, Livy."

"It was painful at the time. Ugly. He wasn't very adorable, let me tell you. In fact, he was lousy company. It was before the first show came through. There was this party." Olivia groaned and sank back on the floor. She rolled toward the fire. Why had she started this? She'd been free of it for months.

Chloe's face was a grimace of sympathy. "What happened, Livy?"

"Shit." Olivia got up and found a cigarette. "Karl got drunk. He doesn't drink much, remember? But this girl was there, and he pulled her into his lap."

"And?"

"I left and went home. I don't know what went on. Later he tried to talk about it, but I didn't want any part of it. Then *he* got upset!" She threw her cigarette in the fire.

"Livy, why didn't you write me any—" Chloe stopped herself. What could she have done? Helplessness was stifling, enraging. "What did you do?"

"What could I do?" Olivia flashed her new rhetorical smile, brief as a comma. "I racked it up to experience. And the next time—take it easy, Chloe, it wasn't right in front of me, for which I'm thankful. But I knew there was something going on with another painter. That time I talked about leaving. Whew! I won't try that again. You know what he did?"

"Tell me what he did."

"He cried. Sat there on the bed and cried. And said things."

Karl in tears! Amazement quelled her rage. "Like what?"

"I don't know, Chloe. He was nothing without me. He couldn't do anything without me. That. I hated it."

"Did you? Really? Why?"

"Because. You know. It's not true."

"Are you sure?"

Olivia shrugged. "Of course. But that's the way he thinks when he's scared."

Chloe thought of Karl, whimsical in the sun of Sicily, declaring he was a better painter than person. Looking into Olivia's eyes, opaque now, she knew that Karl needed no better argument. "And you?" she asked softly.

"What about me?"

"It's enough for you." Chloe turned it into an assertion.

Olivia was headed toward the sink, but she wheeled around, blazing. "Chloe, for Christ's sake! Let's talk about *your* love life!"

Olivia's anger hit Chloe like a wall, and she rocked with fear and chagrin. "Livia! I didn't mean—I don't want to pry! I thought you wanted—"

"I do want you to know, dammit. But it's not so easy. It's not so clear as you want it to be."

"Oh, I know! I don't want—"

"And I mean it! Why is it so one-sided? How the hell *is* your love life?"

Chloe flinched, but she felt the justice. "You win. But if you're going to glare like that, how can I—" She stopped, determined to face the glare if it blinded her, begging pardon silently until Olivia twisted her mouth, laughed shakily, and asked, "Okay. Really. How are you?"

"There's not much to tell. At this particular moment I wish there were. I'm sitting out the dance for a while. Thinking about other things. Listen, Livia, I'm sorry if—"

"Yeah? What about Gabe?" She was still sore.

"He's just a friend. Really. Men can be friends."

"So I've been told. And this is enough for you?"

Chloe laughed ruefully. "Maybe it shouldn't be, but it's how it is now."

"So then why in hell do you expect so much of me?"

"Ah, Livia," Chloe cried. "Marriage—it seems so hard! But if *you* can't make it go, who can?"

"Oh!" Olivia leaned heavily on the sink. "It has to work. It's what I want. Chloe, I'm sorry, but if you could have seen my mother last night, going over us like a detective, looking for microscopic cracks. It's crazy, because she's so proud of Karl as a son-in-law, Karl the artist, but she can't stop undermining me. It's the habit of a lifetime. Well." She sniffed. "She didn't get anything for her pains." She glanced over her shoulder. "Chloe, you're so red! Listen, I know you're not doing what Esther did. I'm sorry I blew up. But she wore me down. And besides, we're better now anyhow, Karl and me." She eyed Chloe defiantly. "That's the point, we're getting on better than before." But she blasted water into an innocent glass.

"That night before we went to Harlem," Chloe said three years later in Washington, "I wanted so much to show you what you were doing, but I couldn't get up the nerve."

"What did you want to show?"

"That you kept confessing your misery with Karl in serial installments. Each time, you told me it had been rough in the next-to-last period but now it was better. Then the next time, I'd hear that that time had actually been a horror but you were confident now for the first time, and so on. You'd open the door to the past and slam it on the present. And I'd know for sure I'd hear the truth about it the next time, but for now I'd get that heroic smile of yours. It was an effective strategy. You gave the illusion of candor and you silenced me. It drove me nuts."

"It must have. God, I wanted so much to make it work."

"Oh, I know! And you almost convinced me. At least the first five times. That's another reason I said nothing. And I couldn't see how it would help to show you what I saw."

"It might have helped. Poor Chloe! It would have helped you! You must have been bored out of your mind."

"You always say you bored me those years you were stuck in the marriage," Chloe said in Ontario seven years later. "But it wasn't that at all. I was frustrated as hell by all we weren't saying. You laid out all your complaints, but after you'd blown off steam, you trotted back to Karl again. It was like some sort of exercise. All truth and no consequences."

"Sounds pretty boring to me," Olivia said. "But I suspect we were both more confused than that."

"You think so? No. I just didn't have the guts to make you draw the conclusion."

Olivia stood at the sink drinking water, studying the framed poster above it of Fanny Lou Hamer, Mississippi Freedom Democratic Party delegate. "So let's drop it! I want to catch up with you! You haven't told me about the movement. I want to know why you feel discouraged. Make us some coffee and talk to me. Your letters were so euphoric when you were demonstrating in the spring. And then when you went to Mississippi, you were so caught up, so . . . so impassioned! Since then, I've been hanging. What happened?"

Nothing about Olivia is more glamorous, Chloe thought, than her resilience. Her eyes cleared, and as she turned to Chloe, her face, like a lamp, promised that light was warmth. Chloe basked. Nobody else knew how to ask like that. When her colleagues asked about the movement, something—guilt, doubt, anger—clouded their questions. Nothing clouded Gabe, but Gabe asked neither Chloe nor himself. Her two best women friends in New York each gave half of what she wanted. One offered unconditional approval, the other, relentless scrutiny. They made her feel like two different people, neither one exactly herself. Olivia fetched cigarettes and settled at the table, equipped for the duration. Chloe realized so sharply that what she wanted was precisely Olivia—her loving criticism, her critical love—that though her friend was now here looking up eagerly, Chloe grieved as though she had already left her again.

"Maybe I expected too much from the beginning," Chloe said, fiddling with the coffeepot.

"Start there. I don't know how it began."

Okay. If there was truth to be got, she would get it telling Olivia. "It was the Klan bombing that Birmingham church a year ago, murdering those four little girls. God knows why that in particular—there were terrible things before, Little Rock, James Meredith, George Wallace. But this was a shock that stopped me in my tracks."

Olivia nodded, wincing.

"I went to a freezing rally at Foley Square and listened to James Baldwin and some other Negroes I'd never heard of.

They spoke as if all the violence done Negroes since slavery began was one single act. And the way they said 'we'—'We've been slaves for three hundred years!' Seeing it that way, claiming kinship to all those sufferers through the centuries, seemed to empower them. That was another shock." Olivia should get this, she knew what a difference language makes. "Then the idea that they, that *we*—this time meaning whites with Negroes—could work together to defeat that violence and all the rage beneath it seemed preposterous to me, and at the same time right, but *miraculously* right. Because it was preposterous unless so much changed. I mean, it could *only* work by the wildest stretch of the imagination."

"Ah!" said Olivia.

"So, fine! If that's what it took, they'd make the stretch. They decided simply to change everything! Do you see?"

Olivia saw. She saw the old Chloe in Italy, gravitating upward wherever possible to get the big view, usually just when Olivia wanted to flop down and relax. It's vastness that moves her. And improbability. Olivia wondered briefly if Chloe could care, even in a good cause, for the small, the modest, the likely—things she herself negotiated daily. It didn't matter. Sometimes Olivia felt that her own life was on hold. It was for the stretch more than anything that she had come to see Chloe.

"How do you change everything, Chlo?"

"You start by working together, black and white. That in itself is a shock that implies the change in everything. It begins to undo the violence somehow."

Chloe's color was up, her hair was coming out in little spikes, and steam from the neglected kettle billowed around her head. Olivia seized the pause. "Somehow? Isn't it because you found your own rage and that made you able to stand up to the racists?"

"Who knows," Chloe said, making the coffee, "but it felt wonderful! It was a gas!"

Her pleasure was clearly so torrential she couldn't pause over its source. Olivia remembered Chloe's letters about working with CORE, organizing rent strikes every weekend on the Lower East Side. The big voter registration project in Mississippi drew some of the group south to prepare for the onslaught of summer volunteers. In June Chloe went to Jackson to help with the media for a few weeks and arrived on the very night three civil rights workers disappeared in the countryside. Not until August were their bodies found in a mud dam in Neshoba County. One of the three had taught her how to organize tenants. Reading her letters, Olivia thought Chloe had short-circuited grief, burned the martyr again in making him fuel for passionate rededication. To her question "Don't you need to mourn?" Chloe had responded, "Our work is his monument."

"Even so, Livia, in the middle of that tragedy," Chloe was saying, "I thought I was home. Nothing explains it. I was wrong about everything." Chloe tugged her rope of hair for help. "For instance, I suggested to Helen, the woman I was staying with, that the three guys might have had car trouble far from a phone. Helen said—I'll never forget this—she said, 'It's nice you can think that way. We just can't think that way anymore.' And then she went down the list of Negroes murdered over the years and showed me how all their deaths followed a pattern. I began to realize our lives were so different that we couldn't see the simplest things the same way. Yet I felt so strangely at home!"

"It's not really strange, Chloe." Olivia was as excited as she was envious of Chloe's entry without her into another world. "Helen told you what you didn't know and then you knew.

You've never had any patience with the familiar anyhow. Remember all our talk in Rome? You never wanted a snug home, you have contempt for anyplace where you'd simply fit."

"You think that?" Chloe laughed, but she looked alarmed. "I was only following out my taste? But that's repellent. People were being shot up."

"You know it's more than taste. What in hell is wrong with doing what you want anyway? Listen, though, I want to ask you something. It felt like home, but was it? Really?"

"Ah." Chloe drew a long breath. "This is the question. And it's so hard to say. I mean, it *seemed* that things had never been so clear in my life, we lived in this *glare* of clarity, we ate it and we slept it. Do you know what I mean?"

Olivia grunted. If it glared, how was it clarity?

"I mean, we knew what was wrong and what would be right, there was no doubt in it! We knew what we had to do, everything was so lucid!"

Anything so unqualified was alien to Olivia.

"Above all, we were all in it together, risking our lives. Helen's house seemed to rock sometimes with this tremendous high nervous energy. The fieldworkers—they were real desperadoes—would fall in there at all hours, and we'd get up and crowd around to hear about their latest narrow escape. One guy, T.J., won't drive anything that doesn't make a hundred and twenty miles an hour, and he never gets arrested, because no one can catch him. 'You want to stay alive,' he'd say, 'stick with me. I love myself and I'm going to stay alive. Like I always tell myself, I'm my mother's only second child.' "

"Gallows humor," Olivia said.

"Our main fare, breakfast, lunch, and dinner. A Negro from the North, very militant, very new, was going on one night about all a man has to do is look the rednecks in the eye and refuse to say 'sir.' T.J. laughed and laughed and told about the sheriff's deputy who asked him was he a Negro or a nigger. So T.J. said, like this"—and Chloe got to her feet to strut out T.J.'s bravado—" 'I said "Negro!" and he gun-whipped me' "—Chloe buckled—" 'and I said "Negro" again and he gun-whipped me again' "—Chloe arched—" 'and then I was down on the floor' "—and so was Chloe, rolled in a ball, shielding her head with her locked hands—" 'and they were whipping me, and I said, "I'm a nigger! I'm a nigger! Hell! I'm a black nigger bastard! I'm a coon!" ' " Red and laughing, Chloe got up and dusted off her skirt. "He says it worked. God. That story's already dated. I bet T.J. doesn't tell it anymore. The point is, we all told jokes on ourselves, did wild things to keep down the fear. We depended on each other in some ultimate way. It made us whites belong to the Negro community more than ever."

"How do you mean?" How, Olivia wondered, could they know what was real if they had to fake bravery minute by minute?

"Look, to the Klan we were nigger-lovers, we'd forfeited the privileges of our race." Chloe laughed. "Civil rights workers—not including T.J. and the other wild men—got to be the most scrupulous drivers. Someone said, 'You can always recognize a civil rights worker in Jackson—he's the only one who stops at the railroad tracks.' But the cops didn't care what we did. They hated us. They picked up Helen and me for running a light where there was no light and took us down to the station just to scare us. We could handle it as long as we were together. But once—there are two Negro neighborhoods in Jackson, linked by one street. One time I strayed off it by mistake, and there I was in my Indian water buffalo sandals, telltale mark of the outside agitator, surrounded by whites, too scared to ask for directions, a wreck till I found that narrow bridge of a street again!"

"So you won your spurs that day," Olivia said. The edge in

her voice surprised her, she sounded almost like Karl. Jesus, she must be jealous. "I'm sorry, Chloe. All that danger, I guess I've lost the relish for it since Hannah was born. It's not my own life to risk anymore."

Chloe looked so bleak that Olivia stiffened, fearing pity. But something else was on Chloe's mind. "I'm explaining it badly. Risk was never the point. The old hands had contempt for daredevils. What it was about was nonviolence, it was a kind of ethos that bound them together."

"Nonviolence *and* danger," Olivia exclaimed, but she felt admiration too. "What a mix!"

Chloe took her straight. "It made them very special, the Negroes and whites who'd been working together for years. They wanted a lot more than the vote, they called it the beloved community and wanted it simply to spread. That moved me more than anything, but I never felt completely at home, precisely because I *hadn't* earned my spurs, Livia, hadn't gone down when they were only a handful."

"Did they fault you for that?" Olivia was prepared to be indignant on Chloe's behalf. "Didn't the Negroes welcome you?"

"Some did, sure. Some of the poorest people did the damnedest things. I was in a cafe and an old guy asked me if he could treat me to any song I liked on the jukebox! 'You came here,' he said, 'and it's our war.' But other people were suspicious and uneasy, we expected that. And some of the young white girls slept around with the local Negroes, that put a lot of people uptight."

Earning *their* spurs, Olivia thought.

Chloe hung over her coffee mug sorrowfully, reluctant to go on. "I know we did some good, but we confused things too. The movement had been decentralized, intimate, improvisatory. And based on the idea that leadership was inherent in the people. But with all us whites around, some of the younger Negroes began to wonder what their role was. We couldn't see that at first, so much was happening, people were needed who knew how to handle the press—there was so much press. And people who knew how to get through to the Justice Department, people who had any office skills or administrative experience, were indispensable."

"Slow down." Olivia was getting impatient. "What has all this got to do with you?"

"A lot. The movement had gotten so unexpectedly big. And the press was usually more comfortable dealing with white folks. The Negroes couldn't help resenting it, and the whites were in a bind."

"The whites, the Negroes, it's so abstract! How were you *feeling?*"

"I'm trying to tell you." Olivia had been so far away. "I wasn't in this alone. Maybe I didn't feel anything independently."

"What a thing to say!"

She doesn't get it at all, Chloe thought. "It's exactly what I mean, though," she said. "We were so consumed by our dream of black and white together, of living it out and working it through, we thought we were the same." Her voice caught. That's what hurts most, she realized, not the defeat of the Freedom Party at the Democratic Convention or the confusion now, but the damage done to the dream of unity—unity against all odds. "Yet because of the way we divided up the work, some of the Negroes began to think they'd been better off doing it alone. But we'd been through so much together!" It was still so raw. She sprang up and began to pace.

"From *your* point of view," Olivia said. "But they must have seen you as birds of passage."

"They did, and they were *right*. We knew all along we were setting something in motion that most of us wouldn't be able to see through. But they *had* wanted us to come, and our being there made the world pay attention to what they suffer, for the first time. So it hurt! I understood what they were saying, but I was hurt too. And then I began to doubt my own seriousness."

"What? How in hell did you arrive at that?"

"Well, I wasn't ready to throw it all over and go live in Mississippi. I don't have the guts."

"Chloe, stop pulling your hair! Don't be so hard on yourself! It's all right to want to stay out of a war. And you said yourself you aren't sure where the movement is going now and whether you belong in it."

"Maybe you're right." She *was* right, but Chloe's throat ached with sorrow for herself.

"It's rough. But sit down, Chloe, can't you? The dream— you can't know yet what will happen, can you? And what about working here? Is it so much harder?"

"It's harder for *me*. I can't find the movement. It's shrunk and split up, and I am too. I tutor a kid in Harlem two afternoons a week, but we're only a couple of atoms, there's none of that thick context."

Chloe hated interruptions when she was with Olivia, but the phone's ring now swamped her with guilty relief. Gabe had managed to borrow a car, he'd be there in half an hour.

"I've got to change," she told Olivia. "Never dress up except when I'm going to Harlem."

"You and Gabe go often? Is that where he works?"

"Some of his clients are there. Most are in the Bronx." She pulled a black skirt from the closet and slipped out of her denim. "He didn't go south, by the way. He *wouldn't* go." It was easier to talk about Gabe, though his good sense was not much comfort. "He said he stands a fair chance of understanding his own community but he'd take years figuring out Mississippi. Gabe knew all along what we came to realize down there, that if we meant to do anything at all, we'd have to prove it where we live. This skirt didn't use to be tight."

"It looks good, though. What's his stake, Chloe? How come he's so interested in Harlem?"

"He was bred to it. His parents were Communists, and they were all wrapped up in the race question in the thirties and forties. Even though everything they did fell apart, Gabe's best memories are of that kind of work with people. But it's complicated. Gabe has bitter feelings about the Party. His parents both quit, but at different times. Do you know what a big deal that is? The ones who quit in '56 won't speak to the ones who quit before or after—"

"Please. The Italians in the anti-Fascist movement were torn apart by that kind of thing."

Olivia's been everywhere, Chloe thought, coiling her beads on the shelf and pulling off her blouse. She takes all this stuff for granted. "Okay. Well, Gabe's parents left the Party at different times and left each other over that. Their divorce hurt him a lot. So Gabe is forever leery of anything that smacks of sectarian rhetoric. Even the New Left—you'd think it would be perfect for him, participatory democracy and all, but he says he'll wait and see. He's allergic to what he calls nonlanguage, the kind of mesmerism that drew his parents together and the hairsplitting that drove them apart. Yet he can't imagine any life but in the streets." She shook out her dressy peach sweater.

"Sounds like he's sorted things out. How old is he anyhow?"

"Only thirty, and quite spry for one so wise. He's very pragmatic. So realistic sometimes"—Chloe giggled as her head popped out of her sweater—"it makes me itch!"

"That's why he's just a friend?" Olivia asked slyly. She brushed her hair at the bathroom mirror.

"Leave me alone," Chloe grumbled. But she didn't like to hold out on Olivia, so she tossed her a scrap. "He's not *hopelessly* realistic, he has a redeeming illusion once in a while." She caught herself in the corner of the mirror. Her braid was a shambles. "Take this woman we're seeing tonight. Ronnie. She's a friend of one of Gabe's clients. Ronnie herself is a respectable, married, middle-class woman, and wants you to know it. A white man propositioned her on a street corner late one night, she wheeled on him and told him to get his hands off her, and a cop crossed the street to arrest her for hustling. She cursed out the cop, he hit her, then her husband Tyrone turned up, and within seconds they were both knocked down, cuffed, and taken in for assaulting a policeman. So of course when Gabe heard about her case, he looked her up."

"Of course!" Olivia laughed. "I begin to see the redeeming illusion."

"What? No, that's not it. Anybody would look her up, the case was irresistible—"

"Chloe, you're too much! Does this Gabe look like you too?"

"Hush. The *illusion* came in later, because when he met Ronnie, she told him that a couple of prostitutes had witnessed the whole thing. They all wanted to nail those cops. So Gabe made the rounds of the bars every night for a week and eventually found the women. They corroborated everything Ronnie said. But they had just been released from jail and weren't about to go near a court. They absolutely refused to testify. Gabe felt like a fool."

Olivia stopped teasing. "He sounds lovely. I can't wait to meet him."

Giving up on the comb, Chloe started a fresh braid. The sight of Olivia busy with eyeliner confounded her briefly. "I'm sorry Karl's not coming," she said, though she could not picture him and Gabe exchanging two words. "You think he'll have any luck tonight? Who is this guy who knows the art dealer?"

"Who says it's a guy?" With her little brush poised aloft, Olivia tossed a smile bright as a shield over her shoulder.

Only in lack of height and electric profusion of hair, Olivia decided, sitting opposite them in the booth at the end of the bar at the Purple Manor, did Gabe look like Chloe. He held himself so straight, his head was so massive, that he didn't seem small. Chloe's hair was already wrestling out of its new braid, but his!—the brown beard, the tangled brows over cavernous eyes, the little hairs springing down the backs of his hands—his hair outdid hers. But Chloe and Gabe took the same pleasure in Ronnie, who had insisted in her deep-chested baritone that the three of them couldn't sit at the bar, she would take care of them herself at the booth. She bent over them now in her lavender jumpsuit and gleaming black wig, serving drinks.

"Be careful, Olivia," Gabe said. "Ronnie gives three shots to a drink."

"Why, is there another way?" Ronnie asked in falsetto. She winked at Olivia. Chloe said she wanted to toast Ronnie for getting a suspended sentence.

"I'm going to drink with you later, honey, don't worry, when I get done. You go ahead and have a good time, but don't be toasting me for no suspended sentence. Remember, I got a conviction on my record now. This here will *not* happen again. If I'm going to be arrested, you better believe it's going to be *for* something!"

When she was gone, Olivia asked why Gabe had believed Ronnie and Tyrone's story.

"You mean, do I swallow everything I hear about police brutality?" Gabe grinned.

His mouth, eyes, nose, were big, and a little crowded in his face. Handsome-ugly, she decided.

"I don't. And I wonder sometimes about Ronnie. She's worked so hard to get where she is that if someone suggests she can be bought—well, I wouldn't want to bet on that person's good health. But Tyrone saw everything, and he said the cops swung on both of them so fast they didn't have time to do anything. Then he said, 'You know, man, I'm good with my hands.' That persuaded me. Tyrone is big. You'll see. If he'd started using his hands, we'd see damage."

This man *was* pragmatic. When Olivia asked if he'd always done social work, he and Chloe looked at each other and laughed.

"I fought it for years," Gabe said. "My folks were old lefties—Chloe told you?—and I thought I was inoculated forever. At City I stayed away from anything mixed up in politics. I majored in classics."

"That's about as far away as you can get!" I should have tried something like that, Olivia thought, taken up Chinese, maybe.

"I even lived in Greece for a year and a half. But as soon as I came back, zip! I was a social worker."

Then Gabe asked Olivia about teaching, her students' background, how much they could learn, how deep the school's support for the program went.

"My students are very poor," she said, "have to be to qualify for this program. A lot are Chicanos, some part Indian, hardly any Negroes. They've had almost no education and are supposed to be ineducable. Actually the ones who were cynically passed all the way through high school are harder to reach than the outright failures, because—" But Gabe was nodding, and she skipped the explanation. "Their attendance stinks. I'm supposed to drill them in grammar, and that sends them away in droves. But it's unpredictable. They're also proud of the smallest achievement."

"Can you tap into that?" Gabe asked.

"I'm trying. One night a guy was talking about his grandmother, she was trying to keep him out of school, and we got into a discussion about grandparents, parents. So we closed the books and I got them to tell stories, the stories of their lives, beginning with the oldest relative they could remember."

She liked Gabe's throaty chuckle. Why wasn't Chloe going after this guy? In a full semester, Olivia thought, Karl hasn't attended to what I'm doing the way this man does after fifteen minutes. Even Chloe hadn't asked much, though she seemed pleased to hear it now.

"It was riveting," she went on. "They looked at themselves in a new way. Now they're writing their stories down. Maybe they'll never be grammatical, but I'm gambling on it."

Chloe shook her head. "Pavese never prepared you for this," she teased.

Olivia didn't respond. *Had* Chloe written her off? She didn't even ask anymore whether Olivia was still thinking about graduate school.

"How far we've come, Livy!" She turned to Gabe. "You wouldn't believe how literary we were in Italy. We thought we could find our destiny in a poem."

"What a travesty!" Olivia snorted. "We thought no such thing!" Gabe grinned. He was not about to enter in. Why was Chloe doing this? It was easy for her to put down intellectual work. She had a full-time job, a career all laid out. But Chloe laughed so good-naturedly it was hard to stay resentful. She had never seen Chloe so happy, and Gabe obviously enjoyed her. Men can be friends. She's better off with a friend like this than a half-dozen lovers and a snake. Olivia thought briefly of Karl. She was glad she hadn't asked about his evening plans.

A band began to squall from the smoky depths of the room. A dapper black man asked Olivia if she would like to dance. Everything stopped, everyone was watching what she would do. She smiled and turned him down. Without missing a beat, he asked if he might join them. Glancing at Gabe and Chloe, she said, "Sure." He held up one finger for patience, then pulled a plastic Santa Claus from his pocket and set it before her. This was not like Chloe being offered the jukebox treat. It was some kind of test. Slipping in beside her, the man squeezed the Santa, which bleated. Then he set it in front of Olivia. She made Santa bleat to the rock 'n' roll beat of the band. The man nodded deep approval. She glanced at Chloe and cracked up.

While Chloe, Gabe, and the man, Floyd, bobbed with the band, Olivia watched Ronnie orchestrate life at the bar. She poured drinks for one customer while teasing money out of another. Hands on hips, she shouted a taunt at a joker at the end of the bar. The men hooted, Ronnie stamped her feet. Still laughing, she whisked up her tray and delivered another round to the booth.

"You can handle it, you can handle it, you're just getting started. Isn't that right, Gabe?" She poked his shoulder. "You all have a good time, that's what you're here for. How you keeping, Floyd? I'm going to be off in five minutes, Chloe honey, and join you. Used to be I did two shifts, back to back," she told Olivia. "That's after our place burned, had to get ev'rything new. Now I'm getting off midnight." Her voice dropped menacingly. "*Better* be."

At that, she turned and disappeared through the swinging door behind the bar. A minute later she was out again, steaming and muttering. She dove back in and flashed back out, radiant with indignation. She stepped to the booth and said to Gabe, "I'm a *bar*maid, not a whiskey pourer. There's a difference."

"What's going on, Ronnie?" Gabe asked.

She glared at him. "I am not going to kiss tail. I never did acquire a taste for tail." Gabe laughed, and she went banging through the door behind the bar again. A few minutes passed.

"I've seen this before," Gabe told Olivia. "I get the feeling she likes to fight with the boss."

The door behind the bar opened. A stout white man with a bulldog face held it for Ronnie. She sailed toward the booth with the man in her wake. Floyd pocketed his Santa and bowed out. This had to be the boss.

"Sol," said Ronnie with a majestic wave. "Sol, these are my friends."

Sol's voice was a wreck. "Pleaseta meedja," he said. "Next round's ona house."

It was all theater, and they were to be audience, nothing more. Chloe was very high now and eating it up.

When Sol left and Ronnie went to order the drinks, Olivia asked, "What's she trying to prove, Gabe?"

Gabe thought that was funny. "Herself, that's all. Every minute."

Then Ronnie was next to Olivia showing her a photograph. Against a mural of champagne glasses and bubbles, there was Ronnie in a plunging white jersey, breasts in high profile, head full-face to exhibit a comic-book shiner. Ronnie tapped the shiner with a blood-red nail. "You heard about how I got that, honey? Yeah? And did you hear how much trouble your friend Gabe went to for me? Yeah?"

"Well, Ronnie," Chloe giggled over the photograph, "if you're going to go around looking so gorgeous—" But she stopped short, seeing her blunder.

"I was *not* wearing that dress that night." An ice queen, Ronnie repossessed her photo. "My coat was buttoned to my—and *whose* business is it *what* I wear—"

"Hey, Ronnie," Gabe said, "she was just trying to make a joke!" He clasped her arm and shook it gently, smiling into the haughty mask she turned on him. "Ronnie! Take it easy!"

Ronnie tucked her face behind the photo an instant and covered his hand. "Gabe." Her voice was gruff. "Let me make the jokes, sweetheart."

Gabe laughed, and Olivia searched her face, but Ronnie's gaze slid over them. "Gabe," she said brightly, shaking off his hand, "how many girls you got anyhow?"

"Yeah, Gabe, how many?" asked a tall brown man in tweed, grinning from under a natty hat.

It had to be Tyrone. Not a moment too soon. He gave Gabe a gymnastic four-part handshake—Gabe knew his part—bowed smartly to the women, and pulled up a chair. Ronnie brought the free drinks. More liquor was impossible. Olivia tried to signal Chloe, but Ronnie intercepted her.

"You be all right, honey. This just one for the road. Then you all coming to our house."

Gabe laughed. "Not tonight, Ronnie. We're going home."

"That's what she's saying, man. Home." And allowing no answer, Tyrone began to question Olivia. "Are you an English major like Chloe?" When Chloe tried to say something about comparative literature and linguistics, she got it all garbled, but Tyrone nodded, saying he was a linguist too. "I was born in Haiti—you know that, Gabe?—and I used to only speak French." He downed his drink and offered them a taste of his patois. Everybody looked at Olivia.

"Don't ask me, I don't know Creole," she laughed.

"Italian. I speak Italian"—Tyrone smacked his chin with the heel of his hand—"as easy as that." And he flapped his long palm out to show how the Italian would flow. *"Come stai, signorina?"* When Olivia responded, he threw his head back and roared.

Then Ronnie was urging them up—it wasn't easy, they all were wobbly—and getting them into their coats, talking about what she wanted them to see at her house. His Italian petering out, Tyrone pulled Olivia toward the door. He was nice. Behind her Chloe asked softly, "What would you like to do?" Solicitous, but her eyes were dancing. Olivia wasn't tired, and the thought of Karl returning to Esther's apartment before her was delicious.

"Chloe, Gabe," she cried gaily, "I'm with you!" Tyrone gave her a little hug.

"And they're with us!" he said.

They piled into the car, with Tyrone insisting on sitting in back between her and Chloe, his long legs folded up to his chin. Olivia got a fit of giggles, so Tyrone turned his frenetic energy on Chloe. He wanted to know whether she taught the works of Oscar Wilde and why not, whether she taught Shakespeare and why. Didn't she know that Shakespeare was a bad writer and Wilde was a great one?

Chloe must realize he wasn't at all interested in her answers, but Olivia couldn't see her face. She felt abruptly sober. The mood in the car shifted. Tension fought with sullen drowsiness. Except for giving Gabe directions, Ronnie was silent in the front. The air was dense, but it was not the thick context Chloe craved. How much she must need community, Olivia thought, to seek it in such a way. No one spoke but Tyrone, who refuted objections no one had raised and argued that Wilde's superiority turned on his having served time. His arms slung across the back seat, he thumbed her shoulder absently. She pressed her knees to the door to avoid his legs, now wide ajar.

When the car stopped, Ronnie revived and relieved Tyrone. Catching Chloe and Olivia each by an arm, she pressed them up the stairs. Then she propelled them on a tour of the apartment, showing it off as if it were for sale. "Look! Look!" She made them tiptoe into a room where her daughters slept—"Look, my daughters"—and one of them lifted herself in her sleep for a hug.

What in hell, Olivia wondered, am I doing here? She yanked Chloe into the hall. "Can't you make her cut this out?" she whispered.

"How? What can we do?"

But there was Ronnie behind them again, pushing them into the bathroom. Chloe rolled her eyes at Olivia, but she smiled at Ronnie. Olivia felt savage.

Sinking onto a red toilet seat, Ronnie gestured to the ceiling and walls. "Look!" She had papered them herself in red velvet brocade. There were pastel dolphins in a gilt shell—"My soaps!" A shelf charged with gleaming phials and bottles— "My perfumes!" The phials were unstoppered one by one and rotated from nose to nose. "Try that one, go ahead, put some on. Look at the price on this one. Try it." Olivia could bear no more and backed out of the room.

Ronnie pursued her to the living room, where Tyrone was declaiming "The Ballad of Reading Gaol" to Gabe on the recliner. She threw open a closet and pulled out a mink stole. "Try it on," she said to Olivia. Shaking her head and fending Ronnie off, Olivia pointed to Tyrone rocking on his long feet in the throes of recitation. Tyrone stopped instantly and couldn't be made to go on.

"All *right*! Everybody's here!" he cried jubilantly. "Let's eat."

He laughed at their shouted refusal and headed for the kitchen. "Come on, Gabe, we got caviar. We got red caviar and we got black caviar. I think we got lobster tails." Gabe didn't budge. Tyrone wheeled, menace narrowing his eyes. "What's the matter, Gabe, you prejudiced?"

"Go to hell, Tyrone!"

"My food ain't good enough for you, man? You prejudiced, man?"

"You can't scare me like that, Tyrone."

Tyrone jackknifed with laughter. "Man, I ain't trying to scare you. I'm trying to *feed* you!" Then, in a high whine, "Come on, Gabe. We got snails, do you *believe* that? Now, I never had snails and you never had snails, let's us have some *snails!*" And he disappeared.

Ronnie was on the couch with Olivia, tucking a fur-covered pillow behind her and trying to unzip her boots. In self-defense Olivia stripped them off herself, and she saw that Chloe was pulling off her own shoes just in case. Gabe stood with his hands pocketed, observing. In a hot wash of apprehension, she took in what a short man he was. Ronnie pinned Olivia's wrist to the couch. "Look," she said, "my wedding ring," and shoved a row of diamonds under her nose. Olivia yanked herself away.

"Let me go! I have a wedding ring too." And with her hand curled in a fist, she thrust her wide gold band at Ronnie's face. Ronnie started back in genuine surprise.

"Oh!" she exclaimed, making a face. "Why, that's like one of those things—one of those things they wear in their nose!"

"Her reaction to my ring! It was too much!" Olivia said the next day. She was phoning from the airport.

Chloe was relieved to hear her laugh, shaky though it was.

"You had me scared. I thought you were going to punch her out, gold knuckles and all."

"*That* would have broken the spell! I kept wondering why we were sitting there taking it. We were drunk out of our minds, I know, but I kept thinking Gabe should get us out of there."

She had been so eager to go on to their apartment, Chloe thought, then all she wanted was out. "Gabe wasn't having such a bad time. He likes Tyrone, and Tyrone was telling him about his stint in prison. That's where he'd learned those poems. But I feel awful, it got so late. Was Karl worried?"

"He was asleep, and he's pretty down today. I don't think his evening was great."

"*His* evening. Livia, I don't know what to say. I felt terrible."

"Well, I didn't feel terrible. I was furious. I can't stand being pushed around like that. I don't care if they invited us. To sit there and take it is just racism in reverse."

"Um." Chloe's hangover steered her away from that one. "I don't know what went wrong. Ronnie seemed so desperate. And you—well, you were having a good time at the bar, weren't you?"

"I *was*! It was just what I wanted, far from Karl and babies and Arizona, being up there in Harlem, being with you, meeting Gabe, even squeezing that gruesome Santa! It was fun in the bar. And then it *wasn't* fun at their house. They got real hostile. It still makes me mad. If anyone was racist, it was them."

"Oh, I don't know about that."

"What do you mean? How can you *not know*?"

"*That night with Ronnie and Tyrone?*" Chloe answered three years later in Washington. "*It was like a shadow play. The bar was like an island out of the stream of history, an hour we were granted to be real. But we overstayed it, and history seized us by the throats."*

"God!" said Olivia. "I'm glad I didn't miss it!"

"I'm serious. It was like something just got hold of us and shook us. And then none of us were real, we were all—black and white—using each other to prove something. Tyrone was proving he was a great performer and didn't need an education, he had more culture than those ofay English majors and linguists. And Ronnie was outconsumering us, your suede dress was a red flag."

"I knew that suede dress bugged you!" Olivia crowed.

"It didn't. I got dolled up too, remember? So Ronnie had to prove she was more respectable than we could pray to be. She liked Gabe, but we were all as white as the guy who thought she was a prostitute and the cop who slugged her. She was still proving they had the wrong lady. And I, like an idiot, tried to kid her about her photo—"

"Yeah, but that's because you wanted that Mississippi movement high—to say whatever you felt and it would be fine."

"It wasn't always possible even there—"

"And besides, you were tense. I was, I know that—why do you think we drank so much?—and that distorted things. I think about Ronnie sometimes. I didn't get her at all then. All that bravado—I missed the pain. But what a bind, trying to put herself together and being taken for a whore!"

"Gabe had a beer with Tyrone a while ago," Chloe told Olivia in Ontario seven years later. "He and Ronnie are still together. He's got his own window-washing business now, the only thing he ever wanted, and Ronnie's messing in local politics."

"So they're doing well? I'm glad. What a great evening that was! A real Arizona antidote! You were my lifeline in those years, you know, even if sometimes you had to yank me bodily into the larger world."

"This is a mellow version! The larger world made you pretty claustrophobic that night, as I recall."

"Really? What I remember is being moved by you. You were gambling on finding the movement again, weren't you? Home, the beloved community?"

"Not consciously, and the Purple Manor would not have been a great place to look for it. But I did want you to feel the ferment, and sure, if possible, the promise."

"That wasn't so important to me as it was to you."

"Of course. So if you saw it, I'd know it was really there."

"Ah! I can understand that. After all, I wanted you to see what I was trying to do with Karl. We were both out on a limb and needed confirmation."

"Even for a preposterous long shot?"

"Especially. What are friends for?"

"But then neither of us came through, Livia. Not all the way. We each only half confirmed the other."

"Thank God! Each of us had a better friend than we wanted."

August 1966

"Yes, in a manner of speaking, I'm alive. I went to Mexico for a you-guess-what. Home now, find your letter. Karl needs a break from Hannah and me and is off scouting out something for his next painting. Isn't summer fun? Don't be sore. I love you. Letter follows."

The last sentences were squeezed onto the large postcard and there was no signature, but Chloe recognized the round black script, and she knew the picture on the other side because Olivia kept sending it to her. A rock like a steeply pitched haystack, standing off the Oregon coast, stained garish red by sunset.

Slick with sweat, Chloe read the card three times climbing the stairs to her apartment. She opened her door, only to slam it again on the even hotter air waiting there in ambush. Back in the street, still holding the card, she moved slowly toward the trees of Washington Square, seeking a breeze. Everyone was moving with underwater languor. Opposite the big arch, a wild-looking old man in a knit cap and an eye patch stood on the sidewalk before two easels. He was busy with two canvases, nearly identical landscapes, two red barns on two snowy hills. Though she only glanced at him, he stopped work to glare with his good eye so violently that his whiskers trembled. He shook his brush after her. "You fucking paranoid," he muttered.

* * *

"Look, Mama!" Hannah shrieked, holding up her hand. "I got a duck paw!" Flour paste webbed her fingers.

"Quack," said Olivia listlessly, and then, with all her heart, "You're dripping! Stay on the newspaper. Get that stuff on the rug and you're in big trouble!"

The afternoon was clogged and gummy, the sky cold clay. Why didn't it rain and get it over with? Time itself was mired, and Hannah, refusing her nap, had painted the kitchen counter with a thick sludge of peanut butter and jelly. When Olivia set her up with paste and magazines, Hannah disdained them, pursuing her own experiments.

"Hannah," she pleaded. "If you don't want to paste pictures, let's clean up! Wash your paws and I'll make you some chocolate milk!"

"Oh, good! Let me smush it."

"I'll smush it. Wash your hands!"

"Smush it good," said Hannah at the sink.

"I'll smush it perfect," said Olivia, pouring milk on the chocolate powder. "I'll splush it, see? And smush and squush it." Hannah loved the bursting clots of beige powder, the rich brown swirl.

"It's munging, Mama. Keep splunging."

Olivia handed her the glass. "It's one big grunge."

The phone rang, and Hannah ran, slinging milk onto the floor. "No," she said sweetly, "I don't know you and you don't know me."

Olivia took the phone. "Hello?"

"Livia. Can you pick me up at the Portland airport tomorrow at three p.m.?"

"Chloe! For Christ's sake, where are you?" Olivia threw a dish towel on the spilled milk.

"Are you all right? When did you get back?"

"Ten days ago. Yes, I'm okay. Really. Where are you?"

"In New York, so have pity. The heat is making everyone crazy. Take me in. I don't have to show at school till Tuesday."

"Tuesday? You're mad. That's no time at all. It's so expensive!" Chloe was so precipitate. She would come, Olivia knew it already. Did she want this? No? Yes?

"I just got a raise. I want to see you. And look—here's an argument. I slew the monster thesis and deserve it."

"But that's fabulous! Congratulations! Why do you sound so—"

"Don't congratulate me, please. It's pathetic. I got through by pretending it wasn't me writing it."

"What do you mean? Who the hell else—"

"It was an act of ventriloquism. I impersonated a straight academic. Let's not. I'd rather not talk about it. The thing is, it's over. Done with. I got my union card."

"But—"

"Can't I come see you? Are you busy?"

"Hannah and I are here alone, and we have nothing to do but put flour paste in our hair." Olivia glanced at her daughter, now glazing the floor with milk. Chloe—did she really exist? Her picking up and flying here—the sheer assumption of entitlement in it—oddly made her seem more distant. Had Chloe sprouted wings, it would not be harder to grasp.

"This is the last big hill." Hannah sprang around the back of the car. "We're almost there!"

"Guess where we're going, Chloe."

"To the coast, you said. Oh, you mean—we're going to your rock?"

"Yes. Karl's rock now, actually. You saw the gouache series."

Chloe had noticed the paintings in the hall of the house in Portland, but frustrated by the need to defer talk, she hadn't looked at them.

Karl's name hung in the air like fog. Hannah was looking out the back window, so Chloe whispered, "You have no idea when he'll come home?"

"Sure I do. Tonight, tomorrow, or the next day. And if he gets home when we're not there"—she paused for a seraphic smile, then mouthed the words—"fuck him!"

Olivia leaned into the mountain curves. She made the little car an extension of her body, swinging it like hips. The tails of the long green scarf she had wound around her head flew in the wind. Trouble only burnishes her glow, Chloe thought, and she said, "You look so amazingly terrific."

Olivia laughed. "It's you, Wonder Woman, and your flying rescue mission."

Hannah thrust her face between them. The auburn hair might be Esther's, the grave eyes, wide-set, Karl's, but her mother had given her the broad, expressive mouth.

"You know about the rock, Chloe?" This anxious curiosity was Hannah's own.

"Know what, sweetheart?"

"I was afraid of it, when I was little."

"Really? How come?"

"It was so black. I cried. I had bad dreams. Didn't I, Mama?"

"You did, lambchop."

"When I was little," she reassured Chloe, bobbing her head. "And now?"

"Now I'm not afraid anymore. Now it's my rock," she said. Chloe thought her claim the best. "I'd say it is."

It was dusk when they dropped down to the coast and approached the A-frame house on the dunes that Karl and

Olivia shared with friends at the museum. Behind it, set in the sea and against the sky, softened by no red light, was the rock. Through Hannah's eyes Chloe saw its uncompromising blackness. There was no measuring its distance. It loomed, it might be marching on them. Then Olivia snapped on a light at the door, and it fled.

It was not until after supper, when Olivia had put Hannah to bed in the only room with no view of the rock, that Chloe could ask, "Does she understand? What does she know?"

Tossing Hannah's dirty trousers in a sack, Olivia said, "She thinks I went to see Gram Esther. But maybe she suspects something. Remember the Russian dolls you gave her? She used to set them out in a row, but now she keeps them all inside each other. I don't know. Maybe it only means she wants to get back inside. That goes on forever, you know."

Chloe was startled—it does?

Olivia bundled Chloe into one of her huge sweaters, wrapped her head in a big paisley scarf, and gave her the same humming hug she had given her daughter. She smelled of musky rose. They went outside to stroll on the gray beach. The air was heavy, and the black rock watched them across the darkening water.

Starting after so much time is always a leap, Chloe thought, a pitching forward into the void. "So this is the rock on which you build your family," she began self-consciously.

"Or on which we split," muttered Olivia. Chloe's stomach dropped. Olivia stopped and stood facing the rock.

"Split," Chloe repeated to steady herself. "Is that what's happening, then?"

Olivia turned away. "Maybe it should be," she said to the sand.

"But?"

Olivia glared at the rock. "I can't imagine it." She groaned. "I tried, it's not that I haven't tried. Lying in my hotel room in Mexico City after the abortion. I had a lot of pain, a lot of blood. Blood instead of a baby. I lay there imagining my life pouring out and away like so much dark waste."

Gripping her crossed arms, Chloe felt her nails in her flesh. The blood was awful, but worse, not having been there.

"I guess it didn't last very long, but it seemed forever. And I got mad. I got so angry I didn't mind the pain. I kind of used it. To feed my rage. I tried to imagine it was the pain of separation. I was on my own, acutely on my own. It was a ghastly dirty hustling place. Exactly right for the way I felt. Beyond the city limits of society. Like I'd gone over the edge of marriage. I wanted to stay that way."

With nightmare lucidity, Chloe saw Olivia reaching for her life to the abyss but unable to loose her hold on the cliff. "Karl—had he thought of going with you?"

"He offered, but I didn't want him." Fury began to buzz in her throat. "He would have thought that gesture made it all right. It would only have made me madder. Besides, someone had to stay with Hannah."

"Wait. Can we go back? I didn't even know you were pregnant, or wanted to be."

"I can't write when I feel this messed up."

Chloe was bloated with angry helplessness. "But I'm your friend, goddamn it! You can't leave me in the dark."

Olivia faced her in silence. "You must be exhausted. I'm tired, and you've been up forever. Let's sit a bit." She led Chloe to a log, and they squatted on it, still facing the rock.

Choking back her anger, Chloe clung to Olivia's hand a moment. "I'm sorry."

"Listen. It's good for me that you've come. But I can barely think about this, let alone write." She lit a cigarette, pulled on it hard, and exhaled long, rolling her head around her shoulders. "Last winter was really rough. It's better for me here than in Arizona, but still—I don't know. I began to have dreams about babies. I really wanted another. Hannah had turned three. It would be a big gap, but she could seriously use a sibling. That wasn't why, though, it wasn't for Hannah."

"And it wasn't for the marriage?"

"No. It's true Karl was best with Hannah as a baby, and I wanted to see that side of him again. But I've always thought the idea that a baby binds a family together is a lot of hokum." She snorted smoke.

Chloe agreed. But she couldn't make sense of Olivia's wish for another child. "So"—trying not to sound glum—"you wanted one for you."

"Yes. And I knew Karl didn't want another kid, I didn't have to ask. I just got a little careless, a little absentminded on purpose, and there I was." She slapped her belly.

"Were you testing him? Let me have a cigarette too. Did you hope he'd change?"

"Here. Not consciously. If you'd asked me, I'd have said that would be crazy."

"But—" How could she have hurt herself like this? Chloe ached to turn back the clock.

"I wasn't thinking a whole lot, Chloe. But it occurred to me he'd at least notice how I felt."

"Did he?"

"No. We had a big fight, but it all got centered on his feelings. He felt tricked, he felt betrayed, he was outraged, then he was cold." Her own coldness drove rage from her voice. "He wouldn't talk to me for days."

"Jesus, Livy." Chloe tossed a stick toward the rock. "I wish

I'd known. Did you ever think of keeping it and moving out?" Her voice was a squeak, as if it originated in her neck.

Olivia laughed bitterly. "And do what? With an infant and a three-year-old? Come camp out on you?"

Chloe was stung, and Olivia instantly contrite. "I'm sorry. You see how fucked up I am. I don't know. I had wild ideas, none of them made sense."

"And your schemes in Mexico City? Of separation?"

"They were hardly schemes. They led me right back to Karl. I left Mexico full of steam, but I was tired when I got home. And he did the one thing I wasn't prepared for. Apologize. And look scared. I could tell how bad I looked from how white he got. He put me to bed and waited on me. Whatever steam was left in me, that knocked it out. I was too wiped out to deal with any of it. All my feelings were—they just canceled each other out. I couldn't respond to him at all. And when he saw that, he froze up and cleared out in a hurry."

"Oh, Livy! You said you wanted his attention." The image of Karl white, so late and at such cost, confused Chloe into unwelcome compassion.

"Chloe, I don't know what I want anymore." Her voice was thin as smoke.

"God, Livy, you're all beat up and I keep you talking. Let's go in and get some sleep."

They walked back slowly then, leaning together, like people much older. Chloe felt that the rock monitored their going.

Chloe was up on her elbows blinking, her face disheveled by sleep. Childlike in that huge T-shirt and looking not quite sure where she was. For the first time in days, Olivia had slept hard. It was a glistening morning, and her ardent friend had come all this way to see her. She was unequivocally glad. We're still so young, she thought. She bent over Chloe, laughing.

"If you're really awake, we should get right out on the beach. There's a neap tide."

Chloe glowered at her scarf, jeans, boots, and smile. "How do you manage to look like that?" She groaned and fell back, pulling the pillow over her face.

"Why is she hiding, Mama?" Hannah asked.

"She's grouchy, lambie."

Chloe yanked the pillow off. "If you think I'm going to ask what a neap tide is, you've got another think"—she tossed the pillow—"coming."

"She has a frog in her throat," noted Hannah. "That's why she's grouchy."

Chloe leaped up and for Hannah's astonished benefit did several deep knee-bends. She was as elastic as ever, her posture zealous, holding her own against the fate of shortness.

At breakfast Hannah took inventory of Chloe's imperfections. She had buttoned her shirt wrong, one of her front teeth was very, very crooked, she needed to brush her hair a lot more, she should drink more orange juice to get rid of the frog in her throat. To Olivia's surprise, Chloe knew just what to do. She grappled shrieking Hannah across her lap and said she was a girl-eating frog.

Since they had a few hours before the tide—the lowest of the lunar month—began to come back in, Olivia drove them several miles up the coast. She parked above a bay the ocean had abandoned. It gleamed at them from the horizon and sparkled in little pools in the middle distance. The emptied bay was littered with jagged freestanding rocks, some as tall as buildings. The sight always shocked her, as though the earth had done itself violence in the night. Chloe's gasp at her side made her feel buoyant.

"Remind you of anything, Chloe?"

"Nothing in the world."

"They remind me of the rocks we saw near Lipari when we were approaching by boat."

"Really? Oh, wait! You mean before we saw the harbor. Yes, sort of. But those were surrounded by water."

"So will these be, when the tide comes in. Got your bucket, Hannah? Let's go!"

They stripped to their suits, keeping only their heavy sweaters on, and set out fast in the cold air, with Hannah between them straining forward.

"You know what I think, Chloe? Karl always envied us our week in Lipari. And he's become addicted to these giant rocks. He calls them god-droppings." Chloe's delighted yelp startled her.

"Funny Daddy," said Hannah. "Daddy's funny, isn't he, Mama?"

"Karl always liked rocks," Chloe said. "I remember that from Sicily. Didn't he grow up on the coast of Maine?"

"He did. He says he'll die before he goes back, but you're right, he's always on the lookout for the rockbound coast. But this is different from Maine."

Rising over the continent behind them, the sun was clearing the hill. Color began to burst from the big rocks. "Maine in Technicolor," Chloe breathed. Olivia laughed, and Hannah peered curiously up at Chloe, trying to decide whether to succumb to her charm.

"Karl is always in top form at the coast," Olivia said. She felt expansive, she wanted to be fair. And when she was generous, she was rewarded by hope. "We came out here nearly every weekend last summer and fall. Nothing stimulates his painting like hanging around these rocks, and when he paints, he's happy. And it's true, he can be very funny."

"Funny Daddy," said Hannah, vindicated.

Olivia sent Hannah ahead to look for sand dollars on the dimpled beach. "We never talk about our week in Lipari, you and I," she began, "but I think of it often now." Chloe looked surprised, but when Olivia recalled the night boat from Naples, it was as if she'd pulled a string. Images toppled out of Chloe— the crooner Ciccio, the night fishing, their fruitless scrambles for privacy—embellishing, correcting Olivia's memory, and stirring it afresh. The five-year interval, vast as the ocean, shrank, swallowed itself, and Lipari lay over the Oregon coast, a luminous transparency that they saw together.

"Everything was so simple, Chloe, wasn't it?"

"We didn't think so then, but now, yes, it seems—"

Olivia conjured up their hike, their retreat to the cave, the magical woman by the well on that remarkable last day. It had never seemed more beautiful than now, beside Chloe, who believed in her so steadily. But rising with the memory, this compression in the chest, denying her air.

"Do you remember how we felt?" Olivia asked. "Like our lives had filled up and we could do anything? We didn't think we were crazy. But now it seems so far away, so impossible."

Chloe sighed. "Ah, Livia," she said, and no more.

They caught up with Hannah, impatient at the edge of a tidal pool that surrounded a lone crag. The sun had warmed the shallow water.

"The rocks are Karl's thing," Olivia said, "but these pools are what get me every time."

"These pools are *my* thing," said fickle Hannah.

So Olivia stood back to let her daughter show Chloe the limpets clinging to the rock. "Pull him, Chloe! Pull! Pull harder!" Hannah laughed at Chloe's failure to break the suction. She had a feeling for nature's comic drama, and Chloe, playing straight man, was like another child. Hannah showed her a starfish, apparently dead, but palpitating with a thousand legs on the underside. She sent tiny sand-colored crabs skittering sideways into crevices. She bothered a snail into weary progress and chased a fugitive bit of kelp, like lettuce-green smoke, through the water. Then, with a silencing glance at Olivia, she danced in front of her green-gray favorite, hanging from the rock.

"Is it a pincushion? A pillow?" obliging Chloe asked.

"Touch it, Chloe!"

The roguish leer was exactly Karl's. Did Chloe see it?

"Touch it!" Hannah giggled uproariously when Chloe recoiled. "Isn't he squishy?"

"It's a sea anemone," said Olivia.

Hannah jumped at her. "Tell her what Daddy said, tell her!"

"Hannah, it's just silly."

"Tell her, tell her, tell her!"

Olivia sighed. "Karl said it's like a scrotum." Chloe's gape of recognition made her laugh. Hannah doubled over, grabbing her round thighs for support. "She doesn't understand it, but she knows it's a good one."

"I do too! Mama! I do too understand it!"

She splashed off in a temper. Chloe stood arms akimbo, bemused.

"You've always dug Karl's outlandishness, Chloe, haven't you?"

"I don't know. Yes. But today it's—too much."

"I know. He's everywhere. I can't get away from him. He even owns the sea anemone. Ugh." Suddenly stifling, she stripped off her sweater and stuck it in a string bag. Chloe peeled off hers. She too had a bikini, brilliant green. They inspected each other, grinning as they candidly measured the body's resistance to the work of five years. Chloe's bikini set off the extravagance of her figure, plummy fullness of breast, sculpted hardness of bone and muscle. Was it possible she was still ripening? Or was her waist nipped in by daily exercise? Olivia's fingers spread automatically over her stretch marks, taut ribbons she used to fancy were filaments binding her spirit to Hannah's. Chloe's belly was smooth. Still a virgin in the way that mattered. And did she feel no emptiness? she wondered.

But what she said was, "What a shape! That bikini was made for you."

Unnerved by the way Olivia had spoken of Lipari, as if she held only the husk of that ripe readiness, Chloe was cheered by her bravado in wearing the skimpy black suit. Her deep olive tan was perfect, and the new line above the belly curved down like her droll mouth. But the hollows under her shoulders, like those come back in her cheeks, were sobering. She's postponed her life long enough, Chloe thought. What if she gets old before she's had the chance to try herself? Chloe was fervently glad there was no second child.

"You look great," she told Olivia. "You got yourself some hips. Just what you needed. You were too straight up and down."

"Yeah? But see this pod?" Olivia pressed her belly with her thin fingers.

"I see it. It's cute," said Chloe.

Olivia grimaced and veered away. When she turned back, her gaze was calm and level. "You wondered why in the world I wanted another child, didn't you?"

Their thoughts were on one line, straight as the horizon. "I didn't want to say it. But yes, I did."

"I thought so. It's better to say it, Chloe."

"Hey, I don't know if I'm right! Hannah is a wonderful person! But I hate to think of you tying yourself down that many more years, Livia."

"I know." Olivia's voice was low. She stared at the sand drifting over her feet.

She knows, but she's grieving for the unborn babe, Chloe thought. Olivia's pain washed through her for the first time, but so intensely Chloe felt she might be nesting inside her. She feared to say more, but silence was scarier.

"I know you feel differently, Livia. There's something left out of me. I'd never have the patience to be a mother."

Olivia looked up. "Never? Are you sure?"

"Oh, 'never.'" Chloe disclaimed the word. "Who can say never? Who knows what they'll feel next year? Next month! Not me." How juvenile, how absurd!

But Olivia smiled indulgently. "You're so good with Hannah! Frankly, I didn't expect—"

"Ah, Hannah! She's no test! If they all came ready-made like Hannah—" She stopped. She wasn't being honest. She didn't wish she had Hannah.

"You've never felt even a little tempted?" she coaxed.

For Olivia's sake at this moment, Chloe wished that she had. "I'm sorry. No," she said.

For some reason Olivia seemed pleased by whatever she said. She took Chloe's arm and steered her to the next tidal pool, where Hannah stood yelling and waving. Olivia waved back.

"Walk slowly, you voluptuous thing," she said, "and tell me all about what's going on with you and my friend Gabe."

Chloe was abruptly shy. She knew how much Olivia had liked Gabe in Harlem. In her infrequent letters, she always asked about him. But the thought of Gabe now was his face popping out around the shower curtain, suds in his hair, yelling, "*What* did you just say?" Was Gabe on his elbow in bed with his look of hilarious incredulity, saying, "You expect me to believe that?" Was Gabe massaging the back of her neck with strong, patient thumbs. So she said, "It's nice," gave Olivia a placating smile, and told her about his work, which she really did find exciting.

About a year ago Gabe had become convinced that the welfare system was a hopeless farce. No one was helped, and everyone, even the most indefatigable caseworkers, was demeaned and made crazy by it. If Gabe weren't so addicted to people in the streets, he'd have cut loose long ago, gone and built himself a house out of a barn in the country, a lifelong dream. He was good with his hands. Instead he and his buddies were cooking up a welfare revolution. Only half the people eligible for welfare were getting any help, so Gabe wanted to track down the other half—thousands of people—and organize them to apply for aid, forcing the city offices to close and the feds to provide a national minimum income. "The time is right," Chloe said. "With the antipoverty program and the riots keeping up the pressure, they may just bring it off."

"It's hard to believe, Chlo. But if Gabe goes for it, it must be all right."

"Everyone trusts Gabe." She told Olivia how she'd gone with him to see some of his clients. Neither credulous nor cynical, he had the touch. She was in the middle of a story about a Puerto Rican grandmother who had foiled the whole welfare department when Hannah interrupted.

She wanted to show Chloe a rock with an arch you could walk through. The tide was coming in, and Chloe ended up lifting Hannah awkwardly to help her through. The heft of the child pleased her, but the chicken-bone shoulder blade was surprisingly complicated and alien. Once through the rock, Hannah wriggled free like a fish. Fresh out of demonstrations, she began to whine for her mother to carry her. Olivia refused, reminded her of some agreement, and gave her her bucket. She asked Chloe to finish her story. When Chloe started again, Hannah planted her feet and screamed, "Mama!"

"Hannah! Just goddamn stop this!" shrieked Olivia with a harshness Chloe had never heard. Hannah stopped and looked up at her mother, tearless but rigid. Olivia kept yelling, and Hannah rocked with each blast, her mouth stretched wide, her eyes fixed on her mother's. Olivia stopped as suddenly as she'd begun. "All right," she said, but her teeth were locked. She bent to lift her child.

"Livy, let me carry her," said Chloe. But Olivia strode on through the shallow water. At the sand's edge, she set Hannah down sharply. Chloe reached for her, but Hannah turned away with icy dignity.

"I can carry myself," she said.

"That barnyard screech of mine," said Olivia in Ontario five years later. "It used to scare me half out of my wits."

"It scared me too at first."

"I'll bet. I felt like I'd confirmed your doubts about having children. But I was scared because I sounded like my mother. It was her changefulness, not her temper. She could swing from incredible sweetness to—repulsion, a physical disgust. I swore I'd never raise a child the way she raised me and Andy."

"But you didn't. You stuck with Hannah. You never farmed her out. You didn't run off."

"Oh, I know. But the price came out in that screech. I felt trapped when Hannah crowded me too much."

"Mmmm. Like when she covered your legs with sand."

"Yes. I got claustrophobic. She'd hang on my arm or my leg and I'd feel hobbled, like I'd lost the use of my limbs. It was worst at the coast, where I wanted to feel free. Well, you saw *that. I'd bite it all down, and then my mother would screech through me. It was like being possessed. And I was devastated, like I'd been fooling myself about being different. When my guard was down, I was just as harsh and selfish."*

"Except you weren't. You were in trouble, and Hannah was jealous of the attention you were giving me. And you gave her a lot. Maybe she wanted more, but I think she understood what you were going through. I watched her watching you. She watched you like a hawk. I was scared for her a little, frankly, more than for you. But she showed me that afternoon that she understood more than I did."

"Just don't hover like that, Chloe," Olivia snapped. "If I say I don't need a nap, I know what I'm talking about." This new head-nurse pose of Chloe's set her teeth on edge. Swooping in from New York and picking away at Olivia's sores last night, then holding out on her about her own private life—that was all bad enough. And now, when Hannah was out of the way and they could talk freely, this condescending solicitude.

Chloe thrust out her jaw. "The hell with you, then," she said. "*I've* got jet lag, I have to catch me some *z*'s." And she marched off to her room.

We're all three-year-olds, Olivia thought, and fatigue sprang like a cat on her shoulders. This is ridiculous, she said to herself as she stretched out on the couch, why would I be tired?

Hannah had to shake her awake. Olivia gave Chloe a rueful look. "Ah, well," she said.

This time she drove them farther up the coast to a spot where the woods extended out on a high narrow cliff. Once they had seen deer here, so Hannah instructed them to creep like Indians down the path to the point. They saw no deer, but out on the point they could look for miles north and south along the coast at what the wind had carved for centuries on this edge of the world, and its up-to-the-minute work on the lacy shawl of surf. Chloe pointed to some large birds gliding over the water, and Hannah told her they were pelicans. Olivia made them see some minuscule specks and swore they were sea lions. She bathed in content. They stayed there until they all saw exactly what each of the others had seen and heard what each thought it looked like.

Then they doubled back and climbed down to the beach. Summers in Canada had made Chloe a cold-water enthusiast. When she came back from her freezing dip, she stretched out next to Olivia on the blanket. How is it possible, Olivia wondered, that I'm tired again? Wearily she told Hannah okay, she could bury her legs, but only up to the knees. A fatal compromise. Sand pelted both women, thigh and back. Hannah didn't stop even when they cried out. Her face was tight with concentration. Olivia fell back exhausted, and Chloe took over, but to no avail. Hannah was deaf to her proposals of walk, sand castle, splashing contest. But when Chloe suggested they walk along the beach to collect things for a restaurant, Hannah looked at her as though she had suddenly been graced with real wit.

Reluctant to let Chloe go, Olivia lifted her head. The two of them were engrossed with a large purple-hinge shell.

"What do you think?" Chloe was asking. "Is it a teacup?"

"Nooo, silly!" Hannah laughed, tossing it in her bucket. "That's a—it's a soup bowl. Come with me and I'll show you, I'll find a teacup!"

Olivia fell back and sank heavily into the sand.

When Hannah landed astride her, Olivia was lost in the back streets of Brooklyn, her mother's voice repeating a warning over and over. Yelling and flailing, Olivia caught a glimpse of Hannah's jubilation just before it faded. Then even Chloe could do nothing to recover it. Hannah spurned her, refusing to resume the game. The bucket of crockery and fixings for a fantastic dinner was just old shells and seaweed. Hannah wanted her mama to go for a walk with her right now, with her by herself, she wanted her to run in the water, she wanted her to swing her, she wanted a piggyback ride. At the water's edge, Olivia felt herself drowning. She ripped her hand free, wheeled away from Hannah, seized a heavy stick of driftwood, and swung it high over her head, so high she felt it could lift her right in the air, then brought it crashing down on a boulder. The stick exploded and flew apart. The smarting in her hands brought her full awake. She felt Hannah behind her to the right, Chloe to the left. They made a triangle on the silent beach.

Olivia took the course that kept them behind her. There was no sound but the blood banging in her ears. She stopped at the base of the cliff and sat pressing her back to the rough stone, her hands worthless on her bent knees. No tears came. Only then did Chloe and Hannah in the distance break out of their trance. Chloe walked toward the water, calling faintly to Hannah. Hannah stood irresolute a moment longer. Then, without glancing at Chloe, she walked straight and steady toward her mother, her face, as it grew visible, grave, delicate, mastering many things. Sitting down softly between Olivia's knees, she took the same position as her mother. She just fit there. She leaned back gently against her mother's chest.

"Why are you so hard on your thesis?" Olivia wanted to know. She was putting away the supper dishes as Chloe dried them. On the floor with her crayons, Hannah was coloring like a model child.

It made Chloe tense even to talk about it. "Innocents

abroad—what a fraud! What a dupe I was to take it all straight! In the very years James was developing his late style, America was hoking up reasons—with all the sheen of innocence, naturally—to build an empire. Save the little brown brother! Remember the *Maine*! And there was James, slicing American innocence ever more exquisitely fine, grinding out the classiest dust ever thrown in American eyes! Hell, it blinded me!"

"Is it James' fault," Olivia asked, scouring a pot, "that you didn't use to care about American history?"

Olivia was sharp. "Of course not, but I should have scuttled the thesis if I wasn't going to take it into account." This was uphill work, filling Olivia in. She felt sweat starting at her temples. "But I wanted to be finished. I don't know how to do lit crit politically—most attempts are awful—and if I knew how, maybe I wouldn't dare." There was the cautionary case of her old friend and colleague Noah. She told Olivia how he'd been slapped down for "harping" on Yeats' conservatism in his thesis and "neglecting the formal justification," how he might give up on the thesis altogether and jeopardize his chance for tenure.

"I think you've polished that platter enough," Olivia said, taking it from her. "Why are you so defensive? It's great you finished, and I'm sure it's better than you let on. But is the goal to keep teaching? Do you like it better now? Remember what you wrote me? 'Teaching in these times is not honest work. More service or more art!' "

In Olivia's mouth, her words were foolish. That was last fall, Chloe thought, before Clem. "It's not that I didn't like it, but I sometimes thought I should plump for outright self-expression or else deal more authentically with students' real problems—"

"That's just the way I feel with my foreign-born students, that it's not basic English they need but basic counseling, how to deal with culture shock and the gap between them and their parents—"

They weren't talking about the same thing. "No, Livia. I don't have foreign students. You're talking about family psychology, fine, that's service. But my students need basic political service, and I mean *basic*." She thought of Jake and his repressive father. Jake wouldn't be at the college Tuesday—oh, where was he now? I'm running, he said, and if the army catches me, okay, maybe they'll lock me up, maybe they'll make me dead, but better my own life and lose it than live off my dad, because that's already death. "Parents," she said. "The kids are better off with the gap—"

"Oh, swell. Chloe! You think that's not a problem?"

Chloe panicked. Why was this going wrong? She had to make Olivia see. If only she could bring Jake, Clem, Frances, under the steep walls of this A-frame. "To me, it's not," she said. "The kids are the only ones willing to look at what's really going on and see how it all hangs together. In fact, it's my students who got me past that service-art nonsense. Look, I know how to dry. Give me back the towel."

Olivia shook her head impatiently.

"They make much more sense than their parents. I'd love to tell you about one boy in particular. He's mad for Kafka, and he's applying for conscientious—"

"Great, now you're going to tell me we shouldn't trust anyone over thirty!"

Was this Olivia? "That—Livy, you know that's just a silly slogan the media loves to milk. *I'll* be thirty in November."

"So where does that leave you?"

"I'm learning with them and from them. These students are a hell of a lot smarter than we were in college." With Olivia so hostile, Chloe had to mind her tongue. "Than *I* was, anyhow.

They pull things together that I kept in little compartments. Like, the best poet in the college organized to keep ROTC recruiting off campus, three off-the-wall comics taught me what Chase Manhattan is up to in South Africa, and Clem, the kid who loves Kafka, anticipated the invasion of the Dominican Republic—"

"Will you please not count your fingers at me!" Olivia grabbed Chloe's point-making hand in her dish towel and squeezed. Chloe glared at her, but Olivia held on.

"I hate it when you talk fast and make political speeches at me," Olivia said a year later in Washington.

"I'm damned if I know why you see it that way. You don't agree with me?"

"It's not that. You know in many ways I do. It's just that you get so strung out. You sound like a student newspaper."

"I don't know what the hell you mean."

"What's happening, Chlo? Why are we fighting?" Still pressing her hand, Olivia took a deep breath and tried to smile.

"I suppose," Chloe said stiffly, "we don't agree."

"It's not that. I'm still twisted out of shape, but I can't talk about it anymore—and I want to know what you're up to. You've come all this way."

"What's that got to do with it?" Chloe hated the sound of her own voice, like Hannah in a sulk.

"Tell me," Olivia coaxed, and the smile came to life, "about the kid and Kafka. Please."

Olivia dropped Chloe's hand and hung up the towel. She lit a cigarette and gave it to her. Clem had done that for her last spring, when they sat together at a talk by an ex–Green Beret. When Chloe asked him if he had a cigarette, he went scroung-

ing through the auditorium and brought her one lit. She relented now and told Olivia about it.

"When I offered to share it with him, he blushed, and I
realized we were a little sweet on each other."

"What did you do?" Olivia asked.

"Ah," said Chloe—the memory of sacrifice was delightful
now—"I found him someone his own age."

We aren't kids on the island of Lipari anymore, Olivia
thought, we're mid-ocean. Chloe's life is so different, and yet
she believes in me enough to come thousands of miles. Olivia
didn't like the way Chloe had dismissed her foreign students,
but she couldn't pretend she cared as much for them as Chloe
did for hers. So she didn't begrudge her her story, but she
listened less to the lyrics than to the tune of Chloe growing
happy. She knew Chloe had to work off the fresh enthusiasm,
tell the passionate tale, before she could concentrate on anything more elusive. And the way to the Chloe she wanted to
hear was through the Chloe who needed to tell. It was a
comfort to know their workings so well.

Chloe was describing a party she had given on the spur of
the moment for Jake, a marvelous student who was going to
run from the draft the next day. Olivia thought of the difficult
girl who gave Chloe the snake. Why is she always so juiced by
trouble?

She invited Clem, Chloe said, because he was such a loner.
Clem had been agonizing all spring about whether he was
authentically a conscientious objector. "He kept a diary on the
state of his conscience and fell short by his own measure. Kafka
impressed him too much. He felt sure Kafka wouldn't have
served, but he feared he wouldn't have gone after CO either."

"Surely Kafka would have been 4-F," Olivia observed.

Chloe laughed. "I thought Clem's scruples alone should qualify him, but I doubted he could explain himself to Selective Service. Then at my party Jake moved him so much he began to think it was unfair for him to get deferred. Fortunately, I was short of cups for the wine punch, and Clem had to share one with Frances, this keen dark girl from a repressive Irish Catholic family, easily the sharpest critic in the class. So they met, and they left together. A month ago, he called to say Frances had helped him write his application, they were going to file it first and then go to City Hall to get married, and would I be their witness!"

Olivia felt a brief pang for her students, too old, too Asian or Mexican, too up against it, for adventures of defiance. She liked the story, but she wondered why Chloe warmed herself so at the fires of others. Would she rather fix Clem up with Frances than work out her own life with Gabe? And did this dewy community of students stand in for her own children? Or was she herself unfair? It had to be awful, knowing the boys they sent to Vietnam. Still, she could not shake the feeling that Chloe was squandering her freedom.

"My goodness, Hannah," Chloe exclaimed in real astonishment. "It's spectacular! Show your mom!"

From a choppy green sea a red and purple tulip yearned upward toward a vaulting rainbow just out of reach. The sky was so black it curled the paper, and the stars in it were ragged shards.

"Because it's night now," Hannah explained, deeply peaceful, "and time to sleep." So often she searched her mother's face for approval, but now she was still absorbed in her solitary journey, and her look reminded Olivia that the child was not altogether hers. As if in compensation, Hannah surrendered the drawing, and Olivia hugged her.

"How daring she is!" Chloe marveled after they had tucked Hannah in. "A rainbow in the *night!*"

Daring, yes, Olivia thought. Brave. But does it cost her nothing?

"And see how completely she forgives your temper," Chloe added.

Olivia said yes, but she knew it wasn't exactly that. Hannah had access to some place beyond forgiveness and accusation, where the flowers stretched confidently to the dark. She could speak of it no more than Olivia, but she labored to show it to her.

In silent accord, Olivia and Chloe made for the side of the deck. There they could still make out the shore tapering down to the sea, they could hear the ocean, but they could not see the rock. Our last evening, Olivia thought, lies smooth before us too, but not infinite. Tomorrow, back in Portland, she would find Karl, or his absence. But for these hours, she could banish both.

She lugged two long cushions out, and Chloe brought the burgundy and the glasses. Traditionalists, they snubbed the house cache of pot.

Chloe lay back and began with the sky. "Look at those stars, there're so few of them."

"Often there are none. The fog moves in after dark."

"Look. The fog is going after those two stars."

"I see three, no, four."

"Hey, you're right! They're rallying."

Then Olivia played too. "Which holds the balance of power, the fog or the stars?"

"Ah!" Chloe was touched. "Who rules the heavens? Foggy U.S. imperialism or—"

"Wait!" Olivia spread her hand over Chloe's face to gain time. "Or—starry anarchism!"

"Yay!" Chloe cheered. She kissed her bunched fingers and tossed the kiss to the stars. They lay there peacefully while the fog shut up the sky.

Rolling onto her side to contemplate her friend, Olivia geared up. "Chloe, are you afraid to talk about yourself and Gabe because I'm in trouble with Karl?"

At first Chloe denied it. Olivia waited for a better answer, and soon she admitted she was a bit inhibited. "Besides, there's not a clear story to tell."

"Who cares about clear stories? This is not the nineteenth century. I favor little incoherent fragments myself. And I like Gabe, you know."

"I like Gabe too!" Chloe wailed. "I like him a lot! Now that you mention it, that's the problem." She went into a shoulder stand and pedaled the impassive sky.

Olivia sat up, poured the wine, and did some more conspicuous waiting.

The wine drew Chloe, who sat up too, sipped, and sighed. "I tell myself it's childish to want that rush all the time."

"You get it sometimes?"

"Yes. You know this afternoon, at the point, looking at all those layers of coastline? Well, it reminded me of a time—Gabe and I had been going around together for nearly a year, and I didn't want it to change, I liked things the way they were. And him, I liked him as he was, so sweet-reasonable, even if I did argue with him about it. He seemed satisfied too, mostly. He asked me once or twice if I didn't want to go to bed with him, and it's funny, it made me like him more than ever, the way he asked, but"—she shrugged—"there it was! Precisely because I liked him so much, I said no."

"What did you want him to do? Grab you by the hair"—
Olivia grasped the hank hanging over Chloe's shoulder—"and
drag you off?"

"God, I hope not!" Chloe swung her head free. "But. I
sometimes think he is too respectful."

"So," she prompted, "something at the coast reminded
you—"

"Right." Gabe had a Japanese friend at City College, Chloe
said, who had taught him to love Japanese landscape painting.
A few years ago, he happened on a collection of scroll paintings
in the back of an unprepossessing shop. "That's typical. Gabe
loves to roam around neighborhoods he doesn't know, sniffing
and poking. He prowls the sites of newly torn-down houses for
trophies. There're half a dozen gorgeous stained-glass windows
in his apartment that he got that way. His place is full of found
objects."

Chloe loves everything mismatched, Olivia thought. Back at
the Portland house she'd turned up her nose at Karl's Danish
modern.

"So he ended up buying a Japanese scroll. He didn't hang it,
he kept it protected in its long wooden box, a beautiful object
in itself, with a sliding grooved lid. It was like a ceremony to
take it out and look at it. One night we were at his place and he
brought out the box. He had to take down a poster, move the
couch, and stand on a table to hang the scroll from a high nail.
He didn't say a word, and for once I kept quiet too. He cradled
the scroll in his hands as it rolled slowly down. It extended the
whole length of the wall." Chloe was trembling.

Olivia whistled softly.

"The painting doesn't look like this coast at all, except that
you can see so far. At the bottom, you see people hiking
through the woods. An old man has already arrived at a little

waterfall. You're looking down at them, but you see them clearly, the old man's stick, the pale blue packs on their backs, even the folds of their clothes. Maybe you're on a cliff above them. The point is, you're near, near enough to call out, say, and they'd hear you. But then—I'm not sure I can explain this—above them in the painting is a craggy mountain, and above that you see a river forking in a plain beyond the mountain, and then there are more hills with clouds of fog tucked between their layers, and then, highest up on the scroll, is an island out at sea, it has to be miles and miles away, but it has a scrawny fir tree and you can see the way the wind has bent it all to one side, you can see its cones and even the needles!" Chloe's voice rattled. She gulped her wine. "Do you get what I mean?"

Stirred by Chloe's excitement, Olivia didn't want to speak. "Um. Yeah, I guess. The perspective is all out of whack."

"Utterly. And yet it's so convincing. Everything is so real! I kind of lost my bearings and said something about how the globe would have to be curling up for us to be so close to the people and still see that island so well. He just smiled calmly— this was his treasure and he knew everything about it." Chloe moaned. "He said, 'Yeah, the world is round, but now we're inside it.' I was thunderstruck, Livia. It was as if I'd never seen him. I couldn't get at him fast enough."

Olivia was reminded of something. In a moment she knew what it was. "The universe as your own cave. My!"

She is my best listener, Chloe thought. This is happiness.

Then Olivia asked, "Chloe, do you seriously expect me to believe you're not in love?"

"I'm embarrassed," Chloe confessed. "It turned me on just to tell you." She cooled her cheeks with her hands. "It got to be a joke between us. When I was stalling once, Gabe got out the box. Another time he just said, 'Do I have to show you the scroll?' But the great feeling doesn't stay."

"Why not? When you make love—"

"Sometimes it's all I could want. Other times I just—it's like I stop myself without intending to. I go away."

"You don't want the great feeling?"

"I don't know. I think I want it. But sometimes it's as if I don't. I think maybe I'm scared of losing my friend by letting us be lovers. Then I realize that's just crap, at least as far as Gabe is concerned, because he hasn't changed. It does no good to reason with myself."

"Sounds like you're afraid"—Chloe held her breath while Olivia struggled for the phrase—"of the force of your feelings, if you really let them out—"

She kept very still to make Olivia go on.

"You're so intense. Well, you know that. But so *very* intense, Chloe, your feelings are so strong that I think you're afraid to let them go in one place. Maybe that's why you spread them around in so many places—"

Olivia's attention to her feelings gave Chloe deep pleasure, until the question chilled her: Was there something else? Could *she* find them too much, fearful?

"But if Gabe's in no hurry, why should you be?"

Now she was distracted by a shift in Olivia's tone, like the sound of the wind when it changes direction. "Livia?"

"You're very lucky, actually. He gives you room and cares for you the way you are—"

Chloe heard and thanked her for what she said, but she kept hearkening to the shift in Olivia, who, facing her, seemed also turned away.

"Livia, you're not afraid—"

"What? Of you? Oh, no! Not of you"—and the wind in her

veered again and gained momentum. It lifted the hairs on Chloe's neck. "I'm afraid of myself! If I'm not using everything—everything in me—to make this go with Karl," Olivia cried, gasping for air, "I don't know who the hell I am." And the storm broke.

Amazing how my tears made Chloe rally, Olivia couldn't help noticing as they subsided. So frightened of her feelings minutes ago, and now so determined to make me believe them, full of words for who the hell I am without—especially without—Karl. Who in fact I am for her. The grinner at skulls who has been in the dark places—"your voice comes from there"—fearless by instinct, the ground of Hannah's daring. Who has only to try herself now. The one who knows how to live—oh, not to make each choice come right or do all she can, wants, should, but who is whole, nothing left out, who can reach out of the core of herself with the surest touch.

At that Chloe's small cool hands touched hers, then moved again in the dark, almost the only thing Olivia could see, palely shaping her picture, raising the mirror so Olivia would know she was there. When Karl painted his willed chaoses, he always portrayed himself at last, and Hannah crayoned her excruciating trust. Chloe had looked at her hard, but what she traced now was the friend she wanted. There's no disinterested knowledge, Olivia thought.

Yet as the night chill fell around them, she was tempted to live according to this friend's sight. On the Massachusetts farm there was a root cellar where as a child Olivia took comfort from the glinting jars of preserves, the suspended cabbages ghostly in the dark, the moist breath of earth. She liked to ferret the carrots, beets, and turnips out of their flats of sand, to lift and smell them and tuck them safely back. Chloe's mind was a cool storehouse sunk in the earth, and within the shelter of its smooth round stones, Olivia was kept ready, fresh and pungent.

"I wondered if I'd done right to rush out there," Chloe said a year later in Washington, "until the last night at the coast when you broke down. I didn't know what you should do about Karl or what was right for Hannah, but as for you being somebody in, of, and by yourself, on that I was an expert."

"It made a lot of difference, Chloe."

"What did? What we talked about? But did it stick?"

"Your coming made the difference. What you said moved me enormously. It was such a fabulous tribute."

"Oh, hell."

"No, Chloe, I loved it. You came charging out to Oregon as if it were some kind of emergency. I thought you were out of your mind until I realized that it was. You felt the crisis before I did. And you brought it out, by taking me so seriously."

"You brought me out too, Livia. Maybe that's what it's about. Friendship is emergency. Makes you summon all your faculties. Rise to the occasion, go beyond your strength."

"There's an ideal! Friendship as ordeal."

"But did what I said do you any good?"

"Well. I thought about it plenty. You said I had to believe I could survive and thrive on my own before I could decide anything real about Karl. See? I heard you. But you always think saying things will make them happen, Chloe. It helps to know you see me that way. What happens is something else. But it made me feel good, and it set me up."

"I suppose that's something."

Olivia laughed wickedly. "It set me up for Michael."

"Oh, Christ."

* * *

Chloe didn't notice Michael at first, though she remembered later the odd symmetry between him and Karl when she and Olivia walked in on them. Karl was tipping backward in his chair, his legs stretched out in front of him, his arms folded behind his head, and Michael, facing him, was leaning forward at just the same angle, legs tucked under his chair, arms and palms raised in demonstration of his point. The tableau held for a second before both men turned toward the women and the child. Karl rose as Hannah leaped. She climbed her father like a tree, and he held her easily, dispassionately, gazing at his wife over the brown head squirreling at his neck. He managed to look both hunted and guarded, Chloe thought, like a stag at bay but still king of the forest. Olivia was white about the mouth, but her look, cool and unembarrassed, matched his.

It was Chloe who was awkward, as if she had burst in on intimacy. She glanced at the other man. With the spell of the wilderness still on her, he seemed bearish in his bulk, full black beard, plaid flannel shirt and hiking boots. He was openly enjoying the silent reunion, and Chloe felt he was equally ready to make an exit or continue his explanation. Hannah's fervent chatter chipped away at Karl's silence. The first thing he said, as casually as if he had seen her only last week, was "Hello, Chloe."

She had prepared herself to withstand waves of pity for Karl, but his coldness was bracing. Fair enough, she thought, I never liked you either. Karl didn't even introduce them, so Olivia took over. She dropped the stuff from the car, told Hannah to get herself cookies and milk, introduced herself and Chloe to the stranger, and sat down. Calling the shots, she clearly felt good. Chloe sought to catch her mood, but Olivia's performance chilled her a little. She and Karl had struck a kind of truce, it gave them space and time. Their shared skill at shelving things was oppressive. It proved their durability.

Olivia told Michael she had heard of him and his program for black high school students, and Michael had heard she was doing good things with English as a second language. Olivia pulled out her cigarettes, gave Chloe one. No thanks, Michael didn't smoke. Didn't smoke, but he was as warm as he was ruddy. Everything in his program, he said, was about language, about looking for one they could speak together that didn't seem second. In fact, he had come to see her as much as Karl.

Next to Karl, this Michael was a forest fire. His program was for bright teenagers who might make it to college if they were pulled out of high school in time or given a mighty antidote. "We've been working with only a dozen kids, and it's taken half the summer to unteach them boredom. It's the one skill they've really been taught, you know, to tolerate boredom." Holding classes in people's homes, a half-abandoned bakery, a park—all that began to help. Olivia hummed with sympathy.

"How did you put in the other half of the summer?" Karl asked. Chloe knew that little smile.

Michael looked at him sharply, then laughed a big belly laugh. "We got them to ask a question. Doesn't sound like much, does it?" Laughing again, he opened his mouth so wide Chloe could see his teeth were bad. But he exuded health. This guy is capacious enough, she thought, to engulf Karl's satire.

"But now they get the whole idea: the only questions that matter come from them, school might actually turn itself around to answer their questions, and they have to think of themselves in an entirely new way to ask them. Now they won't let us stop." He had heard that Olivia got her students to write their own histories and asked her about it.

Olivia hesitated, but Karl's smile seemed to goad as much as

Michael's drew her. "It's an obvious thing, really. My students don't think of themselves as readers. They've never written anything. They just want to become real Americans and make it. They come to me to make them over." She sparkled with indignation.

"Hmm. Yeah. But—you must have won their trust," Michael noted shrewdly. "Didn't you dig that?"

Olivia was struck. "Oh, I liked *that*. I was so green I didn't expect them to trust me at all. But when I saw what they were after—it was really demeaning to both of us. Like all they wanted from me was a new coat of paint. They don't believe me at first when I say they each have a history and I want them to find it. Every time a few of them suck their teeth and walk out."

Chloe held Karl in the corner of her eye. He was keeping his little smile at the ready. Oh, didn't he get tired of it all? Evidently not. He had the patience of a fisherman.

"This is far out," Michael said. "Do you realize how much you're bucking? The school, the economy, the whole fucking system. You imagine they have lives, each one different. That's already a conspiracy against the state! You imagine they can find their histories. In school! Write them! In school! It's an incendiary act."

Olivia wrenched her mouth in self-disparagement, but Chloe caught her eye and they grinned. Then they were laughing, all but Karl, and he could keep silent no longer.

"At this rate, they should have locked her up years ago and thrown away the key."

Michael rubbed his face with both big hands and gave Karl a disconcertingly long look. Then he turned to Olivia. "You say 'their history.' Well, is each one fixed? Is it always about the past? Does each person have only one? Do you?"

Karl smiled with satisfaction. The fisherman had got his fish.

Chloe could read his thought as if he'd spoken it: What a cute
come-on!

Ignoring him, Michael told Olivia they were trying to enlist
well-known people to get mainstream backing for an evening
program in the winter.

Karl broke in. "So you want me for your list because I'm at
the museum?"

"I'm chiefly interested in getting good people to work with
the program," Michael said coolly. "But the museum's name
and yours too would do us good."

Karl's laugh was a whisper. He sat forward and slapped his
thighs. "Chloe, you better beat it out of here! You're stuck with
the squares. He wants me for my respectability! To bait the fat
cats!"

As a matter of fact, Chloe remarked, it *was* time for her to be
going. They all got to their feet.

Chloe was being irrational. "Stop dithering," Olivia said.
"These flights never leave on time. Rushing out there like this,
you'll only be stuck in the airport for hours."

But Chloe was right. The man at the check-in counter said
the plane was on schedule and she should board as soon as
possible. She shouldered her bag, snatched her boarding pass,
and wheeled on Olivia, fuming.

Olivia threw up her hands. "Okay! I'm sorry!"

Apparently Chloe was fuming about something else. "You
heard it," she blazed. "Out of his own mouth! How could he
have put it more clearly? *He's* the one who'll lock you up and
throw away the key."

"What?" Was it possible that Chloe was so literal? "He was
kidding. Chloe! You *know* that. Not that it was very funny—"
But when Chloe still glared, rage prickled her skin. "Why do

you obsess so about my relation to Karl? You want me to have a life, but you don't care about the rest of it. You—you have contempt for my work!"

It was Chloe's turn. "What!"

The poor man behind the counter beseeched her to hurry to the gate. Olivia trotted slightly ahead of her across the terminal. Oh, why did that slip out, and where had it come from? Everything had been great! Chloe talking on the deck last night—how had they gotten into this mess at the last minute? Thank God, thank God she was leaving! How dare she fly in on the spur of the moment, tear everything up, and then take off? *How dare she come and go?*

Chloe was so rattled she showed the man at the gate her book instead of her ticket. That jerked a harsh laugh out of both of them. She threw her bag down and hugged Olivia, groaning. "Maybe I shouldn't have come! It's so damn hard—"

It is. It is. All Olivia's rage had gone into sorrow. "It's the stop and start of it," she complained.

The man motioned Chloe through the door, but she spun around. "Livia, of course I care about your work," she called past him. "I'm sorry I didn't—"

"I know," Olivia called back.

"Do you?" Throwing placating looks at the flight attendants, Chloe took small steps crabwise. "Forgive me?"

"Yes, yes," Olivia said. She wanted forgiveness too. "I'll write," she said instead.

"What!" yelled Chloe, but this time she was laughing over her shoulder even as she scowled. Her open raincoat flapped like wings. "You expect me to believe that?"

"This time I will!" Olivia cried.

October 1967

And she did. In the fall Olivia wrote that Hannah was well, she and Karl had reached a tacit understanding, she had lots of time for herself and was surprisingly content. Chloe wrote back guardedly that it sounded like a transition to something else. She and her friend Noah were organizing a teach-in that fall, and Gabe was out every day with the welfare rights demonstrations. In the winter Olivia wrote that she had gone to see Michael and had begun to teach in his school. Chloe replied that she was glad. She'd taken a terrific trip with Gabe to Jamaica. With a letter of introduction, they had visited a maroon colony in the mountains, a holdover from the times of slavery. Now they were talking about war tax refusal. In the spring Olivia wrote that Chloe should hang on to Gabe, she felt good knowing they were together. Michael and his school were even more radical than she had imagined. Her students were coming to visit her at home and were good for Hannah. Karl was making himself scarce. Chloe wrote that the news from Vietnam was keeping her awake nights. She had begun doing interviews on a local radio station, had talked with draft resisters twice, and hoped to locate a disgruntled Vietnam veteran. She was about to take a course in draft counseling. In the summer they both stopped writing.

*   *   *

In August Olivia drove alone to the coast. Karl's mother had come to visit, taken one look at her, and told her she needed a day off. She parked at the A-frame house and walked for a while down the beach. When she realized a mist was rolling in, she turned back. Everything began to look like the dunes near the house, but behind them was never the house. Disoriented, she thought she had overshot and doubled back. The world felt evacuated, the few gulls on the beach seemed to stare at her, the ocean mumbled its menacing comfort. Olivia felt something spread in her chest, widening her ribs. This is not fear, she said to herself, it is something new. No sooner said than she knew it for something old, older than memory. Then, behind the tall grass, she saw a wrecked vessel, its hull canted up high and over, the deck sloping down the other side. How had it gotten so dangerously far from its sea? Pity rooted her to the spot. No one could have survived, she realized, and pity gave way to relief and calm. Now I will be all right, she thought. She stepped toward it tentatively. The hull flattened. It was covered with something like shingles. Olivia tried to fend off knowledge, to forestall the loud regret already tearing at her lungs. She felt her chest shrink as she stared at the pitched roof of the A-frame, sunk as if drowned in high grass.

She started a letter to Chloe. "I had a hallucination at the coast. I couldn't find the house. When I did, I thought it was a wreck and I was all alone. And I was glad." Frightened, she tore it up. Chloe was so far away, and busy with God knows what. But the torn paper blocked the way to another letter.

A friend of Gabe's had a Doberman named Praxis. He said Marx had written that a dog has no praxis but he was wrong. The friend had to be out of town most of August and was worried about his dog. Gabe liked Praxis, and Chloe loved

Praxis' Tompkins Square apartment. Sitting on its big slatted deck under the spears of the ailanthus trees in a wind made her feel as if she were in the tropics. She had been dreading summer in New York, some friends wanted her to share a place on the Cape, but she was determined to work with the antidraft groups. Gabe had suggested living together. Chloe was stalling. When Praxis' master offered the apartment with the dog, Gabe said, "This is our cue." At first, cohabitation was all kidding around. Chloe tried some fancy cooking while Gabe walked the dog. Once Gabe got to talking to some hippies who virtually lived in Tompkins Square Park and Chloe's sauce was spoiled. She tossed it at him, astonishing them both. Gabe laughed. She belonged with the people in the park, he said, and he took her out to meet them while Praxis licked up the béarnaise. A week later, a meeting of Gabe's ran into the night and he didn't call. Chloe could not remember how she had spent evenings alone in her own place. At midnight she wouldn't be soothed, and Gabe went back uptown to his place to sleep. They made it up, but they were both glad when Praxis' owner came home.

Back in her own apartment Chloe had trouble sleeping. She put on the light to write Olivia. I'm not independent enough to live with anyone, and I may have forgotten how to live alone, she thought. What made me so possessive all of a sudden? She turned the light out. She couldn't write that to Olivia.

Olivia had no intention of calling Chloe until she got to Andy's house in Washington. But the first thing she always did when she came east was call Chloe. It was that simple. Was Andy annoyed? She would keep it quick.

"D.C.?" Chloe's voice pealed. "But I'm going down there Friday!" Only then did Olivia recall the big Pentagon demonstration. "But why are *you* there?"

With Hannah in earshot, Olivia simply said they'd come to visit Andy. Chloe was already calculating how she could get there Thursday. Didn't she have to teach?

"I had to rearrange the week anyway to get to the draft-card action at the Justice Department Friday. A lot of my students will be there or at the Pentagon on Saturday. What could be more educational? Noah's canceling classes too—maybe you can meet him at last. And Clem—remember my student? He's going to turn in his draft card Friday."

"Clem? Isn't he the conscientious objector?"

"Livia, that was more than a year ago! There've been ninety-nine stages since." Chloe was aghast at the density of time. "I'll explain it when I see you. Better, I'll take you with me. But what's up really?"

Hannah was two rooms away. Olivia reduced it to the barest outline: affair with Michael, Karl's discovery, need to flee home, Michael's offer to join her, need to flee Portland. It rang in her ears like a five-act melodrama. Chloe took it like a series of rabbit punches, moaning, then said she'd come Thursday morning on the air shuttle. Good. Olivia had no illusions that Chloe would make things easier, but she could hardly be in more trouble than she was already.

They were awkward at first. Chloe had been arguing politics in the taxi from the airport and was having trouble shifting gears. She stood in the tiny yard of Andy's house and chattered.

"It must sound ridiculous, but I didn't know there were houses like this in Washington. Clapboard, I mean, not to mention blue! And a garden!" She sank into a springy metal chair. "For me, Washington is the march route—parking lot, Mall, monuments, White House, and the parking lot again at the end. Once I slept over, but on the floor of a church."

"I thought an old college chum of yours lived here."

"Yes, but I don't see her here. The marches are their own world, you know. You pack into buses—this is the first time I've flown here—and by noon you can't imagine you've ever *not* known the people in the next seat. You worry about each other if you get separated. You can't just mix in ordinary social life."

Olivia laughed. Chloe was as ever, all rush and tumble, but crackling with eccentric little rules. "I'm glad you made an exception for me!"

"Since when are you ordinary social life?"

Olivia reached across the garden table to clasp her hands. "Chloe, Chloe, I am so glad you came," she said. "I couldn't write any of it. I tried and tore it up." She needed to be gazing into this scowl, she realized, precisely this scowl now unfurled to deplore lost writing.

"Tell me. You can start wherever you like, as long as you leave nothing out. I haven't got a thing to do till the demonstration tomorrow."

Olivia started there. "I'm not sure I can go with you, Chloe. I'll have to see how things pan out. Tomorrow afternoon I'm going to Andy's shrink. Condition of asylum."

Everything in Chloe settled down and drew to attention. For her mobilization was restful.

"What's Andy's scheme? Does he want you to stay here with him?"

"Only long enough to figure out how to save the marriage. He bought round-trip tickets for me and Hannah."

"But—help! Livy, give me a cigarette. I thought Andy didn't like Karl."

"Don't you ever buy your own?" Olivia grumbled, but she was glad that hadn't changed. "He doesn't. He thinks he's a big baby, but he knows better than anyone how much I've wanted to make it go. Andy and I have the same mother."

"Ah."

"And he's worried about Hannah."

"How is Hannah?"

"She's okay. I don't think she knows what's going on. She's having a good time in kindergarten. And she came with me a lot to my school. She's made her own friends among my students and even talks like them. She says this trip is outasight!"

"Livia, it would be great if you could stay and sort things out. What do you say?"

"I can't say anything about anything. I don't even have clothes, just what I'm wearing. I packed up Hannah's bag and went blank. Tonight I'll have to wash this shirt out to wear to Andy's shrink."

"Okay." Chloe stamped out her cigarette and sprang to her feet. "Come on. Let's go shopping."

Olivia burst out laughing and went around the table to hug her friend's head to her shoulder. I rely on this mossy head, she thought, rubbing Chloe's hair, short now and brushed out like an Afro.

"Don't be ridiculous," she said, though she was touched. It was understood that Olivia was the clotheshorse and Chloe didn't have the patience to shop. "Andy's taken Hannah to the movies, so this is our best chance to talk."

"We can talk while we shop. We just have to be efficient."

"Chloe! I haven't seen you for over a year. You're all fired up by this new political action. I want to hear about it. And I have so much to tell you!"

Olivia looks so good, Chloe thought, her crisis is hard to credit. She's losing flesh, and her smoky hair looks thinner, even heaped in a bun, but her color is strong and the teal blouse sets it off. She lives in her own drama and draws me in with those eyes.

As a person who had just flown to Washington, Chloe felt full of executive panache. She dismissed Olivia's objection with a flourish of the hand. "We'll make an agenda! I don't want you to have any excuse not to stay east. Do you know where to shop in Washington?" As it happened, Olivia had noticed an ad for a big sale. "Fine. We'll take a taxi."

When they had told the driver where to go, Chloe wedged herself comfortably in the corner of her seat and said, "Okay. Start with Michael."

"Michael," Olivia sighed. "I'm not sure he's in it."

"Didn't you say on the phone he would go with you anywhere?"

"Yes, but it's out of the question. I can't leave Karl for another man."

Chloe saw the rightness of this immediately. "You're not in love with him?"

"I don't even know. *Can't* know. My leaving isn't about Michael. He just made everything happen."

Chloe laughed. "That's all! Come on, Livia. I saw Michael all of thirty minutes. All I know is he heads the program, he hired you. What's he like?"

Olivia rolled her head against the seat and closed her eyes. "He's just the most immediate person in the world."

Chloe felt a jolt, as if Olivia had accused her of deviousness.

"I've always thought I was pretty direct, but with Michael it's a creed. He was in Vietnam in the early years before the escalation, and—"

"In Vietnam! How come?"

"He's a country boy. Got married early, without knowing

what he was doing, had a kid too young, and when the marriage broke up, he let himself be drafted. Vietnam changed his life. He says he can't afford ever again to do something that's not his own idea. He came back and tore through college. And realized that he needed more than anything to reach kids who were in danger of being acted upon without knowing how to think. Now it seems like nothing gets between him and—anything! What he thinks should happen. What he feels at the moment. It's like something physical, in the way he moves, the way he watches you—"

"In his belly laugh?" Chloe remembered that.

Olivia smiled like a cat. "He's not afraid to seem foolish. He detests temporizing, mediation of any kind. He goes after things with this wild abandon! That's what gives the program guts. It's also what freaks out the white community. I never met anyone who simply believes that if he's honest with himself"—the corner of her mouth dipped—"he can't go wrong."

"Well, does he? You sound—does he go wrong with you?"

"I can't say. He always seems to know what I'm thinking. Not that he thinks the same way. I can't explain it." When Chloe pressed her to try, Olivia said she'd have to know all about the program to understand.

"That's all right, I want it all!" She did, too, more than any time before. "The program's next on the agenda anyhow."

Olivia told how the program had gone through a crisis when the riots burst on Detroit. With a glance at the bristling Irish neck of the driver, she lowered her voice. "This guy came to talk about black power. Tremendously forceful speaker. All of a sudden everyone was painfully conscious of their pigmentation. A roomful of people peering into their pores!" Olivia snorted.

Her distance struck Chloe. It's her European background, but can it insulate her from American madness?

"The white teachers and the few white kids were devastated. But no one was thinking about the black students. A couple of black girls in my class were seriously upset. They couldn't talk about it in class, they each came to see me alone and felt bad about doing that. Everything was so damn politicized—if I tried to reassure them, it only confirmed their guilt."

Chloe wanted to know what the girls were like.

"Okay. This actually leads to Michael. Look at this traffic. Well, I don't give a damn about shopping anyhow. Are all these buses your people?"

"Can't be, not yet. This is only Thursday. The black girls who came to see you," Chloe prompted.

"Right. Let's see. Eileen. She felt she was being driven away from her parents, from all sorts of people she respected, in the name of this new unity, this apparently unique way of being authentic. It can be a kind of bigotry, you know."

Sure. Chloe had plenty of mixed feelings about black power.

"The other was Sharon. Sharon was so upset she could hardly speak. We just sat together till she could. The stuff we were studying had made her aware for the first time of just what she and her family were up against as blacks, how hopelessly things were stacked against them. She finally blurted out, 'Why do you want us to see all this? What good will it do?' "

"Oh, Livy!" Chloe had few black students, and she had never won such trust. "I'm so glad they have you." And that Olivia had them. "How did Michael feel about that?"

"Well, that's it. I didn't know how he felt. I went to talk to him. I was feeling pretty embattled, but"—warming up, Olivia sat forward—"he listened. I said I didn't see how the kids could handle this stuff emotionally, maybe it wasn't liberating at all to just dump black power on them and go home, and he surprised me. He said he really needed this, he didn't agree entirely, but he needed me there to say these things. And he called a meeting and got everyone talking in small groups, breaking down the idea into little personal parts so we could sort it out. He's very good. But he said he wouldn't have come to it without me."

"He does sound good, sweetheart, and decent besides, but you"—her throat clicked—"sound terrific."

"But it's great work—ah, Chloe!" she cried, seeing her friend's wet eyes. "The kind of thing you've been trying to show me for—how long now? Stuck at home, I never really understood. Never had your nerve, anyhow. But now I think I get it, and you know what I'm talking about better than anyone. It's the work and the kids themselves that force you to question everything. But"—she winced—"it's going too fast. It's exciting, but it costs, especially the black kids. They're in an outrageous bind, being adulated after centuries of neglect and abuse. Grownup white folks looking to them for moral leadership. Some of them are swept away and don't know what they're doing. The bright ones get cynical or scared. And there's no slowing it down. It's overwhelming. Do you know what I mean?"

"I'm not doing anything like what you're doing. I don't get that many black students. But in your place, I guess I would try to trust the kids, the process."

"You sound like Michael." Olivia smiled dolefully and shook her head. "But I—sometimes I turn against what we're doing. Even during the summer some kids couldn't take it and left. Now we may lose the evening program before we accomplish anything. And a few of the kids are being punished already."

"Punished?"

"Yeah. For raising a ruckus back in high school, demanding black history and all. Two have been suspended. And before they can begin to figure out what they really want, they're forced into the center of some demonstration or other. They're being used. And the stakes keep rising."

"What does Michael say?"

"That he trusts the process! But he always wants to know whatever I'm worried about, and he incorporates it somehow."

"Sounds like he makes you part of *his* process."

"Yes!"

Chloe caught an edge of exasperation in her tone. Would Michael consume her?

"He can be in the middle of an impassioned argument, about anything—Vietnam, education—and suddenly he'll stop short, look at me, and say just what I'm thinking. How I disagree and why. That's how it started. We had this terrifying rapport. Long before we became lovers. Sometimes he'd express what I thought before I'd even formulated it. As if he were ahead of me, or so close, like in the Groucho Marx joke, that he was on the other side of me."

The driver was pulling up to the curb by the department store. The figure on the meter was staggering. "I've got it," Chloe said, digging in her wallet. "Really. This was my idea. Just keep talking. Terrifying rapport, you say. Can that be rapport?"

Halfway out of the cab, Olivia was laughing at her. "What?"

"I mean, how good is it really to have someone ahead of you?" Bound all these years to a rejecting man, was Olivia going to flee to one who would swallow her up? Chloe tipped the driver and climbed out. "Even if it's your thoughts?" She fumbled her wallet into her bag. "Or especially if? Oh, I'm not making sense. Forget it, Livy, forget it. Just tell me what happened. Now why are you laughing?"

"Madwoman! Are we shopping or not?"

We have no dailiness, Chloe and I, we can't hang out in the laundromat or the playground like other women, Olivia thought, rejecting a whole rack of dresses. The distance and our quick, intense meetings make it all unreal. So shopping is not a bad idea.

But Chloe was too much. She held up a scarlet dress with an enlarged black zipper that ran top to bottom. "Hey, Livy! How about this one?"

"That's not a dress, it's a cartoon!" It was startling how formed their tastes had become, and how different. Only mad costumy things caught Chloe's eye. Surely she would never have chosen any of the subdued dresses Olivia was now throwing over her arm.

But in the dressing room, they looked awful. Her bust didn't begin to fill out the first dress, though she was feeling oddly bloated. She tried another. "Ugh! Karl would love this one." Ladylike, expensive-looking, self-satisfied. She glared at Karl's ideal and nearly ripped the dress yanking it off. In the third dress, a beige wool, the mirror seemed to stop working, and the swollen feeling brimmed as tears. Chloe, who had just been saying this one wasn't bad, looked thunderstruck.

"Olivia!" She smacked her head. "I'm an ass! What a dumb idea!"

Olivia sank onto the stool. "It's not that," she bawled, but she couldn't say more. Chloe stooped over her, hugging her awkwardly, clucking in distress. At her neck, the wool was prickly.

"Jesus!"—her voice came back fast—"I'm going to stain this dress! Do you have a kleenex?" Chloe ran to get one. Olivia changed back into her own clothes and breathed deeply till her heart stopped lunging.

"Just sit a minute, and then we'll beat it out of here," Chloe said.

That enormous patience, Olivia thought, looking at her, over years. I want to try to tell her.

"Chloe. You know what it is? I just don't know what the hell

I look like." So Chloe sat on the floor of the tiny dressing room
while Olivia told her about the day at the coast when she lost
her bearings and imagined herself homeless and alone in the
world. "And it felt so natural. That scared the shit out of me.
And now this!"

The curtain jerked open and a yellow head popped in.
"Girls!" it said in a voice like a foghorn. "If you have no use for
this room, please show some consideration for those who do!"

In a dingy bar around the corner, Olivia sipped the house
wine. Bitter.

Chloe was solicitous. "It's pretty awful. Do you mind?"

Olivia shook her head. If she and Chloe had been fastidious
about wine, they would never have become friends.

"Livia," Chloe coaxed, "go back a bit, will you? What was
going on at the time you went to the coast?"

Leaning toward her, one round hand atop the other, Chloe
was concentrated and confident. A friend like this, Olivia
thought, is a perfect witness. She really would try. "Let's see. It
was a couple of weeks after Michael and I had started to make
love. And then—"

"Take your time, don't rush," Chloe said, failing to repress a
smile.

"It was nice—very nice, actually. But it's funny. It had been
so intense between us before, he'd brought me out so much,
that when we finally went to bed it was like a continuation."

"He brought you out?" Chloe urged her on.

Olivia closed her eyes, and right behind her lids was Michael
kissing her anklebones, Michael licking the insides of her elbows, in fervent demonstration that no inch of her body didn't
want loving.

"It was more than that," she admitted. "He made me feel my
whole body was delightful. It was a revelation."

Chloe's "ahhhh" was both sad and happy.

"It was lovely. And I certainly didn't feel guilty. Karl was being such a bastard." Is that true, she wondered, or wasn't he the same distant way he'd been from the first, posing the same puzzle? Since it was finished with Michael, she could afford to go over it one more time. "I saw myself through Michael's eyes. He told me I'm a real independent thinker. Original. Creative. Me! He thought I sold myself short and set about putting me right. He was awfully good to me, really." But a mighty sigh rose in her chest.

"Good for Michael."

Chloe sounded a bit dry. Olivia's untiring advocate for so long, she must feel jealous. She had on her scrutinizing scowl.

"So what was wrong?"

"I had a strange reaction once. I'd been feeling wonderful, and then all of a sudden I felt dead."

"Dead! In what way? Where?"

When Chloe was agitated, she asked the damnedest questions. "*Where*? In the kitchen, in the pantry, in bed." Chloe didn't smile. "At home. In the marriage, I suppose. Hmmm." There was something there, and Olivia went after it. "What it is—I'd been telling myself all year that things were tolerable. There's Hannah. And so many things I still love in Karl."

"Really?" Chloe's eyebrows shot up. "I never hear about that."

It was true enough. Olivia let the thread she was following go slack. Karl was always at his worst with Chloe— competitive, self-absorbed. And every time she tried to tell Chloe what held her to him, a wall went up. Was it that she needed Chloe to complain to, or that she wouldn't understand? Did she herself?

"That's because it doesn't make much sense." She tried now

to explain how Karl gave her lots of room. She wasn't sure why, but it was indispensable. The rest was harder to say, because it was what she did for him. Understand him and explain him to himself. Back him up in his work, press him to carry it to the next stage. As if she were custodian of his inner force, the most vulnerable and the best in him. She said, "He lets me help him. I've actually gotten creative satisfaction from that for years." It sounded pathetic and stiff, and it hadn't been true for a long while. The Karl she ached for was receding as she spoke. Well, let him go, she thought, suddenly hot, let him go.

"Karl *never* encouraged me in anything I care about. And Michael did. So one night—wait! It was the night, it was the very *night before* I went to the coast!—I came home from being with Michael, and nothing seemed tolerable anymore. Especially me. It was—as if I was dead. And right after that—I'd forgotten this." She had the thread again. "I had to go out for milk. I was walking toward the store, and I just stopped dead in the middle of the street. A car slammed on its brakes and skidded. There was almost a wreck. I didn't even really think about it, and like I say, I'd forgotten it. But the next morning I drove to the coast and lost my bearings!"

Chloe paled, and her hand clasped her throat. In her fright, Olivia saw what she had almost done. Chloe swallowed. "Has this—have you acted like this again?"

"No, no, no. Oh, no. And I don't think I will. I'm all right, really. It was just the shock, the shock of—"

"The shock of having someone care for you!" Chloe's color rushed back. "Isn't that it, Livy? You'd just been with Michael. Karl never let you know you're delightful. And you'd been so willfully complacent in your marriage. No, the word is—complicitous! You'd worked so hard to build the illusion, and when Michael came along and showed you what real caring is, it was shattered, and—and—and you didn't know where you were!"

I was dead all along, Olivia thought, but I couldn't realize it until Michael made me feel alive—yes! She felt the shock and the joy too, as if the car had leapt and swerved again. And Chloe—with her hair standing out in a kind of aura, a vindicated if slightly comical prophet—had helped her see it. Lightheaded, Olivia reached for her wine. But she had to reassure Chloe. "I don't think any of it can happen again."

"Let's drink to that, even this junk." Chloe was vehemently herself again. "But"—she arrested the glass at her lips—"this lust for outer space, for standing on the edge of the planet! What was that?"

"I don't know. But I don't want it. It's too goddamn scary. I don't want to be *out*. I just don't know how to go in. I'm not sure I have the courage."

"Courage? Now, you listen to me, Olivia! If you had the courage to marry Karl in the first place, you can find the courage to leave him. You're not going to tell me you have more courage to do what's crazy—!"

But maybe I do, Olivia thought. Maybe I have courage only to do something for him. Chloe doesn't lack for courage, God knows, blazing her truth that way. A mixed blessing, such a fierce friend.

Chloe blinked and stumbled in the blazing sunlight. She'd drunk almost none of that red ink but felt gloriously high. Then, at the same instant, she and Olivia saw a dress in the window of a shop next to the bar. "*You* like that?" they asked in unison, and laughed. "It's my color, old gold," Chloe said, and the big low-slung belt was good too. She should have known Olivia would go for the subtle line, the cowl neck. What an admirable dress! It was incredible but entirely right that this should happen. The shopkeeper warned them she was about to close. "Give us a few minutes," Chloe begged. "We're serious shoppers!" Olivia snickered. The woman snapped her gum, and they dashed at the racks.

"All over Washington, shopkeepers will rejoice when we leave town," whispered Olivia, flipping hangers to find the dress in black, size 10. Chloe found the gold in an 8. Heady and giggling, they tried them on in adjacent booths and came out to show each other. Chloe whispered that she didn't need a dress, she was just playing. "But it's your kind of dress, just the color of your hair, and you look great," Olivia said. Chloe had to admit she looked good, even a bit taller. She confided that she'd brought lots of money, she and Noah had some thought of getting themselves arrested at the Pentagon. But she probably wouldn't risk it, she had to get back to teach Monday, she'd already missed too many classes.

"Of course you're not going to get arrested," Olivia coaxed. "And it's not smart to carry a lot of cash around!"

"All right, you've sold me," she said, "but what about you?"

Olivia hooked her hands on the belt jauntily and pivoted before the mirror.

"You look sensational," Chloe told her.

Olivia cocked her head, twisted her mouth, and grinned. "I look the way you see me!"

Chloe considered this. Olivia did not look like the ardent girl who had sat up all night six years ago spilling confidences. She was thinner, and her cheeks more dusky with shadow. The Garbo slump she used to assume for fun was permanent. Chloe struggled against the drag of loss. She told herself Olivia was somehow more beautiful, the light in her eye had traveled a longer distance. And the years had given her a stunning resilience. However she had seen Olivia, it was never better than now. She had a reckless whim. The dress was good on Olivia, but black was sad, determinist.

"You know," she said speculatively, "you've been neglecting your tan. The black is almost too dark for you now. What do you think? Would you just try the gold?"

The shopkeeper walked noisily to the window and stood glaring into the street. Chloe was already moving toward the rack, but Olivia stopped her.

"No, Chloe. And not because of her"—she jerked her chin at the shopkeeper. "I can't wear gold. Nothing drains me more. And it's not just that." Chloe was tossing up her palms in surrender. "No, listen. It's your color, that brassy optimistic shade. I can't wear your color, Chloe." She hugged her quickly as the woman turned impatiently. "I can only wear my own."

"I had a dream once that Noah and I had matching scars—I mean, he's practically my brother."

Collapsed in the corner of the taxi with their packages, Olivia wanted to ask about Gabe, but she let Chloe fill her in first about Noah.

"We weren't friends in Syracuse. I knew him in high school, bright as hell, too analytic by half. I kept out of his way. But he was also the class comic and a real actor. He did accents better than anyone. And then he turned up twelve years later teaching in the classroom next to mine. The point is, we were both raised in the same ignorance—the same black pit of darkness, he calls it. It was the standard backward fifties upbringing, you know, but Noah says we have to beat it back every day. He likes to carry on, calls for eternal vigilance and so on." She laughed. "Anyhow, we help each other along."

Chloe's a pushover for performers, Olivia thought irritably.

"He puts it all to use in our teach-ins," Chloe was saying,

"working up skits with the students. But the real payoff comes with draft counseling. When a guy wants to go for a psychological deferment, he's got to put in a convincing appearance before the draft board. And Noah's such a clever actor, he coaxes out whatever's already a little wacky in the guy and coaches him—"

"Sounds like you two are inseparable!" Olivia burst out, surprising herself. "What's going on?"

"Look." Chloe sighed and shook her head. "He prefers men."

"Oh!" Had finding this out cost her? But Chloe took Olivia's sharp glance calmly.

"It's fine, Livia. We're good friends. Or closer—but in the way of sibs. We go back so far. We give each other strength."

Forever filling out her family, Olivia thought, touched. "Ah, Chlo—" Without budging from her corner, Olivia blew her a little kiss. And, taking advantage of Chloe's soft gaze, "I want to hear about Gabe."

"I know you do. And I need to tell you. I couldn't write you. We tried living together in August." Without meeting Olivia's eyes, she rushed through an account of the Tompkins Square experiment. She made much of the comedy of dog and sauce, but Olivia could see she was shaken.

"You're giving up the idea?" Olivia asked.

"We're taking a breather."

"Chloe." Olivia peered under her mass of hair. "You wouldn't give up Gabe."

"We see each other. But to need any man that much—" Chloe looked baffled. "I want to be free to move. Not that Gabe would hold me back. But I'd fetter myself."

"Move where? Chloe, if you need him, you have to work it out—you can't will your feelings away."

Chloe looked resolutely past her at the street sliding by. "A lot of things call on my feelings, not only Gabe. I have to be free to choose."

"You chilled my blood in Washington," Olivia said three years later in Brooklyn. "Holding out on Gabe so you could dedicate yourself to history."
"I never said anything of the sort!" Chloe protested.
"It's what you meant, though. If not history, some cause, something impersonal."
"It was never impersonal. That's what you don't seem to get. It was always profoundly personal, because it was about a need for connection to—okay, call it history, justice. Ordinary relations couldn't touch it. But if you went with that need, you found people like you everywhere. You recognized each other in a flash by what you were willing to do together."
"What does that say about the rest of us, the old friends you knew before?"
"Frankly, some old friends were a problem. It chilled my blood that they could see what was happening and sit back. Friendship like that was up for grabs."

Olivia didn't press it. The important thing, she said despite herself, was that Chloe and Gabe had survived the attempt. She hoped that was true.

"Okay," Chloe said roughly. And after a while, "Something you didn't explain—how exactly did Karl find out?"

Olivia wanted to give Chloe a fair view. He had been tangled up in himself all year, she said. His work was in a holding pattern—he filled up sketchbooks but never touched a canvas. He wouldn't talk about it. If *you* get sick of me, Olivia, think how I feel! he'd say. Pity *me*! He kept pushing her to Michael's meetings, day or night, making no secret of the fact that he preferred to be alone. So, hurt and a little vengeful, she went even when she didn't particularly want to. And then Michael made her want to. Karl noticed nothing and they talked less and less.

"A few weeks ago, he went on an elaborate camping trip to the Olympic Peninsula. I've never seen so much equipment. All the same, he caught an awful cold, complete with high fever, and just lay in his tent. For the first time in months, all his defenses were down and he thought about me. And he knew. He got himself up somehow and drove home. He charged in, shaking and sweating, and said, 'You're having an affair with Michael.' "

"Jesus Christ," Chloe said hoarsely. "Every damn time, he's so melodramatic."

"What drove me nuts," Chloe said in Brooklyn three years later, "was feeling sorry for Karl. I did my best to hide it from you. He and I had never been able even to fake a friendship, and yet he moved me so. It seemed like wretched weakness in me. Inexplicable and infuriating. He'd been so awful to you."

"Inexplicable, Chloe?"

"Yes! I know I'm soft on artists. And his work is so good. But still."

"C'mon, Chloe, it has nothing to do with art. It's his being such a difficult man."

"Why should I like his being difficult?"

"Chloe! Are you really asking!"

They leaned back in the cab and looked at each other, mirrors of glumness. When they neared Andy's house, Chloe roused herself to ask, "Do you have any idea what you're going to do?"

"Karl said, 'Either you leave or I will.' He was so sick, he looked so desperate, I was afraid he'd do something mad like go to the papers. Their favorite sport this season is attacking Michael's program. I had to be the one to go. Then Michael offered to take me in—or me and Hannah—so I had to leave town!"

"Can you stay here?"

"Andy would like it, I'm sure. His old girlfriend moved out, and he's alone."

There was Andy's house, and Hannah was at the garden table.

"That blue house, driver," Chloe said. "Livia, quick! No time for complications—do you want to work it out with Michael?"

"In one word?" Chloe's urgency made her laugh. "No!"

Hannah was running to the house, the taxi was drawing up to the curb.

"Do you want to work it out with Karl?"

Hannah and Andy were coming toward them. Olivia couldn't speak, but she shook her head vigorously. Now Hannah and Andy were opening the door of the cab, grinning quizzically. Chloe's hands were clasped like a supplicant's.

"Then work it out with yourself, Livy! Stay, stay, stay!"

"This hand," said Chloe to Hannah, squeezing it a little, "when I held it last year, it was still a baby's hand. It was soft here and puffy here, and here it had bones that belonged in the wing of a little bird. Now, I do believe, I am holding the hand of a real big girl."

Hannah got over her shyness in a flash. The best part of kindergarten so far, she told Chloe, was beating up a bad boy without the teacher finding out. Chloe regretted her fatuous bird's wing, but Hannah was amiable. She remembered their game at the coast and told Chloe that whenever she went to the beach she picked up shells for the restaurant.

"That's great! Do you think they'll have good shells here?" Andy had brought them to a Japanese restaurant with a tatami room, a tiny elevated cubicle formed by screens, where they sat on cushions at a low table.

"Oh, Andy, you're a genius!" sang Olivia. "This is better than the playhouse, right, Hannah?"

At twenty-six Andy looked like a lanky bespectacled teenager, but it was with the gravity of a young father that he helped Hannah take off her shoes outside the cubicle. She climbed in, made herself a huge nest of cushions, and pulled Chloe down beside her at the table. Not for love of her, Chloe realized, but to have unimpeded access to her mother across from her. Olivia and Andy were having trouble arranging their long legs in the small space. "Can't eat under *this* table, Liv," Andy said. Olivia laughed and knocked her knee against the wood.

Hannah beat the table with her palms. "What are you talking about, Andy, what are you talking about?"

"Well, Hannah, you're old enough to know the truth," said Andy, folding his legs into the lotus position. "When your mama was just a little older than you, she thought the thing to do was to serve me wonderful little messes for supper under the table."

"He's kidding, Ma, isn't he? Isn't he, Ma?"

"No, he's not. I'd forgotten all about it, but it's true!" Olivia gave up and thrust her legs to the side. "It was because Gram Esther had a beautiful big tablecloth."

"That's the reason, Hannah," said Andy solemnly. "You get it? It was because Gram Esther had a beautiful big tablecloth."

Olivia elbowed her brother. "*Zitto!*" A vision of bilingual infant brawling dazzled Chloe.

"The tablecloth hung way down over the sides," Olivia said, "so if you ate under the table, you felt like you were in a cozy little room of your own. Rather like this one, in fact."

"How come you made supper, Ma?" said Hannah, jealous of her mother's past. "Where was Gram Esther?"

"Oh, you know Gram Esther," said Andy airily. "Always gadding about."

Hannah ignored him and riveted her gaze on her mother.

"She was out a lot, Hannah," Olivia said. "I don't know."

A sigh passed through the tatami room. Then a waiter gleamed at the opening with a tray of drinks, three tropical concoctions and a Shirley Temple.

"Surprise," said Andy. "And welcome, you outside agitators, to the capital of your country."

After they ordered, Olivia asked Hannah about the movie she and Andy had seen, and Hannah proceeded to give her a frame-by-frame account. That freed Chloe and Andy to get to know each other.

After a series of jobs in government, Andy was with the Job Corps. Chloe asked him how it was going.

"Backwards," he said. "Strafed in the crossfire of the War on Poverty." In telegraphic spurts, he painted a picture of bureaucratic backbiting, incompetence, and cynicism.

"What about the war budget?" she asked. "Isn't that the main problem?"

Andy lifted a brow. "I'd look to the war itself."

Chloe opened her mouth and closed it. Andy smiled.

"I'm against the war too, Chloe, probably more than you. So I hope you can get the Viet Cong to cut it out."

She was aghast. "Do you really believe—"

"You didn't come to Washington to argue with me. You came to see my sister and go to the demonstration. Tell me, which faction in the Mobilization is your favorite for Saturday?"

It was a sporting event for him. Chloe tried to get her bearings. Andy was up on all the quarrels between what he called the old-guard marchers, the young turks who wanted to invade the Pentagon, and the acidhead crazies who proposed to exorcise its evil spirits. Chloe could only play it straight. The infighting was bad, she admitted, but the press's fixation made it worse. The truth was that things were connecting up, the war was driving everyone together.

"The pacifists and the politicos are both going to the Pentagon. The old-time peace ladies *and* Abbie Hoffman."

"Bucket always half full for you, huh, Chloe?" Was it always half empty for him? "Doesn't every new coalition cost? SANE started these protests, right? But now it's split straight down the middle. What I hear, half the leadership of SANE will quit if Spock won't condemn civil disobedience."

"Well, then they're wrong!" Chloe felt herself getting warm. "CD may just be the only thing that will work. Look, a year ago the civil rights movement wouldn't touch antiwar issues, but now King himself has come around. Black guys are beginning to think twice about killing their yellow brothers."

"And who's going to be thinking even once about how these *brothers* will eat if they stop drawing army pay?" He was hot. Chloe liked him better.

"What's going on here?" asked Olivia.

"Ma," Hannah complained. "You're not listening."

Olivia grunted. "Just tell me how it ends, baby."

"You didn't say who you'll march with Saturday," Andy resumed.

"That's easy," Chloe said. "The Resistance. Their action tomorrow is more important to me than the march itself."

"The Resistance," Andy mused. "Where have we heard about that before, Liv?"

"Hold it a second, Hannah. Here, want the fruit out of my drink? Andy's thinking about the war," Olivia informed Chloe.

So was Chloe. They looked at each other blankly for a moment, and then Olivia got it.

"Oh! I mean the big one! And Andy means the *other* Resistance." She glanced slyly at her brother. "He thinks it stole our mother."

Andy flushed. "I do not." Frowning, he shot a look at Hannah, obliviously collecting swizzle sticks. "But people then were willing to fight and die for what they believed."

He is thinking about their father, Chloe realized, that's why they still call it "the war." Andy sees it the way I did in Rome, when history was an emotion set in Europe, something that culminated in a moment of epic sacrifice and was no more, leaving us to live through featureless time. So instead of protesting, she offered Hannah a sip of her drink. But doing nothing means now what it did then, in their big war, she thought. Collaboration.

"So is our Resistance," she said. Andy stiffened visibly. Chloe wondered if Olivia was skeptical too. She felt herself sputtering. "They're facing jail terms, for God's sake. They're tired of *reacting* to the government piecemeal. They want to do something whole, and maybe that way disrupt the entire machine. They want to put their bodies where their mouths are." At that Andy guffawed, and Chloe felt the blood rush to her face. Oh, what a ridiculous image!

Olivia came to the rescue. "That sounds a little contortionist, Chlo, you have to admit," she said gently. "But the rest is

Thoreau all over again, isn't it?" She turned to Andy. "After Chloe taught *Civil Disobedience* last winter, she found it impossible to pay her income tax. Gabe too, right?"

"Gabe too, wrong." Why did Olivia have to bring him in? "Gabe said the feds would get the money sooner or later and he couldn't see anything gained by slowing them down. I guess he had a point. Eventually, when they were about to attach my checking account, I gave in and paid. The only stall left would have been to hide my money in Syracuse, and that would have meant telling my father—"

"Chloe!" Olivia was wide-eyed. "You wanted to express yourself to the government, but you wouldn't tell your father?"

Chloe hadn't thought of it that way. There was no real connection, was there? Or was there?

"Well, think about it!" Olivia said cheerfully.

"Yay! Here's our food!" Hannah clapped. "Let's eat!"

"You were about to put your body where your mouth is, weren't you, Hannah?" asked Andy. The child liked the chopsticks, but she couldn't really pick up her food with them. Andy, demonstrating, said it was a question of mind over matter.

"Is it?" Olivia asked. "I just think of the chopsticks as extensions of my fingers!"

Hannah gleefully began to test her sticks' potential as fingers, tickling Chloe, picking her nose.

"Cut that out right now!" said Uncle Andy.

When she had eaten less than half her meal, Hannah sprang to her feet. "Look! Those grownups! They're eating with their fingers! Or maybe," she said slyly, "their fingers are chopsticks!" She shouted with the success of her joke.

A young couple outside the cubicle was lost in a dreamy haze of hair and cowhide. The young man, who wore a chrysanthemum over one ear, gently wiped a corner of his lady's mouth with his thumb. She took his hand in hers and sucked the thumb. Then he tongued the other side of her mouth.

"Eeeeh!" squealed Hannah. "They're like puppies!" She fell back on the cushions, stretched, and sighed like a voluptuary.

"And you're a kitten," her mother said, stroking her hair. Hannah smiled and licked her lips. In minutes she was asleep.

"What a brilliantly appointed restaurant!" Chloe exclaimed.

"It's that Mickey Finn you slipped her, Chloe," Andy said.

"A stroke of genius," declared Olivia. They ate in happy silence for a while. "Now, what were you two talking about before?"

"The movements." Andy said promptly. "Whether they really connect up. Let me take another tack. You were in Mississippi, right? Liv said you knew one of the three guys who were killed."

"A little, yes."

"Been following the trial of the Klansmen in Meridian? Radio said the jury was deadlocked this afternoon but the judge lectured them and sent them back. What do you think?"

"Me? Same as everybody. I pray they'll be convicted, but it drives me wild that they're being tried for a civil rights violation instead of murder. What do *you* think?"

"Take what you can get. Bird in the hand. Conviction of a white for killing a black in *that* part of the country? First time since Reconstruction. Can the antiwar folks dream up anything to touch that?"

"Yes and no. It's hard for black people to bridge civil rights and antiwar in practical terms. For the reasons you said before, Andy. But for whites, there's a chance. That's what I think the Resistance is about."

"Ah, the Resistance!" Andy chuckled. "Now you'll excuse me. This is true. I really have to go to the john."

"Is he upset?" Chloe asked.

"Maybe he's allergic to the word. Probably he has to pee. But explain it to me, Chloe. I really don't get it."

Fine. It was Olivia she wanted to tell anyhow, and badly. Now that she was so caught up in things at last.

"Okay. Look, when you see it for yourself up close—when you see a black sharecropper being told his family will be hurt if he tries to register to vote, or a white kid about to be inducted, when they're driven to the wall and finally open their eyes and see something they've never seen before because it's always been called, for generations, by names that hide what it is—"

"Like what, Chloe? Give me an example."

Easy. "A draft card. We were in the cafeteria, and one of my students had his draft card in his hand. He said, 'You know what this is? I just realized this! We use it for ID, but it's not an ID at all! It's a death warrant.' He said, 'I'm not signing any more of those. I'm going to put myself between the state and this death warrant.' Okay?"

Olivia nodded, and Chloe felt herself taking off. "He looked like life was just starting up in him. I saw it in Mississippi too. In the instant when they really *see* the violence done to them, they know what to do. And it's as if they begin to—inhabit their lives. Their real lives, I mean, their whole lives. Because they weren't whole before they saw. And they can't *get* blind again if they want to. They have no choice but take their own lives in hand if they're going to stay real. And the fire of that, the fiery *intelligence* of that turnaround! It burns through all conditioning, Olivia, nothing moves me more."

"I understand. It's great."

"Do you?"

"I think so."

"Have you seen it too, Livy?"

"Something like it, yes, maybe."

"It's contagious. You can't see someone making that turn and remain unchanged."

Olivia started to speak but checked herself. Her jaw shifted. A chill touched Chloe, and Olivia flew into a rage.

"Chloe! Stop pushing me!"

"What?" Chloe was astonished. "How am I—"

"You're jamming me. You want me to take some action."

"I'm not. If you see it yourself—Livy, you said so!—how am I pushing you?"

"For Christ's sake, Chloe! You want me to have seen it *just* as you saw it and to feel it just as you did and take action just like you. What's so goddamn free about that?" Olivia's eyes stretched so wide the whites showed all around them. Chloe could hardly breathe in that stifling little room.

Andy's smiling face was in the opening. "Ready to go home?"

"That was the pits, that supper in Andy's cutesy little padded cell," Chloe said three years later in Brooklyn.

"Claustrophobic. Especially at the end."

"In the afternoon I'd thought our lives were beginning to move in the same direction, and I was thrilled. But that evening everything I said sounded foolish or seemed to enrage you."

"You infuriated me. I'd wanted you to come, and you had done me a lot of good. But in the restaurant all you could do was argue with Andy. At the end, I wished you'd just disappear. It was like our connection was some kind of curse."

"But—why the hell is that, Livy?"

"It makes you mad all over again, doesn't it? Well, I've thought a lot about it. It's only recently I began to understand what was really going on between you and Andy."

"What was really going on. Oh, good."

"Do you think you can hear me out on this, Chloe? Yes? I think you and Andy were fighting over me."

"Maybe you could spell that out a—"

"I will. You were fighting over me, over what I should do. You were playing the firebrand, do or die, and Andy was so accommodating, the reformer. He thought I should work with what I had, and you thought I wouldn't begin to know what I had if I didn't take a risk."

"My God! I was arguing with Andy about politics. And you, I wanted to make you understand how I felt about politics! I wasn't even thinking about you."

"Oh? Do you hear what you're saying?"

"I'm sorry, but I needed so much at that moment for you to understand what was so important to me. But—fighting over you! Well, which of us won?"

"Neither. I heard both of you negatively. I thought you wanted my blood—wait, this is how I heard it, Chloe. You were saying it would be good for me to camp out on the front lines, while Andy, Andy was—"

"Andy was telling you to crawl under the table!"

"You know what Andy asked me after the Japanese restaurant?" Olivia said four years later. *"He wanted to know if you were religious."*

"Oh, my God! So to speak! That's wild. Hey, Olivia! You don't believe that, do you?"

"I know all about your walking out of your parents' church, if that's what you mean. But that zeal that sweeps everything before it—look out! Andy and I had seen enough of it in our mother, and she didn't belong to any church either."

"Oh, Christ, Olivia. Your mother!"

"Well, of course, you were different. But you seemed to have changed so since Italy."

"How do you mean?"

"I don't know. In Rome you were all—appetite. Hungry for the world. It seemed to have gotten twisted around somehow. You didn't want the world anymore. You wanted utopia. And you were in such an apocalyptic hurry, you couldn't see what was in front of your nose. It broke my heart. Actually, it made me angry. And what happened to your friend the next day confirmed my worries."

The new black dress was perfect for this brisk, beautiful weather. Olivia felt uncommonly agile as she wove her way past the sound truck on Constitution Avenue, past the police barricades and the five black-clad Nazis chanting, "We want dead Reds," and stood on a step to scan the sunny crowd of a few hundred people. There was Chloe, smack in the middle, in turtleneck and jeans, hands thrust in her hip pockets, back so straight it arched.

Olivia felt a rush of love. Last night she thought she needed a continent at least between them to keep from falling into Chloe's fire, but today that seemed absurd. She was glad she had put the quarrel behind her and come.

A man on the Justice Department steps was addressing the crowd, but Chloe was listening intently to a young woman in striped overalls. That had to be Clem's Irish wife Frances, Olivia decided. Next to them was a thickset guy in horn-rims who looked nervous even from a distance, but he was too old to be Clem, and the thin young man behind them looked too exultant. Chloe caught sight of her and cheered. "You made it, Olivia! You came!"

The radiant kid was Clem after all, and the girl was indeed

Frances. The heavy one was Noah. He had gorgeous sea-green eyes.

"Livia, this is my infant pal from Syracuse."

A smile organized his rather lumpy face, but his eyes belied it. "Ah, Chloe's other half," he said, taking her hand. It was as if he sniffed. He reminded Olivia of one of Esther's friends, a man vain for no reason but that he held a grudge against society.

Feeling rivalrous, she replied, "Ah, Chloe's *twin*."

At that his grip crushed hers and he laughed, but his eyes kept their own counsel.

"How was Andy's shrink?" Chloe whispered. Olivia said he was fine, and Chloe's friends turned away discreetly.

"I like him. He seems to understand me. He thinks there's hope I'll understand myself. Imagine!"

"Wow!" said Chloe. "You look better already."

"He wants to see me Monday."

"So you'll stay?"

"Well, till Monday. But yes, I think I'll stay a while."

Chloe hugged her. "This is a great day!"

"So what's happening here? And is your friend Noah always so tense?"

"You just missed the Yale chaplain. Fabulous. Talked about the ethics of the nonbeliever. Noah—he's very wrought up about all this. He and I and Frances are turning in antidraft cards."

Frances showed her a statement signed by people not eligible for the draft, promising to counsel, aid, and abet those who were eligible in refusing or evading it.

"Can't you all be prosecuted for this?"

"Exactly!" Frances beamed. "We're making ourselves just as vulnerable as the guys turning in their draft cards. They're going to have to deal with all of us. Whatever happens, it's a relief to be in this with Clem. I felt awful at first when he joined the Resistance. Especially when he said he was doing it for me."

Clem wheeled and gave her a diabolical grin. "That's how I caught you!"

Swaying and tilting toward each other, they were a winsome pair. With her heart-shaped face, large breasts, blue eyes, and black braids, Frances had a redundancy of charm. Clem, small and lean, bobbed about her. She was the anchor for his buoyancy.

"Chloe, you started this, right?" Olivia asked. "You gave them a cup to share at a party?"

"It's true!" Chloe was ebullient too. "It's all my doing."

"It is in a way, Chloe," Clem said. He spoke softly, almost apologetically. "Getting me to marry Frances made me political." A knot of people behind them raised a cheer for the speaker, and Clem appropriated it with a little bow. They all laughed.

Noah has a laugh like raking gravel, Olivia observed, watching his face fall back into a grimace. What's wrong with him? Too analytic by half, Chloe said. Is he jealous of Clem? Or contemptuous? Impatient, she turned to Clem, who slung his arm around Frances' neck. She wanted their secret.

"How did that work?" she asked.

Clem measured Olivia for a moment, caught Chloe's eager nod, squeezed Frances, and said, "Well. I was going to apply for CO. Go it alone, the way I always did things. I worried about the guys who hated the war as much as I do but *weren't* getting deferred, but I figured I'd get over it. I probably could have gotten CO too—I actually *am* a pacifist. I might even have gotten alternative service working with kids. That's what I want to do with my life anyway."

"I'm confused," Olivia confessed. "Would that have been bad?"

Clem paused again before speaking. This was his way, then—to search the face of the other for the way to formulate his answer. "Yeah. I think so. If I'd gotten a job with kids at this government's pleasure, while their dads were serving and getting killed, I'd have been neutralized. What could I have given those kids? When I was with Frances, no longer *alone*, it all became clear. I mean, what I want is to work with kids in a free place, as a free person. But now there are no free places."

"Except," said Frances, sweeping the scene with her arm, "on the other side of all this! And look, there're so many of us!"

Olivia did look. She didn't like crowds, but this one was unusually quiet and serious. Some were beaded or bearded, others Quakerish or priestly, several wore the steel-rimmed glasses of the left intellectual, but some were housewives, jocks, California surfers. All turned the same way, their faces were unguarded. She fancied they were listing toward a future where their best selves would be summoned every day.

"Look, Clem," Frances cried, "they're beginning to collect the cards." Two boys ahead in the crowd hailed Clem.

"They're part of his group," Chloe explained. "They practically live together. They've talked through all their doubts and terrors, even tried to anticipate jail—"

The crowd surged toward the steps, and Olivia started to follow, but Chloe was hanging back. Noah was clutching her arm. "Chloe," she heard him say, "don't let Frances hear. She's blissed out by the antidraft pledge. But the government isn't going to *deal with us*." He almost snarled. "I heard that a lawyer for the feds called it 'a charming gesture.' They're not going to prosecute us."

"Well, why so grim, Noah? Don't we hope they won't prosecute?"

Noah shot her an angry look. "But if they just laugh at us and really go after the resisters?"

A yell distracted them. A kid from Boston Resistance announced that he had more than two hundred cards or photostatic copies of cards that had been burned. He dropped them in a bag held by a slender black man in shirtsleeves.

"That black guy's from SNCC," Chloe informed Olivia, plainly relishing this proof of continuity. "No, I didn't know him in Mississippi. But he was talking earlier about how we had to sit down and figure out other kinds of resistance so this won't be a one-shot deal." Chloe imitated him, " 'Like how many times can we be turning in the same old draft card.' "

The guy was lithe as a cat, he looked as if he'd been places and was on his way to more. He sent something electric down into the crowd. Yet there were almost no other blacks here. Olivia said so to Chloe.

"Oh, I know. This isn't an action for blacks. They don't have the deferments to forfeit. But don't you see? It's what I was trying to explain last night. This is how *we* inherit Mississippi. White folks take the risks on themselves, instead of just encouraging the blacks to."

Noah, on her other side, groaned, and Chloe turned to him. He was in some kind of state, Olivia had no idea why.

The crowd drew her now. All of them seemed polished by the moment, lifted up, like Clem and Frances, by doing this thing together. The electricity was in them too, and flashing between them, and a kind of erotic sympathy tugged Olivia forward.

Young men representing different Resistance constituencies lined up to mount the steps, deposit their cards, and say a few words. It was like a commencement exercise wonderfully reversed. They were getting rid of Uncle Sam's ID and assuming their own. It was what Chloe was saying. Behind her somebody was chanting the running tally, 183 cards from New York, 25 more from Union Seminary, plus those from Yale, Kansas City, Berkeley, from L.A. and Chicago and Portland, Oregon—Chloe hugged her for Portland's sake, and Olivia felt foolishly proud, as if she had taken part.

Noah was looking better. He was audibly sipping the air through parted lips with each new offering of cards. Cincinnati, Detroit, Cedar Rapids. A couple of guys gave in their own cards on the spur of the moment. There was an almost reverent pause when the last student had made his drop, then someone yelled, "Nine hundred ninety-two," the black guy swung the bag over his head, and everyone roared.

An older man came forward, his bald dome catching the sun, and took the bag from him. Chloe said he was a radical poet who had led a walkout when Humphrey spoke at the National Book Awards ceremony. Two men in suits climbed the steps and announced through the mike that they were faculty members who were turning in their draft cards too. After a general stirring in the crowd, more older men went forward.

"What's the deal?" Olivia asked. "Look at that gray hair! They can't be draftable."

"Hey, look, that guy's giving back his honorable discharge papers!"

"What the hell is going on? I feel like I should donate my Social Security card!"

Chloe was giddy. "You? You should give them your marriage certificate!" She doubled over, cackling.

Fuck you, Olivia thought. Three more faculty members were surrendering their cards.

"Dynamite!" Chloe said. "You're supposed to carry that card to the grave. You die without it, they exhume you, right, Noah?"

"What?" Noah was staring up at the steps. "Chloe," he said, grabbing her wrist.

"What?"

"Chloe, I—" His voice shook, but his face was glowing.

"What? Noah, what is it?"

"Chloe!" He wrenched his gaze from the steps and stared at her, breathing harshly. He pulled his wallet out of his pocket.

"Noah—oh!"

"I have to do it!"

Without a word, Chloe threw her arms around him. Noah turned, and his big shoulders swung through the crowd. Still wordless, Chloe hung on to Olivia. Together they watched the forward progress of a spot on the back of Noah's head where the hair was just beginning to thin.

Noah took the mike. He said his name with a rich resonance Olivia hadn't heard before and thrust his card into the bag. Then he stood aside to let the next man take the mike. Chloe cheered while tears streamed down her cheeks. But Noah seemed to be having trouble negotiating the steps.

"Chloe," Olivia cried, "look at Noah!"

"Is he dragging one leg?" Chloe asked. It looked like it. At the bottom of the steps, he made his way to the edge of the crowd. Alongside the barricades, he tripped or lost his balance, and his arm flew up. Olivia rose on her toes.

"He's falling against one of the barricades!" she reported. "He's knocking it over!" Three policemen started forward, but the barricade righted itself. "No, wait, it's all right, he's on his feet." A cop held his arm while Noah nodded his head vigorously. Chloe was already squeezing through the crowd.

When Olivia caught up with her, the cop was backing away with an eye cocked at Noah. "Yes, yes," Noah was saying vaguely. "Fine. He's really a nice guy."

"Are you hurt?" Olivia asked.

"No, no, no," he said wagging his head thoughtfully. "Very decent."

"Who, the cop?" Chloe's laugh was jagged. "He's not bad, but you—you're a hero!"

Noah made a choking sound.

"What's wrong, what's wrong?" Chloe shot Olivia a look of alarm.

Clutching his throat, Noah peered anxiously into Olivia's face. "Aren't you terribly thirsty?" he asked solicitously.

Contrition gripped her. The man was in some kind of awful pain. "Yes, as a matter of fact," she answered promptly, "I am. Are you? Should we go find something to drink?"

Chloe stared at her. "What the hell—"

Couldn't Chloe see the guy was crumbling? Olivia gave her a meaningful frown but said as brightly as she could, "Where do you suppose, Chloe, we could find a cup of tea?"

"I don't have a clue!" Chloe almost yelled at her. So Olivia stepped around the barricade and politely asked the cop. Chloe and Noah waited frozen until she took them each by an arm and steered them the way he said.

Chloe jerked her arm free. "These are his people," she hissed at Olivia. "Why should he leave?" Stepping in front of Olivia, she grabbed Noah. "Wait! Do you really want to leave now?"

"I think, I think, I think"—and then Noah's chest seemed to hollow out. He gave up on his voice, but he nodded.

No one said a word all the way to the coffee shop. Then, sliding into the booth next to Noah, Chloe turned away from Olivia across the table.

"Let's all have some hot tea," Olivia proposed. "It was really a lot colder out there than we realized. And maybe a muffin. Or how about soup?"

Chloe gave her a white glare. "I'm just having coffee! Black!" But Noah ordered tea, and when Chloe tried to get him to say what was wrong, he only groaned softly.

"It's very upsetting," Olivia began.

"Will you let Noah speak?" Each word seemed a separate act of Chloe's will.

Olivia felt the violence of her fear and kept still. But Noah couldn't speak. His big shoulders bunched forward, he drew his right hand repeatedly through his left. As if—as if what? wondered Olivia. As if he wanted to pull off the skin? "I shouldn't, I shouldn't," he began, working his hand. As if to undo its deed! He'd stumbled onto the wrong stage, poor man.

The waitress brought the tea in a pot. Olivia poured some for Noah and, monitoring his nods, spooned in the sugar.

"Shouldn't have done it?" Chloe squeaked. She sipped her coffee to bring her voice down. She looked so small beside Noah. "Is that what you mean?"

Clutching the mug, Noah brought the trembling of his big hands under control. He stared into the tea for help and began to mutter in a stifled voice. He might have been reaching into a dark sack and pulling things out. Some of it he meant, the rest was the trash of terror. He shouldn't have done it. The fucking draft card. What would happen now? He should call his father. No, God, not that, above all not that. The cop was so decent, did they see? What would happen? Maybe he should call his bank. Could they get at his pension? The fucking card. It was burning a hole in his pocket. He couldn't not, he couldn't *not* do it. But it wasn't right. It wasn't the thing. Not for him. No hero, an impostor. Too old. It just happened, like that. He hadn't even meant to. He couldn't not.

Chloe sat hugging her misery. Olivia felt abruptly like an intruder. She could see that Chloe wanted to touch Noah, but

he was so wrapped over himself she didn't know how. Finally
she put her little hand on his hunched shoulder. Noah stopped
talking. He lifted his head sharply, turned to her, and frowned
as if he couldn't quite place her.

"Noah! Noah!" she cried.

"Chloe, for Christ's sake," he said, and his natural voice
came back full of agony. "Why the hell didn't you tell me to
stop and think?"

Chloe didn't return to Andy's until late in the evening.
Opening the door, Olivia got a foreglimpse of Chloe old. Her
flesh blurred over her cheekbones, and even her hair had abandoned the fight. Hannah had been giving Olivia hell, demanding and refusing attention with inexhaustible energy. Even
Andy had fled the scene. Drained dry, Olivia was trying not to
face how upset her daughter was. Chloe might have been
another harried mother, her love spilt, but the way she held
herself warned Olivia not to touch her.

She poured them red wine instead, Andy's best, and led her
to his leather sofa to tell what had happened. Chloe's voice had
been battered flat. She had just left Noah at a friend's apartment. On the way there, they'd passed some of what she called
the shock troops, rows of army trucks, riot gear, and she'd been
afraid they would really upset Noah. But instead they'd had a
bracing effect. She hoped the thought of the march would pull
him out of this paranoid funk.

For Olivia's part, the thought of the march doubled her
fatigue, but she only asked, "Where do you think it comes
from, the paranoid funk?"

Chloe could barely shrug. "We kid around about how our
students leave us in the dust. They make Noah feel sorry for our
generation, he said that once. Another time he said they didn't

make him feel old, just tardy. Maybe he was trying to catch up somehow. But he seems to feel like he acted in some criminal way and has simply ruined his whole life." At his lowest point, she had called Gabe in New York. "Gabe said to tell Noah he could probably get his card back if he decided he wanted to. I didn't think I should, I was afraid he'd feel so defeated. But Gabe said just plant the idea, it'll give him a little breathing room. So I did."

Olivia said Gabe's approach sounded smart and sensitive. Was he a friend of Noah's? Noah was her friend, Chloe said coolly, but Gabe liked him and everyone liked Gabe. Yes, Gabe was going to meet them and march with them tomorrow.

Olivia was glad, but she noticed that her enthusiasm for Gabe made Chloe go a little wooden. Was it something about him—his sweetness, his pragmatism? Or was it her own praise of Gabe that bothered Chloe? A little wary, she changed the subject. "What was Noah saying about his father?"

It was the wrong note. Chloe was practically hostile. "I can't make it out. I always thought he despised his father."

We're like people with bruises so fresh we're afraid to move, Olivia thought. They could neither talk nor give it up. Finally Chloe asked, almost politely, if she wanted to tell her anything about her talk with the shrink. Olivia had indeed wanted to, it was one of the reasons she'd rushed to find Chloe at the Justice Department. What he said about Esther had piqued such startling interest. The doctor's conviction that most of her puzzles would find explanations there was exhilarating. But now, fronting Chloe's weary face, as blank as a stranger's, she found it a little frightening. They heard Andy at the door.

"Not really," Olivia said, "no."

Chloe seemed relieved to talk to Andy. The jury in Mississippi had brought in their verdict, exonerating one of the worst guys, but seven Klansmen had been convicted.

"Do you realize," Chloe asked, her voice reanimated by rage, "that the possible sentence for those murderers is five thousand dollars or ten years in jail, exactly the same as what all the guys who turned in their draft cards today are facing?"

Chloe finds more coherence in historical irony than in any personal thing, Olivia noted sadly. The talk was winding down. Everyone was wiped out. They all said goodnight. Olivia couldn't believe that she and Chloe were going to ignore the tension, but it was so. The loss of candor between them made her heavy climbing the stairs.

"I wanted to thank you after you took care of Noah, but my heart wasn't in it," Chloe said three years later in Brooklyn.

"I thought you were sore at me for interfering. Being officious."

"Oh, I was! I thought you were insufferably matronly. But I didn't know Noah was so upset. Didn't want to know. I couldn't help knowing later when they threatened him with induction unless he took back his card. But that weekend I just prayed he'd snap out of it and start drawing strength from what he'd done. I wasn't tracking well, but you were. What was really beginning to bother me—I couldn't bear your having called it so well at that wretched Japanese dinner. About how the contagion of ideals was really pressure, manipulation. I'd been in all this stuff up to my eyebrows, and you just waltzed in with your cool detached judgment."

"It wasn't so detach—"

"The fact that it was my dear friend who proved you right the very next day," Chloe went on, "I couldn't handle it."

"I wasn't detached, Chloe. The issue for me was influence, not your influence on Noah, but Michael's on me. And yours. I was awfully scared that that kind of loving influence canceled out genuine choice. That's why I got up such a head of steam."

"Oh. I had no idea—"

"Anyhow, you're too preoccupied with being wrong or right."

"I am?"

"Are you kidding? You mean you don't know it?"

"Is that wrong in me?"

"You know in Washington when we talked ourselves speechless and neither of us could hear what the other was saying?" Olivia asked four years later in Ontario. *"I think we were each trying to tell the other the same thing."*

"Really? Let's hear."

"It didn't look the same, but there we were, both living entirely through others. Neither of us could stand it in the other. You couldn't bear my surrendering myself so to Karl, his work, and I couldn't stand it that you kept living through some hero or other outside yourself."

"But I was trying to find a way to engage myself more directly."

"And falling short of the mark. They didn't prosecute the women for aiding and abetting the draft resisters, after all. Only the men."

"Whew! So it was vicariousness. We saw it in each other, but not in ourselves. Murder! How did we ever communicate?"

"Calamitously! Remember the phone call?"

When Chloe called late Saturday afternoon, only Andy was home. She said it had taken her hours to find a phone, so she probably wouldn't call again until tomorrow. She didn't know when she'd get back to his place, she was going to stay and help out the demonstrators who were making a night of it around the Pentagon. Andy said nothing. "Tell Olivia I won't get arrested, I can't afford it, she'll understand." Andy said he would. Only after hanging up did Chloe realize she'd forgotten to ask how Hannah was today.

Sunday afternoon she waited on a line of muddy, ragtag demonstrators to use a phone set up at the edge of a scarred field. Her calf muscles screamed with fatigue.

"Livia? Listen, there's a guy here driving to New York, give me a ride if I can leave in ten minutes. I don't know what to do. I want to see you, so much to tell. But I gotta get some sleep, teach tomorrow. I'm so sorry. Yeah, I'm all right. Exhausted is all. We went back and forth all night getting food and blankets for the ones keeping the vigil. Crossing the fields and bridges, going around the lines, now we know the Viet Cong can go on infiltrating forever. Did you hear about the tear gas?"

The connection wasn't good. Chloe had to hurry. "I can't hear you very well. Can you hear me? The police said they had no tear gas, but they did. Mean stuff. But the spirit was great—"

Olivia was shouting something about Noah. "Noah? He went home last night with Gabe. Much better, the anxiety fit passed, like the twenty-four-hour flu—"

"Who did he go home with?"

"I said with Gabe. Gabe! He's going to be all right."

"Are you saying Gabe went home with Noah and you stayed?" Now Olivia's voice came sharp.

"It was so chaotic. We were exhausted, especially Noah. We weren't going to get arrested, Gabe didn't see the point of staying."

"And yet you stayed and let Gabe—Chloe, I don't understand you."

Someone behind her in line began to curse softly. Her feet were numb, her legs were begging her. "Livia. I gotta go in a minute. But I have to tell you the most important part. It's so exciting, it's worth everything. They should have stayed, Noah and Gabe—"

"Chloe—"

"Wait, Livia. Just listen, because the press missed this. There were these troops flush up against the kids sitting on the ground, and the kids were trying to talk to them. We all tried, it was a chance in a million. They're victims like everyone else. Some of them so young you could weep. And scared! But they were under orders, wouldn't crack. Then, in the middle of the night, two of them crossed the line and sat down with the demonstrators! They were yanked back and whisked away. Word went around like wildfire—"

"Chloe, I can't listen to this. I can't understand how you—"

"For God's sake, Olivia! This is the most important thing to happen in the whole movement! If the Pentagon can't hold the army, if we can get these guys to start thinking for themselves—don't you understand the implications? I've got to find those two, publish their story. It could stop the war! I still haven't found the people who saw them, but I'm on their trail. I know it wasn't just a rumor—"

"Chloe, shut the hell up!" Olivia shrieked.

"What?"

"Shut up, shut up, shut up! I can't listen to this. You sound completely crazy. You miss the point of everything. I don't understand you at all!" Olivia seemed on the verge of tears.

"What? Olivia?" In the silence, she was afraid she'd hung up. "Are you worried about Noah and Gabe? Livy, they're not going to mind when they hear—"

"Chloe. I can't talk." And Chloe heard her gasp between breaths. Was she crying? "I'm going home."

"Home?" For a minute Chloe couldn't remember what the

word meant. She repeated it desperately. "Home? Home? You mean—"

"It's Hannah. She's too upset. I can't take a chance."

"Home? To Karl, you mean?"

"To Karl. We've been talking all weekend."

"I don't understand. You were going to stay. Sort yourself out. What about the shrink tomorrow?" she asked hoarsely, as if Olivia had simply forgotten her appointment.

"You're not listening. Hannah's wild. We have to work it out there so she can stay in school. I don't know what's going to happen."

"Oh, shit!" Chloe yelled. "How's it going to help Hannah if you—you can't do it this way, Livy! You can't go back. What about your life? What are you doing to your life?"

"Damn you, Chloe, if it's *my* life—"

"Livia, say you won't go!" Chloe fought for calm. Her eye swept the line of stony faces stretching behind her like a defeated army. "Not like this. I don't know how in the world I can get back to you—"

"Don't. I have to go." And Olivia hung up the phone.

October 1967–
November 1969

In the next days the thought of Chloe sent the blood pounding to Olivia's head. She heard again Chloe's voice on the phone, raw with fatigue and ecstatic with the fantasy of renegade soldiers. That high—how she goes after it, like an addict!—the more abstract, invisible, the better. Real people she doesn't want, least of all those she knows, Noah, Gabe, even— *especially*—me. Chloe would reform me out of existence.

Then Olivia raged at herself for having trusted Chloe, having imagined her capable of really seeing her point of view. Chloe was trapped inside her own passionate obsessions. What about your life? she had howled. How did she dare? Ruthless! A blackmailer in her zeal to rescue.

Inevitably, outrage crested and ebbed, and Olivia saw her own injustice, her partial vision. Finally she was numb. As she turned her energy to her marriage, she thought she had forgotten Chloe.

Two weeks later she realized she had not. For as long as she could remember, Olivia had loved to stand in the shower, turn the water on hard, and listen to the sound of the rain on her own roof. When she was six and Andy four, she explained to him that for children to grow, they needed showers as much as supper. As steam filled the bathroom, she would slide into peace, and beneath the benign drumming on her skull hear her own feelings. Even Hannah learned young that she interrupted her mother's long showers at her peril. Now what swam under Olivia's lids, closed against the hot water, was the outline of Chloe's scowl of concern in the dressing room, in the bar, her lips pursed, asking, What? Olivia found herself musing aloud, as if she were showing Chloe something.

"Like, take today," she argued under the water. "Wasn't that decent? He's trying, he *can* think of someone else! He sees Hannah, how rough it is for her. And he did something. This afternoon while I was teaching, he took her to buy a fish tank, a forest of plants, and six tropical fish—they each chose three, like equal partners. Then they set up the tank together, and Karl talked to Hannah more than he had for a long time." About what? How he liked their flat eyes. Why? "Hannah stood there, agreeing with everything he said."

"Ruse," she hissed under the beat of water ten days later. The sharing of the fish hadn't lasted a week. "You feed them too much, Hannah," Karl had said, taking over. "You'll make them sick." Then, when Hannah sat on the couch to watch the fish with him, Karl became so still, so absorbed, that she soon left and went into the kitchen to sit near her mother. The next time he sat rooted there, Olivia stood behind him watching the Siamese fighting fish sail from wall to wall in that smeared green water, flinging his cloud of blue tail after him. And today, when Olivia came home early, Karl was not in his studio. He had fallen asleep on the couch facing the tank, body curled, mouth open. The fighting fish was still measuring his cell. "Despair." Olivia said the name in the shower. Under her lids Chloe's face was sad, like when she said, And what about you? "All right," Olivia said. She would see about help.

A month later, hot tears flowed before the shower was warm. "Long, long, long ago, should have started," she told

Chloe. With the therapist today, Karl had suddenly seen how sealed off he was, and terror made his lips gray. Then he cried in great dry heaves, just like that time early in their marriage, so long ago, when they were hopeful. "When he breaks like that, when he breaks like that, when he breaks," her own voice drummed. "Nothing, nothing, nothing." Chloe peered, mouthing, What? "I," she answered. "Am nothing, grudge nothing, withhold nothing." But her arms ached from not holding him right there in the office. At home her throat ached from waiting for him to speak to her. The hot stream worked at the soreness in her shoulders, and she caught some water in her mouth and held it there.

Their next session with the therapist precipitated three sleepless days of talk, mostly Karl's. Fear chased fear too fast for him to heed Olivia. He paced the house, following and talking at her, or making her follow him, falling silent only when Hannah carefully entered the room. Then he'd walk the roads to come back dogged by a new fear. He couldn't paint, couldn't remember how, couldn't eat, couldn't fuck, couldn't care, never could, couldn't touch, couldn't keep people in mind, couldn't remember them sometimes, couldn't see—and that seemed to be the worst—he could barely *see* anymore! Then, suddenly, he slept. He slept two nights and a day. Olivia got up to take Hannah to school, then returned to bed. After she'd held him for an hour, he reached for her, rolling half his body on hers. Her flesh quickened from head to toe, but he was only heavy, his chest and belly cool and lifeless. Olivia lay still, taking his dead weight and willing her blood to quiet, until it was time to get up and go teach her afternoon class. "Like abandoned children," Olivia whispered in the shower, "we lay." Chloe's face said, Like you and Andy. "Yes," said Olivia, "I made myself young. A sister."

"Closing up, shutting down, fending off," the water drummed the next morning. "Worse than ever before." Because when Karl came out of that sleep at five in the morning, he said, "I'm going to the studio." After driving Hannah to school, Olivia stopped by the converted garage where he worked. Karl met her at the door, saying, "Don't come in just now. Please." Happiness made him gentle. "I think I'm just starting something." Olivia turned on her heel, speechless, but she called out from the car that she would pick him up in two hours to go to the therapist. She was at home stripping for her shower when the phone rang. "Olivia," Karl said. "Don't come. I can't go today. I can't stop now. I've just gotten started. You know how important that is to me." The kindness was gone, and Karl's patience was wired to a time bomb. Panic made Olivia rigidly polite. She asked what to do about their appointment. He said, "Don't ask me that, Olivia. You go if you want."

In the shower, Chloe's face grieved. "Painting is the beginning of everything for him," Olivia pleaded. "I should be glad. Everything may follow from this." But Chloe's face didn't change. Its look said, What about you?

"Hannah said it." Olivia's voice spoke against the driving water on Christmas night. She said it at Karl's studio, where he asked them to come at last, Olivia and Hannah, to see what he'd been painting. He was being nice to Hannah, finally alert to her wildness after she plunged down a hill on her sled and smashed her arm against a tree. Three large canvases stood against the wall, the beginning of a new series, striations of ochre and purple, a canyon, a chasm, and a desert. All rock, only rock, no growth, no sky, no water. No peace. Hannah was the first to respond. She shoved up the sleeve of her sweater, baring the violent colors of her elbow. "She said it," Olivia told Chloe in the shower. "Daddy, look, they're like my bruise."

Karl's hand flew to his mouth as if he were stricken, but Olivia saw he was covering a smile. "Deep pleasure, the kind he rarely took in me." It was all so clear. "He's found his pain and he wants to marry it."

Chloe often groaned aloud when she thought of Olivia that fall and winter. Her frantic flight back to Karl in the face of all she had come to know and feel shocked her each time she recalled it. And the memory of Olivia's wrestling with herself tormented her. It was like a gift—confiding her trouble and letting Chloe work at it—now withdrawn. Olivia's reserve was deeper than she had known. And she had fled, dynamiting the path behind her.

The first week back in New York, Chloe phoned people all over the country, seeking someone in the demonstration's diaspora who had seen the soldiers cross the line at the Pentagon. She called before, after, and between her classes. She phoned late at night and set her alarm to try again early in the morning. It was maddening. She found eight people who swore it had happened, though they had not seen it themselves. Once, listening in a half-sleep to a phone ringing interminably somewhere in Wisconsin, Chloe had an uncanny feeling it was Olivia she was really hunting. She dismissed the notion as the work of fatigue. In their infinite regress, the soldiers grew smaller and smaller. They became toy soldiers. They became gunsmoke.

Even if their defection wasn't real, she argued in the insomniac night, the point is, it might have been. The scared faces of the boy soldiers nearest her at the Pentagon burned in the dark. Nothing but khaki cloth set them apart from the kids who would do almost anything to free them from fear. How many of those soldiers might be lying awake now, dreaming of cross-

ing the line! If the whole thing was a group hallucination, she
thought, more power to the group. Their revolutionary imagination would make the deserting soldiers real. It was only a
matter of time.

Suddenly, like a tower of matchsticks, the fancy collapsed
and Chloe grieved. But for what loss—the soldiers, or Olivia?

Why, she protested, pounding her pillow—why should I
grieve for her? I've been wrong about her, devotedly and per-
versely wrong, all these years. Projecting on her a misty dream
of growth and truth—a vestige of my James period—sustained
intact even when I put James behind me. And sustained why?
Because of Olivia's beauty, the astonishing intelligence of her
beauty, because she deeply knows me? No more, she moaned,
than that?

Chloe fought pain with anger. *How* does she know me?
Olivia sees only the ways that I'm excessive, preposterous. Who
needs a friend for that? What kind of radical is not willing to be
foolish? What was truly foolish was losing sight of what might
be accomplished. Preposterous was keeping on in the old way
when the world was crashing around your ears.

No matter how she cast it, Chloe couldn't finish the argument, and anger gave way to despair.

Olivia's reproach about Noah rankled. Chloe invited him
over often and, to help him sort out his feelings, fed him heaps
of linguini. There seemed no easing Noah's shame for what he
had done or for his desire to undo it by asking for his draft card
back. "Ignominy either way," he said. While he paced and
pulled at his hands, Chloe felt Olivia's watchful presence. Over
pots of coffee they took apart the crisis in Washington the way
in other years they'd worried the meaning of a poem. "A
syntactical error *en fin*," he said, rolling a cigarette. "I confused
acting with action." Chloe balked. How *do* we change our-

selves, she wondered, if not by plunging, taking the part we want to become? "It's simple," he said at last. "Prison would destroy me." He threw over draft counseling and started going to workshops on nonviolent civil disobedience. "You have to learn everything about your motives," he explained, "or they won't let you play."

Chloe's first arrest effectively drove Olivia from her mind. With three upstate Resistance organizers who had camped in her apartment, she met Noah, Clem, and Frances before dawn on a corner near the induction center. A little family of conspiracy. Since celebrities were blocking the building's entrance on Whitehall Street, Chloe's group was sent to squat on a forlorn side street that Noah said only someone too demented to be draftable anyhow would use to approach the center. Huddled on newspaper on the cold ground, they wondered if they were going to be forgotten. No inductees showed, but police vans and horses did, and Noah, an expert now on nonviolent technique, gave instruction on going limp. Everything was sweet and wholly absorbing—the heaping of triumphant bodies in the van, the good humor of their arresting cop, who flashed his jacket to show them Camus' *Rebel* in his inside pocket, the mass of supporters cheering their arrival in custody, and the scuttlebutt passed down the line of women about frisking protocol: "They snap your bra and make you drop your jeans, but that's all."

The women were put in a cell that seemed full with twenty. Fearing separation, they squeezed to make room for ten, fifteen, twenty more. By ingenious leg folding and back propping, they made themselves comfortable on the cement floor. Dried fruit circulated, and bread and cigarettes were tossed across the human carpet. Someone with a headache found nine offers of aspirin, and better, a slender girl who knew how to make the headache pass by pressing the base of the skull. A general massaging began. Low and off-key, someone started to sing. "Gonna lay down my sword and shield, down by the riverside." Holding Frances' head against her shoulder, Chloe closed her eyes and sank into the deep bosom of a woman whose first arrest had been for opposing American entry into World War II. She smelled of talc and dust. "Ain't gonna study war no more." Chloe felt sleep coming like an extended hand. She lowered herself down the rockface and into its dark rounded palm. "This is the cave of camaraderie," she told Olivia at the warm stone bottom. "This is what I meant."

She woke to cheers. The women were struggling to their feet. "They say there's too many of us to jail, they're going to release us today!" someone cried.

"We've done it!"

"There's too many of us! We'll burst the seams of the joint!"

"Jailbreak!" Frances sighed blissfully.

The women filing out of the cell in front turned and hushed them. To be processed they would be led past the regular male detainees, and speaking to them was forbidden. They were marched swiftly past a bullpen where a stocky brown-skinned matron said, "No talking no talking no talking no talking." Almost all the prisoners were black.

Then they had to wait in a corridor by a cell full of women hanging on to the bars and yelling. The matron drew her stick across the bars, and the women backed away from the clatter. She shook the stick at an ashy black woman with an orange wedge of hair, hips hugged in brief black plastic. "Darlene, you watch that mouth!" she scolded. But her voice softened before a woman small as a child, golden flesh poured in an emerald sheath. "How are you today, Honey?"

Honey dimpled. "Just fine, Miz Moore, how you keeping?"

Miz Moore moved on down the line of demonstrators, herding them against the wall.

Darlene was the first to press back to the bars. Her long arm shot out, her liquid eyes swept the line, her whisper crackled. "Hey, baby, you got some reefer for me?"

All at once pink palms and brown knees broke between the bars the length of the cell. The room was raucous with requests. A leggy hooker fixed her bloody eye on Chloe. "C'mon, darlin', cop me a drink."

From thirty feet away, Miz Moore barked them into silence. A torpor fell over the cell and the passageway. The two rows of women eyed each other across five yards of concrete. Under the hostile longing in the prisoners' gaze, Chloe felt her group stripped to their whiteness and mobility. The younger hookers stood with their arms laced around each other. A couple of the demonstrators resumed their shoulder massages. Honey watched from under drooping fuchsia lids. "Oooh, mama," she bleated softly, doing a little shimmy at the bars. "Do it to me!" Frances strode abruptly to the cell and whispered something to the startled woman, who turned and offered her nape. Frances worked her neck and shoulders through the bars, and Chloe heard Honey coo. Darlene was watching, hand slung on shot hip, sucking her teeth.

"Here come Miz Moore," someone hissed, and Frances scooted back into line. Her black eyes blazed in her white face. Miz Moore came and stood in the space between them, looking from Frances to Honey, clucking. Then she reached into the cell and cupped Honey's cheek in her hand. Honey lifted her lids slowly.

"Okay, move out," Miz Moore said sharply to the demonstrators. Chloe looked back. Honey's face was blank and Darlene's purple lips composed. Arms crossed, she nodded coldly, beyond surprise or expectation.

Chloe could not recover her good feeling or share Frances' giddy pleasure in her defiant gesture. There was too much Frances was ignoring. While she was being processed, Chloe was surprised by the gentle way the officer took each finger in turn and rolled the print off onto the paper. She reproached herself: You can appreciate these things only because it's your first arrest and you're not going to do time. In the courtroom, her spirits were lifted for a while by their sheer numbers and the comic exasperation of the judge as he released them on their own recognizance. Then her dismay spread. Everything had gone too smoothly, there was no real opposition, no edge of peril. The war seemed less real than before.

Spent though she was, Chloe slept badly that night. Olivia joined Darlene, Miz Moore, and Honey nodding coldly in every corner of the room. You miss the point of everything, Chloe, they said.

When Gabe came over early the next morning with a sack of bagels and the *Times* folded back to the story on the demonstration, Olivia spoke through him. "What? You weren't going to tell your parents?" His astonished hands knocked over the carton of orange juice. He grinned. Gabe always got a kick out of Chloe's quandaries. She wondered sometimes—did he take her seriously? After a quarrelsome day with the welfare rights people, Chloe's projects refreshed his spirit, he once said, teeth glinting in his beard. Like the panels of stained glass he uses to brighten up his apartment, she thought. But now he stuck by his point. "You've gone to all this trouble to get maximal publicity, to make people think. And you've succeeded. And now you hope your father doesn't pick up the *Times* in Syracuse! Whatever did you do it for?" Gabe mopped the juice, poured the coffee, and leaned back in the sunny chair, ready to be entertained.

Chloe deprived him. "You're absolutely right. I'll write to them. No, I'll call. I'll call tonight."

But she didn't. Instead she tried to start a letter to Olivia. But she couldn't write a word, she realized, until she had called her parents. And she kept putting it off.

Olivia broke the silence. It was a day when heavy snow threatened, a day at the stony heart of the Portland winter when a hard dry wind was blowing from the east. Driving down into the Willamette valley, she saw the complex of arterial highways undulating to the rhythm of the new bridge. The span across the river was finished, but there was only one approach and no exit. The cables of the half-made ramps waved in midair like tendrils, like antennae seeking connection, she thought, thrilled. Sole witness, Olivia sped down the road. Then, as if in an aerial shot of the scene, she saw herself, a woman in a car driving into a valley, a woman who might have missed this vision of the bridge and kept a wounded man so before her eyes that she forgot life itself. She wanted to sing. After so many years, she could summon only a few phrases of Bach. She switched on the car radio, but everyone was obsessed with the coming storm, and she turned it off. Thinking suddenly of Chloe, she missed her with the clear intensity that belongs to a blue summer sky.

Her high mood was ebbing fast by the time Olivia reached her apartment, but she wrote to Chloe anyhow. "They're expecting a record-breaking storm, but all I feel is thaw." Oh, but what if Chloe didn't? She tore it up. Better to start with what Chloe would most want to know. "We had a little remission, Karl and I, but the whole business was terminal." She wrote quickly, racing with the weather.

"We went together to a therapist. There were days when I thought it would work, moments when Karl was suffering, but I found out eventually that the suffering has little to do with me and I can do nothing to help it." Olivia paused, astonished: it was perhaps that simple.

"We were both afraid of losing something, but the things were different, I guess. A few sessions unfroze his painting, and he was incredibly relieved, but then he was afraid more therapy would make him lose it again. He refused to go back. He wants to hoard the pain, like a great natural resource. I didn't know there were so many ways for a guy to say 'I can't.' It's all clear enough: his painting is more important than everything else combined. Seeing it that way at last, really sitting and looking at it, made everything I had done seem different. (It's like what you were trying to explain in the Japanese restaurant, the moment when everything gets redefined, I realize it now!) For years I thought I was helping, but I was pouring myself into a bottomless pit. It bore in on me today I don't want that anymore. I want connection with someone who will meet me halfway.

"I'm the one calling it quits. This is *crucial* for me. Karl's about to move out, he can take a room in the house next to his studio. The nights I teach he'll stay with Hannah. She's very upset, but I'm gambling on her feeling better now that things are clear. The days are numbered for Michael's program, and I've got to find more work anyhow. I'm trying to pick up classes for spring term at some of the other colleges around.

"I'm so sorry about the way we parted in Washington. I think of you more often than I can say. This morning you were so close I felt as if I had bought the gold dress after all."

Reading the letter, Chloe was weak with remorse and gratitude. For her their quarrel was tangled up with more and more of her life, but for Olivia it had simply vanished. Olivia was changing her own life, touching at last its hard bottom and pushing off for herself. Chloe was torn between pride and regret that she hadn't had more to do with it.

But Olivia needed work! Chloe rushed to call everyone she knew who might know someone teaching in the Portland area, then strangers recommended by acquaintances. She learned to gear up for their change in tone upon understanding that Olivia had not completed an advanced degree—and they weren't even doing the hiring! When she had a little list of contacts, she added a note to Olivia.

"Good luck with all these bastards. They'll be lucky to get you, but they probably won't know it. As for Karl, I'm glad you took the first step! You don't need to be left behind ever again. He may have found a vein to mine for a while, but he's the one who's losing. I wish I were there with you. I feel so useless here. How are you coping? Are you going on with the therapist alone? I wish I could help with Hannah. How is she doing?"

Chloe paused, acutely aware of the suffering Hannah and her mother must be feeling. Olivia's pain was like a bar between them, and Chloe's inability to really imagine it frightened her. All she knew was to try to mend it, and suddenly her frenetic inquiries seemed like evasions. Is the wish to change things only fear of helpless pain?

Upset, Chloe ended the note and jammed it into an envelope. Then she spotted a letter begun a month before, still in her desk drawer. Hardly relevant, she thought, but she stuck it in with a new note on top of the page: "So you'll know I've been thinking of you too and our fight in Washington. I was a mess then, still am, but it's different." She'll like this mess better, Chloe thought, rereading the old letter.

"I just called my father to tell him I had been arrested for sitting in at the induction center. Both you and your agent in New York, Gabe, have urged me to take this course, and I could no longer deny the sense of it. I hadn't been frightened in the least of the mounted police, but it took me a week to muster the courage to pick up the phone. My mother answered, and my father got on the extension. Livy, it was bizarre. He simply couldn't understand what I was saying. He doesn't track as well as he used to, and he'd read nothing about the demonstration. 'What's that? What's that?' he said. 'You went to watch them induct them? You went to watch them arrest them? Not the soldiers, you say, but the picketers?' 'Simon, just listen!' my mother said, and translated. When he finally got it, all he said was 'That must have been interesting. Has it snowed yet down there?' My mother cracked up. It *was* funny.

"But after I'd hung up, I felt the way I did in Ontario years ago when I had just learned to drive and the brakes failed. A dog ran into the road, I pressed the pedal, and nothing happened. I drove right off the road onto a fairly level field and stopped in a thicket of raspberry bushes. The feeling of free fall, of pressing against nothing, *no resistance!*—it came back so violently I had to lie down on the floor. I felt as if I had done nothing at all at Whitehall Street. It's made me wonder how much I've counted on his opposition to clarify my choice of action."

And who would you be without it? Olivia added, reading the letter late at night. But she was delighted. Chloe was listening to her body at last, learning what she felt. Olivia climbed into bed and began to write: "I'm sorry about your father, but fascinated by your line of thought. I've always thought you and he were symmetrical. If you've needed his opposition to shape your own, you may be more alike than you want to admit. You may take some comfort in this in the long run. And in theory you should be able to make clearer choices now." I'm always lucid for others, Olivia thought, and went instantly to sleep. It was a couple of weeks before she returned to the letter.

"You asked about Hannah. It's not easy to tell. She's so variable, she has me jumping to keep up. I don't know what I'd do without Sharon. I told you about her in Washington, remember, the student so upset from really seeing racism? Now she's racing to make up for lost time, taking all the history she can at Portland State. Hannah and I meet her at a deli near there for supper, then she takes Hannah home while I teach the night shift. It works well for Sharon, who needs the cash, needs to get away from her family, needs to talk to me. I like her, she's tough, and she has a good take on Hannah. Yesterday, when we were waiting outside the deli, Hannah and I had a fight. She's so angry with me about Karl and so afraid she'll lose me too that when she saw Sharon coming, she just tore off down the street, took a great slide on the ice, and cracked her chin open. When we'd mopped her up, Sharon told her that after you cut your chin you become brave. Hannah just looked at her, drank it in, and took her hand to go back to the deli. She's so suggestible, so utterly at all our mercies, it was all I could do to keep from running off and bawling myself. When I got home, Sharon said I should be thankful Hannah's so scrappy. I think she wishes she'd started fighting that young herself."

Hannah will manage, Chloe thought, but Livy says nothing about Karl, Michael, the therapist, or her own feelings. Olivia's notion that Chloe and her father might meet with comfort was outlandish. Like two cars whose brakes failed simultaneously meeting in a field and scorching raspberry bushes for acres around.

"I haven't spoken to my parents again," she wrote in March. "I suppose my father is just getting old, wearing out. As for 'clearer choices'—I worry. The Tet offensive proves the NLF and the Viet Cong know how to make choices clearly enough. But nothing I'm doing seems right. It's as if you're always at my elbow asking, 'Is this a clear choice for you? Clearer than before?'

"I'm getting great people on the radio, a Vietnam veteran, a *black* Resistance organizer, SDS types and others who think resistance isn't political enough. Each of their choices seems clear to me, but I don't know where I stand. For interviews, I don't have to know, and I used to think the format was perfect—it legitimates my nosiness and forces me to stay at a remove. But now I feel like I'm cheating.

"And then draft counseling—we rescue the desperate and the clever, but we also insure that more of the poor and the black get shipped to Vietnam. Gabe helped set us up in a storefront in Harlem, but almost no one came, and some were hostile, as if we were sneaking in a new way of talking them out of a living. We sat up there three Saturdays, then we closed up shop.

"I don't know, Livy. I saw Gabe the other day. Welfare rights is petering out, but he's hanging in. He says no one ever said it was supposed to be easy, that's why it's called *struggle*. I can grasp that, but I feel sunk. I'm getting sour. Johnson's not going to run, great, but where does that leave us? Can't go gaga for McCarthy, can't believe in Bobby, can't quite cry revolution with the students. The danger out there is more ferocious than ever, and meaningful (to me) options scarcer. It's harder than ever to know what to teach my students, and it looks like Noah, who takes a strong line, may not be reappointed. The dean hates his guts. Clearer choices, huh? And how about you?"

* * *

Good God, Olivia fumed, now she's measuring herself
against the Viet Cong. But she was pleased by Chloe's puzzle-
ment. She scrawled a postcard.

"Who says sour isn't clear? Hannah's all right and I'm okay.
It's just incredibly hard to write."

The next day a letter and a package arrived for Hannah, a
box of bright squares of paper and a book about origami. Chloe
lives out her sweetness on a level she can't credit, Olivia
thought. Sharon and Hannah were bent over the book when
Olivia left to teach, and when she came home, she found a lime-
green crane suspended on a thread above her pillow. Chloe had
repeated her questions: How did Olivia feel? Was she talking to
anyone, friend or therapist? Olivia sprawled under the crane
and made a list.

"1. The family therapist believes in marriage, not separation.
He won't see halves of couples: alone, I'm invisible.

"2. Two friends have suggested other therapists, but I can't
afford them and have no time. I teach four nights now.

"3. I saw Michael and it was awful. He avoids me. He
doesn't want me as a friend. It turns out I don't want that
either.

"4. A couple of men at my jobs are all excited about my
separation. They see me as half-person they can make whole.
But their eyes glaze over when I mention Hannah. Moral:
Separated mother who thinks she can confide in man is not just
separated, she is dissolved.

"5. I let it all out to a good friend here, a woman, and
afterwards Hannah could see I'd been crying. She blames herself whenever I cave in. Fatherless child needs double mother,
not half-person.

"6. Andy wised up Esther, who dashed off a note saying it
was 'a pity to lose such a gloriously handsome man!' She hinted

that I should expect less of marriage, adopt the French model—i.e., take lovers. She never stayed with any man as long as I've been with Karl, but she can't get over her disappointment in me for *losing* Karl. (She wrote Karl to tell him she would always consider him her son.)

"7. A student who likes to talk to me in my office said I'm a good therapist. So all I need is myself, right?

"8. I sit by myself and watch the fish Karl left behind. No need for talk. They swim around in the unconscious.

"9. I talk to you in the shower."

Then Olivia tore up the list. She stripped and went into the bathroom. "Chloe," she said before she even turned on the water, "shut up."

"Why don't you write me, Livy?" asked Chloe in June. "Do you have to be wearing the gold dress to communicate with me? That would be a fat irony, wouldn't it—if we dare show only what the other wants to see? I expect things are rough, but I want to know." I do, too, she told herself.

"Noah got the boot, and I'm about to get tenure. Imagine how compromised I feel passing their muster when he didn't. I should get out of this wretched place. A friend of mine says I have it backwards—thinking tenure means they have me in their clutches instead of my having them. But having them is having nothing, and these days it seems shameful to be secure. Noah's going into full-time organizing. He's in better spirits than I am. I used to say that understanding literature and doing politics were the same—learning to make connections, see the thing whole, and trust your vision. But I feel the gap something awful.

"I'm half ashamed to write you about my troubles when you don't yours. But I send this to set you an example."

* * *

In July, Olivia sent a postcard. "Bad times, couldn't write. Writing underscores everything. I think I've found a terrific therapist. Things are looking up. Forgive. Letter follows. Write to me."

The letter didn't follow.

Chloe knew she should be happy Olivia had someone to talk to, but she felt shut out. She reminded herself of Olivia's predilection for solitude—that's what she'd loved in Pavese. In those ignorant days Chloe had believed she liked solitude too.

When she talked it over once with a friend, the woman said, "Why don't you just write again? Or call her?" Chloe only said she couldn't. She understood then the depth of her fear: she might actually lose Olivia. In a dream Olivia appeared frail as bone china, and Chloe knew that to touch would be to violate her.

Besides, Chloe had nothing to say. Clem had gone to jail, and after an evening of trying to buoy up Frances, Chloe went home and wept. The Resistance, like everything else, was dividing under the strain, and when she was tired, she felt scored by the shards of things she had once dreamed whole. One night, at a late meeting, the arguments became pure noise, and for an unclockable moment Chloe could identify no one. It was like the bad afternoons in Rome before Olivia had rescued her, except that then the outer world, though alien as a postcard, had kept its coherence. Now the jeopardy was general, and escape without meaning. Olivia had never seemed more remote. How strange, then, and beyond all earthly use, was the memory that surfaced through half-sleep, of the afternoon at the coast when Hannah went after her raging mother—only it was Chloe who crept into the circle of Olivia's limbs.

* * *

"Are you still there, Chloe?" Olivia wrote in October. "I had a dream I was standing at a train station, somewhere in Sicily, and one of those funny little trains came along. You were sitting at the window looking at everything with the greatest excitement, everything but me. The train slowed down, but it didn't stop. I didn't even call out." Olivia had trouble remembering dreams, but this one wouldn't be shaken, try as she would. "Why I couldn't write: Karl wanted to try it again. Hannah wanted us to. I was very wary. It turned out he came back because he was too puzzled by himself. He counts on me to tell him his secret—as always. Odd. The very thing that drew me to him in the first place drives me away now. Other people's secrets draw me these days. I have a teaching job with some counseling on the side. I love it more than any teaching. At best, it's like getting another person to unriddle his mystery. Sounds cerebral, but it's not. I may be saving my own neck in this work. And (surprise) it makes Karl nervous that I do it. I told him to leave. He said, 'Oh, I was just going.' But I had said it first."

Setting it down alarmed her. What if it was another illusion. She tore up the letter.

"No illusion, he's gone and staying gone, and I'm fine," Olivia told Chloe in the shower some weeks later. "But Hannah is paying." She got into bed and started a letter.

"Last week Hannah hurt herself three times. Then, on Friday, when I kept her home with a cold, she refused her crayons, her most ancient consolation. Not thinking, I coaxed her to draw a picture for me, and her refusal was so emphatic I had to respect it. It's taking me longer to figure it out. She's always made me pictures and presented them to me with some ceremony. I've guessed she was partly emulating Karl, and competing, too. Because Karl's painting has been a strong bond between us. She's seen how intense he is when he gets me to look at his work, she's looked at it with me since she was a babe in arms. Her own work is very dear to me—it's gorgeous and unpredictable like the thing you saw at the A-frame. I realized long ago I have a responsibility to protect that wild invention of hers from being socialized away. This refusal to draw worries me. Is she too angry to give me anything? Or does she think painting is cursed, destroying what it meant to bind? She must have hated painting as a rival. Now she may despise it for its failure. Whatever the reason, it's borne in on me how she's suffering."

A month later Olivia found the letter in the drawer of her bed table. She wrote on the back, "A reason not to send these scraps: everything changes. I didn't know what to do. I wanted to tell Hannah she didn't have to draw for my sake, but the words stuck in my throat. I loved those gifts and was sure she missed making them too. Everything I thought of was clumsy, too direct. She clamped shut and I sank down beside her, waiting. We brooded together for a month or more. Then she lost another tooth.

"Every time she loses a tooth, she leaves it with a note under her pillow for the tooth fairy, specifying the candy she wants the fairy to leave. Hannah plays by strict rules: she shows me the tooth, but her communications are only with the tooth fairy, and I have to be on my toes to get tooth and note out and candy under before she wakes up. This time the tooth fell out of her pocket before bedtime. She couldn't find it and went to bed worried, but she let me see her tuck a fold of paper under her head. As soon as she was asleep, I retrieved it. On the outside it said, 'For the tooth fairy (just for the tooth fairy),' and inside, 'Dear Tooth Fairy: My tooth fell out, and I don't know where it is. So please, can you see if you can do something about it anyway? Love, Hannah.' The tooth fairy came through with the goods, and Hannah looked very pleased the next morning. That night I checked under her pillow again. There *was* something, a wonderful drawing of the tooth fairy shooting sparks and rockets, and the message 'I love you tooth fairy.' My ingenious girl had found a way out of our impasse! The drawing was replaced again by candy. For three more nights now, we have kept up our own outlaw game (no teeth change hands)—I'm so relieved, so admiring."

"You had a problem in magic and, between you, found a magical solution!" Chloe wrote swiftly. It was Olivia she admired, her gift for empathetic hibernation, for hunkering down to Hannah's size to wait out her pain and bewilderment. I could never do that, she berated herself. Selfish, selfish. She wanted to tell Olivia how sharply she'd been missing her. Sometimes Olivia's absence was palpable, a column of air beside her. But her longing seemed regressive. She finished the letter and sent it, prepared herself for silence and got it.

I should write Chloe, Olivia told herself, driving to work the next summer. The way things unfolded with Amy—Chloe would want to know. She rehearsed a letter in her head.

Amy. Her daughter and Hannah so close all this while, and I'd never troubled to know her. Wrote her off like those Arizona wives. Mother of four, aspiring as far as the next hairdo. But her look one day when she dropped off her child made me offer coffee. In the pantry, so the girls wouldn't hear, face in her hands, fighting for breath: "Just got back the test results. I waited two months, we were using protection! I can't stand to have another. Impossible to tell Jack."

I remembered a journalist friend, furious with her own findings: "You need two psychiatrists to certify you have suicidal tendencies—I made the rounds with a woman, saw her rejected by *seven* before she found two who would. And then you begin the long hunt for a willing doctor and—good luck—for a hospital." She quit the paper and opened her own abortion referral service. When I told Amy, she straightened right up, utterly calm: "How do I reach her?"

That night, looking at Hannah asleep, two thoughts abruptly clear in the dark: the rightness of my own abortion (only the way it happened wrong), the absolute rightness of Hannah. And one question: By what grace do my fumbling non-choices work their way to sense?

Amy had to move fast. She learned her options. To keep her husband ignorant was to forgo his health insurance, their joint account. "I thought I had everything. In fact I'm poor. All they can do is send me up the hill." A wan smile for my bafflement. "That's the medical school. Where the welfare mothers go." Was she punishing herself? I worried until I picked her up.

"It's over. The worst part was the exposure—so many people!—and finding we were only teaching tools." Shaky and white-lipped, but vivid in a way I'd never seen. "I'm all right. I got something no one can take away." She made me understand. "Because I'm a woman, I'm poor and powerless." She'd found a starting point, the only real one in her life.

And yesterday—Olivia spotted a parking place—Amy went to work as a volunteer at the referral place. I really must write Chloe.

In August, Chloe wrote to Olivia again.

"I'm in Ontario at the place I've told you about—the cottage my great-grandfather built on the St. Lawrence River. I've just put my parents on the plane, and Gabe won't arrive until tomorrow. I'm exhausted but can't sleep. Wish I could talk to you. I've felt bad all year that you haven't written, but I can't bear being alone right now, so I write for my own sake. Since my father's seventy-first birthday my mother has been telling me he was deteriorating, losing his memory and his wits, and then he got fixated on going up to the cottage. She asked me to go ahead to open it for them and spend a few days together. I haven't been here for a decade, so I drove up. I had a full day to take down the shutters, put up the screens, start up the pump, clean out the wasp and mouse nests, air everything out, bring in firewood and supplies, and I got up the next morning to swim as the sun rose, incredibly happy. Then I went to meet them at the airport.

"I was completely unprepared. The airport here is tiny, and they take the luggage out of the belly of the little plane as the people climb down the steps. Before I could get to him, my father had seized someone else's luggage, and when my mother protested, he swung it, trying to hit her. Right then and there my proper mother forced two big Valiums into his mouth like a farmer dosing a horse. We got him into the car somehow, and as I was fastening him in place—thank God for seat belts!—he fixed me with his eye and confided sadly, 'I'm afraid your mother has gone berserk!' Have I told you he has the fiercest big monitory eye? I say 'eye' because you really can only bear to look at one at a time. My mother snickered, but I was in stitches. I started off down the road feeling a kind of lush excitement that made no sense, as if we were launched on a fabulous adventure, as if—this sounds crazy, but you have to take my word for it—we were a family at last.

"But I was still unprepared. The Valium took hold, and we had a reasonable evening, sitting outdoors, watching the ships in the channel. My father got calm and cogent. He told old stories about how his uncle, during Prohibition, used to watch for a flag on the American side and row across the river at night loaded so heavily with crates of bootleg liquor that you could barely see the gunwales. I used a technique I've cultivated in the last few years to get through visits to Syracuse—I think of him as someone else's father, crotchety, salty, engaging. He went to sleep early, and my mother and I washed up and collapsed half an hour later.

"I woke up suddenly to the sound of my mother pleading, 'Don't go, Simon,' then shouting, 'Simon! Wait!' It was still dark, though the sky was whitening, and by the time I got up, he was going down the path through the woods, tying his grandfather's oriental silk robe around him. My mother was running after him in slippers and gown, tugging on her raincoat. I took off after them barefoot. I could tell he was leading us into some different time frame, because we never use that old path since we built the laneway. The path used to lead to the farm where his childhood friend Eddie lived. And sure enough, when I said, 'Where are you going?' he said, 'To the farm, to see Eddie.' I said, 'Dad, don't you remember? The farm is gone. Eddie lives in the village now!' He stopped in his tracks, turned slowly, and drew himself up to what seemed (he's no taller than me) a magnificent height. He managed somehow to look down on me, his eye more formidable than ever, and said, 'You! Go home and write a dissertation!' I looked at my mother. 'He says we locked him up, we're trying to steal from him. I don't think we can dissuade him, darling.' He went on down the path, slippers flapping, bone-white legs flashing, skinny but strong.

"Since the path now ends at the highway, we decided she should follow him and I should go back, get the car, and cut him off. I slipped jeans on over my pajamas and took off. I was scared, but I felt a manic thrill again, like at last I was in on it. In for the kill, I almost wrote. There was something of that. I felt like a cowboy going to head off the varmint at the pass. But he went so fast that by the time I reached the highway, he and my mother were already there, stooped in their nightclothes, arguing at the edge of it. The highway confused him. It didn't fit with the time when there had been a farm.

"I drove up, but I shouldn't have. My father summoned all his resolve and strode away down the shoulder of the highway. I swooped around and threw the car door open in front of him. I said I would drive him to Eddie's. He said, 'Bah!' and slammed the door, with the ultimate curse: 'Oh, go home and talk to your father!' Then, cagily, he stepped right in front of the car and across the highway to walk on the other shoulder. It was light now. There still wasn't much traffic, but my mother and I were frightened. Those trucks expect an empty highway and barrel along. He was heading toward the little road on the other side of the highway that leads to where Eddie lives now. We followed on foot, praying he had remembered that. When he got to the road, he hesitated. A big van thundered by, sucking us after it, and my mother yelled, 'Go up the road, Simon, for God's sake! That's the way to Eddie's!' 'You are a false wife,' he said sorrowfully, 'and you,' to me, 'have nothing to do with me!'

"I was finally terrified. And when he set off again along the highway, I told my mother to follow him quietly while I drove as fast as I could to Eddie's house. Farm or no, Eddie is still a farmer, and he was up. He grasped it all immediately. 'Let me get my hat,' he said, and we were off. My father was still tearing along, half a mile further down the highway, his ragged robe splendid in the rising sun, and my mother was trotting behind.

As we pulled alongside, Eddie hailed him in his gruff basso voice, so warm. 'G'day, Simon.' My father stopped, and when Eddie climbed out, he grinned like a kid. 'Eddie! Am I glad to see you! They were all trying to lock me up! How are you?' Then he glanced left and right and lowered his voice: 'Let's go to your place.' Eddie was brilliant. He stood there smiling too, hands in his pockets tugging down at his suspenders, hat tipped forward. 'Hell! Ain't nobody *at* my place. Let's go to yours. Let's go see Jean and Chloe.' My father looked at Eddie uncertainly, repeated his request, and Eddie spat tobacco before answering in the same good-humored way. 'Oh, all right,' my father said, completely at ease now. 'You want to walk or ride?' Eddie asked. My father gave me an utterly neutral look. 'Let's ride!' he said grandly.

"My mother and I made the men a big breakfast like a pair of farm wives while Eddie pulled my father back into the world. I've always loved this old farmer. He's never left the province, he's reactionary and bigoted, but his instinct is surer than the most worldly man's. Stirring the eggs, I had a passionate wish to ask him to be our father, father for all of us. He left eventually, but only after everything was calm. We got through the rest of the day quietly, my father taking his Valium so docilely we weren't sure it was necessary. We acted like a gentle kindly little family, but it didn't upset me or make me cynical like my performances in Syracuse.

"Livy, I feel as if I've just swum two miles, across the river and back. There's more to tell, especially a horrifying little encounter yesterday afternoon, which also fills me with wild energy. But it's too much, and I don't need to tell it now. They've gone and I feel burned clean, as though I'm shedding light. What a mystery! I'm not at all frightened as I was when I began the letter, thanks to you, Livy. Good night. I love you."

* * *

Why thanks to me? Olivia wondered. And why such manic joy, so little pain? But she wrote, "Of all the wonderful stories you've told me all these years, this is the one I love most. Thanks for writing it to me—especially after I've been so out of touch. I never understood before how mad your father could be. From such a man I don't wonder you've had so much trouble. I trust your mother is getting some medical help with him? It's like one of those great nightmares where everyone is truer than life. You and your mother both were very brave. I didn't realize she had such dimension, such humor. The harmony between you! Cherish it." If I'd had that for five minutes with Esther! she thought.

"How much you find out by writing! It's not that way for me. Writing's only salt in the wounds. But *you* should keep at it—I never knew you could write like that! And I want to know what you were too tired to write, the 'horrifying little encounter' that filled you up with energy. And you mention Gabe—are you together again?"

Olivia had no stamps and put the letter aside. A large book was set down on it, and when she found it again weeks later, she put off sending it until she could write more. In November she had a short note from Chloe.

"Dearest Livia, my father died last week in his sleep. He was in a nursing home these last two months, mostly out of his head, so we can't be sorry he's gone. But there were moments of the strangest lucidity, which left us with a lot."

Olivia wept for the abyss that opened between her and Chloe, then for the formality of the note and her own failure to send off her letter, then for Chloe's closeness to her mother betokened by her unconscious "we," and finally for her own losses, father and mother. She dialed Chloe's number for the first time since her flight to Washington two years earlier.

"I'm *sor*-ree," the operator in New York sang without a trace

of regret, "that *num*-ber has been discon-*nec*-ted." Panic
stopped Olivia's tears. Heart pounding, she got the operator to
find Gabe's number. It had been changed. Chloe answered, but
the connection was bad, and she sounded distant besides.

"I've been living here with Gabe since the summer. How are
you? How's Hannah?"

Olivia said they were fine. "I'm so sorry I haven't written. I
actually did write after your wonderful letter but didn't get
around to sending it. It's inexcusable. I feel terrible." Chloe
murmured something unintelligible and fell silent. Swamped
in sudden shyness, Olivia asked how Gabe was. Chloe's voice
began to come alive.

"He's been great. We're working together right now. We've
moved into this old building off Franklin Street. Below the
Village, below Houston. You know the section of old cast-iron
facades? Old warehouses, streets jammed with trucks? All these
buildings were slated for demolition, but they've been saved,
people are finding ways to move in and live here. We have a
whole floor of what was a sweatshop. The sewing machines
have been taken out, but there's still a lot to fix up. It's good.
Gabe likes finding out how to do things." She seemed to laugh.
"Here he is now with a crowbar. We're prying bolts out of the
floor—" But she stopped suddenly, as if she'd lost the thread.

Were they going to say nothing about her father? Her
moving in with Gabe? Or their friendship? Olivia felt the
weight of silent seconds. Static broke it. "Your father," she
stammered.

"Small. Just a few friends." She must have thought Olivia
said "funeral." After a pause she added, "Cremation."

Chloe's bitten-off words grieved Olivia more than anything
yet. "Your mother," she tried again.

Now the line produced a metallic echo of Olivia's words.

Through "mother" she heard Chloe saying, "She's okay. She's—all right. We both had plenty of time to get used to it." Was her voice fading again, or was it the connection? "I think she'll do well on her own. She's going to visit her sister in Florida. Maybe she'll stay the winter with her."

"I wish I were there with you," said Olivia, and through the mocking echo, ". . . there with you," she heard Chloe say nothing.

There was a pause, and then they both spoke at once.

"Are you ever going to come here a—" "Are you really all ri—" They both laughed diffidently, then both answered at once.

"Very possibly, because my mother—" "Yes, I've had time to get used—" Then, "What did you say?"

Olivia said, "You finish."

Chloe said, "Never mind, I was just repeating myself." Her old vigor rushed back. "I *hate* talking on the phone. It makes me repeat myself. It makes us unreal. Did you say you're coming east, Livy?"

"I think so. Esther thinks she may have—my mother's not been well, she wants to see me. I think she'll even pay my fare."

Olivia hung up a few minutes later, chilled, her questions shriveled. One remained: What if they should not be able to talk anymore?

January 1970

When Olivia opened the door of her mother's Park Slope apartment, it was like the collision of two pasts. Here was Chloe, a trifle thicker around the middle, her hair grown out again and darkened to khaki, but flamboyant as ever in black turtleneck and red scarf, the same outrageous cheekbones blazing from cold, her head cocked in question. If Olivia were blindfolded and twenty years had passed instead of two and a half, she would know whose was that brusque hug. And there, behind the glass-paneled double doors, was her mother giving a voice lesson. The double doors permitted her to hear, now as twenty years earlier, Esther enthralling yet another student. "No, angel, there's no point in going on this way," she was saying as voice and piano stumbled to a halt mid-phrase. "Feel where I'm pressing. Put your hands on mine, that's right, here, this is the place. Now—do you feel the song? The song starts here or it simply doesn't exist." The rise and fall of Esther's hidden voice, by turns imperious and indulgent, but ever intimate—it was the background music of her adolescence.

Then, leading Chloe by the hand from the foyer through the dining room and kitchen to the maid's room where she was staying, Olivia might have been leading Andy to the point most distant from their mother's luxuriant voice. Ignorant of the ritual, Chloe shattered it.

"How strong she sounds! How dynamic! I expected the opposite."

"*Boh*. She's always strong," Olivia said. "And strongest when she's in trouble." She brought a pot of coffee and two mugs from the kitchen, and they sat at a little table under a shelf heaped with vocal scores. Chloe looked at nothing but her. "How dreadful," she had said on the phone. "Can I see you right now—just, say, for half an hour?" Olivia was overcome. "*Can* you? It would be wonderful!" But now they had to go through it.

"Chloe, thanks so much for coming. I know it's—"

"Forget it. I had to come."

"I feel terrible that I wasn't in touch when your father—"

"It's over with him now, Livia, but your mother—it sounds bad. Tell me."

Olivia had been tense before about this conversation, but a different fear nerved her now. "I will, I'll tell you all about it, but we can't just ignore what's happened between us. If we don't clear it up, nothing we do will be real."

Almost word for word it was what Chloe had said to herself a year before when she thought she had to confront Olivia about her silence. A friendship like ours is over if we duck its difficulty; to have it at all, I have to risk losing it. Then she had recoiled from such rigor, checked in part by her growing sense of Olivia's vulnerability. Our friendship is rare; it has to be shielded from the harshest scrutiny. In the end it was the force of her own need laid bare to her that made the prospect of loss too devastating.

Chloe dealt her a pale, grave look. "I'm not sure it can be cleared up."

"We have to try," Olivia insisted. How strange, she thought, I sound like Chloe, and now she's the doubter. "I feel I hurt you badly."

Chloe's blood swept from neck to scalp. She could put her feelings aside, but discussing them was unbearable. "So why do you want to put me through it again?"

"Because I'm so sorry. I want to be sure you understand—"

"I understand that you're sorry," Chloe said flatly. "Okay?" She picked up a spoon and stirred her unsugared black coffee. In a moment, seeing what she was doing, she dropped the spoon. "What do you want me to say? I felt like an idiot prying apart the mailbox to see if something was stuck in back. When I wrote you about something important and you didn't answer, I'd try to think, Well, we're different, and I'd end up thinking, Yeah, one of us is crazy! Either you've lied to me or to yourself—or I have. Friendship with you is like a test of sanity or a leap of faith! Like, can you believe in the face of all contrary evidence. So I'd force you out of my mind for days at a time—"

Olivia moaned. Whatever her faults, she would never do that to Chloe!

"Do you blame me? It *hurt* too much to think of you."

Olivia tried to grasp it. At her angriest she had never stopped thinking of Chloe. And knowing that Chloe kept her in mind strengthened her hold on reality. Each kept the other fresh in her root cellar. She said nothing, and Chloe relented.

"It didn't work. Every time I took that little metal key in hand, there you'd be again."

Olivia blessed the mailbox key. "I knew I should write," she said. "I knew it mattered to you, but I didn't know how much." I don't have Chloe's need to reach out, she thought.

"I didn't know myself. That winter after Washington, I tried to make it not matter at all. I told myself friendship was a luxury, a false one, and only the people who endured the movement together had a claim on me." This was a cheap shot. That attitude now seemed grotesque to Chloe.

"You were willing to sacrifice me!" Olivia cried, and her guilt fell clean away. "Without a hearing! It's not fair! You had no right, you could have no idea what I was doing—"

With an unhappy laugh, Chloe pounced. "Precisely!"

"Ah, Chloe!"

"That didn't work either," she said hoarsely. "I don't believe it at all. I had other ideas about us"—she wasn't about to disclose her temptation to risk all or her fear of loss—"but none of them covered it."

"Ideas don't have much to do with it," Olivia hazarded. "It's just dumb loyalty."

Chloe looked at her. It wasn't that simple, and Olivia must know it. But her appearance bespoke her fragility. The svelte charcoal dress and careful makeup didn't conceal her gauntness. And her smoky hair, bobbed short for business—emblem of the earnest single working parent—was thinning. Chloe glimpsed the yellow scalp beneath.

Chloe's wan smile was more piercing than any accusation. Olivia had to make her see her side. Did Chloe know what separation was? She understood worry, overwork, distraction, but not the main thing.

"I'd seen myself as Karl's wife too long. I had to find out who I was on my own. I relied enormously on you, on your believing in me, but I had to go it alone."

"Okay, I can see that, but my believing in you—what does it mean?" Chloe laughed shortly. "What was I supposed to believe in? My fading memory of you?"

Olivia winced. She wanted to say, The real me, the inner me, like you always have. But who was that, after all—the long-gone me? the pathetically potential me? Instead she said, "There's another reason too. I've thought about this a lot. I don't have your need to tell, Chloe, to discharge the story. And to talk about some things, I need the comfort of your presence. I wish you could accept this difference. I don't care less than you do. I carry you around with me all the time."

"Now you're unfair," Chloe said, but tenderly. "You don't know who you're carrying unless you're in contact." She sipped her coffee. Comfort of your presence, words like balm. "Please"—she touched Olivia's hand—"how bad is it with Esther?"

Olivia registered the touch, the tone. This was almost forgiveness, the best they could do now. Still shaky, she borrowed her mother's fluency, and Esther's story told itself. She had no symptoms but the tumor—the "neoplasm," the doctor liked to call it—and there was a possibility the biopsy to be done in two days would show it was not malignant, though that would be extraordinary in a woman of fifty-five. Olivia had gone with her mother to Downstate to see Dr. Friedlander the day before. His partisan manner, the feeling he let show in his face, and his unorthodox intelligence won her at once. She knew all about the hereditary risk factor in breast cancer, and if Esther's news proved bad, Olivia would go directly to Friedlander herself. She could tell that Chloe knew nothing about it. Just as well. Her own danger was the last thing she wanted to think about.

"I liked him very much. It's a great stroke of luck that Esther found him." She explained how the first doctor had told Esther she needed a biopsy but had waited till the last minute to mention that she would have to sign a release permitting him to remove the breast if he found cancer.

"The way Esther tells it, she said, 'You mean you wouldn't wake me up to discuss it?' He laughed at her. 'We could have that discussion right now. I could ask you if you'd prefer to live or die.' Esther walked out and has never spoken to him again. She says she only regrets that she didn't laugh back and say,

'And you? Would you rather live or die without your mighty prick?' " Taking Esther's bold words into her mouth made Olivia almost proud of her, until she saw Chloe's face. "What is it?"

"The doctor was a brute. Something about the medical profession is unhealthy for the people it trains. But Esther! What does she—is she willing to take such a chance? To keep her breast?"

"It's incredibly important to her. What counts for her is the impression she makes. By now she's confused the impression with her essence. Obviously she couldn't answer the question. What she did instead was blitz the medical community. She saw a dozen doctors, each more arrogant than the last, all scoffing at her attempt to understand the procedure, let alone alter it. She kept notes on their contradictions and challenged them. Esther has limitless energy for organizing around a crisis, you know. She set about organizing the rescue of her breast as if it were, I don't know"—she threw up her hand—"an Italian Jew!"

"God, Livy! She saw cancer as fascism? But what courage!"

"Yes!" Olivia wanted to give Esther her due. "It's very moving. But it wasn't so much about cancer, her fight. It was against the medical community, the doctors."

"So long as she could turn her rage on the doctors, she didn't have to face the cancer?"

Olivia nodded. It was what she thought.

"It *is* terrifying, isn't it?" Chloe whispered. The way she sagged back in her chair now was something new. Olivia scarcely recognized her face. The look of insistent expectancy that always came with the thought of Chloe was gone. Olivia felt disoriented, and then, remembering what Chloe had been through, ashamed.

"Oh, Chloe, you've been here and back, and I—"

Chloe held up both hands. "Later. We'll talk about all that later. My father was different. Tell me the rest about Esther."

"And then you'll—? Ah, Chloe, I'm so glad we're together again. I can't tell you how much it means!"

"Me too," Chloe muttered awkwardly. She had always loved and envied that husky directness, but now she held back. How could Olivia cover the ground between them so swiftly? Chloe still needed more time, but she wasn't prepared to say so. It was strange to be talking this way, jumping right into the middle of things, after all that had happened. But it was what they had always done. This friendship, thought Chloe with a shock of painful love, will never be perfect, and it will never be over.

At the end of her rope, Olivia was saying, Esther found Dr. Friedlander, who asked if she was sure the lump was not a cyst. "Esther said it made her fall in love with him instantly. As it turned out, it wasn't a cyst—he lanced it and it was solid. The point is, no other doctor had raised the question. They all said 'mastectomy' as if it were the only word they knew. Friedlander told her what no one else had mentioned, that there were two kinds of mastectomy, radical and modified radical."

Startled, Chloe fought back the thronging associations of the terms. Her friend Annie's frantic eyes, when they quarreled about the Weathermen, flashed before her. Modified radical— it could be her own label. Scandalized by herself, Chloe forced her attention back to Olivia.

She was explaining that in both operations the breast and the lymph nodes in the armpit were removed, but only the radical mastectomy took out the muscles of the chest wall as well. The radical, Friedlander said frankly, was mutilating, the modified was not. He referred to Esther's "splendid carriage," which he hoped to preserve if surgery proved necessary. "I think Friedlander is terrific. He took Esther's measure perfectly.

I don't know which matters more, her physical vanity or her belief in her intellectual superiority. But he's working them both. His candor makes her want to match him, to be equal to anything. Last week he asked her, 'Would you deprive your friends of the pleasure of your conversation for a few ounces of fatty tissue?' "

"But he's fantastic!"

"He is. But I don't know how much she's really taking in. She's bravest in front of people she wants to impress—it's all about conquest."

"Ah, Livy," Chloe said, her throat aching. "If she finds a way of being brave, what do you care about her motive?"

Olivia glanced at her sharply. "You've changed."

Chloe had to agree.

"I care," Olivia went on, "because if it's all front, what will prop her up when the reality hits her? Won't she suffer more?"

"She'll suffer in either case," Chloe said.

The French doors opened, and they heard Esther's vibrant voice. Olivia started to her feet and moved involuntarily toward it. Chloe followed, but in the kitchen Olivia held out a detaining arm. They could see Esther's proud back in the foyer, her hands on the shoulders of a young woman with hair scraped back into a ponytail, who stood covering her eyes.

"It's what you always lose sight of, angel, isn't it? We've talked about it so many times, Daphne. You've said it yourself, you live in the shadow of Schubert, wasn't that it, darling? Wasn't that it." The girl's head bobbed, unable to resist the rhythmic force of Esther's remarkable voice, by turns cajoling, bullying, and inspiring.

"And what did I say, angel? I said brava, Daphne, brava. Because there is nothing more splendid than living with great-

ness. Beneath it. In its shadow, angel, precisely in its shadow. *If
we go about it the right way.*" Her stage whisper forced the girl
to uncover her large pale eyes to Esther's. "If we go about it in
the *right* way. Which is not to use greatness as a knife to slash at
ourselves, a light to show us our flaws. We're not to use greatness to make ourselves suffer, and we *mustn't* break our heads
trying to dominate greatness." Here the girl ducked her head
again, but Esther raised it by the chin. "Look at me, darling."
Chloe looked away from the girl's flayed obedience. Olivia's
face was twisted, unreadable. "No. It's not for *us*, greatness, is
it, angel? It's we, the fortunate ones, who are for *it*." From the
way Olivia dropped her lids at that, Chloe knew she'd over-
heard the formula countless times.

Old training had made Olivia pause in the kitchen while
Esther finished her spiel. Once, as a child, in a fury of jealousy,
she had interrupted Esther's talk with another whispery dev-
otee. She would never forget her mother's indignation. But
now she was paralyzed with pity. Esther's performance was
paper-thin. When she had closed the door behind Daphne, her
shoulders slumped, and her face in profile was bland, almost
simple. Chloe was holding her breath, as if she too feared to
intrude on what must be Esther's few moments of rest.

But Esther caught sight of them. Immediately her back
straightened and animation complicated her face. She bustled
forward, both hands extended. "Olivia's Chloe!" she cried
brightly, "come at the perfect time! Lessons over for today!
What a relief!"

Olivia was repelled, but Chloe kissed Esther's proferred
cheek. Was she taken in?

"I hope you didn't overhear my little sermon to Daphne.
Oh, but I think you did! How mortifying! I do go on and on
like a fool, Olivia will tell you that, won't you, darling. But
then, they all count on it so."

When Chloe remarked that it sounded like sensitive advice, Esther shifted her tack. "Oh, Daphne's a treasure. But if she's going to be a singer, she has got to learn to live every day with tremendous insecurity." If Esther heard the irony of her words, she masked it. "But why are we standing like dolts in the hall?" she exclaimed. "Let's have some tea, shall we?" When Olivia said she'd make it, her mother sounded a warning. "I guess I can manage *tea,* Olivia."

Esther put the water on to boil, and Olivia took cups down from a shelf. "Not those, darling. Just get out the tea tray and sit, I'll do it." While Esther measured tea, sliced lemon, set out milk and sugar, and explained her work, Olivia, swallowing rage, perched on a kitchen stool like a child. "They're not all like Daphne, heavens, no! Daphne's *intelligent,* I can explain things to her. The others want their little tête-à-tête too, but that's just whoring. All I have to do is look at them and parrot their favorite cliché. It's like writing horoscopes or those little paper fortunes for Chinese cookies." Esther loved to frolic with danger, Olivia knew, but this wholesale contempt smacked of despair.

She sat on the couch swinging a shapely leg, holding first Chloe and then Olivia with her large liquid gaze. She used her sweeping stare to haul in and sort out the people before her like fish in a net. Some were daunted, others aroused.

"Your Chloe doesn't understand about singers, darling. I suppose she thinks they're musicians! Now, now, don't feel bad, Chloe, it's a widespread misunderstanding. But singers, my dear! Half of them don't even know how to read! What? Books?"

Esther set down her teacup, threw back her head, and barked in happy outrage. She was flirting hard now, working to mock Chloe into adoring submission. "Of course not, they don't read books! *Imagine* a singer with a book. With a newspaper! An informed singer! It's a contradiction in terms! I'm talking about *music*, they often can't read music! They aren't musicians, they just have a freak gift. They don't have instruments. Their bodies are their instruments." And with a comically solemn look, Esther spread her white hands across her breasts. The way Chloe bent toward her, smiling, made Olivia feel anxious and isolated. Chloe always enjoyed a character, the more audacious the better. "That's why they make a fetish of the body." She lifted her hands abruptly, as if she had burned them.

As she watched her mother circle her terror, Olivia's own rage was chilled. She listened to her croon and coo and marked the freighted gestures. As if inviting Chloe to her very bosom, her hands scooped the air toward those aquiline breasts, which arched, now as always, like the necks of Arab steeds. And one might be taken from her—from Olivia too, jolted by sudden pain beneath the ribs—irrevocably, in two days' time.

"You like her, don't you?" Olivia asked. She was walking Chloe along leafless Prospect Park to the subway station at Grand Army Plaza. The great arch loomed before them, with its goddess of the Yankee armies driving her four horses into the gray sky.

Chloe glanced at her friend, handsome in square-toed boots and gray maxicoat. Olivia's helpless resentment rang so close to the surface that Chloe took her arm and pressed it to her side. After a moment she said, "I like to listen to her. She's clever, she's witty. I've never met anyone just like her. She moves me, I'm not sure why. Those big yellow eyes—so conscious!" Yet there was something wrong in them, she thought, as if at bottom they were blind. "And she has so much style! But—"

"It's true," Olivia said unhappily, "she's remarkable."

"But—let me finish—it seems forced. She must be terribly frightened, as you say. And I also saw that she'd be murder as a mother. Livia, you're twenty times the mother she is!"

"What's the good of that?" Olivia wailed. "She won't let me do anything for her. She didn't give a good goddamn about those cups, but she had to make me useless! Hell! Why did I come?"

"I suppose she wants to feel self-sufficient. But why she does it at your expense—"

"It's typical. She doesn't actually need me at all, but she wants me there somehow. She's got all these doting students, and Don—he's been her pet for years—he'll do anything for her, she lets him. But not me. Like, get this! The night I arrived, I gave her a present. I'd spent some time finding it. It's a lovely Italian scarf, heavy silk, you can wear it over your shoulders like a shawl, or tie it or drape it. I was showing her the possibilities, and she just sat there, sort of stroking her breasts in this way she's taken up. She's always been so proud of her big handsome breasts, you know, and finds ways to remind me that mine are small. I don't care, but it's exasperating. Anyhow, she just sat there smiling in this almost tender way, and then she chuckled. 'You keep the scarf, darling. You need it more than I do.'"

They had reached the arch at Grand Army Plaza, and Chloe stopped in the street and stared at her. Traffic wheeled before them. "Livy, that's incredible!"

Olivia relaxed perceptibly, as ever when Chloe grew indignant on her behalf. "Isn't it?" She took Chloe's arm, steered her through the traffic to a tiny circular park, and began to saunter around its edge. "It's almost funny."

"Funny! It would be outrageous if it weren't so sad. Jesus, Livy! Don't you see now why she needs you here?"

"What do you mean?"

"She needs you to see she doesn't need anyone, in order to convince herself she can handle it. Of course she doesn't consider what it does to you."

Now Olivia stopped. "You think that?" she asked, eyes stretched wide.

Chloe thought that and more. For instance, that this transparent look of trust was what had won her in Rome. The gaze between them was a string on which their thought moved, an old and indispensable resource. Although she did not yet understand it, Chloe also glimpsed the uncanny oneness of Olivia's life in all the years she had known her. Olivia on the beach in Sicily, begging for Karl's response. Her haggard face in the steamy hotel mirror. Brooding before the fire in Chloe's apartment. In the drawn woman grieved by her mother, Chloe saw the girl puzzling over Karl.

On Chloe's face Olivia read her love and her sudden sadness like written words. How had she done so long without her? She looked up at the four columns at the entrance to the park, each topped by an imperious eagle, each eagle's wings aloft. Out, out, up, and away! She had an inspiration.

"Listen. Why don't I ride back to Manhattan with you. Don's with Esther, and he'll be there all evening." She drew Chloe's arm resolutely through hers and strode toward the subway.

"That would be great! What's with Don and Esther—are they lovers?"

"Years ago, sure. Now it's anyone's guess. She makes it seem that everyone and no one is her lover. But she's fine, let's go! You saw how she waved us away, ever the grande dame. 'Take Chloe to the museum!' Well, I'll take you home instead. Pop in on your new place and see Gabe, okay? Then leave you to prepare your lecture. I'll get back in plenty of time for dinner."

"Our place is unnavigable, full of construction junk, and we're still figuring out how to heat it. I want you to see it when it's done. And Gabe's not there."

So Chloe was keeping her at a distance, rattling on about Gabe's rush construction job in Jersey. The intimate story would have to wait. Olivia asked about Gabe's work.

"He's doing carpentry till he figures out what he wants. Maybe union organizing, maybe printshop work, it's all up for grabs. Meanwhile, carpentry's not bad. He likes it. And I'm flush. The new job may lack prestige, but it pays better."

It bothered Olivia that Chloe had left her old job because they fired Noah. What did Chloe want for herself? The remade friendship was too new for her to ask. "How is it otherwise?"

"I like it. I teach more blacks and Hispanics. The students are less prepared, but more of them are awake. Half the school turned out for the memorial meeting for Fred Hampton."

"Horrible! Outright murder!"

Chloe looked surprised. "And shameless," she said, nodding angrily. "The cops didn't even bother to set up a pretext."

"And they say he was one of the Panthers' most talented leaders."

"He was."

At the subway's maw, Chloe turned to Olivia. "Will you *really* ride me back? The subway's my home away from home, you know, and we've never ridden it together, do you realize that?"

"Has that been a failing? Let's fix it now!"

On the platform a gang of schoolgirls, giggling and gossiping, made Chloe ask, "What's Hannah like now?"

"She's a handful, as ever. It's been rough, but we're in the clear." Olivia was proud. This was her lifework.

"Rough? What kind of handful?"

"Impulsive, feisty. She did some harm to the furniture in kindergarten after Karl and I split up. And then she ran after older boys. The boy at the soda fountain was no problem, because he tired fast of having a kid hanging around. But the shop teacher was more patient—and I was more worried. She'd sit in his lap and stroke his beard. She can be very seductive."

Chloe scowled. "Did Hannah know about you and Michael?"

"I did my damnedest to prevent it, but she might have. Why?"

"Could she have wanted her own secret love at *her* school?"

Chloe was quick. "Maybe," Olivia said. "But I think mainly she needed to replace Karl and to best me."

"Help! What did you do?"

"I cultivated the guy a little—not much, he was Hannah's friend, just enough to see he was sensitive and let him know I saw. And I made more time for Hannah. It took its course—"

"Ah!"

"—and now she loves only her karate instructor."

"Karate! Little Hannah!"

There were no double-takes as gratifying as Chloe's. "Not so little anymore. You'd want to stay on her good side."

"And this teacher—is he okay?"

One of the girls was shoving another down the platform. "*Max* is cuter!" The other shoved back. "No, *Dan's* cuter!" Hannah would hold her own here.

"He's great," Olivia said. "I think he's tamed her. No hitting other kids all this year."

Chloe whistled. "So he deals with all the problems in one stroke."

"We'll see. But Hannah's also making friends her own age.

Especially two kids with divorced parents, who make her situation seem more normal. And we mothers take turns with all the kids. Divorce is civilized in Portland. Even some of the dads—not including Karl—are good for rotation."

"Doesn't Sharon help anymore?"

"Sharon has a little Panther baby. One of the brothers made her a mother." Chloe flinched, and Olivia felt herself heating up. "Sharon thought he would take her and the baby on, but so far it's only her mother pitching in. I'm sorry, Chloe, the Black Panthers may be handy with the free breakfast, but they're all thumbs when it comes to diapering their own son." Chloe was not about to give her an argument, she noticed. Contrite, Olivia added, "I miss her. She comes around once in a while, but she feels guilty around me for quitting school."

The train rushed into the station, and Olivia felt the old thrill of rescue from Brooklyn. The girls swung like rag dolls from the straps, spun around the pole, and shrieked as the train careened around the curves. Olivia hadn't ridden the subway for years, but this underworld was exempt from the vicissitudes of time. Her body knew by heart the rhythm of the lurches. When the doors rattled open at Atlantic Avenue, the girls burst forth, and the mere clatter of the train then seemed bucolic.

Chloe sat sideways to face her, one bell-bottomed leg stuck in the aisle, the other tucked up under her. It was her natural habitat, Olivia thought, and she was simply herself, inured to the lidded looks she was getting. *They* were getting. Olivia felt light, young, like when they prowled Rome, dark and fair, tall and short, making heads turn.

"Three more stops to Clark Street," Olivia reminisced, "then we dive under the East River, the tracks get straighter, and the ride gets quieter, faster, smoother. As a kid, I took it as proof of Manhattan's superiority to the squalor of Brooklyn.

So Chloe, can we talk? Over this racket? And without props? No smoking, no alcoholic beverages?"

"With you? With nearly three years to cram into a couple of hours? Anywhere. No problem."

As long as they could talk they would come out all right, Olivia thought. From old habit, Chloe took over the agenda.

"You have to tell me fundamental things. For starters, are you and Hannah all alone?"

Olivia balked. "You have a list? How long is it?"

"I'm years out of date," she said tartly. "What can I do? My friend is illiterate."

So the rancor was working its way out, like the splinter in Hannah's heel. Olivia wanted to speed the reconciliation along. "I've started seeing men, if that's what you mean."

Chloe took heart. "Anyone special? Do you see Michael?"

"Not often. We've tried to become friends, but it's difficult. We never got over that business."

Chloe was sorry. She'd liked Michael more than she realized.

"But oh—listen! Michael's set up housekeeping in a commune with three women, a therapist, a Marxist economist, and—wait!—a family planner! And they're going to take on clients together, serving their various needs in turn. Michael is going to work on their 'expressive energy'—he'll do yoga and poetry. They're calling it the Hokey-Pokey Institute!"

"You're putting me on!"

"I'm not! Remember the dance? Vintage fifties, I think. 'You put your right foot in, you put your right foot out, you put your right foot in, and you shake it all about!' And then you put your left foot in and so on, until finally—"

"I remember! 'You put your whole self in!' "

" 'And you turn yourself about! That's what it's all about!' "

"It's magnificent, Livy! The revolution West Coast style!"

"Radical change for the seventies!"

Chloe sobered for an instant. "The seventies, God! Can you get *ready* for it? The sixties are over! The *seventies!* What can they possibly be?" Then she giggled. "Who knows? Maybe the Hokey-Pokey Institute is the wave of the future. Maybe it's"— she pressed her hands to her heart and intoned—"the next phase of the struggle!"

Olivia cocked an eyebrow.

I'm overdoing it, Chloe thought. "I don't know why I'm picking on Michael," she said. "I still believe in turning yourself about. But you can't institutionalize it. Still, it sounds like fun!" Olivia looked unconvinced. "Doesn't tempt you, huh?"

Then Olivia told her that in fact she wanted to ditch teaching altogether to do therapy, but real therapy. She had been apprenticing in Gestalt with a therapist she liked, and was beginning to talk with patients. It sounded so right to Chloe, she was abashed not to have suggested it herself.

"But apprenticing is not enough, frankly. I want something more rigorous. I have fantasies of going to a psychoanalytic institute or graduate school in psychology." She added grimly, "Just as soon as I can afford it."

Chloe started to tell about an acquaintance in a program in New York, but Olivia stopped her.

"It makes me nervous to talk about it."

She seemed firm about that, so Chloe lowered her voice and asked again if she'd met anyone special.

"Nobody special. Just, you know, the Creature Comfort, the Foreign Movies Man—"

That barbaric time! Chloe shrank from the reminder. "Seriously," she said.

"I am serious. More or less. I'm making up for lost time, the way you did years ago. You had the Reichian, I had, briefly, the Transactional Analyst. Very frisky in bed, but unh! when he talked about his work! There was also, still more briefly, a superannuated flower child on his way to dealing dope, and—"

"Liv-ya!"

"Oh, they're not all so awful. At least not until they absorb the fact I have a very real and complicated seven-year-old. There's one nice Divorced Dad who grasps that—"

"Yeah? How nice?"

"Nice enough. But"—Olivia started to laugh—"it's over. He used to complain to me about his ex-wife, and I found myself taking her side. In fact, what he told me about her began to fascinate me. So I ended up making friends with her and dropping him—"

"You're unbelievable!" Should I back off? Chloe wondered. But she had a hunch and ran with it. "Livia. Are you and Karl talking about divorce?"

"No. He's happy with his gallery lady, but they have no plans. Why roil things up? It's not that I want to try it again, but—if neither of us is going to remarry— Why? You think the divorce matters?"

"Yeah. Symbolically, anyhow. I guess I'm wondering how far you've put him behind you."

Olivia dropped her guard. "I don't really know, Chloe. But I can tell you have something on your mind. I'd like to know what it is."

Chloe could see she meant it. A blind man playing an accordion inched his way down the car, legs spread wide. She fished a quarter out of her pocket, then said, "I thought of something in Brooklyn, but I may be off the wall."

"Never mind. I want to know."

When Chloe hesitated, Olivia tugged at her red muffler. "This is me and you! I don't want you not to say what you feel."

A warrant of safety? "Really? Even with all the time we've been out of touch?"

"That doesn't disturb me as much as you, Chloe. I wish you would understand. You're one of the very few people I have let know me. And with me, that lasts. I think I can take anything from you. I hope I can. So let's have it."

There was Olivia's no-holds-barred smile, and this was what it had always promised, and why Chloe could never resist it. The train was crowded now, so she had to say it right in Olivia's ear. Watching her with Esther had made her see why Olivia had been attracted to Karl in the first place, and why it might be hard to leave him. Esther and Karl were two of a kind, weren't they? Olivia's sharp intake of breath was assurance enough. Out of the corner of her eye, Chloe saw the white tiles of Franklin Street, her stop, fly by. She'd forgotten to change to the local at Chambers. "When you decided to marry Karl, did you think of Esther at all?"

"Only that I was getting away from her at last!" Olivia muttered.

"Only that?" Chloe's hunch was clarifying itself. She plunged with the dangerous confidence of a gambler. "Nothing was being redone? Revenged, redressed?"

"Oh!" The question was startling, especially from Chloe. The train screamed, and Olivia closed her eyes to concentrate. Had her decision really been so complicated? Karl's back waiting for her outside the door in Milan always came to mind as the very image of fate. What is fate anyhow, Chloe had grumbled once, what does it feel like? Rather than answer, Olivia had teased her, pretending Chloe's optimism cut her off from yet another visceral mystery. You think nothing's inevitable, Chloe, she'd said, everything can be changed.

But she asked herself now. Fate—it fills you without your

choosing, it's like knowledge in the bones. And what is *that* but recognition, if unconscious. Unconscious familiarity. The train stopped, and she turned to Chloe.

"What I thought at the time—when I did think—was that I had found someone who listened to me as Esther never had. Karl put me down plenty, but when we were alone, he seriously wanted to know what I thought. Of his work, his ideas, of him! I think I believed"—the marvel of it made it the more likely—"that doing that for him was what I was made for."

"What you were *made* for!" Chloe cried as the train started up again. "But *Esther made you* that way!"

You keep it darling, Esther had said so tenderly, extending the scarf. It was such an old gesture, Olivia thought, she *never* accepted anything from me. And Karl's seeming so different was *precisely* what made me fall for him. Redress, Chloe said. But in the long run, he shut me out just as much. More.

"Do you mean that Esther trained me," she said at the next stop, "to seek rejection?"

"I don't *know* what I mean," Chloe smiled. "*Did* she?"

"No. Not so simply. But she taught me to tolerate tantalization. To live in hope of a connection next time."

"I can believe it! She gets a kick out of whetting your appetite, isn't that so?"

The roar resumed, and Olivia only nodded. And Karl seemed to feed the hunger Esther had instilled. And made me think I'd be valued, if not right away, eventually. Gave me the illusion I'd become my own self at last. When in fact—oh, it was remarkable. She felt excited and calm at once. How surprising that Chloe saw this.

"Oh, yes," she said as the train slowed again. "There's something there."

"You know, Chloe," Olivia said the next year in Ontario, "I think I ran from Andy's shrink because he wanted to talk about my mother and I wasn't ready."

"Uh-huh!"

"Had you thought of that too? You thought of everything else that day. I couldn't get over how clearly you saw—"

"Umm. After such inauspicious beginnings."

"Come on. You have to admit you'd changed a lot. Going through all that with your father—you were popping with connections."

"I'm smart about you, you're smart about me. It's our thing."

"It's true. But you put me in a trance. And never mentioned we'd gone way past Franklin Street—"

"I was having too good a time to break the spell."

"And I noticed nothing till Penn Station. And then! What a reception!"

Olivia heard the women yelling, but she couldn't make out the words. "Livy, you have to see this!" Chloe pulled her down the platform. By the turnstiles a girl in combat attire was leading a crowd in a chant. Olivia caught it now.

". . . should be FREE! Don't pay the FARE, subways should be FREE! Don't pay the FARE, subways should be FREE!" There was one man in a business suit, and a few hippies, but the rest were suburban women with Macy's bags, looking pleasantly surprised at themselves.

"Do you dig what's hap—," Chloe began.

"It's because of the fare increase, isn't it? I read that people were jumping turnstiles—"

"Oh, we're past that now. Look!"

Beyond the chanters, kids were haranguing the people lined

up at the token booth. A cheer went up when a girl turned away from the line. A lean Hispanic man in leather jacket and beret opened the Exit Only door for her. He had to be one of the Young Lords she'd read about, Hispanic brethren of the Panthers. As the girl passed, he took a sweeping bow, the maître d' of liberation.

Now almost no one was paying. The line was veering away from the booth. Olivia pulled Chloe's sleeve. "The token seller's cracking up!"

"He's getting into it. Gabe should see this. He loves this part, the gates of the underworld swung wide and everyone going down to party—"

"Gabe's involved in this?"

"Even Gabe!" Chloe laughed. "Gabe more than me!"

"Is he here?"

"No, he must still be in Jersey. But he digs this action because you don't need a lot of heavy rhetoric to explain that no one should pay extra for a ride, that transit could be free if we taxed the bankers and developers. And all over the city local groups are springing up. It's an anarchist's dream. And oh! Guess who's one of the leaders!"

It had to be Noah. "He's all right, then?"

Chloe said quickly, "He's fine." They didn't have to name him; Noah was the name of their quarrel. It was long ago, but not quite behind them, not yet.

"Do you think he's here?" she asked. "I'd like to see him."

"I doubt it. He's running all over the city."

"He's *really* all right?" Olivia repeated foolishly.

Chloe smiled, and the tension broke. "He's the most nearly happy person I know in the movement. You know what he does? Gives classes in getting arrested. No one knows more about it. If they gave a Ph.D. in arrest, he'd have the first one."

Just then a group of new arrivals began to leap like acrobats over the turnstiles, back and forth. A girl with a tambourine and a guy with cymbals accompanied them, chanting a line from a song: "Break on through to the other side!"

Everything was about everything. Olivia's head was spinning.

Chloe looked at her anxiously. "Are you okay? What do you want to do now, Livy?"

"I want to break on through to the other side," Olivia said. Then she laughed. "Let's ask about Noah just in case."

Glad to oblige, Chloe approached the crowd. She seemed to know every third person. "Maybe he split," a girl said, "when the pigs came through to bust the cats from YAWF. They had these big sticks, you know? With banners? The train came in and they jumped on it, man. We got a perfect mobile tactic going."

An old anarchist Chloe knew from civil rights actions said nonsense, Noah never ran out on an arrest. He had gone to Broadway-Lafayette to see the women from the factories at rush hour. Best example yet, he said, of people's capacity to rebel spontaneously. "Sit eight hours behind the machines, you can bet they'll cut loose when they can. Rumor has it they turned it into a party. When the exit gates were locked on them, some of them began to limbo under the turnstiles."

The improvisatory genius of New Yorkers, Olivia thought, is boundless. Only remarkable things happen here. "C'mon, Chloe, let's join them, just for a few minutes!" she cried, unaccountably exhilarated. Someone offered Chloe a placard. "I'll take it," Olivia said. "What does it say?" The legend was scrawled in red and black crayon.

Chloe read aloud: "Mass Transit Is Free If You Are!"

"I love it! But Jesus, we paid our fare! I feel terrible." Olivia slung the string over her head, laughing. It was a childish gesture of peacemaking, she knew, but she was euphoric. "We have to do penance, or we'll never be free!"

"You don't have to do this, you know," Chloe said. "This action is no big deal for me."

"I want to, I want to," Olivia said. Chloe hugged her, and the string of the placard broke and had to be retied.

Circling for twenty minutes, they had persuaded a dozen people to use the exit gates, but many more lined up to buy tokens. They had just decided to leave when a cherubic girl ran up.

"Hey, Chloe!" Three years ago, someone like this would have had flowers twisted in her hair, but now she wore fatigues. "Isn't it wild?" she cried hoarsely. "The shopping crowd is outasight, man!" She punched a palm with a fist. "The more ladies we get the more the TPF keeps away. But there were some busts across town. Rush hour's beginning. Maybe we'll have a showdown at the height." She glowed at the prospect. Olivia laughed openly.

Chloe introduced them. Karen was one of her students, clearly an acolyte.

"Your friend Frances is here," she told Chloe. "We've been talking. She's great. She let this Puerto Rican dude have it, said if they're so big on women's participation, how come they're called *Lords*? She's sharp! And she sure knows how to sock it to the Macy's ladies. Wait, lemme tell her you're here." She dove expertly under the turnstile.

"Never mind!" Chloe called, but the chanters drowned her out.

"Frances?" Olivia asked. "The Frances I met in Washington?"

"Yes, but she and I—"

Karen was back, Frances in tow. She was the same black-eyed Irish beauty, but her hair, freed from a lifetime of plaiting, snaked out wide. A leather cap came down tight over her eyes. She greeted Chloe flatly, but her gaze burned. Chloe was stiff.

"Oh, yeah," Frances said to Olivia. "We met at the draft card action, right." She turned to Karen. "This woman was in Washington when Clem—" Karen nodded. "We broke up, Clem and I, did Chloe tell you?"

Olivia was shocked and showed it. Monitoring Chloe's response on one side and playing to Karen on the other, Frances explained. "We just couldn't hack it anymore, me and some of the other women. We supported what the guys were doing, right? But for some of them—*a lot of them*, Chloe!—support meant the works, from being gofers to getting laid." Karen's snicker spurred her on. "It was all supposed to be about freedom, they were locked up for a 'larger freedom,' right? But meanwhile the chicks were their prisoners on the outside!" Chloe turned sharply away, and Frances glared at the back of her head.

Olivia jumped in, incredulous. "But what about Clem?"

"Well, Clem, he's on a communal farm up in Vermont"— and Frances glanced slyly at Karen beneath thick lashes— "grooving on cows!"

Poor Chloe, Olivia thought, all her protégés running amok. But Karen's snicker was exasperating. "I meant did Clem treat you so bad? I can't imagine him—"

Chloe broke in harshly. "Clem wasn't even there—he was doing his time in jail!"

"And left me out there alone with those animals, Chloe!" Frances snapped back. "You don't want to see what's in front of your face! There's more than one kind of sentence!"

Chloe walked away. "Fuck it," Frances muttered, and she too turned on her heel. "I'm going back to the Macy's ladies." Looking a little frightened, Karen followed her.

Chloe stopped abruptly. Damn! Why did I lose my temper? In front of Livia! Breathing deeply, she slowed the racing of her heart. Olivia stood where she'd left her, looking quizzical. "I'm sorry, Livia. Maybe I'm not fair, but I get so sore when I think of Clem." The demonstration seemed inane. "Let's get out of here. What do you want to do?"

Olivia snorted. "I want to hear what happened between Frances and Clem, and between you and her. But let's go outside. Get a coffee or something."

Their fight in Washington was obviously on Olivia's mind, and she was confident they could straighten that out too. Climbing the stairs, Chloe could scarcely remember what it had been about, things had changed so.

The outer city was gray and anonymous, and there were no appealing coffee shops in sight. Olivia stopped impatiently in front of a fast-food place. "It doesn't matter, let's just go here. At least it's quieter." Her nostalgia was clearly not for *this* New York.

Sipping the watery coffee, Chloe said she couldn't understand Frances, she'd tried. There were some idiots in the movement, as usual, and Frances had taken guff from some SDS heavies. But Chloe didn't believe they had much to do with it. "What she said was she felt her whole identity wrapped up in supporting him!"

Olivia put down her cup and studied her. "Maybe she did, Chloe!"

"With *Clem?*" Chloe cried out despite herself. "Who adored her? Who did his time, got out, and found nobody home? How did he deserve that? The whole thing was about standing for something, sticking by each other, bringing a new idea into the world!"

Olivia clasped Chloe's arm. Her voice was low. "Can we just *talk* about this?"

"Oh, God." Chloe dropped her head on Olivia's shoulder. "I'm really sorry, Livia."

"Don't be sorry," Olivia said sternly. "We have to talk, is all." Chloe sat up straight. "Now. Why do you get so hot? Is it really so one-sided?"

"No, not at all! But Frances' change—this business about women, I don't like it."

Pushing away the foul coffee, Olivia ordered a Coke. "Why not?"

"I don't know. There are so many groups in New York—" What she'd heard about the Witches, the Radical Feminists, and the bunch that took over the movement newspaper on the Lower East Side swam together in her mind with the SCUM Manifesto. "But either they know nothing about the movement and couldn't care less, or they say they've suffered in it so much as women that they wash their hands. I can't bear to see women turning away from the world. That's what happened to Frances—"

"So. You get hot when the one thing that made sense to you is questioned."

"What one thing?"

"The Resistance."

Oh, that's not it, Chloe thought. Even the Resistance can't summon what's needed now.

"Chloe, listen. I have a friend, Amy. Completely conventional so far as I could see, four kids, never held a job. She had an abortion without her husband knowing, and it split her life open. Now she works every morning at an abortion referral service. Busy as hell, and she's just joined this group where women, all kinds of women, talk about their lives, things each one thought were her problem alone. And they found out they'd all been through similar stuff. It's giving them a new way of thinking about what happens to them. Makes them less passive. I would think you'd like it. And would see why *that* makes more sense to *them* than anything else."

Chloe nodded. She really wasn't fair. "It sounds good," she said, "but here it's such a tangle. The women's groups don't even agree with each *other,* and they have no use for the left." When her father got sick, she'd given up the radio work and discovered she wasn't sorry. Believing each group had a piece of it, she'd tried to keep up with them all, the feminists and the draft file bloodiers, the conspiracy trial analysts and the Weathermen. But now there was no news she felt driven to publicize. "It's impossible to see it as all one wonderful explosion. There's no unifying idea anymore, just proliferating enemies."

"What if seeing *that* is seeing what there is?" Olivia touched her arm. "Is it your responsibility to make it all come right? Maybe it makes no sense to try to think of it any one way."

That's what Gabe says, Chloe thought, and he makes more sense than our friend who said that without a complete analysis he was paralyzed. Still, I need *something* to steer by. The stakes are too high on both sides. Fear collected around two obsessions: the photos of Fred Hampton's door shattered by police bullets, and Annie's frantic eyes when she said she was joining the Weather Underground. If we'd taken a stand when they shackled Bobby Seale, she told Chloe, they might have been afraid to kill Hampton. Grandiose nonsense, and who would protect Annie?

"The way things are now—either we're controlled by doing

nothing or we're flying out of control. It's scary," she began. Then she stopped, startled by the revelation that she'd said all she needed to: Olivia couldn't solve it, and it was in no way essential that she understand the details. Relief washed over her like a wave.

Olivia listened with growing wonder to the silence Chloe was letting happen.

"*Boh,*" said Chloe, in grinning imitation of her friend. "Let's stow it."

She's upset about Esther, Chloe thought, watching Olivia roll and reroll her placard as they waited for the southbound train, but she can't bear to think about it. That's why she threw herself into the demo, that's why she's asking me now about Gabe.

Gabe had been depressed for a long time, she said. "It began with his disappointment in the New Left." Olivia smirked because she started with politics. "Well, it did," Chloe insisted. "Just when the New Left was about to bring something new into the world, he says, it mutated back into the Old Left, and now every faction, when you scratch it, is some kind of Marxist-Leninist."

"*Avanti!*" Olivia broke in. "When did you start living together?"

"When everything fell apart for him. After the government got wise to welfare rights," Chloe explained. "A couple of years ago, remember? Gabe's group staged these big collective grievances almost daily to get welfare people the special grants they were entitled to. Then Welfare abolished the grants. Bit by bit, they blocked whatever the activists tried to do, and now the movement's dead in New York. Gabe saw it coming, but he was crushed. He'd believed in it more than he meant to—"

Far better that generous error than holding back, Olivia thought. Olivia was very tired now, and hungry for the inner story and the happy ending. "That's how you got together, then?" She grinned wickedly. "You're always turned on by guys in trouble, Chlo. A crisis in faith would be irresistible!"

Chloe laughed. "It's true," she admitted. Just as Olivia fell for the blind narcissist only she could understand. Suddenly she wanted to tell Olivia everything. After all, it had begun with her, Chloe realized—the rawness of her own longing for Olivia had precipitated somehow the long slide into feeling for Gabe.

The train came, and they found virtual privacy between a hippie, drunk and sleeping, and an Irish woman absorbed in *True Romance.*

"I always liked Gabe," Chloe went on, "but he seemed so much surer of everything than me and so much nicer! It put up a terrible barrier. I had this idea that the man was supposed to be thorny and ill-tempered, and the woman the sweet forbearing one."

"Like your father and mother."

"What? That would be crazy!" I grew up, Chloe thought, alarmed, by being *not* like my mother, and my father has been my tormentor.

Olivia shrugged. "They're what you know best. But Gabe could hardly be less like your father."

Yes, Chloe thought, but then he changed so. And so did my father. Here comes my darling Chloe, he said, and at the same time Gabe became so surly. Forget it, he said, it's no good. "You know," she reflected, "they sort of swapped places. My father changed just when I made my stand with the Chinese takeout."

"What?" Olivia laughed.

"It was when Gabe was up to his eyes in hash."

Olivia's smile faded. *"What?* Chloe, what happened?"

"When the welfare thing caved in, Gabe did a lot of drugs. He felt he'd gotten no clearer than his parents, just been blind in a different way. He felt he'd betrayed his welfare clients. And he didn't know what in hell to do with himself. One night—" Chloe scanned the glazed eyes of the straphangers, the woman reading, the hippie, very young under his beard, lean as a rake and snoring.

"One night I showed up at his door with a big bag of Chinese takeout," she said in Olivia's ear. "There he stood in his underwear, unshaven, wiped out. He hadn't slept in God knows how long. He didn't want to let me in, he told me to forget it, I was wasting my time. I said the hot-and-sour soup was steaming, I was damned if it would go to waste, and I just served it up. He ate it on condition we didn't talk and I leave right afterward. I was too nervous and excited to eat. I must be perverse, but it came over me right then and there that I was crazy about him and would die if he sent me away. So I went and stood behind him and rubbed his head. He loves that, he's like a cat. But I was scared out of my wits, my fingers were stiff, my heart was banging away!"

Olivia was wagging her head as she listened. She sighed deeply and murmured, "So I guess he didn't send you away."

The hippie stirred in his sleep and cried in a high nasal whine, "No fucking *way,* you jiveass—" and then subsided again.

They started and burst out laughing. "Right!" said Chloe. The Irish woman peered over her magazine, the straphangers stared and tittered, two Puerto Rican boys called out, "Tell it, brother!" but the motion of the car swayed them back into semiconsciousness.

"You moved in then? Yes? That night? Oh, I love it!"

Chloe jumped up and slapped her head. "Chambers Street!" She pointed to the sign sliding offstage left. "We've missed Franklin again."

Olivia felt no compunction. "So now you're riding *me* home. What's wrong with that? We've got to ride extra anyhow to punish the Transit Authority."

Chloe said that when she was fourteen her best friend in Syracuse would walk her home from her neighborhood, and then Chloe would walk her home, and sometimes they'd spend half the evening walking each other home. Olivia felt light again, like a fourteen-year-old.

"Only then I didn't have classes to prepare," Chloe added plaintively.

The hippie sleeping at Olivia's side lifted his head to mutter, in a wind of cheap wine, "Fucking motherfucker, go fuck yourself." He let his head fall again.

"Umm-*hmm*," affirmed Olivia. "Your friend here is not impressed with these excuses, Chloe."

"Tough. I've got to go home. Term begins tomorrow, and I'm doing a new course. I have to give a big lecture on the historical background. I've been reading for months, but I've got to pull it together."

Olivia hadn't seen Chloe yank at her hair that way for years, and it did her good.

Chloe had begun to talk about her course—Racism in American Literature—when the train ground to a halt between stations.

"Holy Mother of God," True Romance exclaimed. "Not again." The lights in the car dimmed, flickered, and stayed dim, leaving the car in thick dusk.

"It's because we're going to Brooklyn," Olivia said cheerfully. "Didn't I tell you?"

The guy next to her stopped snoring, sat up, and said in a perfectly natural voice, "This is ridiculous!" He rose and made his way easily down the car through the gloaming.

A woman's voice shrilled, "For this we got a fare increase?" and one of the boys yelled, "Right on, lady." The other said, "Hey, folks, how's about some entertainment?" After a little static, salsa rocked the car.

The subway never used to be so romantic, Olivia thought. "Now, Chloe," she coaxed. "We have all the comforts, let's make the best of it. I promise to let you head back home whenever we get to a station. Meanwhile we're stuck, and it's as private here as a nightclub. You didn't finish what you were saying, anyhow. About your father and Gabe swapping places."

"Oh! You have the most amazing memory, you're going to be some fantastic shrink! You're right, no one can hear me over this. Let's see. Gabe's crisis was just when my father was going around the bend last fall. And his senility, whatever it was, made him as sweet as Gabe was bitter. Did I write you about this?"

"You wrote me a great letter about his mad visit to Ontario. But he was anything but sweet—"

"Oh, right. And when they got back to Syracuse, he was uncontrollable. We had to put him in a hospital, and then in a nursing home. The first weeks he was in an uninterrupted state of fury, it was torture to visit him. Then one day everything came unstuck, he seemed to sail backwards in time. One week he treated the nurses like secretaries, saying he was proud to have them on his staff, and the next he talked like a boy. *That* week I was in Syracuse and saw him every day. He didn't know where he was, but he knew me. The third time I went, he cried out, 'Here comes my darling Chloe! Isn't it strange how we keep bumping into one another in all these different places?

Three times now! Isn't that remarkable!' He was lucid—he had the count right—and affectionate in a way he'd never been when he was well. Never! It must have been senile dementia, but I decided to take it as true. As if all the layers of disappointment and antagonism built up over the years just peeled away to expose something more real, you know what I mean?"

Very moved, Olivia squeezed Chloe's arm. "Yes."

"And then he tried to make it up with me about the Ontario visit. His confusion gave him his chance. He looked at me sort of sideways and said, 'We had terrible weather up north, didn't we, Chloe?' When I allowed that the weather had been pretty bad, he just beamed, as if between us we had pulled off a spectacular practical joke."

"Amazing! Do you think he was asking your forgiveness?"

"Something like that. Without really asking."

"Or without acknowledging he'd done anything."

"It was complicated. But it acknowledged something, and I liked it that way. No sloppy tears."

Chloe was remarkable, converting darkness itself into light, but Olivia couldn't help thinking she had gone through the tunnel too fast.

"The point is," Chloe went on, "I was so used to his being tyrannical and impossible that I had trouble believing in his gentleness. And the trouble itself seemed to explain so much."

"Like what?" Olivia leaned toward her voice.

"Like I'd had some kind of stake in his being impossible—"

"You *did*! You constructed your life around it!"

"You think so? Really? Well, I simply didn't need that anymore. But it was scary, kind of like waking up naked on top of a flagpole. I didn't know what came next!"

The train lights flickered on, off, on. Chloe blinked. When the train moved tentatively forward, the Puerto Rican boys booed.

"Moving in with Gabe came next?" Olivia suggested.

"It did! And Gabe was terrific about my father. His own father had died in an institution, so he knew what to do and how everybody felt even before we did."

"When the people I work with in the clinic get stuck and can't see how things link up," Olivia said a year later, *"I wish Portland had a subway system."*

"How's that? Ah!"

"You're still up?"

"Livia! Everything all right? Yes? Yeah, I'm almost done with the lecture. Gabe's in bed—"

"I won't keep you more than a minute. Esther's finally called it a day—"

"How is she?"

"Fine. In her fashion."

"What do you mean?"

"Oh, you know, busy and charming as hell. Showing Don old photos, getting out old records, fussing about repainting the hall, bitching about the landlord. Never once mentioning the hospital tomorrow."

"I thought it was the day after."

"The biopsy is. She has to go in a day ahead. But I'm calling to say how wonderful everything was, your rushing out here, the demo, even the breakdown. Talking was so good, Chloe, I can't tell you how much better I feel."

"So do I," said Chloe heartily. "But wasn't it a funny scene? Gabe says we must be out of our minds trying to catch up on the IRT, bellowing our secrets—"

"He's right. But we had no choice. We packed in so much I'm dizzy. We have to talk more about everything. But listen, what you said about Esther and Karl knocks me out—I had to let you know. It keeps spinning webs in my head." She wanted to add: I felt you really saw me, you used to idealize me so.

But Chloe was laughing, delighted. "Webs?"

"Yes. The idea of her training me to bear rejection, to keep taking the bait. I remembered what Andy used to call her game: Come close but don't touch. It could have been Karl's motto too!"

"*What?* What did Andy say?"

"Come close but don't touch. Esther's always had her hands all over her students, but she rarely touched us. And we've learned never to touch her."

After she'd hung up, Chloe put away her notes. She always overprepared anyhow. Even sitting under a quilt between the oven and the new space heater, she was chilled.

Come close but don't touch.

That was Esther. My father never touched either.

Chloe was back with her father in the nursing home. It was the next-to-last day. Dozing and waking, he was going in and out of coherence as if through a window. A window on what? Watching him sleep, Chloe thought about Thoreau dying, how they wanted him to report on the next world. Henry, they whispered, what do you see? She imagined Henry putting up a broad palm as he answered, One world at a time. Her father too, it turned out, was hanging in to report on this world, but with his mad true vision. When he woke, he stuck out his big rope-veined hand. Without thinking, she took it in hers. He recognized her then and snatched back his hand with a look of pure concentrated terror. When it subsided, he said, slowly and patiently, as if she were a retarded child, "Don't ever do that again, Chloe. You almost *realized* me! That would be a terrible thing to do." Then he smiled broadly and fell asleep again.

Gabe was lying curled on his side. Chloe crept in, crooked one elbow up under her head, and inched toward his back, knees to his legs, until the length of her was flush with his warmth.

The bickering couple in the waiting room annoyed Olivia, but when they had left her alone there, she wished them back. All the magazines exhausted, she was staring into the airshaft, practicing numbness, when Chloe came in.

"No word yet?"

"Chloe!"

Dropping a paper bag and her briefcase in a chair, Chloe hugged her. "I didn't say I'd come, because I wasn't sure I could really get away from school. Obviously, you're still waiting."

"I'm supposed to hear any minute now. They're testing the frozen section. Your timing is spectacular."

"Have you seen her?"

"Only this morning, just before she went in for the operation. She was absolutely silent, but it was a relief after last night."

"What happened last night?"

"She was wild. I think she'd had a few drinks at home when my back was turned. Don came with us, and first she threw a scene because he wouldn't smuggle in some more liquor. Then she recovered and said that if they took her breast, we were going to give it one hell of a wake."

"Don was there? He heard her?"

"Yes, and he got a little green. He's known her for years, but she can still make him blanch. If you ask me, that's what holds them together. She said, 'Oh, Donny, love, what can we do? This guy'—she never says cancer, she calls it 'this guy'—'this guy,' she said, 'is a rapist and a thief, but we can't call the police on him, can we?'"

"This *guy*? She's something else! She talks tougher than death."

"That's it! She thinks she can stare it down. She's always acted like an Amazon, and now she's getting ready to be one. The orderly on night duty said, 'That your mama? She *bad*!' "

"Oh, man!" Chloe said. She pulled off her coat and reached for the paper bag. "I thought you might be sort of camping out here. I brought you a coffee, a Danish, and—"

Olivia caught her arm. "So tell me, Chloe! Will you, please? Is she facing it or is she running from it? Will you please tell me that?"

She doesn't care if I answer or not, Chloe thought. Clairvoyant of the sickroom, she knew that if she hugged her now, Olivia would start to cry. She knew too that Olivia was not asking what she really wanted to know: Would Esther ever face *her*? "Oh," Chloe answered, "she's doing both. And neither. She's doing what she can, Livia." Then Chloe hugged her anyhow, and Olivia clutched her shoulders and sobbed.

With Olivia's slimness in her arms, Chloe couldn't down any longer the words of her colleague that noon. "But then your friend is at risk too. Don't you know the odds jump when the mother has breast cancer?" Olivia must know. But this was not the time to speak of it. Beginning to tremble, she eased Olivia onto the pink plastic bench. "Livy, wouldn't you like your coffee? It's still warm. And I brought you a pack of your cigarettes."

"For Christ's sake, Chloe!" Olivia blew her nose derisively. "Haven't you noticed? I've quit smoking!" She laughed. "It's bad for your health!"

Had it not been for his white coat, Chloe would not have recognized the doctor, he had so the lively reality of a layman. The rosy flesh of his face was rumpled, his lower lip stuck out, and he squinted at Chloe beneath a gray tangle of brows. But when he saw Olivia, he spread his hands in such a welcoming gesture that she sprang toward him, still hugging herself with both arms. He steered her to the hall, but Chloe could see him speaking to her, his hand on her arm. Olivia listened with her narrow shoulders hunched high like a seabird's, nodding violently. Her bent neck made her exposure to danger vivid, but the doctor's hand stroking her arm made Chloe feel a keener pang for her friend. Then Olivia gasped or laughed, kissed the doctor's cheek, and wheeled toward Chloe, head high but looking ready to cry again, and as Chloe rose, she caught the word "benign."

"A benign neoplasm!" Olivia cried, swinging Chloe in a little circle. "There's absolutely nothing to worry about, she can go home tomorrow! It's over!" She stopped. "I can't believe it, Chlo. It's the one thing I really wasn't prepared for."

"Me either! And Esther—she'll be stunned! Dr. Friedlander seems lovely, Livia. He hadn't guessed?"

"Isn't he wonderful? He had guessed, but it was such a long shot. I mean, it's common enough in a young woman but rare in someone Esther's age. Another proof, says he, that she's an exceptional woman."

"Ah, we knew *that*!" said Chloe. "*We* should have guessed!"

Still in shock, Olivia chattered on. Esther wouldn't come to for a while, and Friedlander suggested she wait till evening visiting hours to pop in on her. So she had nothing to do except make a few calls, but she wanted to get out of the hospital. Was Chloe free?

Chloe was, and she could no longer recall why she hadn't invited Olivia to the loft. "I guess you can step around boards and wrenches as well as anyone else," she said. "We just got two space heaters, there's good heat in the bathroom, and there's always the kitchen stove, so you'll survive. I'll give you an early supper so you can get back here. You may even catch Gabe. He'd love to see you, and you can make your phone calls there."

Olivia liked the protocol that went with living in a loft. The little door cut out of the huge one, and then the big open elevator that let her see the brick innards of the building while Chloe hauled them upward by a cable to the sixth floor. The red sock hanging just inside the door held the extra key to be thrown out the window for visitors.

She stepped into a great shadowy cave. "Don't move," Chloe said, "till I get these lights on." She turned on a Tiffany lamp near the door to reveal a little island of civilization in the vast expanse: a makeshift kitchen, two overstuffed chairs, and a bit of rug. But it was *cold*. Was that her breath she saw?

Chloe stepped off into the darkness and snapped on a row of photographer's spotlights clamped to a bar the length of the wall. The ceiling was of embossed tin, and marching down the center of the room were three Corinthian columns painted bright yellow except for the glossy green acanthus leaves at the top. Gabe's heaped workbench stood before a wall of windows. Through the warped glass Olivia made out the pilasters, capitals, and pediments of the iron facades across the street, as elaborate as anything in ancient Rome.

"Help! I forgot the blackout!" Chloe pulled a cord that drew a huge black curtain over the windows. "These private rentals are illegal, you know. That's how come we got this place cheap." She bustled back to the stove, turned on all the burners, and pulled one of the chairs close. Then she disappeared into a maze of lumber, wallboard, and wire, and emerged with an extension cord. Olivia helped her drag a big space heater to the other side of the chair. "It takes a while to warm up. Keep your coat on."

Olivia put her gloves back on too. "Chloe, do you realize what you've done? You've figured out at last how not to live in a house! How to bring the outdoors in!"

"I warned you, we're camping out."

"You're frontiersmen in the middle of the city!"

Fetching a phone with a long cord, Chloe put it on the arm of the chair. "More like cavemen. And you're in luck. This is the day we discover fire!" She rubbed her hands in front of the space heater. "Oh, Livia, welcome, welcome!" She gave her a quick squeeze and led her to the chair. "You'll feel better as soon as you've told Andy and talked with Hannah. Why don't you make Don call the others? Sit here and call in comfort— would you believe Gabe found this chair on the street? Not too worn and only a century or so out of fashion." Suddenly weak with fatigue, Olivia sank into the chair, and Chloe covered her legs with a big shawl. She brought a glass and a jug of red wine and set them beside her. "I'm going to run out to get some stuff for supper. Chicken okay? It's quick. Will you be all right? Do you need anything else? Make your calls, have a glass of wine. Would you rather something hot, tea or coffee? No? Oh, why don't I warm some wine for you? Gabe and I have taken to mulling wine—cinnamon sticks and lemons—no?"

Olivia was content. "Beat it," she said.

"I'll be right back and show you the rest."

Olivia didn't budge. By the time Chloe got back to the loft, it had warmed up enough for her to shed her coat. She lay back in the chair, legs stretched out on the cable spool in which Gabe had envisioned a coffee table. She was gazing up at the stamped tin ceiling. "It's so beautiful," she told Chloe. "Everything. The ceiling, these fancy columns, those windows. This was a sweat-shop?"

"Those things were all cheap then," said Chloe, dumping her groceries. "They must have packed the workers tight and worked them hard. And they sure did stint on the heat."

"Well, it's warm here already. I figure it's your good insulation."

Chloe threw on an apron. "What?"

"Gabe called. He'll be here in an hour. He sounds just great, Chlo. I can't wait to see him. He told me this used to be a pennant factory and you keep finding felt under the baseboards, cotton balls in the lathing. I figure your walls are stuffed with flannel."

Chloe laughed and started to cut up the chicken. Olivia told about her calls. Andy flew into a rage at the doctor for letting them worry so. But Don said he wasn't a bit surprised, Esther would bury them all. According to Olivia's mother-in-law, Hannah had been fine the whole time, but as soon as she heard her mother's voice, she begged her to come home. "She said she'd make me a chocolate cake if I did." There was no reason now to stay on, so Olivia had made a reservation for the next day.

Chloe set aside the seasoned chicken and dusted her floury hands. "How about it? Are you bushed, or do you want the tour?"

Olivia was on her feet. "I'm bushed, and I want the tour." Chloe led her past a mountain of book cartons to the back of the loft, where the bed stood between huge potted canes.

"Gabe picked up the carved headboard years ago. We bought a bed to fit it," Chloe explained. "It may be the only thing we bought."

Olivia laughed. "You may be forgiven that," she said.

"And now the one finished room!" She swung wide a shutter and ushered Olivia into a warm bathroom as big as a sitting room. It was a phantasmagoric jungle. The floor was green tile, and ivy hung from the pipes and coiled around them. At the end of a shower stall made of Gabe's famous stained-glass pieces stood a deep shelf where tall feathery ferns caught the light from the airshaft. On a platform, like a throne, was a gigantic tub with a brass spout and four leonine clawed feet.

"I like baths and Gabe likes showers," said Chloe, as if that accounted for the splendor. "Just now the shower doesn't work, but we're both mad for the tub. Lots of welfare people live in the midst of disemboweled buildings, and Gabe still sees some of his former clients. He told them he was looking for a tub, and one of them called when this beauty showed up on the street."

"I like showers too, but I'd love a bath in your tub."

"Of course, perfect," Chloe said. She should have thought of it.

Olivia said, without conviction, "I should help you with supper."

Chloe laughed and turned on the water. "What you should do is soak until Gabe comes." She got some towels. "I wish I had bubble bath!"

She went back to the kitchen, snapped the beans, and measured the rice. Risotto would be nicer than plain rice. She peeled an onion and rummaged for some saffron in the wooden box where all the spices were jumbled together. There was none, but the sage had broken from its bag; furry leaves curled ghostly white and sent up their ominous odor of dust, dank woods, earth. How close they had been that day to death—Esther's, and even Livia's. Olivia would be gone after supper. Chloe closed the box and fished in her bag for the cigarettes she had bought for Olivia. She lit one, but it tasted acrid. She rubbed it out in the sink and flushed away the ash. No fun smoking alone. She poured herself a glass of wine and sipped it. Olivia's glass, a stain of red in the cup, stood before her. Chloe filled it and carried both glasses toward the back of the loft, where steam was wafting out over the bathroom shutter.

Olivia filled the tub with water as hot and deep as she could take it. Only when the tension began to ease from her back did she realize how tightly she had been gripped. Massaging herself with the soap, she took the steam deep into her lungs. She imagined Esther getting the news, seeing her life swim back full-color like the features of a photograph rising through the developer. But by evening, when Olivia arrived, she would have arranged the event for maximal effect. She'd be as armored as ever. In the middle of relief, Olivia mourned the loss of an opportunity that had never existed. She would have to take this in. And then learn to break Esther's sway over her life.

A big tub was delicious, entirely different from a shower. You kept your eyes open. In its own medium, your head seemed more separate than usual from the rest of the body. Olivia's scalp felt grungy. Dirt glommed onto hair twice as fast in New York. She slid down deep, scooting up her knees and immersing her head as long as possible before bobbing up for air. Another difference: Chloe's face didn't waft around her with its questions. But then, how Chloe in the flesh had talked this week. How on the mark she had been about Esther and Karl. Whatever else, the loss of her father and gain of Gabe had slowed her down and made her keener. She must have some shampoo here somewhere. She was about to call when she heard Chloe's step.

"Olivia." Chloe knocked the shutter with her elbow. "How is it? I've brought you another glass of wine."

Olivia's voice hesitated, then sang, "Come in!"

Through billows of steam, she saw Olivia in the tub, hair

matted to her head. She was deep in the water, only her pointed shoulders out. When she reached for the wineglass, Chloe saw one breast beginning its downward slope.

Olivia saluted her. "How you indulge me!"

"I wanted to say—" Chloe's voice was clogged. She sat on the toilet seat across the room, giving Olivia the privacy of the tub rim. "Do you mind?" Olivia said no. "It's so wonderful, such a relief—about Esther—" Coward! "So great, I mean," she tried again, "that you, that you're all right too. I was scared, Livy, more than I realized."

"Ah!" said Olivia.

In the long, level gaze between them, death came close again, and together they watched it retreat. All that was left then was their parting.

"I hate to let you go," Chloe said.

"I know. I'll miss this. And we started so many things—"

"The time was so short, Livy!" Chloe wailed.

"Packed, though. Intense." A little unreal too, Olivia thought. "We couldn't have sustained it much longer. But it was good for us, Chloe, wasn't it? I feel so much better."

"Oh, yes, but I want it to go on—"

Olivia set her glass down on the green tile floor. "Ummm. It's hard not to be near each other. But for me, it goes on, it goes on and on." She thought of her talks in the shower with Chloe. The water was cooling. She ran a little more hot. "Listen, no one knows me better than you. I realize it when I see you. You go so far back and remember so much, it's sometimes a burden. You know what I hoped for and you've seen me fail and fail." She cut off Chloe's protest. "But you hang in. Even when you're not there! That's my point." She laughed. "You look mystified. Well, you talk to me sometimes. I mean, you just appear and say the kind of thing you would say." Overwhelmed, Chloe clasped her chest, so Olivia added, "Sometimes you're a real nudge," and asked for some shampoo.

Chloe produced a green gel. "You haunted me too after Washington, but that just made me miss you, the *real* you. Oh, Livy, can't you come here to live?"

Olivia massaged her scalp furiously. "Don't even start, Chloe. It's not fair. It's a miracle I have a job without a degree, you know that."

"Okay."

"Then there's Hannah, her school, her need to see Karl, my work with the therapist—"

"Stop!" Chloe was on her feet. "How are you going to rinse that? Hold on and let me get a pan."

Chloe filled the pan from the sink. "Do you remember," she asked, "how strict you were in Lipari about rinsing your hair three times with fresh water even though you had to fetch it from the well basin by basin? How pissed you were when I questioned it?"

"I'm still a pain about my hair," Olivia said. She could have taken the pan herself, but it was lovely having the warm water cascade gently, having Chloe rub her hair softly, lift it to the water, turn her head from side to side, tip it back. "I used to do this for Hannah, years ago," she said. But no one had done it for her.

Two pans were sufficient, Olivia knew, now that her hair was so short, but Chloe was filling the third silently. Olivia felt like her own Hannah, who used never to want the baths to end, and she knew it was because of the other pouring water. She thought of Chloe, happy now with Gabe, and me, but still wandering, striving restlessly. Oh, Chloe, Olivia thought, if only you would give yourself peace!

Carefully blending the hot and the cool, Chloe filled the pan again, and stood behind Olivia pouring slowly so the water didn't go in her ears. When Olivia leaned forward, she saw the mortal core of her, the chain of her spine, the shadow of ribs. She clasped Olivia's thin shoulder as she poured, her forefinger on the little point made by the bone. Finger on bone and love rising like steam, she felt fullness and limit at once. This is as close, she thought, as we get.

August 1971

Olivia raked the river. That was her job. The second morning at the cottage she told Chloe and Gabe, "While you all are making breakfast, I'm going down to rake the river."

Gabe looked up from the box he was filling with kindling, his thick brows lifted over his round spectacles. "Bring us back some water in a sieve, would you?"

Olivia picked her way down the steep path. The trees growing dense to the shoreline brought to mind for the first time in years a thicket on the Massachusetts farm where her mother had sent her during the war. A place where her stone seat was cool in midsummer, where the leaves tossing the light absorbed her wholly. A refuge, she realized only now, expressly for days when Esther's face menaced her peace, where ritual concentration abolished longing.

But the way this path opened to the abrupt hugeness of river and sky—it was wonderful, and there was none of her past in it. Overcast now, the sky reduced the American shore to a dark line. On the long ramp to the dock, she imagined she was the only living thing between that great concave bowl and its flat mirror in the river.

The trash of the night, a thick island of floating weeds, bobbed at the upstream side of the dock. Olivia rolled up the broad sleeves of Great-aunt Martha's caftan and jammed the grass rake into the center of the weeds. They didn't move. She had to work the edges like snarled hair to undo it bit by bit. Then she coaxed a bunch along to the corner of the dock, where it caught in the current and whirled away downstream. No one lived in the bay below them, and if the weeds fetched up in Dr. Morse's posh boathouse a quarter-mile below, so much the better, Gabe had said. It might foul up his speedboat and give them a little quiet on the weekends.

The rhythm of the work was good and the weeds were pretty—gleaming ribbons, greener than green, with minuscule snails stuck to them. A swipe of the rake unveiled a large rotting fish. She pushed at it, it sank, but it rose again, leading with a baleful silver eye. When she pulled at it with the rake, flesh shredded off. Its stink jumped into her face.

"Got it all tidy?" Gabe called. He came down the ramp bearing a tray of coffee and mugs. They wanted nothing between themselves and the weather, Chloe had said. It was a defeat if they had to use the cottage. Gabe, barefoot, was wearing a striped robe secured with a frayed silk rope. He took the rake from her, scooped the fish in it, and flipped it far out into the river. The curly hair on his calves was reddish from the sun. A flock of gulls came screaming out of nowhere to the spot where the fish had disappeared.

Chloe paused on the bluff with the steaming tray of food. The sight of the arc of flying fish, the woman applauding, and the man taking a little bow made her think of her parents, Jean and Simon, lithe and young, playing on the dock. Simon, caked in mud from digging something or dingy with soot from burning brush, leaped in the water with all his clothes on. Whooping and spitting water, he tossed his trousers to his wife, his shirt to his daughter, and one sodden sock to each of them. Jean ran up to the cottage for a glass and the whiskey, and Simon sipped while swimming on his back, his toes pointing out of the water. Then Chloe ran for the soap, and he washed right there in the river.

But now it was Gabe and Olivia on the dock, gorgeous in the rags of her forebears. The man, the woman, and the place she loved best, all astonishingly together. The chief miracle was that Olivia had come—drained and depressed from the divorce, overwork, men who mattered too little, and a decisive rupture with Esther. And she took so to the place. She was a good sport about spiders and the chipmunk that got into her room. She and Gabe would get over their shyness, and the river would do the rest.

Gabe met her on the path and took the heavy tray from her. Around Olivia, he had a slightly proprietary air. Olivia clutched her belly, crying, "Eggs, bacon, pancakes! After this, we'll have to swim a mile." Olivia took even to the icy river water, swimming yesterday almost as far as the lily bay.

"Hello, beautiful," Chloe saluted the day. "Will you please burn off that haze?" They sat on the dock around the breakfast trays. "We never used to have weeds. The water was so clear when I was six that my great-uncle found his lost watch gleaming up through twenty feet of water."

"It's the phosphates they dump in the river that make the weeds," Gabe told Olivia. "Chloe, is this the end of the butter?"

It was, but she and Livy would paddle to the outpost for supplies, she said. Last night, when they paddled Olivia to the American side to watch the sun set over Canada, she had clutched the gunwales during the whole ride. As soon as she learned her way around the canoe, everything would be better. But now she was balking.

"We're going to paddle two miles instead of drive to town? Isn't that a bit affected?"

Gabe guffawed into his pancakes. "Affected! Why, nothing of the sort! Just fine family tradition. In the old days there was no road, and Simon rowed the skiff up to the outpost for all the supplies. And before there was an outpost, it was tougher. Great-uncle Guy had to take it out in trade on his booze runs during Prohibition. Great-grandpop Emile shot or stole what he put on the table. We've gone soft. We just paddle to the outpost for the occasional stick of butter."

"Especially if it's not windy," Chloe amended. She knew Gabe got a kick out of rampaging up and down her family tree, now that he'd mastered the branches.

Olivia liked Gabe, but they were still diffident with each other. They both looked after Chloe when she left them to get the paddles from the cottage. Olivia asked Gabe if it was hard living around so much of Chloe's past.

"It's a little tricky," he admitted.

Above his beard, his pursed lips were full and dark. It was a nice mouth. His mouth, his reserve, his caprice—they had been teasing her memory. Now she had it. He reminded her of a lover she had after she left Karl, a man whose passivity she mistook—God, for nearly a year!—for gentleness. Was Gabe that type? His waiting so long for Chloe—was there another side to it?

"You think you're in the wilderness," Gabe was saying, "but there's nothing wild here, there's nothing merely natural, nothing anonymous. Not even that big gray rock with the pink veins in it." He pointed to the water's edge. "When Chloe was a kid, the water was higher and she used to crouch on that rock to brush her teeth each night. And see that big space beyond it? It was a harbor, all old Emile had when he smuggled his furs. Later Simon took his first baths in it." Gabe began to scrape the plates. "It all takes a little getting used to." He watched her out of the corner of his eye. "But you get the hang of it. You just have to tell yourself, That tree's not really a tree, that stone ain't what it seems, that rabbit belongs to the turn of the century."

She laughed. "You've really gone into it!"

"It's a change. Who in New York knows the first thing about his grandparents?" Stacking dishes on a tray, he gave her another sidelong glance. "Do you?"

"Grandparents, yes. But further back, I can trace only the gentile side," she told him.

Gabe nodded. "Mine—on both sides—gone without a trace. My mother's family—pogrom. My father's—we know the name of the shtetl in Poland, but the shtetl itself was razed." He swept the air with his hand, canceling the subject. "But Chloe's family, man! Their history's still alive and about, wherever you look." He peered around, as if spooked.

Gabe is very nice, Olivia thought. If he weren't spoken for, it wouldn't be hard to flirt with him.

"It's strange," he concluded, shaking his head slowly. "For all they knew about each other, it didn't make them close." He picked up the tray.

Olivia said, "No?" and he set it down again.

"No. Simon's father, John, broke with the lot of them. You didn't know about that? Yeah. There's this big kink in the line." Now Gabe sat down cross-legged and gazed into the river, as if conjuring Chloe's ancestors up out of it. "John was too good for his father, who was a two-bit smuggler. John decided to go straight. Translation, he was going to make good money. He went the whole way, left Canada, left the church, converted to marry a Wasp, set himself up in business, built a proper home, the works. And when his kid brother Guy, the bootlegger, got shot up and needed help, John turned him down flat. That's when Simon, a nineteen-year-old kid, made his way up here on his own to take care of his uncle."

Olivia didn't know Chloe's father had ever done anything like that, and said so.

Gabe nodded. "A very contradictory guy," he said, almost admiringly. "Simon is the hardest one to figure. It may have been his finest hour. He got his uncle on his feet and with the help of his friend Eddie found him some work, and then he went back to college. He came here every summer, defying John. But when Guy died and Simon inherited the place, he seems to have changed. Got conservative and proper. Never wanted anything to do with the neighbors but began to live in terror of their disapproval."

"Or, belatedly, of John's?"

"John's. Hmmm. Likely, very likely," Gabe said, and he looked right at her.

Chloe told Olivia to just sit in the bow while she took the canoe in close enough to the shore to see bottom. Flexing her wrist in the J-stroke, she remembered her father's last ride two years before. He had leaped into the canoe, talking nonsense, and her mother was afraid. But when Chloe saw his big fingers making their fine adjustments on the paddle, she told her not to worry. Simon's body still made beautiful sense. Drawing the paddle through the air, Chloe feathered automatically, the way he had taught her. Was that Simon's terrible influence or his good ghost? Or both at once?

"You know I've never paddled, Chloe. No one in my family ever went near boats. They were all afraid of water." Olivia was straining to sound matter-of-fact. "And this boat is very tippy."

"It's as easy as breathing," Chloe assured her. "Gabe never paddled before last month, and now he goes out alone with the double paddle even when there are whitecaps. These old cedar-splint models are very narrow, but if you keep moving forward, you won't tip. And it's the fastest, best, most maneuverable canoe there is."

She told Olivia to spread her hands wide on the paddle for better control and stroke close to the boat without touching it. Olivia took tiny strokes at first, but as she relaxed, they lengthened. To show her how a canoe could navigate a few inches of water, Chloe paddled beneath the arch of the weeping willow. They lingered in its green tent while a sandpiper strutted busily by, its white tail bobbing as its long beak dipped. "That's why he's called tip-up," Chloe said. Olivia laughed at his officious air. Startling as ever, the way the willow's roots turned crimson in the wash of the water. She showed Olivia. She told her the great blue heron often dove into this shelter, but they found no sign of its nest.

They rounded the point and passed the buoy marking the channel's turn toward shore. The current got swifter. Chloe told Olivia they would have to put their backs into it for a stretch until the next bay opened.

"*Ufa!*" Olivia stiffened again. "Why are we going against the current?"

"Well, the outpost is upstream," Chloe said. But I always set out upstream anyhow, she thought, the way my father trained me, to be sure to get home no matter what. Last year Gabe teased her in his hippie drawl: Like man, you know? Let's go with the floooow!

Far ahead, the side of a tall blue freighter gleamed. "Is it coming this way?"

"Yes. And you can tell by the way it shines that it's sunny up there. Maybe it'll bring fair skies."

"Yeah? And what about those giant waves it makes?" Her voice was tinny. Chloe explained that you take the wake diagonally, cutting between wave and trough. "Here comes a motorboat, we'll practice."

Wonderful, the control you got just by taking the right angle! Olivia began to feel more relaxed than she had in months. "Chloe, this is great. I don't know why I've been so jittery. I think I've lost my nerve."

"What are you talking about?" Chloe began vigorously, clearly glad to address this at last. "Who's nervier than you?"

"We don't see each other day to day, Chloe." How different everything would be if they had! But would they have survived? "And you idealize me madly."

"What's this?"

"Really. You remember how I was, or what you imagine I've become, and you project it onto me."

"Oh! Did I project the full-tuition scholarship at Berkeley with living expenses on you? Did I project Hannah into a terrific camp that had already closed admissions when Karl canceled his trip with her? Who's mad? Did I imagine you through your divorce?"

Olivia couldn't explain it. Those things left no residue, and she didn't want to keep up the act. She wanted Chloe to know how unlikely and precarious each victory seemed. She paddled clumsily, splashing herself. "Can we change sides?" she asked.

Chloe steered them into a bay where an abandoned boat-house tilted into the water. Hannah would love all this, Olivia thought. She pictured Hannah on the diving board, looking over her shoulder to check that her mother was watching, the quick anxious look that preceded the big smile. If Olivia wasn't there to catch it, would the anxious look fade? Or never emerge in the first place? Odd not to rejoice at the thought, not completely. Odder to want her here now, after working so hard to get her off on her own. Since saying no to Esther, no visit this time east, no explanation, no promise to call again, the distance from Hannah made her more nervous.

As the sun began to burn through the clouds, they drifted

into a marsh littered with lily pads. Chloe told Olivia to pick one of the big waxy blooms. The stem was rubbery and strong, and the boat tipped fearfully until it snapped. "My mother came up here for her first paddle every year and brought back a single lily to float in a bowl on the table," she said.

Olivia wondered again about Chloe's mother's decision, after Simon died, never to return to the river. Was that grief or something more bitter? Something like her own move with Esther, a locking of the door against grief?

Chloe was musing in another direction. "It's funny," she said. "I stopped coming up here when I went away to college, but this place is like amber. It holds everything just the way it was. I keep bumping into my former self at all different ages. Unnerving."

Olivia turned carefully to look at her. In her great-uncle's lumberjack shirt, with the paddle across her knees, Chloe looked young and dreamy. "It could be nice," Olivia said, "to have access to all your old layers."

Chloe made a face. "Sometimes it's pretty damn regressive." And she started to paddle out of the bay.

Olivia took up her paddle. "Getting the divorce was a little like that."

"Ah—how do you mean?" Chloe was all attention, and Olivia was surprised to discover how much she wanted to tell her.

"Having to see Karl again and again over details," she explained, "it was as if I'd *forget* sometimes what we were doing. Sometimes I'd just see his hands, or that vein in his neck, and it would be like it was in the beginning. As if everything that I *knew* about him was unreal or didn't matter. It was alarming."

"Oh, yes," Chloe said.

"Sometimes I'd think, I'll never know anyone as well as I

know this man, and I'd get terrified." Or never love anyone as well, she thought, but didn't say. "And though I was the one leaving, I kept feeling he was abandoning me. And that brought back the old feeling of failure that I thought I had licked. It was grim!"

"Jesus, Livy. Yes! But—"

"And the only way not to be overwhelmed by waste and loss is to stay in a rage, but then you see through yourself, so it doesn't work and you feel humiliated. Being separated was no preparation. Hell, separation is easy. But divorce makes you *know* too much."

Chloe groaned.

"People don't want to admit this, Chloe," Olivia went on. "Amy kept after me to come to her women's group. I was getting awfully solitary, so I thought I should. At first I just listened. But then this woman fresh up from L.A. starts talking about divorce—never having had one, of course—how easy it is now, no fuss, no muss, a mark of the culture's coming-of-age."

"Murder," Chloe muttered.

"I'd never heard such bull. I threw a fit. I thought it was the most *oppressive* line of guff—and in the name of liberation!"

"I'll say! And you said so?"

"I did, and some of the women were glad. But then I had to go through my whole story, and they couldn't see what it was that had held me so long. And *they* said so. One of them said Karl had used me as his muse. 'Woman as muse,' she said, 'is the oldest form of sex objectification in the Western world.' She's a funny woman, academic but very dramatic. 'Didn't you get sick of playing the muse?' she asked. 'How does your own song go?' "

"Did you like that, Livia?"

"The part about my song, yes. I went out and joined the local chorus the next day, and lo and behold! they were working on Bach's B Minor Mass. It felt wonderful to sing again." She laughed. "Not that the B Minor Mass is my song, but it's a start."

"Oh, splendid! I've missed your Bach! Sing me some."

"No!" Chloe was so distractable. "I'm trying to tell you something. The point is, they all agreed it was my conditioning as a woman that had got me in that bind. You know the argument. Everything in the culture conspires to shape us for dependence, beginning with the nuclear family. That's where I got mad again."

"I can imagine," Chloe said.

"Right. When I told them how iconoclastic and independent Esther was—*and* how undermining of me—it blew away their paradigms. It was good. Finally we could all talk about what really happened, and much more subtly. Eventually I told them some of what you and I talked about on the subway last year—"

"Really? What?"

"About recreating with Karl the way I was with Esther. You can't imagine how much I've brooded over that. And it came out that two women in the group had done similar things with their mothers—*thought* they'd broken away but sought out a man with whom they could reproduce the relation in some convoluted way."

Of course Chloe wanted to hear the stories of the two women. She wasn't so distractable after all. In the end she said, "That's really intriguing, Livia. Maybe you should write it up. But how could you have figured all that out if your nerve had failed?"

They paddled a while in silence. Break away from their mothers, Chloe was thinking. It wouldn't apply to me. My mother was too pliant to permit of any such brittle moment. Besides, there has always been space enough between us, a terrain as calm as a meadow flat to the horizon. It was my father I had to blast my way out from.

"It's always about mothers?" she asked.

"Well, yes. I'm talking about the pre-Oedipal attachment. You'd need a different theory—" But she broke off to explain the theory of the pre-Oedipal phase.

Chloe was glad to skip the different theory. Quite disturbing enough the visitation this morning of her father's funny bath, not recalled before. It left in its wake a now familiar queasiness. You loved him and found out too late? No, never could have, would have, in the flesh. Love him, love him not—as tedious and endless as the slap and gulp of waves in the rocks.

Olivia's excitement about Melanie Klein made Chloe think of Olivia talking in Rome—there was only a world of difference. She was so strong now. Did she really doubt it? But she was making absentminded little dips with her paddle. Chloe asked, "Do you want to rest a while?"

"I'm not tired at all," Olivia said proudly.

"We've come more than a mile."

"Tell Hannah about it. She thinks I'm an awful sloth."

"And she's really a jock? Do you miss her?"

"I do. Especially here. She'd love all this. By now she'd be agitating to swim across the river or hassling me to try some death-defying feat with her."

"Ah, you should have brought her."

"Well, we've both got to get used to being on our own."

"She's become such good company?" Chloe tried to imagine it.

"My biggest booster about graduate school. We take heart from starting new schools in Berkeley together."

"How nice!" Chloe was moved, as if she saw all at once the joys of mothering. "It must be in some ways like getting a second chance, watching Hannah grow—"

"No, no." Olivia shook her head and stopped paddling altogether. "You can't let yourself think that way."

"Why not?"

"Because it's *her* life. It's actually tempting to both of us to forget that—but we don't dare."

Chloe sighed. There were so many things to guard against, such multiple awareness—she would never have managed it. *Her* life—what was Hannah really like? "You said she took the divorce in stride," she began.

"Seemed to. It was so long coming. But we'll see."

"I wish I *could* see her."

"I'll send her to you here sometime," Olivia said. "The perfect aunt for my daredevil kid."

Aunt! Chloe humphed uncertainly. She knew they were both thinking of what she had written Olivia last winter, that Gabe's not wanting kids made her decision easy. It was almost true.

"Gabe is awfully nice, Chloe," Olivia said. "It's lucky he goes for all this tradition. And a little surprising, frankly. He's so different from your father."

"Wait, watch this." Another freighter was passing, and they had to concentrate on knifing across its big wake. The canoe barely rocked. Terns sleeping in the sun covered a reef. Chloe told Olivia to sit still while she worked the paddle underwater Indian-fashion. They came close enough to see pink feet before, with a clatter of wings, the terns lifted themselves away.

Finally she said, "Gabe and my father. What they have in common is loving to work on this place. But my father was up and about before seven, vacation or no, working as if against some deadline. It was like we were part of some contest but only he knew the rules. Gabe takes his time. Like, he said he'd repair the old skiff today, but it's no big deal. Now that the sun's out, I'll bet he's wandered up to talk with the guys working on the highway. Or gone to the boatyard in the village to see about a jigsaw. And then he'll sit down and ask the owner about the bait he uses for rock bass or what he thinks of Trudeau, and finally he'll get to why it's not such a bad thing the guy's son dropped out of school. Before Gabe came here, it never occurred to me we lived in a community."

"How come?"

"We lived like hermits! Livia, see that metal roof reflecting the sun? That's the outpost. When my father first came here, there was nobody else within half a mile. And when people began to buy and build around us, we more or less ignored them. We never got to know anyone but Eddie, his oldest friend—you remember. And my father always acted like the first settler. Everything had to be an epic drama—Man Against the Wilderness," Chloe jeered. "Carving the Laneway! Digging a Well! Roofing the Shed! Ambushing the Red Squirrel!" But it wasn't funny, and her mouth went dry.

Olivia wanted to watch them together, see how they worked it out. Gabe was saying that if he rebuilt the stern of the skiff outdoors, it was sure to rain and wreck the job, so he had to get it into the shed. "The hard part," he said, "is getting the thing through the sacred pine grove." When Chloe made a face, he laughed. "If I carry the front and you and Olivia take the stern, we should be able to do it without harming a branch."

The old skiff was damn heavy. The stern was full of splinters. When Olivia asked how it got smashed, Chloe muttered something about having put too heavy a motor on it. Olivia said she thought they had a thing against motorboats. Chloe seemed out of sorts. "We *don't* like them. We just rent one once in a while." She was so short that Olivia asked nothing more. Not even what was sacred about the pine grove, which to her eye was overgrown and ragged.

In the end, Chloe blasphemed the grove herself. No matter which way they turned the skiff, it wouldn't go between two scrawny old pines near the front of the shed. "Set it down! Set it down!" Chloe yelled. She stood there panting, still yelling "Okay! Okay! Okay!" at one of the trees, as if it were giving her an argument. Sweat stood on her forehead, but she hugged herself as if she were cold. "We'll cut the fucker down!" She was so defiant that Gabe and Olivia burst out laughing. Chloe laughed too, but her laugh turned into a comical wail. Gabe came around the side of the boat then and hugged her. Chloe leaned against him, laughing and moaning, then broke away, red-faced but resolute. "I have to do it fast. I'll get the saws. Stay here, Gabe, it's better if I go myself."

Gabe dropped gratefully to the ground, but he called after her to bring the long rope too.

"How come?"

"So it won't fall on the other trees. You two can pull while I saw."

"Ah! Right!" Chloe cried. "Of course!"

"Perfect!" Olivia said to Gabe. "Whew!" She sank down on a stone across the path from him, and they beamed at each other. Gabe wasn't like her timid ex-lover, not a bit.

After a minute he said, "Quick, before she comes back, let me show you something in the shed."

In a corner behind some lumber, hidden under a tarp, was an old maple chest, freshly sanded. "The lid had rotted around the hinges. It was hopelessly warped," Gabe told her. "Chloe said we had to throw it out, even though she'd loved it as a kid.

She had tears in her eyes, but she insisted I take it to the dump. It was ridiculous. She doesn't know I hid it here." Gabe uncovered something behind the lumber. It was a new and snugger cover for the chest, nearly finished, the edges dovetailed into the top.

"How beautiful! I didn't know you did this kind of work!"

"I don't," he said, grinning. "I've been wanting to try, and there's this guy in town, a cabinetmaker—"

But Olivia had stopped listening. Keeping her eyes on the dovetailing, she stroked it gently while jealousy closed like a clamp around her lungs. It didn't come often, but it was familiar, and she knew that its force might pass only if she offered it no resistance.

Chloe stood on the dock, an old quilt in her arms, and felt the turning of the year. Orange sunlight still struck the American side, but the shadow of Canada fell far out on the river, much farther than at this hour last week. Yet the light wind was still from the west. Getting cool, but not cold enough to go to the island and watch for northern lights. Just as well. They were all tired from lugging the boat and the fallen timber, and from the long swim afterward.

"We have a few more days of full summer," she told Olivia, who was helping Gabe bring the rest of the quilts. "But it can turn like that, any day now. Fall begins, my father used to say, when the river runs the wrong way for twenty-four hours."

"Translation," Gabe said. "When the wind swings around and comes from the northeast, it makes the river seem to run upstream. And sometimes, at the turn of the season, we get spectacular storms. Last year, God"—he turned to Chloe— "remember, kid? We were inside the cottage, grooving on the radio, what was it—Brahms?"

"The Violin Concerto."

"Right! There we were, in by the fire, zonked out on Brahms, when wham!"—Gabe dumped the quilts on the dock to sock his palm—"outside all Beethoven breaks loose! We ran out, but the wind was too strong to stand up in. So we watched from inside, and it came and lifted the boards, the very boards we're standing on, like toothpicks, man, one by one, and carried them into the air!"

Chloe hadn't known Gabe was so proud of their storm.

"Next day," he said, "Chloe and I went out in the skiff and retrieved the lumber, some of it three miles away."

"I had no idea it was so wild here," Olivia remarked.

Chloe spread her quilt on the dock, the one Aunt Martha made and Jean patched. She tucked under the corner the mouse had chewed. "It's wild, but it's on a scale you can handle. The river is more than a mile across, but you can see the houses on the American side." Pointing to windows flaring red in the sunset, she took a quilt from Olivia and spread it over the first.

"This river," she went on, "takes you right up to your limit. I pity people who live on lakes or ponds."

Gabe snorted and flapped down another quilt.

"Really. In a little pond the water just lies there. There's no current to deal with. People who live on lakes and ponds, they just loll around."

"Poor bastards," Gabe chuckled, spreading the last quilt.

Chloe ignored him. "An ocean is overwhelming. You can't paddle in it. There's no other side, no human measure. You're lost. But the river—"

"Ah! The *river*," said Gabe, stretching out on the dock.

Chloe muffled his head with a flap of quilt. "Shut up, Gabe!"

Olivia laughed. "Tell me quick, for God's sake! The river—"

"The river," said Chloe, "is exactly on the human scale. You front it, and it makes you do things you didn't know you could.

It's scary, it takes your lumber, but you can follow the current and find some of it again. And you learn to buck the current."

Gabe bucked for a moment under the quilt, then lay utterly still. Arms folded, Chloe placed a foot on his chest.

In her great white hunter pose, Chloe looked glorious. Never had Olivia seen her so happy. Gabe sprang up and wrestled her shrieking to the quilt. Olivia scrambled out of the way and watched the shadow creep from the river up the far shore. The sky was still cobalt. She felt cold and separate, her lungs caught again in a cage too narrow. Chloe can play out her feelings in this vast landscape, she thought, but I have no place to mourn my losses—father, mother, husband. Letting the bitterness course hotly through her, she imagined it seeping through her fingers and toes into the river's current and out to sea.

Chloe and Gabe respread the quilts in one heap. "This was Gabe's idea," Chloe explained. "We start out posh, on top of the lot. And as the evening progresses, we get under one layer, then two—"

"I told you we're going soft," Gabe said. He beckoned with his friendly nod. "Try it." There was no holding out against such good nature. His invention was in fact luxurious. "Decadence," he declared complacently. "My contribution. Chloe was brought up to stargaze shivering on the bare boards. If she located Antares fast enough, Simon let her put on her sweater."

They laughed, but when Gabe went up to the cottage for cushions, Olivia pressed Chloe.

"My father was always pedagogical, and it's true, he had his little system of incentives. That stuff galls Gabe."

"But not you."

"I didn't mind." Chloe stretched out next to her. "He was unhappy so much of the time in Syracuse, and this place made him relatively peaceful. Besides, if he was teaching me something, he paid attention to me. This is the only place we had that connection."

But what a connection! Olivia thought. Simon was so tyrannical, so egomaniacal. Everything had to follow his script. Chloe's acceptance, her need to affirm Simon, was disturbing.

"I thought what you were doing was bizarre," Olivia said later. "You'd spent your life opposing your father, and as soon as he got sick and died, you made him over. You fell into his arms and wouldn't let him go."

"You make it sound Gothic. I guess it was. Especially at the river that summer when you visited. Because I was swamped with memories of real contacts—"

"It was the last thing I could hear about. I'd put Esther on ice, and at that point it seemed everything depended on keeping her there. Even going after the degree, I realize now."

"So you were doing the opposite—"

"Ech, it's all grief."

The stars weren't out yet, so Chloe offered massages. Gabe volunteered himself. Olivia was stewing over something, lying rather more apart than necessary. Her isolation struck Chloe like a body blow. Gabe's groans of bliss embarrassed her. Sighing mightily to excuse herself, she ended the massage and collapsed between them.

Through a half-drowse, she heard Gabe telling Olivia about their friends who had gone to Chile to make a film about Allende's gunless revolution. He and Chloe had tried to figure out a way to get there themselves. Gabe seemed so comfortable here, but she wondered again if he would have preferred to go. Now Gabe was drawing Olivia out about life in Portland. She said she and Hannah would not be sorry to leave. It was time to move on.

Chloe stirred herself. "Whatever happened to Michael and his turnabout asylum?"

"The Hokey-Pokey Institute?" Olivia laughed. "In the end, it turned itself around. It evolved into a movement restaurant."

"Makes sense," said Gabe benignly. "The way to a man's psyche is through his stomach, everyone knows that."

"But the restaurant doesn't make sense. Or profit either. It's in a working-class neighborhood, and they call it Chickens Home to Roost in honor of Malcolm X. Everything is run on movement principles, so the waitresses won't take any sexist lip, any little feels, and the guys won't fence the usual goods in the alley."

Gabe hooted, and Olivia picked up steam. "Prices are kept low, but they hold ordinary oil in contempt, and the cost of pure safflower is killing them. What's worse, the pensioners in the neighborhood have figured out they're good for credit. Under the old management, it was a perfectly viable restaurant, but with political purity, it'll be a miracle if they last the summer."

"Hey, Chloe," Gabe said cheerfully, "you never told me your pal was such a cynic."

Olivia's no cynic, Chloe thought. She may be depressed, but the vitriol is for exorcising Michael. Chloe hadn't forgotten what Olivia once confided, that Michael was the most loving of lovers. "You know this from Michael?" she asked.

"No. Local scuttlebutt. Michael pulled out. It's his Hokey-Pokey colleagues who run the restaurant."

"Michael pulled out?"

"Went to New Mexico. They say he woke up one morning and thought of his kid. For all I know he's still there trying to find him."

"Well, good for Michael. I guess the institute succeeded with him," Chloe ventured. But Olivia hid her face in a shrug.

"My friend Sharon says grass roots have gone under," she went on to Gabe. "She's trying to get the community behind a daycare center, but it's all uphill."

Gabe remembered that Olivia had friends in the women's health movement.

"Yes, Amy and Naomi, but they're always battling," she sighed. "They opened a storefront self-help clinic in southeast Portland last winter. Amy was determined that the women in the community be drawn in to talk over their needs, give the clinic direction, ultimately take it over. But Naomi—she's a radical feminist—was dead set on pressing feminist issues, especially abortion. Amy thought Naomi should shave her legs, if only for the door-to-door canvassing phase. But Naomi says, 'Look, if we're going to teach them to do their own menstrual extractions, we have to be up front.' And so on."

The only one having a smooth time of it in Portland seemed to be Karl. "His canvases get bigger and emptier and more successful every year."

"Ah," said Gabe. "He's caught the spirit of the seventies."

Olivia laughed and stretched happily. "My turn to play," she said. "Whatever happened to Noah?"

Chloe tuned out to all but the shiver Gabe's deep voice sent through the boards beneath her. It made her wonder, could people who lived together a long time come to hear each other's voices even without sound, the way her body seemed to wake to Gabe's last night even when they were still asleep? Their bodies—so much simpler and even more friendly than the rest of them—were they their truest selves? And how did Olivia manage the stark night?

The sudden sounding of ships—bass call and tenor

response—brought her sitting up straight. A freighter and a liner were sliding past each other.

"Look, Livy! We hardly ever get two ships at night," Chloe whispered. "This is for you."

It's only circumstance separating us, Olivia decided. Chloe would make me co-owner of this place if I wanted it. They watched the freighter dip slowly out of sight, its string of lights curving between the masts, the even thump of its engines growing so faint that they weren't sure whether they heard or imagined it. But the passage of the liner seemed to take forever. All its decks afire with light, it moved, mysterious and ceremonial, like a tiered cake. As it slipped behind an island near them, the lights winked through the trees, blazing their black contours.

It's like a dream, Olivia thought. A pause, the world stepped back. Watching in silence, she was at peace beside these friends. Irritation and jealousy had loosed their grip. The lights emerged one by one on the far side of the island, re-forming the shape of the ship. Its wake clapped and shouted in the rocks under the dock.

"Bravo," said Olivia. "Oh, my! How do you remember the world?"

"What world?" Chloe breathed.

Gabe stood and stretched. "Look!" A single star, blue and quivering in the coldness of space, stood at the end of the extended arm of a pine.

"Is that the world?" Olivia asked.

Chloe was peering into the slip. "Or is that?" In the rocking water, the star's reflection lifted whole on a wave, then dropped and scattered. "Look how it breaks and starts again," Chloe said, "breaks and starts again."

They watched for a while longer before climbing up to the

cottage. When they reached the porch where Gabe and Chloe slept, Olivia kissed them each lightly goodnight and went in.

In bed in the little back room that used to be Chloe's, Olivia could hear the desultory waves on the rocks along the shore. Where Chloe used to brush her teeth. Nearly asleep, she caught another rhythm, a sound that soothed before she knew it for rain, gentle, gentle, on the leaves. So enveloping she almost missed the high squeak, open, the low squeak, close, of the porch door. But heard the soft call, "Oh, it's delicious! Warm! Come on out, Gabe." And his laugh, his low "No way! Haven't you had enough water today?" And her soft "Gabe, come! I'm a naiad!" And his low "I'm a dryad." Laughter light as rain on leaves. Then nothing while sleep edged its dark wall closer. And then his step on the hollow porch, the screen door sighing softly. She imagined a dull thump, Chloe's sculpted calves flying, curly hairs all over his back. Olivia's fleeting wonder— to hear all that and not be desolate—before the full fall of sleep.

Gabe told Chloe he wanted to start repairing the skiff, she and Olivia should take advantage of the calm, the storm predicted for tonight might wreck their chances for days. The clouds now were innocent daubs. Olivia said good, she wanted to learn more about paddling. So everyone's wishes fall in together, Chloe thought, and the air itself, soft as her own skin, called them out on the water.

With Olivia in the bow again, Chloe headed for a shoal where the eddy would spin the canoe if they let it. She taught Olivia how to steer sharply from the bow, using the paddle as rudder. Olivia seemed pleased until she set out across the channel in front of an approaching freighter. "Oh, watch our smoke!" Chloe cried, and three minutes later, when they were on the far side of the channel, Olivia admitted to feeling powerful.

Then she wanted to learn to steer from the stern, so Chloe headed for the sheltered cove of an island, where Olivia climbed out to watch. Chloe demonstrated the J-stroke, and Olivia cheered. "If you encourage me like that," Chloe laughed, "I'll have to show you all my stunts!" Holding on to the gunwales, she crept up to the bow while Olivia gasped. "When you're alone against the wind, you can make headway by kneeling in the bow. The canoe becomes a weathervane," she said, quoting Simon. Turning in her seat, she showed how to make the bow double as stern. And with her legs spread for balance, she stood in the center and paddled. "Of course, it only counts if you do it in a gale!" But it was Simon's showoff joke, and paddling back to Olivia, Chloe felt foolish and depressed.

Sitting in the stern, Olivia worked on the J-stroke. The water fought her when she turned the paddle, making it thud against the boat. "I'll never do it like you," she complained. All at once she got it. Chloe praised her, and Olivia did several perfect J's in succession.

The wish to show Hannah her new prowess came so sharp it stopped her breath. She could almost hear Hannah's loud laugh, benign revision, it often seemed, of Esther's bark. How strange it is, she marveled. Chloe has this place, steeped in family, and I have nothing like it, but I have Hannah, in whom old loves and griefs collide and are remade every day.

"It's so easy now," Olivia said. "Must be no current today."

Chloe laughed. "There's always current in a river. You just don't notice it when you're going with it."

Always current in a river. Of course. That's why you can't step into the same one twice. Heraclitus. For him the river was flux, ceaseless change despite apparent continuity. What I feel is evanescence, loss—and the strange recurrences. But it's the tenacious sameness that's haunting Chloe now. I don't envy her that. Olivia filled her lungs with the exhilarating air, glad all at once for the cleanness of the cut with Esther. I can see better what she didn't do, couldn't give, and the way she *would not see me*. And use it to work against with Hannah—she dipped her hand gratefully in the streaming water and felt the muscle of the current—until, she thought in wry reflex, that proves illusory too.

Chloe was telling her to set her course by the farthest island she could see upstream, "the one that looks like it's floating in the sky."

It *was* in the sky. "How can that be?"

"It's a trick of the light, or the haze. Makes the sky and the water the same limpid stuff. See? There's no seam between them. No horizon, no edge."

Indeed there was none. Olivia loved Chloe the way she was now. Sitting in the bow, white shirt, yellow hair, bright, cool, brimming, like the pale water. She leaned toward her. "The water, what color is it anyhow?"

"Oh," Chloe said. "I don't know how many hours I've spent wondering what color the river is. It's hardly ever just blue. It's never any color the camera can find. If I were a painter, I'd despair. It—"

"Would you say silvery?"

"I don't know, is it? Or is it milky?"

"Milky blue silver," Olivia hazarded. "Isn't it?"

"It's no color at all, it's light."

"What kind of light, Chloe?"

"Early," she said promptly. "Early light. Young. Half born."

"Ah!" The universe was clinging to the womb. The water was without ripple, the shores were half effaced by light, there was nothing linear, there was only this bowl of milky early light. The air caressed her arms, and she dipped her hand, her paddle, in milk. She paddled without effort.

"Chloe," she called. "I feel like I've never done anything in my life but paddle. I could do it forever."

"It's because you're paddling the sky!"

They had come half an hour in near silence, but Olivia said she wasn't a bit tired. Chloe knew the feeling well, but she had never dreamed Olivia would. "What do you think, Livia," she heard herself ask without having decided to, "about love between women?"

Olivia stopped paddling and so did Chloe. "You mean sex?"

"I guess I do. Do you ever think about it?"

"Of course I think about it."

"And what do you think?"

"For myself, you mean?" When Chloe said yes, the forward motion of the boat resumed. "I don't know, Chloe, I don't dare predict. I've changed so much anything could happen. It's not for me now, but who knows?" She paused again. "What about you?"

"I think no too. But it puzzles me sometimes. I'm always easier with women. I love to look at women. They seem to me more endlessly beautiful." She knows I love to look at her, Chloe thought, I don't even have to say it. "But it doesn't seem particularly sexual. I mean, I don't feel like doing anything but look. I wonder if the taboo is just too deep."

"Taboo is taboo," Olivia said. "You're not a hypocrite if you don't break it."

"I know. But I wonder, if I were fifteen or twenty years younger, not so formed, if it would be different."

"Ah, well—"

"With you, for instance," Chloe said. For instance. Coward! "With you, like this, the way we are now—it's wonderful. But it seems sufficient."

Olivia laughed. "I don't need anything more either. And it would probably fuck up the friendship." They both burst out laughing.

"Well, wouldn't it?" Olivia insisted. "And how could it be worth that?" She stroked the water vigorously. "But anything can happen. If my feelings changed, I don't think the taboo would stop me." The boat was veering to the left, so Chloe, reasonably satisfied, resumed paddling too.

After a while Olivia asked about the consciousness-raising group she had joined last spring. Chloe wasn't keen to talk about it. "It was all right," she said. Better than that, she admitted, in the meetings when the women looked back over their lives, trying to make sense of things they had not even known to object to. "Infuriating stuff," she concluded, "but every last one of them has guts."

"You don't sound exactly inspired," Olivia said. "I would have thought this was the movement you've been waiting for. What happened? Did you tell your own story?"

"I did, but they didn't like it much."

"What on earth do you mean, Chloe?"

"Unh! My story—it didn't pass muster as a woman's story."

Olivia refused to drop it, but Chloe wasn't in the mood. "Livy, what can I tell you? I flunked CR! Do you love me just the same? If I'm no feminist, if I'm unreconstructedly masculinist?" But Olivia didn't laugh, so she added, "They said I was 'male-identified.' "

"A male-identified woman," said Olivia. "What a crude approach! As if there were two separate categories of women."

Chloe was gratified. "Thank you, Olivia. It was because all

the 'causes' I've worked for—*causes,* that's how they talk about politics!—were 'male-centered.' You might argue that about draft resistance, but doesn't war damage women a little? And civil rights—I recollect a couple of women there." They were nearing the island with the tall tree where the heron sometimes perched. She told Olivia to steer for it. "One of the women asked me where did I shelve my own feelings when I was in the movement. I tried to explain that sometimes politics *was* my inner life, my own deepest passion. I got nowhere. I still wasn't relating to these movements 'as a woman.' Actually"—Chloe laughed, because dead argument had nearly become fond memory—"it was a little like the way you used to rail at me!"

"So I was the railer?" Olivia splashed her with her paddle. "Well, at least I was ahead of my time! Relate as a woman," she harrumphed. "And said it better!" But in a moment she wanted to know, "Was she really so formulaic?"

"No." Chloe calmed down. "The analysis could set my teeth on edge, but some of it got to me. One woman made a list of my misdeeds, I mean, my contrary acts." She rested her paddle to recall them. "My flight from writing to graduate school, from graduate school—just when I was really doing well—to Rome, from a prestigious job after they fired Noah, et cetera, et cetera. She asked if I was afraid of success. I would have said I despised it, but she made me wonder."

"She sounds a little off to me," Olivia said. "It's true you tend to disown your accomplishments. Once you've done something, it loses its worth. Like you don't recognize yourself in your success. But you're also one of the most ambitious people I know."

"Really?" Olivia was more interesting than any of them.

"Really. Not in the conventional sense. You don't want to be a big muckety-muck in the university, but you're ambitious about life, about leading an intense and dedicated life."

Something in her tone made Chloe turn. "I gather this is not altogether a compliment."

Olivia threw her the wicked grin. "Well," she said after a teasing silence, "it's not all bad. You're always excited, but sometimes you want to live beyond your means, so to speak. Spend more than you have and not appreciate what you've got."

"It's like what Gabe says," Chloe sighed. "Being happy is the real challenge."

"Gabe is a sweetheart!" Olivia said. He must want Chloe to live where she was, closer to her own marrow. Without knowing how, Chloe seemed to want to do that herself, never more than in this place so saturated with her past life. Here she seemed to speak in her native tongue. They rounded a point and entered a shallow bay of the island.

"You know, Chloe, I think you should keep a journal." She warmed to the idea. "Write every day. Not like you used to for the radio. You're a great storyteller, but I'm not thinking of stories. Write about the day, *your* day. Nothing about the world."

"Now we're out of the current," Chloe turned to whisper. "Stop paddling and watch for the heron." She worked her noiseless underwater stroke, inching them up the shore. The island lay still, bleached in the sun. When a cloud passed over, its dark colors swam out, then the sun took them away again.

"He's hiding," Chloe said finally. "A journal?"

No matter the blueness of the sky, Gabe told Chloe at the kitchen door, the radio said the storm was on its way. Down on the rocks cleaning the fish, he'd seen the leaves turn over. She stepped out and had a look. The leaves were quiet again, and the river lay flat as paint. "Remember how innocent it looked before the storm last year?" he asked. He was looking forward to it. What luck to find a man who liked storms as much as she did. He passed her the tin plate of fish and went for an extra load of firewood just in case.

Shucking corn at the window, Chloe heard little snatches of Bach from the back room. Olivia had overdone the paddling and was taking a long hot shower to loosen her muscles. That lilting voice—Chloe hadn't heard it since Italy. Maybe closing the book on Esther lets her sing again, she thought. She wondered—this no to Esther, could it really be all right? Was it final? And why did it frighten her?

In a fresh shirt and jeans, her head wrapped in a green towel and with a splash of lemony cologne somewhere, Olivia took over the corn, pulling out the little strands of silk Chloe had overlooked. She started in on the salad and asked, "Do you still see Frances?"

Lining the broiler pan, Chloe grinned. "You mean Frances Ruthchild?"

"She did a name job too?" Olivia laughed. "So many this year. Even in Portland, we have a Pauline Silverperson. God, if patriarchy were only a matter of names! But Frances—"

"She renamed herself for her mother, even though they don't really get along," Chloe said, seasoning the fish.

"What about you two?" Olivia was discarding the outer leaves of the lettuce. "Are you getting along?"

"Well, we made up the quarrel you witnessed in the subway."

Olivia smiled. She had taken Frances' part.

"Then when Frances decided she was a lesbian, she came to tell me right away."

"Really! I should have figured! And she wanted to run it all by you. Probably to see what she thought about it herself."

"Whatever. I was glad she came. She's a little bumptious sometimes, but she's got courage. I don't like the way she treated Clem, but it wasn't going to work. And she's come a long way from that straitlaced family. Been on her own a lot. Do you have a problem with that tomato? It's spotty, but it's perfectly okay." Chloe put up the water for the corn. "I like it that she tries to keep the tie with me alive. But I almost blew it. I thought her approach was a little theoretical, and Frances was offended."

"Whew!" Olivia stared. "You said that to her?"

"Yes, in effect, I did. She's convinced that domination is embedded in heterosexuality, and she thinks she can get around it all by sleeping with a woman." She poured them each a glass of wine. "I said it can't be that easy. Besides, the other woman—she's just a kid! She's very sweet, but she followed Frances in everything. In the end I apologized for my doubts, and Frances outgrew the affair anyhow. I thought she'd for-given me, but recently she said I'll never understand what she's doing because I'm involved only with men."

"You sound upset, Chloe," Olivia said, dropping the to-mato in the bowl.

"I'm not upset, but it drives me wild when people assume you have to have the identical experience to know where they're coming from. It's so fucking solipsistic. Are we stuck forever in our own skins, like—potatoes? What's imagination for? Just daydreaming? I tell my students that sometimes it's the only thing that keeps me teaching literature, getting inside other people's heads and lives." She *was* upset. "So it's corny, but I believe it. I've always believed it."

"Yeah, and you've suffered for it too," said Olivia sharply, attacking the cucumber.

"What do you mean?"

"I mean suffered!" Olivia slammed down the knife. "Suffering is suffering! Sometimes, Chloe, you don't seem to register what happens to you!" Olivia tossed the cucumber onto the counter. "You were in agony over Mississippi when the blacks felt they had to go their own way. Then you identified so passionately with the draftees it made you sick that you couldn't take their risks for them. And then a couple of soldiers who might have only been figments of somebody's imagination—"

"But Livy, that was dif—"

Olivia shook her head. "And now it's gays. You've got to be let into how gays feel! Chloe, look at it!"

"But you're running together things that—"

"They're not different, Chloe! Each time you think it's something new, but it's the same old thing. You don't let yourself *feel* it, *absorb* it—you just let yourself get caught up in the next excitement, and it turns out to be the same thing again! It has to!"

Olivia clutched her by both arms and searched her face with her alarming white glare. Chloe stammered, "What's the thing—the thing that's always the same?"

"The passion to connect. Sometimes it's so unreal! You want to wipe out distinctions by a sheer act of will! Imagination, it's essential. But you have to imagine the boundaries too."

Wipe out! Sheer act of will! Chloe felt dizzy. She couldn't meet Olivia's eye. Is it possible I'm like that?

Gabe's voice broke in on them from outside the porch. "Hey, kid. Olivia! You guys better get out here! The show is starting!"

Olivia ran back into the cottage at the first crack of thunder. Gabe and Chloe were two of a kind, crazy about the storm. It was exciting to stand on the cliff and see the storm slide like a black curtain along the far shore. But that thunder was not far off.

The gashed cucumber on the counter reproached her. Had she come down too hard on Chloe? No, but she hadn't made herself clear, and now she couldn't. The argument went on in her head. It's not just her willfulness, and she's better, that's changed some. But she doesn't heed her *self*, and so lays herself open to hurt. Olivia thrust the corn into the boiling water and the fish into the broiler. And why does it get *me* so hot and bothered?

Gabe came in whooping. "Great!" He nodded at the stove. "Good thing you started. Electric lines can come down any time! We better get candles ready."

Chloe came in behind him, laughing, then crying out, "I've got to cover the porch!" She rushed to lower the awnings.

"Batten down the hatches! It is going to blow!" Gabe yelled, tugging at a pulley to close the skylight. Olivia ran around banging down the windows. "You get to eat indoors tonight, Olivia!" He pulled a table in front of the fireplace and began to lay the fire.

"Oh, my God," Chloe cried from the porch. "The canoe's on the dock. I've got to lash it down."

"I took care of it," said Gabe. But Chloe was already out the door. Gabe went to the porch and yelled, "I tied it down at both ends!" He stamped back in, muttering about the candles.

Olivia found some sorry green stubs of tallow in a kitchen drawer. "How about these?" Gabe was at the window, cursing under his breath. "What's the matter?" she asked. She looked past him. Through the branches, swinging in the wind, she saw Chloe untying the canoe. "What's she doing, Gabe?" He didn't answer. She smelled the fish and rushed back to the kitchen to turn them just before they burned.

Gabe came in and angrily wedged the candles into an old blackened candlestick. "Smells great," he said, but in a flash he was back on the porch yelling, "Chloe, for Christ's sake!" Olivia couldn't hear her reply. The corn was almost done. She grabbed a fistful of silver from the drainer. Gabe came back and snatched it from her hand. "I'll do that. Fuck it."

"Where's Chloe? Is she coming?" Again he didn't answer. The toothpick came out of the fish clean. She turned off the broiler, leaving the fish on the stove to keep warm. She was pulling the ears out of the water when Chloe came in, red and panting.

"It's about to hit! Livy, you got the whole dinner ready! Fantastic!" But she didn't look at Olivia. She turned to Gabe on his knees at the fireplace. "And a fire! Hey, Gabe!"

He kept his back to her, and his voice sounded weary. "You had to tie it all over again with the stronger rope, right? Because Simon always—"

Chloe's voice was high and pinched. "It's not that, Gabe! It was probably all right the way you—but just to be—these blows are sometimes—"

They both fell silent. Olivia brought out the corn and set it noisily on the table. Then Gabe and Chloe bustled back and forth across the room, bringing plates, glasses, salad, butter, wine, Gabe's beer, and fish. All without a word. The hell with it, Olivia thought, I'm starving. She picked up the spatula to serve and the lights went out.

"I've always thought light overrated," Olivia said later. "People ought to linger in the dark more. The night of the storm proved it. Things were fairly grim until the lines came down. In the dark we began to get somewhere."

"Thanks to you and your question! I felt horribly betrayed. I could have killed you. But I would have felt too guilty."

"Murder often has that effect, I'm told."

"I mean, it would have been ignoble to kill you under the circumstances."

"Chloe, you're too much. Be sure, when you do kill me, that it's in a noble spirit. I didn't mean to be mean, but the tension was driving me nuts. It was like trying to take a jolly vacation in a haunted house."

It was a relief to have to get the candles, Chloe felt, and to fuss over fish bones they could barely see. The dinner was good and the fire was a comfort, with the wind rushing behind the thin-walled cottage. But the clouds didn't break outside, and tension held within. She was wondering how to pull Gabe out of his sulk when Olivia pushed her plate away and asked, "Have you two ever done anything here that Simon would never have done?"

Chloe flinched, but Gabe lifted his head and shot Olivia an appreciative grin. "I wonder why you ask—" He glanced at Chloe. "As a matter of fact, we have." Gabe stretched and tipped his chair back expansively. "We don't talk about it, so it's not a story yet, but it would be a good one. And kind of in the family tradition if you skip over Simon and go back to Guy and Emile."

Chloe tried to catch his eye, but Gabe was turned toward Olivia. "You see, I told you Noah's doing military counseling, but it's a little more than that."

"Hey, Gabe," Chloe warned.

Gabe turned to her. "Yes?" His politeness was a kick in the gut.

"You know we're not supposed to—"

Olivia leaned toward her anxiously. "Listen, if this is something you shouldn't tell—"

"We can trust Olivia, can't we, Chloe?" Gabe asked, smiling as if nothing were wrong.

Chloe ignored Olivia. "Of course," she said bitterly. "But you've already named Noah—"

"I shouldn't have." Gabe was conciliatory. "I won't name anyone else. Olivia, you can keep a secret, can't you?"

"It's my new profession, for God's sake," Olivia said, "but I don't want to hear anything Chloe doesn't want me to."

Chloe stared at the guttering candle. Of course Olivia will keep the secret, she thought, and I wanted her and Gabe to get close. And this was Gabe's adventure. But it was ours too. Am I jealous because he wants to share it with Olivia? Or do I want to tell it my own way? That would be contemptible. It makes no sense. It's just that the timing is so wretched.

She felt tired and distant from both of them. "I don't know what the hell's the matter with me," she said gruffly. "Go ahead and tell it." Gabe looked almost friendly again.

Olivia wasn't sure this was a good idea. Chloe had her back to the fire, and she couldn't see her. Facing the flames, Gabe was lit from below, like an actor. His steel rims glinted, his beard prickled with sparks, and the tilt of his head was determined.

"No more names," he began. "We had to do it all in code anyhow. We got a message from Manhattan telling us to phone home. We knew who to call. We were told some books were in the mail, the package would arrive General Delivery on Friday at the latest, he was sure we'd enjoy it."

"He being Noah," Chloe put in brusquely. "Since the damage is done."

"Okay, right, it was Noah. I guess you're getting the picture, Olivia. Noah's been helping some guys who were, uh, disappointed with military life to get some R and R in Canada. A lot of guys, actually. Somebody calculated there's a desertion every thirty minutes. It's the real antiwar movement, the one that will tell. Anyhow, most of the time it's cool to use the bridges. There's a chain of people in the States and over here, ready to take a guy across and pass him on to someone who will put him up and help him get situated. Great people, like the old Underground Railroad. But sometimes things get hot. The Canadians, for the most part, are glad to have these guys, but once in a while a customs official gets hungry, the FBI feeds him up a little, and then it's not healthy to use the bridges." Gabe pursed his lips in mock perplexity, then his smile spread wide. "That's how come we got General Delivery!"

Olivia was bewildered but fascinated. Gabe relaxed into his tale. "General Delivery means a town on the other side that has a bus station, about eight miles downstream from here. It's an easy row with the current, but coming back would be something else. No problem maybe for Simon or old Emile. And Guy in his prime had a high-speed motorboat because he had to make a few fancy fast moves. It seemed to me we might want to make tracks ourselves. So—Chloe was against it, but I went to town early Friday and rented a motor."

Keeping her face in the dark, Chloe only grunted.

"She was right. I didn't know what I was doing. I got a motor too heavy for the skiff. But there wasn't time to get a different motor, and no time left to row either. So we set out, Chloe practically hanging off the front of the skiff to counterbalance the weight of the motor, and even then the bow shot just about upright if you went fast. We prayed our package would be a heavyweight or have half an armory with him. And it turned out the guy was so skinny he might blow off the boat altogether if the wind picked up."

Gabe's relish of his escapade was irresistible. "You have to understand, Olivia. Noah had filled us up with visions of princes, these natural radicals from the boonies, these political clairvoyants who, give them an eyeful of the sergeant, suddenly can see clear through the military-industrial complex. Well, Noah had primed us. So no matter that our package was scrawny and dour, we figured him for a saint."

Olivia laughed out loud and barely noticed Chloe receding into her shadow. Gabe held her eyes with his.

"No matter he wanted to light up his ganja the minute he got in the boat. He was a free spirit. We tried to explain to him about the Coast Guard, but he didn't get it. Well, how can you blame him, hey, this hero had been through hell! The wind explained better. It was blowing nice and steady by then, and there was no way to light anything. We gave the guy the benefit of the doubt, but he gave us lip. Seems to have expected us to produce I don't know what. A yacht, maybe."

Chloe was beginning to scrape and stack the dishes.

"Poor bastard," Gabe went on. "I don't blame him. He was only eighteen, had never been anywhere, didn't know where he was going, and here he was stuck with people who might have been trying to drown him for all the competence they showed. Turned out he couldn't swim. Confessed it to Chloe in the middle of the river. She told him it was physically impossible to capsize. She told him the life jacket could practically make him levitate. She told him I was a champ lifeguard. She knocked herself out, but there was no calming his jitters."

Chloe padded across to the kitchen with the dishes, saying nothing.

"Meanwhile we were scared shit of the Coast Guard. We had that heavy motor, we had wind, waves, and current against us, and the boat was bucking it all, nosing almost straight up in the air. Real inconspicuous. But there was no Coast Guard out.

Maybe the weather was too rough for them." Gabe rubbed his face ruefully.

Chloe was still in the kitchen, but Olivia stayed, held by sympathy. This was more than a random adventure for Gabe. He'd done something of his own in his own way, joined Chloe's line of smugglers, and beyond that, he must have lived out an old fantasy, doing what he couldn't do for his own obscure family—help a refugee get to a safer land.

"We got home somehow, but it was too late to drop the package at the next address. He didn't really want to stay with us here, didn't want to eat with us, didn't trust us, and he didn't hide it. We were too tired to think about it anymore. Chloe showed him the bed where you're sleeping, and when we sat down to eat, he flaked out. Next morning, we were still asleep on the porch when Eddie drove up to pay us one of his rare visits, yelling, 'Ho! Banker's hours, eh?' We freaked out and leaped up, Chloe ran inside, but the back room was empty. So, by the way, was the fridge. He'd cleaned us out. It was a relief he was gone, because there was Eddie. He would have taken a dim view of it. But to be deserted by a deserter—it was a bitch!"

Olivia thought she heard the porch door. "Chloe?" she called. There was no answer.

The sky was a tight helmet, but the storm had moved on west. On the eastern horizon a yellow smudge was the moon behind clouds. The storm had slid by unbroken, though Chloe could make out several trees downed in the woods. When she came out onto the dock, littered with drift, the wind was down to a stiff breeze.

Her heart was lunging. The house behind her was a horror, she had to get away. The dock was slick, but she steadied herself with the paddle. The bow paddle—she must have picked it up without thinking on her way out. She knelt by the canoe and yanked at her own strong knots. The wet rope bristled like an animal but gave way at last. Now the other end. Heart still leaping. Boards slippery. The other knot came free fast. The boat felt heavier than usual when she flipped it onto its keel and slid it into the slip. Water high, no splash. With the paddle, she dropped into the bow. Beyond the dock the wind was still keen. She headed upstream into it, dropping to her knees. No cushion. The ribs of the canoe, hard against her bones, good.

The hazy moon behind her caught the tips of the waves. She crossed the worst of them, swiftly shifting the ineffectual little paddle from side to side of the bow. Some waves washed in, less cold than she'd imagined. Something dark sprang at her between the waves. A muskrat. No, flotsam, an old board. She dodged it, concentrating on the water, and her heart began to quiet. But her throat was raw with angry hurt.

Worse than strangers, Gabe and Olivia. The way he told her the story, the way she listened to him, as if neither of them had anything to do with her. Jealous of both teller and hearer, was she? That monstrous possessiveness again? But it wasn't only that, it was what Olivia said before, about her will. And Gabe's anger at her retying the boat. Water *had* washed over the dock, caution made sense.

But she was wrong in some other way. It eluded her, but she was sure of it, and pulled her paddle harder. It mixed in with what Livy said—what was it? And then Gabe reminded her about Eddie! She'd buried that, but her face burned now in the cold air. Finding them in bed and almost finding the deserter. When she'd seen the boy was gone, she kidded with Eddie as if they'd done nothing but oversleep.

Nothing happened, so what was so terrible? It was right,

helping the deserter, and I loved that run with Gabe. If Eddie had found out, he wouldn't have done anything. So is it his approval I need so badly? Is Eddie the surviving conscience of the place? Is it my father rising up in me now, saying, *Wrong*? Does his will still live in me?

She grazed something with her paddle. No reefs here. Was it something else broken loose and floating? She couldn't see. *Never at night without running lights or a flash, and a lantern on the dock.* Simon's rule sounded in her head. Rage surged through her. It was her father under everything, and Eddie his surrogate, like every single thing on the place. Everything bore Simon's mark, his rule, his method. Making sense in some way, but for her wrong. Then how *good* to break his rules!

Looking back, she couldn't see the dock. Because there was no lantern, of course. But a light was wobbling down the path toward the dock—Gabe or Olivia come to look for her. Longing for them assailed her. Then remorse. She'd forced their attention back to her. *Just like her father!* She made a broad stroke to turn back toward them, but it only drove her forward. She pulled several times before she remembered that a canoe in a wind with one paddler is a weathervane. Simon again, whatever she did. She wouldn't be able to turn it, she would have to turn herself, pivot on her seat and face the other way. Keeping her weight low, she managed to swing her legs around, but the canoe pitched perilously.

The waves lifted her now and she flew downstream, the short bow paddle barely holding her on course. The cottage lights flared like a beacon on the bluff. Gabe must have rolled up the awning. Now two lights were on the dock, sweeping the river. When they pointed her way, Chloe lifted the paddle and waved, and in the same instant saw the large log almost directly in front of her. She dug in hard with the paddle to steer free, but the sharp turn, her thrown weight, and a wave striking from behind made the canoe roll on its side. It hung there, on the cusp of tipping, for a long moment. Chloe had time to think, If I just lean fast enough the other way I will right it, to observe that she did not move, and to feel a long slide of the will before she went under.

Hanging on to the paddle, she grabbed a thwart of the canoe underwater and pulled herself up fast, propelled too by uncanny elation. "I'm okay!" she cried. She heard something splash. "Don't come in here!" she gasped. "All kinds of crap banging around in here—I'm fine!" She swallowed water, coughed it out. Better not to try to swim. "Current bring me right to you. Didn't lose anything. Don't need help!" But Olivia, arms flashing in the dim moonlight, had swum almost to her, to take the boat from the other side.

Warm now, Olivia couldn't get Chloe to take her place by the fire. "I'm not cold, I'm hot! hot! hot!" she cried, flapping the long sleeves of an old robe and giggling. Her eyes were blazing.

Gabe scowled and felt her head for fever. Chloe took his hand and kissed it. "No fever." She hugged him. "I'm fine, maybe never been better! Took the old river cure—" But when he started to draw away, she held tighter. "Oh! I scared you"— and looking past him—"and Livy! I'm so sorry! I was awful, going out like that. Jealous! Stupid!"

She could admit it just like that! Olivia was astonished, until she realized it was because there was more.

Gabe pulled himself away angrily. "Jesus Christ! Why?"

"That can't be the only reason," Olivia said.

"It wasn't!" Chloe's grateful look was so luminous that Olivia understood she had found something. She'd gone out there like a hunter and found something.

"Take it easy, will you?" Gabe said stiffly. "Sit down here and let me get you a drink." He put her in the rocker in front of the fire, made a worried face at Olivia, and went for the brandy.

Olivia tried to cover her with a quilt, but Chloe pushed it away and grabbed her wrist. "I'm not cold! Don't you believe me? Listen, I'm really sorry. I was acting crazy, possessive, for no good reason. I was possessed—ha!"

"Here, take a pull on this." Without looking at her, Gabe gave her scotch in a jelly glass. "Don't try to talk. Just take it easy. Here's yours, Olivia."

She thought Chloe *should* talk. But when she took the glass and felt the tremor in his hand, she said nothing. Chloe's confession had touched some grievance. She hated scotch, but like Chloe, she sipped obediently. Gabe took a swig from the bottle and began to poke up the fire. They stared into the secret center of the incandescent log, pink, white, yellow, flashes of green.

"I can't," Gabe said slowly between clenched teeth, "fight a dead man."

"Gabe, don't," Olivia started. How morbid! He was making it worse. It *couldn't* be that, Simon was such a bully.

But Chloe was saying quietly, "You don't have to, Gabe. It's over now. I finished it."

He wheeled on her, the poker still in his hand. "You took such a chance! It was so fucking dangerous," he growled, almost choked by fear. "On a night like this! You could have joined your precious father for real!"

It couldn't be that, it was so melodramatic, but his words seemed actually to settle Chloe. She pulled at his arm to draw him down to her, frantic to appease him. "It was the only way, and I went right through. I finished—"

"Agh! He's dead, but you won't cut him loose!"

"Gabe, listen! I did it!" Chloe was tugging at his hand, but suddenly she dropped it, staring at the poker he held. "Oh, God!" she cried.

It was the poker Chloe had thought of when she turned over, caught within the ribs of the canoe, suddenly like her father's own. And it was the thought of the poker that freed her! But it was too terrible to tell. Olivia was rubbing her head with a towel and clucking in distress. Do you forgive me, Livy? Gabe, forgive? Her lips were afraid to form the word. The sight of the poker had made her clammy with gooseflesh, but she had to tell them, make them understand. And not let herself forget it again. A wave of nausea flowed and ebbed.

"Something important happened, and I forgot it." She swallowed hard. "And I remembered it when the canoe went over. I have to tell you. I'm afraid I'll forget again. Because it was so scary. Oh, God."

Olivia sank into a chair and said something to Gabe, and he sat on the floor in front of them.

"It happened the last time my parents came here."

Gabe grunted, and Olivia said, "When Simon went tearing down the highway in his bathrobe?"

"Yes. I wrote you about that, Livia."

Olivia nodded vigorously.

"But I didn't tell either of you what happened the next afternoon. My father had taken a nap in the morning, and he was almost himself in the early afternoon. Then he fell asleep again in the back room. It was a lovely day, and I told my mother to take a walk so she'd get some pleasure out of her visit. I was sitting in this chair right here reading when he woke and came into the room. I saw right away that he was off again, but the way he stared at me I couldn't tell if he even saw me, let alone recognized me. He looked so vacant, I thought he might be sleepwalking. But then he stood not two yards from me and looked at me, and his eyes gradually woke up. They were full of hate. His mouth was twisted with disgust."

"Jesus, Chloe!" Gabe said. His eyes were bright points of pain. "Why have you been sitting on this?"

Chloe felt the tears burn behind her eyes. She was afraid to touch him. She mustn't stop. Olivia's eyes urged her on.

"And then he began to shake with rage! He spat something at me." What was it? Chloe was afraid she was losing it again, it was so like a hallucination. "I couldn't get it at first. But he said it again. 'Who the hell are you?' Then, 'Out, out, get out of my place.' "

The tears streamed now, and Gabe reached up to squeeze her leg. She clasped his hand, shaking her head. She wasn't to the point yet.

"He was furious. He stood there clenching and opening and clenching his hands. I was too stunned to say anything, and afraid to move, because I wasn't really sure he saw me, his eyes were so strange. But I also felt something I'd never felt before. And out of the corner of my eye I saw the poker, and I knew that it was in my reach."

She had to gulp air. She clutched the arm of the rocker. "Gabe, Livia, I knew I would use it to defend myself. I would use it if I had to. I was ready, I was more than ready. I was stifling. And thirsty to defend myself!" She clamped her teeth hard.

Gabe's face was wrenched with sorrow. Olivia's mouth was drawn, but her eyes were vast.

"Wait!" said Gabe. "What happened?"

A groan, half sob, half laugh, escaped. "Nothing! His eyes went blank again, and he wandered back to bed and fell asleep. Maybe he was asleep all along."

Chloe was still quivering with the horror of her memory,

but Olivia was caught in her friend's rage. No horror to her, rage was as familiar as her heartbeat, and if her heart was pounding now, it was because Chloe's rage was so inspiring. She had never seemed dearer. Olivia hugged her, pressing her cheek against her own, and stroked her wild hair. Then she folded the quilt and picked up the poker. Setting it beside the fire screen, she blessed it for helping Chloe find her willingness to act, *this* time for herself.

The firelight danced around the walls and ceiling of the cottage. Gabe paced the room, hands in pockets, absorbed in his own train of thought. He wheeled on Chloe. "Hey, kid, how come you sat on this so long, so *long?*" But he sounded more relieved than hurt.

"I think I was terrified to find out I could kill him."

Olivia remembered how Chloe had cherished those demented scraps of kindness from the nursing home, trying to knit them into a tolerable memory, while she herself had fumed and chafed. But Olivia had not dreamed what Chloe had had to hide from herself, his real confession, the one lying beneath all the others.

They sat together in front of the fire, watching it die. At length Gabe sighed hugely. "Once you get it through your head that the guy wanted to be alone that desperately," he mused, full of his new vision of Simon, "it's hard to hold him accountable."

Gabe was a sweetheart all right. But Olivia sensed that Chloe wasn't listening. Her face was streaked with tears, but calm. She was sure Chloe was taking in the pain of her father's violence, letting it happen to her at last. Chloe looked right at her, as if reading, and needing to correct, her thought.

"I *loved* him, you see," she said, almost inaudibly, "and I would have killed him if I had to."

Winter Solstice
1975

Rocking in the dark in the Mayan hammock, Chloe was hypnotized by Roman facades. At the other end of the loft, Gabe had bedded down early to nurse his flu. Chloe was tired from a long semester's work, but she knew she wouldn't sleep. Too full to sleep, but also oddly empty. Full, empty, full, empty—the rhythm went with her swinging. The light from new lofts playing on the grimy cornices, friezes, and columns across the street made their cast-iron fakery more imposing. Rome and not Rome, full and empty, here and gone. Disappeared. *Presente!* The strange feelings of ten days before began to rise through the clutter of intervening days, and with them a longing for Olivia. Olivia, of course! No point in brooding over her silence any longer. It was Olivia's great failing, a story Chloe knew by heart. But she needed to speak to her now, even on the wretched telephone. She brought the phone to the hammock and dialed Berkeley.

"Chloe! I'm fine—hell, I'm a wreck!"

"What's the matter?"

"Hannah. We've been assaulting one another. You're in New York? Why are you calling?"

"Just to talk, but it sounds like rotten timing. You need to get off? What's happening with Hannah? Can you just say that?"

"Yeah. I can talk. She just slammed out of here, thank God! But what did you call about?"

"It can wait." It really can, Chloe realized, her spirits already lifted by Olivia's voice, wrathful in medias res. *Presente.* "It's eleven o'clock here, the rates are low, I'm good for a real conversation if you are."

"Perfect! Just let me get my coffee."

Grinning in the dark, Chloe sprang up for the wine jug and a cup and lowered herself back into the hammock. "Shoot," she said.

"Chloe, long-distance! You need this garbage?"

"All of it. Dump away!"

Olivia sighed. "What a mess! Where should I start?"

"At the end," Chloe said brightly.

"Okay. She clobbered me with her backpack to make me get away from the door, she screamed, 'Don't touch me, bitch!' and she beat it out of here before I could bash her skull in."

"Mmm. Second thought, better go back to the beginning."

"Beginning." She sucked her breath. "I spoiled her rotten. No, wait. Beginning: I got her the wrong father. No, wait, wait—I had the wrong mother."

Chloe longed to see her face. "Okay. Tell me what's going on."

"It's only puberty. She turned thirteen. I know all about it, got an A on the paper." If she was trying to laugh, she succeeded only in coughing. Chloe waited. "She thinks she's a woman and acts like a two-year-old."

"Livy, what is she actually doing?"

"What is she *not*? She's kicking, punching, screaming curses, running around with a big macho lout who thinks he knows how to drive, not coming home till three in the morning."

"Oh, Livia!" The warm pads of Hannah's hand in Washington. Hannah at the Museum of Natural History last spring, riveted by eland and buffalo, a child dreaming of Africa. The snapshot from last summer of Hannah on a beach. Lovely high breasts sprung up overnight like mushrooms, wedge of bold red hair, a look of shy astonishment about the eyes, and a fixed smile, trying to brazen it out. Maybe it's that? Hannah's got such a stake in courage. Her body running ahead like that—is she making herself brave by pretending? Didn't we all try that stunt? "Lout?" she asked. "How big? Is she out with him now?"

"Big enough to override what authority I had left. But no, I don't think she's with him."

"Are you sure? Do you want to keep the line open?"

"No! If she gets a busy signal, too goddamn bad about her. But she won't call."

Olivia wouldn't be budged, so Chloe asked, "Three in the morning, you said? Was she with this guy?"

"Yes, this guy. And maybe another, I don't know how many—"

"God!" Chloe felt herself floundering. Would that be worse, or safer—more than one guy?

"It doesn't matter who, how many, how late," Olivia said. "The point is to get at me—"

"To get attention?"

"Christ, Chloe, she's had so damn much attention!" Olivia was almost screaming.

"Sorry, I didn't mean—I meant—"

"The point's to get me like this. To make me feel so bad I lose it."

"Your temper? Is that so ter—"

"My temper, my *mind*! To make me lash out, stop thinking, go blind with fury, fear—" She stopped abruptly. Fear of what? Chloe wondered. Olivia was back in the fight. ". . . she's got an exam tomorrow. Been out all weekend, not studying. So I said she couldn't go out tonight. She said I couldn't tell her what to do—but the cold, contemptuous way she said it! It made me yell, and she yelled, and I must have raised my hand, and she grabbed it and we wrestled, she kicked, I shoved. She called me bitch and I told her to get the hell out. But it wasn't the fighting, it was the way she grinned when I raised my hand. Like it was just what she wanted. She'd already won—"

"Because she'd made you lose your cool? Is that so important?"

"She hates that I'm a therapist. If I try to get her to talk calmly, she jeers, says I'm treating her like one of my clients. She won't lay off till she's pulled me down to her level—"

"She hurts your pride and ties your hands. It sounds painful! But what you did, is it so awful? I mean, God, if I'd seen my mother openly angry, I might not have been so fucked—"

"You'd be fucked up in some other way—"

"Okay, okay, but—it sounds like she needed the fight," Chloe said. Why am I babbling? I don't know anything.

"Obviously. She'd settle for nothing less. She can only feel good if she's wrecked me. So what?"

Chloe thought of the daughter of a friend, a girl who had just decided not to go to college. "There are no graceful exits, are there? Isn't it better if they fight free?"

"Tell me about it, Chloe." When Chloe said nothing, she added, "You're so cerebral! You think understanding pulls the sting."

Chloe winced. Am I going to be caught out this way all my life? Terminally dense? Her toes, woven into the hammock strings, were clenched. Rush to reconciliation propelled by fear—it might be her law. Fear. Olivia had said: Go blind with fear.

"Are you afraid she'll get hurt?"

Olivia's voice was wizened. "I think she wants to get knocked up."

"What! Why? Oh, God—the lout, the guys, you think she—"

"I don't know what they did."

"You can't guess? No? You can't—can't you ask her?"

"No."

Whyever not, Chloe wondered, wouldn't Hannah really be wanting her to? The complacent way she said it, the day she visited last spring: My mother worries about me too much. And when Chloe dug out snaps of Olivia in Italy, how she hung over them! "You know how much she loves you, don't you? When she was here, she kept after me to tell her everything about you when you were young, I wrote you that."

Olivia came back into her voice. "Yes. I know, sort of. But I can't push her to confide in me. She's got to make decisions on her own. I can't intrude, I have to respect her and make her believe I do."

A mastery of suspense, a stomach for waiting I'd never have, Chloe thought—and now won't get the chance to try.

"God knows no child has heard more talk about birth control—and since she was six. She knows I'm here, knows she can tell me anything any time, knows how I feel about sex, about everything. And I know how she feels."

"Everything but the main thing you know."

"*Boh,*" said Olivia, unfazed. "It's always like that, beginning with the fetus."

She means the mystery of pregnancy, Chloe realized, when one knows the whole feel of the child, everything but its face and sex. I didn't get that far, but I imagined.

Going full circle, Olivia seemed to have come to rest, and she was crying now. "Oh, poor kid, poor kid, the poor kid."

Chloe pulled it out of her bit by bit. She knew that Karl had married a woman with a baby son, but not that he had become an adoring stepfather. She saw Olivia on a dark Oregon beach mourning her abortion and recalled her own, now inconceivable detachment. "Wait a second. Did it upset *you?* Karl's feeling for her baby?"

"I know what you're thinking. But you know, it seems like the Dark Ages when I had that abortion. So humiliating and so needlessly messy and dangerous—and I had no way of thinking about it."

It was the abortion more than anything, Chloe had long since realized, that had propelled Olivia toward women's health action and perhaps into therapy as well. "I know. But I meant your wish to have another child."

"It doesn't matter now. No, it's better than that. If I'd had another baby, I would never have broken free, never gone to graduate school."

"Um." Chloe was relieved.

"But the way Hannah sees it, her father has up and got himself a new family, a regular picture-book family. When she talks about them, you can practically see them in a circle holding hands, and Hannah and I suddenly seem pathetic, like—I don't know. Refugees! Amputees! Mistakes!" She blew her nose violently. "She's more infatuated with Karl than ever, and she's stuck with me and can't stand it. Can't stand me, can't stand us."

"How is Karl handling it all?"

"Ah," Olivia said bitterly. "Karl's nicer than ever. His wife too. It's the divorce—none of us can miss it—hitting her now, really for the first time, and hard. So they're being particularly considerate, they're being bountiful—Karl keeps taking her on trips—and she comes back from them more savage than ever. She can't attack them, so that leaves me." She started to sniff but stopped to add, "Or herself."

"You mean—oh! God! That's why you think she wants to get pregnant?"

"She would never say so. But her mood is—reckless."

Those watchful eyes gone wild. I could never, Chloe thought, never bear it. I'd grind my teeth to bits. So it's just as well. "God! And you really don't know where she went tonight?"

"No, but—" Olivia took a deep breath and, relaxing, began to feel the real dimension of what had happened. "She wanted to scare me, and she succeeded. You just got a taste of what happens when I let myself be scared—" She could feel Chloe waiting.

"The pregnancy thing—when I get beside myself and panic, it's like falling all the way to the bottom. But"—and the next sigh cleared her sight—"when she swung her backpack at me, I think I saw her pajamas."

"What?"

"In the backpack. If she packed her pajamas, that would mean she had innocent plans. She probably went to a girlfriend's."

"Really? Would you *please* check and see?"

Olivia laughed. Chloe had got herself into such a sweat. She put down the phone and went through the heap on the floor of Hannah's closet. No pajamas. She reported back.

"Jesus," Chloe said. "She left you the clue!"

"Ah, yes," said Olivia, "that's Hannah all over." Hannah's "bad rabbit" look—alert, secretive, on the verge of whooping laughter—swam before her. How brilliantly she wove together father's tease and mother's candor! The parents may divorce, she thought again, but they stay married in the child.

Of course Chloe wanted to know what she meant. Olivia told her about the fight that began in October when Hannah went out slamming the door on Olivia's "Where to?" The next night Hannah met her mother's rage by swearing she would not speak to her again. So Olivia said that settled it, she couldn't go out at all. She thought Hannah had gone slamming to bed—communication was reduced to crashing wood—and eventually went to take a shower. Hannah came into the bathroom for a second, still refusing to speak, and when Olivia got out of the shower, Hannah had left the apartment. But written in the mist on the mirror was the telephone number of her friend Tina.

"Livia, how marvelous!" Chloe said. "She saved face and kept you from worrying too much. And it's all because she counts on you—it's like the time she wrote letters to the tooth fairy."

Olivia had almost forgotten about that. All her tests, she thought, are designed to make me lie in wait for her.

"You two are so incredibly close. How can you hold out? Don't you want to call her?"

"Of course we're close. That's why it hurts so much." Olivia tasted again the gummy rice and black chicken Hannah had surprised her with the night before her Ph.D. orals, remembered the unfamiliar look of all the winding roads in Berkeley when they climbed them together for the first time.

Chloe was wheedling. "Not to check up on her. I trust the pajama clue entirely. But just to be sure she's okay and let her know you know—"

Olivia hesitated. She didn't want to court trouble. "I think she's okay. I want to talk to you. Maybe I'll phone her when we're done talking."

"Call now. And get yourself a drink. I'll call you back in twenty minutes."

*   *   *

Hannah had begun to menstruate last spring when Karl brought her to New York, Chloe recalled, emptying the hammock of phone and wine and stretching out. The day she came to the loft. And at the same time Chloe had gotten her period again after so many months. But Hannah's occasion eclipsed hers: getting the curse for the first time across the continent from her mother! Her own consternation was funny now. After the drugstore, what? She couldn't slap her in the face and say, Now you're a woman, the way shtetl Jews used to. Surely Olivia would not have done that—had any mother really? So she hugged Hannah and took her to an ice cream parlor and the Museum of Natural History. She was only twelve, after all! Hannah was cool to the dinosaurs, but she loved the dioramas, above all the cattle egret promenading on the buffalo's shaggy hide: I want to go to Africa when I grow up. Oh! Chloe had said, your mother and I never thought of doing that.

But Hannah *was* a woman and could become pregnant at any time, just as Chloe had done though trying to prevent it. The thought of her miscarriage hardly hurt anymore, it was an old wound that throbbed in bad weather. Olivia had not even remembered it just now. Are you sure you don't want to get pregnant again, this time on purpose? she wrote last spring. Now Chloe rehearsed it all one more time. But the sorting out of her feelings and Gabe's had been endless, their decision against the abortion so shaky, the grief so disorienting and oddly mixed with relief—so no, no, no, she was not willing to go through it again.

She rocked herself gently.

After calling Hannah, Olivia pulled a sweatshirt, two barrettes, half a tuna sandwich, and a sneaker out of the big armchair by the phone, snuggled under her quilt, and sat there sipping wine obediently, feeling as if Chloe herself had tucked her up. Hannah was all right, she felt sure. She closed her eyes and remembered the sand drawings—was Hannah six? seven? Working out her problems so ingeniously. Sharon had read Hannah to her that time. "You're supposed to look, Olivia, without being asked," she'd whispered, "and quick, before the tide edges up. The drawings aren't meant to last." But the tides were so relentless now—what could Hannah draw, how could Olivia get there in time? Was she even supposed to be on the beach? The phone rang.

"Hannah's fine," she told Chloe. "That was a good idea. Thanks. Hannah and Tina had made hot chocolate and brownies, and now, according to Tina's mother, they're sitting in a heap of stuffed animals studying for the exam."

Chloe laughed. "So much for vice with the hot-rodding lout."

"I think she doesn't really like him. It's amazing how easily she can slip back into early childhood. One of our fights ended with her snuggling in my lap in the big armchair. She's as tall as me now, and so leggy. Like cuddling a gazelle."

"Mmmm! Hang on to these times, Livia. When those legs get a little friskier, you'll have your hands full."

"What the hell do you suppose I've been agonizing over?" Olivia grumbled, but it was comforting to have Chloe absorb a little of the worry. "But the truth is, I can't afford to hang on. The closeness we were talking about? It's been too much."

"Yeah? Sounded nice to me."

"It's confusing. To both of us. Confusing at best. Suffocating at worst. We've lived too much inside one skin, Hannah and I. Whatever separates us is too porous, leaky. Ech!"

"You make it sound disgusting!"

"It ain't great. Female soup. Let her stay in her bowl and leave me in mine, I say."

"Livy? What's up, really?"

She could imagine Chloe's concentrating scowl. "Ah, Chloe! I just want to be done with it sometimes. It eats me up, even when I'm neglecting her—"

"What do you mean?"

"Seems like I keep on coming of age, never get done with it. I'm thirty-six and it's taken me all this time to find what I want to do, and I don't dare leave her long enough to do it. And the irony—it's just this I want to work on, mothers and daughters, what we really do for and against each other. Women are getting smarter by the minute, maybe we can ask better questions now. But I don't know what to do. My plan for next year was to lie low, just finish the thesis and have time for Hannah, but Jenny and Alice—I've told you about them, right?"

"Let me see. Alice was the brightest and sourest woman in your grad school class," Chloe recited in a singsong.

Olivia smiled. She's still a little jealous, that's nice.

"And Jenny's the one with no cervix?"

Olivia laughed. She'd forgotten telling Chloe about her failure with the speculum during her brief involvement with a self-help group. Just by *trying* to use a speculum, Chloe had said, you outclass me.

"You've got it. Except Alice isn't even very sour anymore since she thought up this women's office for family therapy. She and Jenny want me to come in on it. We'd practice separately but also do group. We'd consult regularly, work it all out together, find other women doing related things, have study groups, presentations, the works. We're already handling a number of cases together."

"It sounds perfect. Except—oh!" Chloe cried. "Now you'll never come east! I keep hoping—" She pulled herself up and said vigorously, "Obviously you have to do it."

"It would feed right into the thesis, but it would mean spending less time with Hannah."

"Hannah? Didn't I just hear she's trying to break away herself!"

I fed her the lines, Olivia thought, and she's delivering them well. The trick as usual was in the believing. ". . . only make it worse hovering," Chloe went nimbly on. "When she really needs you, she'll . . . you have to be flexible, of course, but it's a matter of trust . . . independence . . ." My own words, but in that other voice, no matter how ardent, their vulnerability is tangible, they're a whistling in the dark.

"Livia, if you could hear the way you sounded talking about that project—" Now Chloe was speaking on her own authority. "What could be better for Hannah than to see you move confidently into the world?"

A laugh stirred in her gut. "Ah, Chloe, you always want me out there. You think I can do it."

"You think so too, Olivia."

I never really know what I think, Olivia felt, all I know is that *this* sea will break over our heads regardless. "Hell, if I did three years of graduate work with jobs on the side—," she heard herself say. Well, they could swim, both she and Hannah. "If I live only in relation to Hannah, I'll disappear."

Disappear. The word touched Chloe like an icy finger. The very word that had made her call Olivia. But she couldn't speak of it yet.

"Listen, Chloe," Olivia was saying, "it must be after midnight there."

"Who's counting? It's the winter solstice. The longest night of the year. I've missed you. I still miss you. But it's less bad. I had no idea you and I could really talk on one of these new-fangled machines."

"I've missed you too! We're snobs, we care too much about perfect communication—and we've had some pretty bad luck with the phone. This isn't bad, though, you sound almost real. I wish I could see you. Where are you? In your giant tub?"

"I'm lying in a yellow hammock we brought back from the Yucatán. And you?"

"In the big armchair, wine handy, already getting a nice little buzz."

"Your favorite green chair? With the arms Hannah carved on a hundred years ago? Yes? And you're facing the terrace?" Chloe remembered standing on that terrace a year ago, on an evening snatched from a conference across the bay. The terrace looked down on a tangle of wild garden. Chloe approved its neglect. "What do you see from where you are?"

"I can see San Francisco through the terrace door—or an orange smudge where the city is. And I can see you twisting up your mug trying to imagine it. But where's Gabe?"

"Felled by the flu. Three days dragging himself around, refusing to go to bed. Tonight I stopped arguing. I simply knocked him into bed." Gabe had pulled her in after him—always hot when he was feverish—but he fell asleep mid-pass.

"Folks clobbering each other all over America tonight," said Olivia comfortably. "Mmmm. I'd love to see the two of you again. What're the chances of a nice trip west next summer?"

"We've talked about it, actually. Renting the cottage last summer worked out fine, paid for our trip to Mexico. Gabe loves the hot and dry, and we're looking at Southwest deserts. And he wants to see Bryce and Zion in Utah. Maybe you could meet us there."

"Old friends of Gabe's? Do they live in Salt Lake?"

"What friends? Who?"

"Bryce and—who did you say?"

"Olivia! You're putting me on!"

Olivia made no sound.

"Bryce and Zion are national parks!"

"Seriously?"

"They're famous! Wild rock formations—"

They both roared with laughter. "I thought they were some hip couple," Olivia gasped.

"Idiot cosmopolite! Will you never settle in? You're not in Rome anymore!"

"Don't tell Gabe on me, okay? Try to come, and I'll take a crash course so I can talk to you, but don't tell Gabe. Oh, how is he? When he's not sick, I mean. What's he up to these days?"

"Up to his eyebrows, doing two lofts at once and cabinet-making in his spare time. Getting good, too. I'm next to his work table, and judging by all the drapery, I think he's making me something for Christmas."

"Gabe." Olivia sighed. "You lucked out, Chloe. You know that, don't you?"

"Don't *you* think I do?" Chloe asked, but her mind was on that sigh. Strange to be virtually married while Olivia was lone-wolfing it. "And how's by you?"

"With boys, you mean?" Olivia yawned. "That's all they are, the ones who darken my path. Boys. Who needs it?"

"Come on, Livy. Don't tough it out with me," Chloe began, and then she remembered Luc. First *man* I've met in years, Olivia had said a year ago. He's made me lose all patience with American guys. Chloe had never met him, but she rejoiced in the story of their meeting at a lab, when Jenny had involved her in hot pursuit of criminal negligence in the IUD. And in Olivia's high-hearted affair with the Belgian doctor, who teased her mercilessly before giving her first-rate statistics. And then felt helpless sorrow when she heard they'd broken it off.

Olivia had defended him to her: He had only six months here, he told me at the outset he loved his wife, she was waiting in Brussels, so we both promised it would only be fun.

"Is it Luc?" she asked now. "Do you still think about him?"

"Not often. And don't sound so sad, Chloe. I don't mind thinking of him. I knew exactly what I was getting into, remember?"

Oh, exactly! But Chloe held her tongue. Neither of us knew we would come to feel this way, Olivia had told her. I think we were both surprised. It's something else we have in common. And that's why we could end it.

"Look, the point is, I don't regret it. And nothing interesting is happening. I'll tell you when it does." She chuckled. "Meanwhile I'm celibate."

"Celibate!"

"Celibate!" Olivia sang out, clearly relishing Chloe's shock.

"Are you serious?"

"Yeah! When you *choose* it, it feels good. I feel rinsed, braced. Ready for what's next."

Chloe grunted dubiously.

Olivia giggled. "Are you tugging at your hair?" she asked.

Chloe was startled. She was. "Olivia, I'm having a little trouble—I just can't imagine you celibate. I'm sitting here looking out at these cast-iron facades—when it's this dark they sometimes really remind me of Rome, our time there—"

"Ah. It was fourteen—no, almost *fifteen* years ago we met, do you realize that?"

"I do, and my first impression of you, and my deepest, was—well, not celibate!" Juicy would be the word—even so slender, passionate sap coursed through her. "But I guess it makes sense if it's temporary, if it's like a discipline."

Olivia laughed. Just like Chloe to dignify it so she could

accept it. "Discipline—like paddling upstream, right?" Chloe chuckled uncertainly, and Olivia said, more kindly, "You can't imagine how often I think of that: how there *is* a way to resist the current. But this is more like getting into a quiet bay, out of the current. Out of the path of the erotic mudslide."

Chloe hooted.

"Maybe I delude myself, but I think I can see men more clearly," Olivia went on. "Like—hey! Guess who came to see me last month. Michael. With his son in tow."

"Ah, how *is* he?" Chloe asked quickly. "It's been a long time, hasn't it?"

"More than five years."

"Really? How is he—he got his son from New Mexico? Does he have custody now?"

"Yes, for more than half the year. The boy's pretty quiet but seems okay, and he likes his father. Michael's changed a good deal. The vets coming home have shaken him up—he served in Vietnam early on, remember? So he's been working in the hospitals as an occupational therapist. It's not only that the vets have been so messed over, but the cynicism of the government, the cutbacks in benefits, and the total indifference of the left— it was making him crazy."

"It's hard to be fair to the vets who haven't opposed the war," Chloe said.

"No one's been fair. What gets Michael is the hysteria over the boat people, this great outpouring of guilt—it goes hand in hand with the neglect, the outright *hostility* to the vets."

"It's all a mess. And this orgy of sentiment over Operation Babylift! The press eats it up, and there's no knowing what's really happening in Vietnam. I'm worried. I'm afraid some- times we expected too much of the North Vietnamese. Noah has this awful feeling it's going to be rough—"

Poor Noah, Olivia thought, he built his life around the war. It must be like getting a divorce. "How does he feel?"

"Every which way. The celebration is over, isn't it? Now that he's gotten what he worked for so hard, he's at sea. He's working on amnesty for the guys in Canada, but he's nervous, doesn't look good. Occupation gone. I wish he had something like Michael. Occupational therapist! I could use him myself! The question is, Livia, can you?"

"I like to listen to him. He puts in long hours talking to the guys. He's very moved by them. I think he's changed. There's this little pause before he speaks. He's less sure of himself. More thoughtful."

"*He* doesn't sound like a boy, Livy," Chloe persisted. "What do you think? Were you already, er—celibate when you saw him?"

Chloe sounded so wistful! "Yes, and it was just one day and his son was here too." Olivia thought of the bus terminal. "Something strange happened when he came. I wish I could tell you face to face." How odd to miss her so much all at once!

"I'm here."

Okay. "I went to meet his bus. The terminal was crowded, and I didn't see him. But there was a man bending over a magazine explaining something to a plump teenage boy. I noticed him because something about him"—was it his stoop? his patience?—"reminded me vividly of that tender man Esther sent to take me and Andy back to Italy. I couldn't see Michael anywhere, but when the man looked up—well, it was Michael!"

"You hadn't recognized him?"

"No. Not with his big beard gone. And he's thinner. But in a sense I did recognize him. More than if I'd known who he was."

"What a wonderful mistake! Did you tell him?"

"No, dear, only you. But he got the benefit of it all day. It was very nice. We've known each other for a long time, and he seems to have kept track of me—well, he really knows me!" The depth of Chloe's silence made her add, "Not as well as you do, but much better than I'm used to in a man."

Chloe cleared her throat and said forcefully, "Olivia, you will see him again."

"Still so bossy!" The temptation to tease was sweet, but it was sweeter to answer straight. "I think he's coming again soon for a few days, and I don't know what will happen."

"Listen, Livy, I don't know how to say this. When you told me about Michael way back in Washington, I got the idea that he was too intrusive—I caught it from you." She hesitated.

So Chloe wasn't jealous, Olivia decided. Or if she was, she was struggling hard against it.

"But was that really so," she went on tentatively, "or were you afraid—I mean of his coming too close?"

It's what she fears I feel about her, Olivia knew. When she didn't deny it, Chloe drew breath and plunged on.

"Livia, wasn't that the secret of Karl's hold all along? You've hinted at this—he never wanted to get close enough to know you, and so you felt safe? But you're past that now, aren't you? Sounds as if you like Michael knowing you."

Reading Michael by herself, using her longing for closeness to urge it for Michael, loving her enough to let her go to Michael, loving her through him—it was extraordinary.

"I don't know if I can let anyone get as close as you, Chlo," she said. Then she laughed. "Hey, he may not even come! And if he does, and if it takes off between us, it'll be a problem. There's Hannah and his son. And he lives and works in Portland."

"Oh, occupational therapists travel, they're in demand all

over the country," Chloe improvised airily. "And the vets, God knows, are everywhere."

"Now, Chloe, for heaven's sake," Olivia said firmly, "enough about Michael. Tell me what you've been up to. Tell me about yourself."

Which self, Chloe wanted to ask, the one right next to your life now in Berkeley? Or the separate one in New York? Moving back to her single self made the half-forgotten distance odiously palpable. She approached herself from outside, like a stranger.

"I'm in better shape than Noah. I didn't hammer away at the war to the end, like him. And I got some good out of it. It forced me to learn about the Third World and our imperialism. That doesn't go away, there's plenty to attend to."

"You've been doing a course on the Third World, haven't you? And bringing in women too," Olivia said, proving she'd read Chloe's letters even if she hadn't answered. "How's it going? Why do you say you could use an occupational therapist?"

"Because I'm never sure teaching is enough. But the course is good, better than I expected. Most of the kids didn't feel the sixties personally, and that makes it strange. They're old-fashioned students again, in school to learn or to get credentials for work. I miss the ones who wanted to rip everything up, they taught me so much. These—I have to find ways to hook them. But oh, I had two gems in my class this semester."

"You always manage to find at least one to care for, don't you? Beginning with the girl with the snake. You pour so much into your students, Chloe, sometimes I think they're—the ones you love—your children."

"Oh, no, no, not really." It's not just that I'll cry if we talk about this, she thought, it's that I'd need her more than I can bear.

"Chloe? Don't you want to talk about it?"

"Afraid I'm not up for it."

Silence. Then, "Okay," Olivia said evenly. "Can I ask about your writing?"

Olivia's gingerliness made it easy. "Yeah. I'm writing. Not just the essays you've seen, but what you suggested in Ontario. A journal. When I can. Took me a long time to get to it. It was a good idea."

"Oh, I'm glad! How does it work—do you like the way it's coming out?"

"Sometimes. Not often. But I like doing it, I like the difficulty."

"That sounds like you all right. It must have the ring of authenticity anyhow." Olivia's laugh was a caress. At her end of the line, in New York, Chloe knew she could hold back or lean into it. She savored the freedom and wanted to prolong it. Olivia was saying, "Tell me more."

"I can't do it like other writing. I've tried, at my desk in the afternoon, in the evening. But it's not possible. Sometimes it comes to me on the subway. Mostly I write in the middle of the night, like this, facing Rome out there, as often as not in this hammock."

"Adrift, eh? That's nice. It sounds right."

"It's like peeling words. Something happens, I want to catch it, I know I've felt it, I sit down to write, but the words I start with are like bark. Coarse, tough. I have to strip it back, get under—"

"Mmmm. To get at the wand."

"Exactly!" Though she hadn't thought wand. She'd thought marrow, she'd thought wood's flesh, like in Ontario when she'd stripped bark once from a log, it was so resistant and sharp she'd hurt her hands. She'd thought of the pith, naked, wet, alive. But wand was good—when she freed it, it released her. "You understand without my explaining. But I can't get at it often. The wand, I mean. I try more often than I succeed."

"Of course," said Olivia, as if any other account would be failure. "I'm very glad, Chloe."

That low timbre. "Sometimes I'm writing to you." The words were out without her willing. Olivia's surprised "Oh?" prevented retraction. "I mean, as if to you, to make you see what I see—"

"How lovely! Why don't you send them to me?"

"They're not letters. I mean—" What she meant was that she wrote as if Livia were at her side, snug to her ribs, facing the world the same way, seeing not just *what* but *as* she saw. Sometimes she set to work with Livia's name on her lips. Tongue's tip up to the teeth for *L*, the *v* a bite at her lower lip. Surprising when she first noticed it, because she wasn't writing for Livia. She realized now that "Livia"—mouthed, unsounded—announced a need for privacy. For getting nearer herself. But she couldn't say this to that other Livia in California, even now with her warmest voice in her ear. To that one instead, with unexpected bitterness, she blurted, "And what if I did send them to you? I wouldn't know what you thought, I wouldn't be able to stand it—"

"Because I don't write?"

Because you're not *here,* Chloe didn't say.

Olivia sat up like a shot. "Chlo, I've hurt you! I'm so sorry!"

Chloe's voice came from high in her head. "I'm all right. I don't know why I said that! I don't really want you to read—"

"Don't take it back! You mean you can't bear my not answering. This keeps happening between us. I don't write often enough, it's true, I really don't know why, but it doesn't mean I don't care. Why can't you trust me? I miss you too! There's no one else I can talk to like you."

"Livy, this isn't necessary any—"

"Wait. Let me try. I don't want you hurt—"

"I'm all right!"

"Just listen to me, Chlo. I never explain myself well enough. We're different. You don't feel like this, I know, but the fact is I miss you more when I write. Maybe I protect myself by not writing. When I don't, I can summon you and you're with me. Because you're a permanent part—"

"I know, I know, you've told me. It's not really the writing, it's just—God, *missing* you so much. My only recourse till now has been to forget you—"

"Forget me!" Those shattering words again. Olivia found herself on her feet, shaking, her oldest fear black with reality.

"Damn straight!"

Olivia paced as far as the phone cord let her. Why didn't you warn me? she wanted to cry, but panic parched her throat.

Chloe wasn't rushing now to appease her, to take it back. "We each have our way of coping," she said. "Imagine how I feel, Livia, being an idea you carry around with you, like a dead thing. My way has been to forget you, or try to. Because I'm real, I'm here! Life keeps right on messing with us! We're not frozen, we live in *time!*"

"We do, Chloe, but not entirely, not so simply." About this she had words. "You and I, we live in so many times and places, and when we're together it's as if we make it up ourselves, the time, the place—"

"*Make it up!*" Chloe was outraged anew. "You say that so matter-of-factly, but to me it's a nightmare. It's been my nightmare, I mean. Because it's changed, it's changing right now. This is what I called to say, actually, I just realized it."

"What do you mean?"

"That the hurt is done with."

"It doesn't *sound* very done with!"

"No, because once we get in the argument—I've played it out so often in my head—but wait. I'm trying to tell you something's happened that's making me see it all differently."

She *did* sound different. Exhausted, Olivia crawled into her chair. "Will you please explain yourself."

"It's a bit of a story," Chloe said, entirely calm now. "And it must be late even there on the sunny side of the world."

Olivia pulled the quilt up to her chin. She peered at the smear of light that was San Francisco, as if by looking hard enough she could make it New York. She knew where she was: Chloe had a story to tell. "What happened?" she asked, catching her friend's calm. "I'm yours for the duration. Why did you call?"

Chloe stood, kicked a kink out of her leg, poured herself another cup of wine, and eased herself back into the hammock. The facade across the street was now quite dark. What pattern she saw there was made by memory.

"I've been obsessed by disappearance. About ten days ago, we had a demonstration at the United Nations—"

"Ah, your Chile project."

"Yes. We marched in front of the Chilean mission, a much larger group than we'd had at meetings, all women—"

"Great! The synthesis is working!"

"Synthesis?"

"Of feminism and anti-imperialism. Wasn't that the point? The women's movement was becoming so middle-class, so domestic—"

"Oh, absolutely! Did I tell you the National Organization for Women wouldn't let us bring our protest for Chilean women into their march last spring? It's true. On International Women's Day yet! So we still don't reach those women. The ones who come out cared about Latin America before or had been deep into antiwar. But reaching American women was only half the point. The other half was that Chilean support groups weren't mentioning women at all—"

"And isn't some huge percent of prisoners in Chile women?"

"Twenty-four percent, we think. Hey, you really read the stuff I sent you!"

"Damn you, Chlo—"

"I'm sorry, Livy." But how was I supposed to know? "The support groups don't deal with that," she went on, "and for the Chilean organizations feminism is a bourgeois joke. The women may not have been leaders, but they've done plenty. And since the coup, they've been taking the weight along with the male cadre."

"How about women from Chile? Are they with you?"

"It's hard. They may come once to a meeting of ours, but their first loyalty is to their party. Why shouldn't it be? And then some of them are working-class and don't want to come at all. We have to face it—our group may be countercultural, but hardly working-class."

"Whew! It must be frustrating."

"It is, but when you understand why, it's easier to take."

"What about the Chilean women who've lived here for years?"

"Some of them have been involved. But they have a problem too. They're afraid—and who's to say they're wrong?—that DINA agents, the secret police, are everywhere, and that if they challenge Pinochet publicly, they can never go home. So, oh! At the demonstration, none of those women came. It was a heavy blow. But then some other women we'd never seen showed up out of nowhere. We couldn't figure who they were. They looked funny because they were wearing dark glasses. In December! But after a while, we realized they were our Chilenas, all wearing wigs—and wearing them well!—to foil the DINA."

"So wigs are politically useful! I love it! Chloe, things are coming together for you this time!"

"For moments. And it doesn't kill me when they can't—"

"But *this* is good news—"

She's right, Chloe thought, I'm more patient. And there are some victories. She told Olivia how their petition campaign got a few women released from Tres Alamos prison. "The stories they've told! Not here, though, because of Nixon and Ford's restrictions on asylum. It's obscene. The bloodiest coup in the history of Latin America, no other country refuses asylum, but the U.S. pours aid into the junta—"

"They have no shame," Olivia burst in. "They take in the boat people, but not the Chileans. They might as well admit they paid for the coup—"

Olivia kept surprising her tonight. "Yes, well, everybody's wising up now, what with the Senate investigation, but we have to keep up the pressure—"

"Chloe, about their stories—you sent me a xerox, remember? Testimony of a woman who'd been tortured? I'll never forget it. It was so graphic! The insane malice—I couldn't sleep after I read it. The tortures they devised for women—"

"Oh, God! You mean the way they used the electric shock—"

"All of it! Christ! Don't remind me. It was too ingeniously sadistic, too grisly, to be only about political repression."

"What else? What do you mean?"

"It has to come from some primitive terror of the female."

Chloe recalled the books on Olivia's bed table, a tidy heap of feminist theory. "Maybe, Livy," she said, "but when they come together, misogyny and politics, the torture is more brutal. Because these women stepped out of their place—"

"That's it, they refused to be servile—"

"Okay. They're tortured for both things. But for the women it's all one, and when they get out of the torture chambers, if they do, into prison, they start to organize themselves as women. They all care for the babies—a number of them were pregnant. Whatever food they have they share, whatever skill. A professor gives lectures, someone else teaches shoe repair. They cover the walls with their own newspapers, and when those are torn down, they tell it in poems or they sing. They're amazing. One woman said ninety-five percent of them had resisted torture—they've really proven themselves to the men."

"How awful that they felt they had to—"

"Mmmn, but how glorious that they got strength from what was supposed to break them! It takes your breath away."

Phoenix birth. This is the turn Chloe has always loved, thought Olivia, and in some sense lives for. Even now when she's so much more awake to complexity and failure. *Especially* now.

"I can't tell you how it affected us," Chloe was saying, "knowing about the violence. Like you're violated your*self*—unless, as a Chilena put it, you're fighting to become part of the tree of life, feeding it with your own. It's a hard idea—"

"It's beautiful—"

"It's either very crazy or very sane."

"Why crazy?"

"Because there's always death and loss, and the idea means you will never accept that. How can you live sanely that way?

But at the demonstration at the Chilean mission, it came at me another way. And this, at last, is what I called to tell you about."

They both began to laugh—low, bitten-off laughs—but laugh they did, in the middle of grief, right across the continent. It was, Olivia thought, a tiny proof of that tree of life, a little branch, a tendril.

"Okay." Chloe took a deep breath. "The demonstration was not only for the prisoners in Chile, men and women. It was also for the people there's no trace of, no record, people seized in prison, in their homes, in the street, often in front of witnesses! The Chileans call them the *desaparecidos*, the 'disappeared ones.' The situation has twisted the language. 'Disappear' in Spanish has become a transitive verb. They say, 'The police disappeared her.' "

"God, how sinister!"

"Sinister and worse. To me, it's worse than torture and outright murder—because the disappeared person *could* be murdered, but you can't know if it's happened already, going to happen later, or happening at that very second. It must cripple the survivors. No dead to bury, and they don't *dare* grieve, because that would be surrender. And can't fight, because the target keeps receding. Hope—it has to feel like insanity."

Olivia closed her eyes and sank into the story.

"So the resistance is sabotaged in the most insidious way. The junta says the disappeared have killed each other off—or died fighting in Argentina—but the survivors know it isn't true. So at the demo, we concentrated on the disappeared—"

"Can it help them? To show the world is watching?"

"It serves notice. Most of them are dead. But some reappear months later. So we each wore the name of a disappeared woman on a placard on our chests. Mine said, 'Marta Aguilar, twenty-nine, journalist, disappeared, February 19, 1975.' I'd read about her. Some women knew her in Tres Alamos, where she was raped by guards. The women helped her to abort, and then the military beat her for losing 'an authentic son of the fatherland.' Shortly after that she disappeared. She could have been me, I could have been Marta. The identification gets very strong when you know something about a person, and we worked with it deliberately."

"It sounds like it was working with you."

"Ah, Livy, it was! Identification—it's so mysterious. We were marching in silence, and people leaving their offices stopped to watch. One of us would explain quietly what we were doing and offer them a bracelet—the plastic kind they use in hospitals, you know—with the name of a disappeared person slid into the slot. We asked them to wear the bracelet until that person was found or freed. The few who took them—they looked afflicted."

"I can imagine!"

"You can imagine! Imagination is all we've got! So listen— we had planned that at peak rush hour, when the crowd was thickest, we would break the silence and read off the names of the disappeared. One woman stood with a long list, and another with a big drum. You have to understand we'd been marching in silence for over an hour, and I felt in the strangest way close to Marta, as if I really knew her intimately and also— this is bizarre, but you have to believe me—"

"I believe you already, Chloe."

"It was also as if I knew, *intimately*, what it was to disappear!"

Olivia felt the hairs on the back of her neck move. "You mean you thought you were disappearing?"

"I didn't think it, I felt it. I felt gone into Marta and gone altogether with her disappearance. Hollow, not there, invisible, lost. It was morbid, I suppose, but I clung to it as if it were some true thing I couldn't understand yet."

"Oh, Chloe." We're still so fragile, Olivia thought.

"And then the woman with the drum started this heavy roll, and in the silence the other woman—she's a singer with a big rich voice—she started to read the names of the disappeared. The list was alphabetical and her name came first. 'Marta Aguilar, twenty-nine, journalist, disappeared, February 19, 1975.' And then, from one of the Chilenas scattered through the crowd in wigs and sunglasses, there came this fantastic shout: '*Presente!*' I'd never heard that before, but I knew immediately what it meant!"

So did Olivia, as the chill leaped at her even under the warm quilt and tears started to her eyes.

"After the reading of the next name, several of the Chilenas cried, '*Presente!*' and then, after the next name, all of us together. '*Presente!*' It was electrifying! As if they were all in some way restored and we ourselves had become invincible."

Oh, thought Olivia, tears hot on her cheeks, I thought 'fragile,' and we *are* fragile, but the compensations are breathtaking.

"You called to tell me this," Olivia said thickly. "Why?"

"I didn't know exactly why. I had to shelve my feelings at the demo for ten days to finish the semester—but when they caught up with me tonight, I knew I had to tell you, and explain—Olivia, you're crying—oh!" She paused, but her voice was steady. "Olivia, you see it all. No one else. This is what I wanted to say. I didn't understand until—" She paused again, but still she didn't cry. "Olivia, sweetheart. Don't cry anymore. I'm calling to tell you it's different between us now. I've gotten to the other side of that hideous anxiety. Livy?"

"I'm here," she said.

"Listen, I believe you. You're not here, but you're there. You prove it every time. Like tonight. I've thought about it for so long, and I've finally cleared it up for myself. I almost understand it. You can't answer letters, you can't live here, the reasons don't matter. But there's no one else, not even Gabe, who understands exactly everything the way you do. As soon as we start talking. It's something too rare to put conditions on. So this is where I come out: if we never communicate between the times we meet, if we only see each other every five years, every decade, I promise you there will be no obstacle, no reproach, no holdout. I promise I'll feel the same way."

Weeping rose in Olivia like a wind. "Chloe, don't. Don't promise anything so terrible."

Chloe laughed. "Terrible? What's terrible? I'm giving us carte blanche."

"No!" cried Olivia, inconsolable all of a sudden. "I know I can do better. Give me a chance."

"You always have a chance, Livia. Why are you crying?" Something like a laugh was struggling deep in her throat. "But you don't need it, not from me, don't you understand? And if I give you a chance, then I'm locked into waiting for you to take it."

"Chloe, you nearly forgot me! I never forget you!"

"Not even nearly? Livia, the way you remember me, I could have died years ago."

"No! It's not the same! But I know how you feel now, and I promise—"

"Don't promise me anything!"

"All right, I won't if you won't, if you'll retract your promise."

"What's this, now? We both promise not to promise?"

Chloe laughed, but when she heard Olivia laugh at last, tears stung her own eyes. "Livia, why can't you accept what I'm saying? I thought you'd be relieved! Glad! Never mind, I have another idea. I'll write it, then you'll understand."

"Write what?"

"About us, this friendship. How, like you said, together we make up our own time and place, to hell with circumstance! Okay, we know better now. And yet we keep right on inventing each other over the distance—"

"Chloe, I've got a better idea—"

"Hush!" Chloe felt herself soaring, preposterous, joyful. She would put to rest her tormenting need. "I see it all now. I'll write a little story about it. How we've *always* made our own time and space. Where are we right now, after all? And when?"

"*You* hush!" Olivia's laugh rattled around in the receiver, unconvincing to herself. "It's the winter solstice, that's when. And on the phone is where. We've been blind, deaf, and dumb, never thinking of the phone. Here we are, talking for hours, and it's almost like being together. So I promise to call you next—"

"That would be great, but it doesn't hurt my idea. We'll do both. You'll call and I'll write."

She thinks she'll see me best in her writing, Olivia thought. She felt herself tensing in the presence of ancient dread. Summoning her gravest voice, she said, "Don't do it."

A mistake. Opposition only stimulated Chloe. "Livia, whyever not?" she cried gaily. "You just said you'd like to see what I write. You've been my biggest booster."

"Chloe. Write something else."

"Why not this? What's wrong with it?"

"You're going to exorcise me, that's what." Do I *need* her to need me so—is that it?

"On the contrary! I'll invoke you."

"That's worse," said Olivia. "It's my story too!"

"I know that. You think I'd get it wrong?"

"Of course you would!"

"Well, then, I could change things. If you like, I'll make you short and me tall. I'll swap our hair. You can be an American blond, as blond as you like. How's that?"

"Ugh! Horrible!" But ridicule was wasted on Chloe when she got like this. Avid and glorious, she might have been spreading huge wings and swooping clear across the continent. As appalled as she was charmed, Olivia was flooded with energy. "Go transform someone else!"

"You think I'm too bossy? Possessive? Unrealistic?" And she only roared at Olivia's fierce yeses. "My old failings. I never completely learn, do I? Well, nobody's perfect. Let me just try it. I'd open with the moment when it all began, when I was dazzled by the sight of you in that underground boneyard."

"That's not how it began at all."

"*What?*"

Checked at last, pitched toward Olivia but still midair, Chloe was just where Olivia wanted her. As her chest swelled with laughter, she said, "It began this way. I saw you come in from the street. I was intrigued, and when Karl said he recognized you, I made him introduce us."

"No! I saw *you*—Livia, you're kidding, aren't you?"

"I am not! You see, Chloe? You shouldn't bother. You don't know the first thing!"